T0369462

When All Else Fails

Book One of the *Sweet Ever After* series

Elaine E. Sherwood

iUniverse, Inc.
Bloomington

When All Else Fails
Book One in the *Sweet Ever After* series

iUniverse books may be ordered through booksellers or by contacting:

iUniverse
1663 Liberty Drive
Bloomington, IN 47403
www.iuniverse.com
1-800-Authors (1-800-288-4677)

Because of the dynamic nature of the Internet, any web addresses or links contained in this book may have changed since publication and may no longer be valid. The views expressed in this work are solely those of the author and do not necessarily reflect the views of the publisher, and the publisher hereby disclaims any responsibility for them.

Any people depicted in stock imagery provided by Thinkstock are models, and such images are being used for illustrative purposes only.

Certain stock imagery © Thinkstock.

ISBN: 978-1-4759-1541-9 (sc)
ISBN: 978-1-4759-1540-2 (hc)
ISBN: 978-1-4759-1539-6 (e)

Library of Congress Control Number: 2012906716

Printed in the United States of America

iUniverse rev. date: 8/21/2012

This book is dedicated to my good friend, Jack Tidlow,
for graciously and patiently teaching me ballroom dancing. His
zest for life, and unfailing positive attitude,
has been an inspiration to me.

Acknowledgements

Thank you to my family and friends for their constructive criticism and whole hearted support.

Thank you to Dr. Rose Byland at the Falck Cancer Center for her input regarding physician practice and compassionate patient care.

Thank you to Adam Nugent for his computer skills and the cover picture. He was a lifesaver.

Prologue

They were oblivious to the pounding winds and driving snow that had been hammering the house since the wee hours of the morning. The two had become one and that's what mattered.

After a light supper they relaxed on the couch in front of the big stone fireplace where burning logs crackled and popped, sending sparks floating up the chimney.

Taking her hand, he pressed her fingers to his lips. It was a familiar gesture that reassured her that he was there for her. Tenderness filled her dark blue eyes as she gently touched his cheek. The smile on her face was one reserved only for him, and it took his breath away.

With a sigh of complete contentment, she laid her head on his chest, and his fingers were soon entangled in her long curly hair. Was it any wonder she loved him so much? In a million years she never dreamed she could be so happy.

From the safety of his arms, she let her mind drift back to the beginning...

PART 1
Kathy Ann Martin, the Beginning

Chapter 1

∞

It was June 15, 1955 - my seventh birthday. I had invited all my little friends to a birthday party at a local restaurant. I was so excited I could hardly stand still. Earlier that day Daddy had given me my present. He told me I was a big girl now, and he had gotten me a big girl present. He handed me a little box wrapped in pretty pink paper with a pink bow. I carefully unwrapped the little package as my parents watched. When I lifted the lid, tucked inside was the most beautiful heart-shaped locket I had ever seen.

Daddy put the locket around my neck, and showed me how to open the tiny clasp. To my surprise, inside was a picture of my mom and my dad. I threw my arms around my father's neck and buried my face in his shoulder. Then I ran to hug my mom and show her how I could open the clasp all by myself.

Whining usually worked on my dad so I began nagging him to hurry up. I didn't want to be late for my own party. What would my friends think? Besides, I couldn't wait to show all my friends what a wonderful present I had received.

When mom was FINALLY ready we piled into the car. I was sitting in the back seat gazing out the window. The trees were whipping by so fast it almost made me dizzy to watch them. I remember trying to guess what kind of presents my friends had gotten me.

I never saw the truck that slammed into us head on. All I remember was an explosion of flying glass and my mother screaming; then everything went black. I woke up in the hospital the next day confused and frightened. The concussion was minor, as were the cuts and bruises. The doctor said I was extremely lucky to be alive.

A nurse with sad brown eyes explained that my parents had "gone to heaven." Not understanding exactly what that meant, I wondered why I hadn't gone with them. I was inconsolable.

Apparently at the point of impact I had been thrown forward and to the floor behind my father's seat; that's what saved me. My parents had both been ejected from the vehicle through the windshield. They were dead at the scene.

The headache was bothersome, but my injuries were not serious. They kept me in the hospital only a couple more days before discharging me into the care of Child Welfare Services. Since there were no living relatives I was placed in a foster home. Now I was terrified! My heart pounded in my chest and nausea was just a swallow away. Why was this happening? I wanted to know where Mommy and Daddy were! Nobody had ever come out and said they died. They used vague euphemisms like, "they went to a better place" and other such nonsense. This only served to infuriate me. Unfortunately, I had more immediate problems.

Chapter 2

The first thing the foster mother did was cut my long, curly, reddish-blonde hair. She said it was too much work to keep it long. I was heartbroken and tried to protest. What would she do to me next?

"I really don't care what you want little missy," the foster mother said with a cruel smile on her thin lips. "You're in my house now, and you will do what I say." It was a very rude awakening.

There were three other children living in this foster home, two girls and a boy. It was controlled chaos - completely different than anything I had ever experienced. I was definitely NOT the center of attention as I had been with my parents. I had been their only child. The apple of my father's eye.

Mealtime was every man for himself. Not being accustomed to needing to fight for my food, I went hungry until I learned to grab and gulp. I didn't get my little peanut butter sandwiches with the crust cut off or chocolate stirred into my milk just the way I liked it. In fact the peanut butter was slapped haphazardly on bread that was a bit too stale for my taste. There wasn't any chocolate milk.

To this day, I don't know what happened to all my clothes and toys. Or for that matter, what happened to my house. I guess because I was only seven years old no one thought it necessary to explain anything to me.

I was allowed to keep only a stuffed teddy bear that I had gotten for Christmas that year. Someone must have gone to my house, and gathered up a few of my clothes; very few, because everything I now owned fit into a small suitcase. I was smart for a seven-year-old. I hid my locket under my shirt so no one would see it, and make it disappear like all my other belongings.

Every night I would beg God to PLEASE send Mommy and Daddy to get me. I would look at the pictures in my locket and the tears would come. Over the next weeks and months, I learned what "dead" meant. Mommy and Daddy were never coming back, ever. I felt lost and frightened in a world filled with strangers.

The outgoing, fun-loving child I had been disappeared, and in her place was a sober, quiet, thin, little wisp of a girl with huge, sad eyes. When I looked in the mirror, I hardly recognized myself.

School began in the fall, and I started second grade. My teacher was a middle aged, married woman nearing retirement. Since I was a willing student who excelled in most of my subjects, I became one of her favorites. Mrs. Morse gave me a little of the attention I craved, and school became my solace.

Adjustment to this new life had taken a while, but I had finally come to accept things such as they were with this family. One day, for reasons I was never told, I was moved to a different foster home, and a different school. Nothing felt real anymore, and my tummy was upset most of the time.

Chapter 3

Child Welfare moved me five more times over the next few years. I never understood why. Had I done something wrong? Didn't the families like me? I tried to be as good as I could, thinking it would make a difference. I began to realize I couldn't count on anyone so I turned inward and hardened my heart.

My life seemed to be one upheaval after another, and I soon learned it was pointless to become attached to anyone or to care about anything outside myself. I became reconciled to the fact that until I was old enough to control my own circumstances, I would always be alone, passed around from here to there without any regard for what I wanted or how I felt.

My entry into puberty was a rough one. Everything I knew about how my body was changing I learned in health class or from eavesdropping on the conversations of other girls. Not wanting to appear stupid, I never asked questions.

When I was fourteen I was put in a home where there were other teenagers. One was a fat, ugly, pimple-faced boy named Roger. As my body matured I began to understand what my dad had meant when he said my mom had a "good figure." Roger noticed.

Late one night after I had been in bed for several hours I heard a strange noise that woke me up. Before I knew what was happening Roger was on top of me, straddling my hips. One pudgy hand was over my mouth while the other hand roughly ripped my nightgown, and began groping my bare chest!

He found my locket, and tore it from my neck leaving a little trail of blood behind. He stuffed it in his pocket before he continued his quest. Panic filled my mind. I could hardly breathe! I thrashed and bucked, hitting him in the face with my fists as hard as I could.

Being terrified gave me more strength than Roger expected. I managed to bite down hard on the hand that covered my mouth dislodging it long enough to scream.

The foster mother burst into the room.

Roger jumped off me as if I was on fire, and started whimpering. As I trembled from exertion and fear, rivulets of sweat poured down my body. I sprang off the bed, and stood against the wall as I tried to cover myself with what was left of my nightgown.

He told the woman that I had been "teasing" him all day, finally inviting him to my bedroom. When he tried to kiss me, I began kicking and screaming. How he managed to get tears to come from his squinty, near-sighted eyes was the most incredible thing I had ever witnessed. I couldn't believe he was blaming ME!

The foster mother spun around, and slapped me hard across my face. She called me names that I had only heard in association with "bad" girls who "did things" with boys. When I tried to stammer out an explanation, she slapped me again.

The woman's voice escalated as she yelled at me.

"Maybe you were allowed to act this way in other foster homes, but your behavior will NOT be tolerated in this house."

I was locked in my room, and told that I would be sorry for "starting trouble." My behavior? What had I done exactly? Dazed and confused, I slid to the floor.

At first I cried, not able to comprehend what had just happened. My locket was gone along with the pictures of my parents. The thing I treasured most in the whole world had been ripped from me, and the anguish I felt was overwhelming. My nightdress was in shreds. My cheeks were bruised and stinging.

I have to get away, was my next conscious thought. I knew I couldn't stay in this house a minute longer. Sooner or later Roger would try again, and he would keep trying until he succeeded in getting what he wanted. I had learned enough in health class to know exactly what that involved as well as what the consequences might be. I also knew I would be blamed as being the instigator.

Chapter 4

V ery quietly I pulled on a pair of jeans and a tee shirt. I tied my shoes together by the strings so I could carry them around my neck as I tiptoed across the floor. The window was heavy, but I managed to push it up and crawl through, dropping to the ground. I landed hard, hurting my knee in the process. Terror pushed me to my feet. I had to keep going!

Fortunately, it was a new moon and very dark so no one saw my escape. I decided following the highway would be the best course of action. When a car passed by, I hid in the ditch that ran along the side of the road. In the morning when the sun came up I crawled under some dense underbrush and collapsed into a restless sleep.

As I tossed and turned, a realization came over me. Maybe it was the result of losing my locket, but I began to think what had happened to my parents was my fault. I had begged them to hurry that day. If we had left the house later, the truck would not have hit us. We were at that exact spot at that exact moment because I didn't want to be late for my party!

It was MY fault they were dead! MY FAULT! The weight of guilt crushed me, and a deep sadness engulfed me. *Maybe I DID encourage Roger in some way. What kind of person am I? It's no wonder no one wants me!*

When it was finally dark, I knew it was time to get moving. Thirst and hunger were taking their toll. I would soon be too weak to cover much ground. My knee was aching so bad I could hardly walk, but I needed to find something to eat and drink. There was a small stream running parallel to the road. I dropped to my stomach, cupping water into my mouth until I was full.

If there were berries I could have eaten it was impossible to find them in the dark, so I continued to follow the highway. After walking what felt like miles, I came to the edge of a small town. I saw an all-night diner with a big dumpster in back. The top was up. I was short and the dumpster was huge, but I finally managed to pull myself up and inside. They had apparently just thrown out the leftover supper food because I found any number of dried out burgers and soggy sandwiches. I ate as much as I could.

After rummaging around for several minutes, I gathered up everything else I could find that was edible, and wrapped it in a discarded paper sack so I could take it with me. I peeked over the top of the dumpster, and saw that the coast was clear so over the edge I went. I hurried as fast as my injured knee would allow back to the trees along the road and rested for several minutes before setting out again…to where, I had no idea. My future looked bleak.

Chapter 5

I didn't dare stop moving. The child welfare people were probably looking for me. I was pretty sure the foster family had given them a colorful, albeit untrue, picture of my character. They had probably accused me of stealing or worse!

The thought of what would happen to me if I were caught gnawed at the edges of my consciousness making it almost impossible for me to keep focused on what I had to do. I knew it was imperative for me to stick to my pattern of sleeping in some secluded spot by day, and walking at night. I was following a main road and I figured eventually it would lead to a big city where it would be easier to hide.

The little sack of scavenged food was all I had so I rationed it carefully. The little stream frequently wound itself around close to the highway, so finding water was not yet a problem. I was dirty and tired when I took shelter in the early hours of the morning behind a large fallen tree.

The grass was damp with dew, but I didn't care. Before falling asleep that morning I wondered if this would be the day I just never woke up. It was obvious to me that God hated me. After all, he had taken away everything that held any meaning for me. He had turned my life into a living hell so why not just kill me now and be done with it. If I did see another day, I would need food again soon.

My knee seemed to be getting worse making it almost impossible to make any real progress.

I woke up as the sun was setting with my stomach grumbling. I felt lightheaded as I staggered to my feet to begin the night's walk. I hadn't gone far when off in the distance I saw lights. It looked like a little farmhouse. There was a barn nearby with a few cows in the pasture. A cautious look around might be a good idea.

The possibility of finding something to eat gave me a glimmer of hope as I cautiously approached, hiding whenever I could behind bushes or trees. There didn't seem to be a dog, for which I was grateful. I made it all the way to the corner of the barn without attracting attention from the house.

Never having been on a farm before, I was unfamiliar with the routine. Everything seemed quiet enough, and the animals appeared to be content. I finally decided the work must be done for the day. I wedged myself between a couple of loose boards in the back of the barn finding it full of machinery and all sorts of equipment, but otherwise empty.

On the floor near the door was a large saucer of milk. *There must be a cat,* I thought wearily. Tonight he would go hungry. I slurped up the milk not caring that it was warm. As I spit out bits of straw that had been floating in it, I thought nothing had ever tasted so good.

In one corner of the rather dilapidated structure was a stall filled with sweet smelling hay. It looked clean and inviting so I told myself I was only going to lie down for a little while. My belly was full of milk, and I was emotionally and physically drained.

It seemed like I had only been asleep for a short time when a commotion at the barn door jerked me wide awake. I jumped to my feet ready to run, but in the dark I was unable to find the loose boards that had allowed me to enter. All I could see was the silhouette of someone in the doorway blocking any possible escape in that direction.

I was looking wildly around for some place to hide when a woman flipped on the lights. I was caught! We just stared at each other for several seconds. My heart began pounding in my ears, and

I was trembling from head to toe. The milk in my stomach began churning as beads of sweat crept across my scalp.

"Please don't tell anyone I was here," I pleaded just above a whisper. "I'll go away, and I haven't stolen anything except the cat's milk!"

"You should have put the saucer back where you found it. I nearly broke my neck," the woman said, as she folded her arms across her chest. "Why don't you come on inside and tell me who you're hiding from? Then I'll decide whether or not to call the authorities."

Chapter 6

The sternness she intended was contradicted by the smile twitching around her generous mouth.

"I have leftover soup and, maybe, some cookies. It's warm inside and I would welcome some company. Boots, he's my cat, hasn't been very talkative lately."

The soup sounded like manna from heaven, but I was wary. This woman looked harmless enough, even friendly, but could I trust her? Probably not. Nonetheless, hunger outweighed my better judgment and I followed her into the house with every intention of eating and running.

"My name's Harriet," the woman said, as she pulled out a chair at the table and indicated that I could sit there.

Harriet Lewis was a tall, thin, plain looking woman in her 40's wearing funny looking clothes and thick glasses. Her outfit was completed by a pair of high rubber boots. Her hands looked callused with the nails broken off short. Mousey brown hair hung in a long braid down her back.

She must have to work hard, I thought, as I glanced nervously toward the dark corners of the other rooms. *I wonder if there's a man around.* The thought of encountering a man filled me with dread.

"If you want to wash up, there's a sink in the pantry," she said, as she stirred the soup.

Taking full advantage of the hot water, and good smelling soap, I scrubbed my hands and face until my skin felt raw. When the soup was hot, Harriet brought a bowl to the table.

"Mind if I sit?" she asked.

I shrugged.

The soup smelled delicious, and I forgot every table manner my parents had ever taught me as I wolfed it down. Harriet watched with interest, refilling the bowl when it was empty. I slowed down a bit on the second bowl, daring to give Harriet a shy, quick look of appreciation.

As I ate, Harriet told me about herself.

Chapter 7

She and her husband Maynard, "May", as she called him, had been high school sweethearts. They got married shortly after graduation, both looking forward to starting a family and living happily ever after.

They had worked at menial jobs and saved their money. When they had enough for the down payment on the farm, they were so excited. Their dreams were finally coming true!

"We were young and full of hope in the beginning. We wanted to have a family right away, but we were never able to have children."

She did her best to say this matter-of-factly, but I could see the tears she was trying to hide on the pretense of having something in her eye.

"After a few years of back-breaking work on the farm, Maynard became more and more restless. He was dissatisfied that we didn't have more. There never seemed to be enough money for the things he wanted to do and I began to wonder if he liked farming at all."

It was obvious, even to someone as inexperienced in the ways of romance as I was, that Harriet adored her husband. She would have been content here on this farm with him forever.

One day Maynard decided he needed to travel to Boston, an hour away, to look for work. He said he wanted to be able to make more money so he could buy her nice things.

"I told him I didn't need THINGS, I only needed him. I tried to discuss ways we could improve production and increase our income, but he always had a hundred reasons why what I suggested wouldn't work."

With a sad shake of her head, she continued. "The first few times he went, he only stayed a few days, always coming back with cash in his pocket from 'odd jobs' he was able to pick up."

Then he stayed a week, which slowly progressed to a month. He did send her money; enough to keep the bills paid, but she missed him terribly.

She said she worked hard trying to keep the farm going and the animals cared for, not to mention staying ahead of the weeds in the garden.

This time Maynard had been gone for several months. She didn't know when he would return and the money he was sending her had slowed to a trickle.

"I just can't make ends meet working the farm by myself anymore," she said with a shrug of her thin shoulders.

Why is this woman telling me all this stuff, I wondered? *I'm just a kid!*

She didn't seem to notice that I was more than a little uncomfortable hearing her life's story. I had known her for all of a couple of hours!

"I had to sell most of the cows to pay the mortgage payments until only six are left," she continued, as she stared out the window at nothing. "It's a good thing they're still giving milk, and the garden provides vegetables. I'm afraid my flock of chickens is dwindling. The ones that don't lay eggs I slaughter for meat."

I had finished the last of the soup some time ago, but Harriet was still talking. So, I took the opportunity to look around the small kitchen. She didn't seem to need me to respond, she just needed to talk. The walls could use some paint, the furniture was old and worn, but everything was spotless.

"I've tried hunting. May left me his rifle, but my eyesight is poor and I'm not a very good shot," she lamented. "I can't afford to waste the ammunition"…her voice trailed off.

Chapter 8

The warm kitchen, along with a full tummy, not to mention Harriet's droning voice, had worked its magic and my eyelids were drooping.

Suddenly Harriet jumped to her feet. "What am I thinking?" she gasped.

Her sudden action startled me and I came to attention, poised for flight. Thinking she now regretted spilling her guts to me, I was sure she was going to call the police or something!

She must have seen the fear that flashed across my face.

"You probably think I don't have any manners at all. I can see you're tired. Please forgive me for rambling on so. It's just that it has been a long time since I had anyone to talk to except Boots. Let me get you a pillow and some blankets. I hope you don't mind sleeping on the couch."

Before I had time to protest, she was headed up the stairs. *I should go right now*, I told myself, but somehow I sensed this woman meant me no harm and she was alone. *What will it hurt if I sleep on her couch just for one night?*

The couch was wonderfully soft and the blankets were warm. Now I couldn't seem to fall asleep! She hadn't questioned me like I thought she would. She was just really nice.

I told myself NOT to like her; not to get attached to her, but I <u>did</u> like her, and that scared me. I also felt sorry for her. *What am I thinking? I can't stay here! I haven't told her anything about myself so if I were to just sneak away, what could she tell the police? Nothing.* All these confusing thoughts swirled around in my head until I finally fell into a troubled sleep.

I dreamt about Roger and awoke in the wee hours of the morning soaked in sweat, my heart pounding. This had happened frequently since I ran away and it terrified me all over again.

Before I could think about it too long and change my mind, I decided the best thing I could do for myself was to get away before Harriet got up. I didn't realize cows wanted to be milked REALLY early.

Chapter 9

"Oh, I see you're awake," Harriet said brightly as she came down the stairs. "I'll put on the hot water so we can have some oatmeal for breakfast. You like oatmeal, don't you? I like mine with cinnamon."

I jumped to my feet, my knee buckled, and I dropped back onto the couch with an agonized moan.

Harriet hurried over to me, and demanded I show her "where it hurt." She pushed and probed my knee until I wanted to scream! She finally concluded nothing was broken, probably just badly sprained. All the walking had made the problem worse because there was definitely swelling around the joint.

She went to one of her "junk" drawers, and pulled out an elastic bandage, which she carefully wrapped snugly around my knee. She acted like she knew what she was doing, and I was hurting too bad to interfere with her ministrations. She told me if I continued to walk on it, it would only get worse, possibly resulting in permanent damage.

When she had finished, she put her hand under my elbow, and helped me stand up. I gingerly took a few steps, managing to hobble to the table.

"I can't pay for any of this," I mumbled as I sat down.

She smiled at me. "You can help me do the chores if you want to."

OK, I can do that. I can pay my way by helping with the morning work. I had enough on my conscience already without adding free-loading to the baggage. This woman had been nothing but kind to me. I couldn't just run off without helping.

Harriet gave me some easy things to do to spare my knee as much as possible. At the same time, she made me think these were very important tasks. She showed me how to scatter feed for the scrawny chickens, and how to collect the eggs, assuming there were any.

As she sat on a stool beside one cow after another, with the milk spraying into her bucket, she very nonchalantly asked if I knew how to shoot a gun.

My eyes popped, and my mouth flew open. *OH NO,* I thought. *What have I gotten myself into?*

Harriet chuckled. "I don't need you to rob a bank or anything. I just wondered if, after your knee is better, you could help me hunt. Like I told you last night, I'm a terrible shot. I can't see worth a damn and we really need the meat."

She had said "we." I wondered what that meant exactly. Did it mean she wanted me to stay? She didn't know anything about me! She didn't know what I had done.

Now I was really suspicious. Was there some reward for turning me in to the Child Welfare people? She obviously needed money. No one was nice for no reason. There was always an ulterior motive. My past experience had taught me that much.

But the fact remained; I wouldn't get very far with my knee like it was. It still hurt when I walked, and I certainly didn't want a permanent disability. How would I take care of myself if that happened?

We had sandwiches for lunch with cold fresh milk. I had never tasted "raw milk." I kind of liked it.

There was some ironing to be done, so while Harriet attended to that, she said I could lie down if I wanted to and rest my knee. I hadn't realized how tired and weak I had become, and the couch was sooooo comfortable.

She tucked a blanket around my shoulders, brushing a strand of curly hair from my forehead. In those minutes between drowsiness and sleep, I thought she was my mother, and I was safe at home. I sighed deeply and drifted off.

After a couple weeks of rest and good food, I was feeling much better. I wasn't dizzy when I stood up anymore and my knee didn't hurt. Best of all, fear was no longer my constant companion; however, nothing lasts forever.

Every day I reminded myself that I should leave. Every night I slept on the couch.

Chapter 10

The rifle was heavy for me and I missed the mark over and over again. I wanted so desperately to be able to do this for Harriet; especially after all she had done for me. Tears of frustration were soon running down my cheeks, as I jammed one shell after another into the chamber.

"Whoa there girl! Slow down," Harried said with a chuckle. "Those shells cost money you know. Take your time. Squeeze the trigger, don't jerk it. You can do it. Now take a deep breath, and try again."

The first time I hit the target I couldn't keep a smile from spreading across my face.

"Dimples! Maybe that's what I should call you since you have never told me your name," Harriet said with a grin.

"You haven't asked me any questions. How come?" I asked sheepishly.

"I figured when you were ready to talk, you would."

"Can I trust you, Harriet?" Deep in my heart of hearts, there was still a part of me that was untarnished and innocent. I wanted to trust her so badly it hurt. I wanted to tell her everything. I needed someone to understand.

"Can I trust YOU, Dimples?" was her serious response.

That was the last thing I had expected to hear. It gave me pause. She had opened her home to a stranger and she had treated me like family. How could she be sure I wouldn't take advantage of her kindness?

At supper that night, I decided I would tell Harriet everything and let the chips fall where they may.

I started at the beginning. With a heavy heart I explained how I had been responsible for the death of my parents.

She shook her head and gave my hand a little squeeze. "No, honey. That wasn't your fault. You were just a little girl excited about your birthday party. If there is blame to be placed at anyone's door, it's the guy driving the truck. It sounds like he swerved into your lane."

I slowly raised my eyes to meet hers. There was no condemnation in her steady gaze.

The foster homes, my locket, Roger, it all came pouring out. She didn't interrupt me; she just let me talk. The weight of this burden slowly fell away and that night the unrelenting dreams were kept at bay.

In the morning, the day held promise; my hope was restored. When Harriet came downstairs, her eyes filled with tears as I ran to her and hugged her tightly for a few seconds before pulling away.

Chapter 11

⬯⬯⬯

It was the big day. We were going hunting. It made my stomach churn to think of killing an innocent animal, but I didn't want to let Harriet down. We traipsed around in the woods for quite a while before we finally spotted a young deer. *Darn!* I had kind of hoped we wouldn't find one. I knew I had to try my best no matter how it made me feel. After all, Harriet was counting on me!

Harriet had already loaded the gun. She quietly told me to lean against the tree to steady my arm, sight down the barrel, and squeeze the trigger.

I did exactly what she told me, and when the shot rang out, the deer fell. Harriet was so excited! I had "bagged my first deer," as she called it.

We had brought a wheelbarrow, some rope and a couple of sharp knives with us into the woods, just in case. That was Harriet's favorite expression, "Just in case." She told me she always hoped for the best, but prepared for everything. It made perfect sense to me!

It took both of us pulling on the rope attached to the deer's hind feet to haul it up over a low hanging tree branch, and that was the easy part! When Harriet took the knife and slit the deer's throat, my stomach heaved. I turned quickly away from the grisly sight, and vomited into the grass.

My tears flowed unchecked as Harriet showed me how to gut and skin the deer. I thought I was going to be sick again, but I managed to see the whole process through. We wrapped the chunks of meat in paper that Harriet had brought and headed for home.

Harriet was beaming. "I'm so proud of you! That was a fine shot. I know the whole thing was hard for you, but you persevered."

I didn't know what persevered meant, but it sure <u>felt</u> like a good word! For the first time in my life I had helped someone else without regard for myself. I remember wishing at the time that my dad could have seen me. I knew he would have been proud too.

Venison was soon cooking on the stove and it smelled SO good. The rest was in the big freezer in the pantry. I couldn't stop smiling as we ate dinner together and did the dishes. It made me feel good inside to see Harriet so relieved, and I knew I had a part in making it happen.

The weeks flew by, and soon, I had been at the farm for several months. I had gained some weight and my knee was completely back to normal. My cheeks were pink, the old sparkle was back in my eyes again, and I was happy. I didn't dare think beyond the moment!

There was no indication that Harriet was anxious for me to leave, so I flirted with the idea that maybe I had found a place for myself.

I wondered if Harriet would ever feel the need to go to the city and live with Maynard. My suspicion was that she really didn't want to know what was going on in Boston. Denial was a beautiful thing, I guess.

Chapter 12

One afternoon a police car drove into the driveway and an officer walked up to the house. Harriet told me to hide in the pantry, and keep quiet.

She smoothed her hair and gathered her wits as she went to answer the door. Officer Bradshaw politely asked Harriet if she had seen a 14 year old girl, small for her age, with blue eyes, and reddish blonde hair.

"I can't say that I have, officer," responded Harriet politely.

The officer handed her a card.

"If you spot this runaway, call the number on the card immediately," he said briskly. "According to her foster mother, this girl is a consummate liar and a thief."

WHAT! That is NOT true! I had left with only the clothes I was wearing. THEY had stolen from ME. The last time I had seen my locket, it was in Roger's possession!

The officer tipped his hat and left with Harriet's promise to be on the lookout for this possibly violent teenager.

They were still looking for me!!! I thought enough time had elapsed that they had given up the search. I was just beginning to feel safe. I sat on the pantry floor with my knees drawn up, my eyes tightly shut, and my hands over my ears. I rocked back and forth thinking, *no, no, no. Please not again.*

I knew I would have to run. No matter what Harriet said to try and persuade me to stay, she soon realized it was no use; I had made up my mind. I couldn't stay at the farm knowing it would mean trouble for Harriet if she were caught harboring a "criminal." Someone was bound to see me sooner or later. Sadly, Harriet knew this was probably true.

We came up with a plan to get me to Boston so I wouldn't have to walk or hitch rides. Harriet said "hitching" was much too dangerous. Since the police were looking for a girl, we decided I needed to change my appearance enough to pass for a young boy.

Harriet's nephew had stayed at the farm one summer, leaving some of his things behind. In the back of a closet we found some shirts and pants, a hat, jacket, and a pair of lace up boys work boots. Perfect!

Everything was a little big, but that was okay because I was growing, which presented another problem. Harriet thought the best solution was to cut some rags into strips and bind my breasts. We hoped this would make me appear flat-chested and more boy-like.

I cried when Harriet cut my hair, but it had to be done. There was nothing we could do about my brilliant blue eyes and feminine little nose. Harriet told me to keep the hat pulled down low and not to look anyone directly in the face. With some heavy socks, the boots were good.

A friend of Harriet's on a neighboring farm frequently made trips into Boston. A phone call verified that she was going this Saturday. Harriet asked if she would mind picking up some things for her at the market. Beverly readily agreed. It was only about an hour's drive into the city and she would stop by the house around ten o'clock on Saturday morning.

Harriet knew her friend drove a pick-up with a canvas cover over the truck bed. She would distract Bev long enough for me to slip over the tailgate and under the canvas. When the truck stopped at the market, I was to wait until Bev was inside before I slipped out the back.

Harriet wrote her husband's address and phone number in the city on a piece of paper. I memorized the information, just in case I lost the paper. I was to go directly to Maynard's address, as Harriet was sure he would help me.

She had tried to call him several times, but he never answered. She figured he was probably out job hunting. This struck me as a little odd. He was job hunting even at night? Oh well, I had other things to worry about right now!

Friday night came all too quickly. Harriet and I didn't talk as we tried to eat. It was impossible for me to swallow past the lump that was lodged in my throat. My heart was breaking. I could tell by the look in her eyes that Harriet felt exactly the same way. We were each dreading the inevitable separation the next day.

The dark circles under my eyes served as proof that I hadn't slept at all. I felt so incredibly angry! *Why God? Why, why, why are you doing this to me again? I was just beginning to feel secure! You must hate me. Well, I hate you too!*

I dressed in my new disguise, and with some luck, I would pass. Harriet put the extra clothes, food, and a jug of water in an old knapsack that had belonged to her husband. As her friend's truck turned into the driveway, she quickly helped me put my arms through the straps before hugging me tight.

Right before she pushed me out the back door, she pressed twenty dollars into my hand. I knew what a sacrifice this was for her and I didn't want to take it.

"No, you keep it," she whispered, her voice thick with tears. "Just in case."

With a tight smile on her face she went out to greet her friend. I climbed into the back of the truck unnoticed and cried all the way to the city.

Chapter 13

The truck stopped at McGrady's Market. Bev went inside to get the things she needed, plus the purchases for Harriet. I waited several minutes before carefully lifting the canvas flap for a quick peek. I didn't see anyone close by, so I cautiously slipped out over the tailgate.

Pulling the hat down low over my forehead as Harriet had instructed, I tried my best to assume a loose-jointed, cocky walk, which I hoped made me look more like a boy.

The first order of business was to find "May" so I looked for street signs. He had told Harriet about shopping at McGrady's Market so that had become the foundation of our escape plan. Harriet knew her friend did her shopping at the same market, so Maynard must live in the vicinity.

As luck would have it, the market was on the same street as Maynard's address. I saw a post office up ahead. Someone there should be able to give me directions to his house.

There was a bald headed older gentleman behind the counter, and when I gave him the address he got a surprised look on his face.

"This address IS the post office," he told me with a condescending smile. "Your 'friend' must have a post office box here. As you can plainly see, this is not a residence."

"My mistake. I must have written the address down wrong," I stated in my best boy voice. I hitched up my britches like I'd seen the boys in the foster homes do and left.

Oh, this is just great. Now what am I going to do? I thought as I started chewing my bottom lip. It was a habit I had developed when I got nervous and was trying to think things through. My dimples winked in and out.

Harriet had shown me several pictures of Maynard in various poses. I thought I would recognize him if I saw him. Since there was a park across the street from the post office, I sat down on one of the benches where I had a good view of the front door. My hope was that he would come to check his mail sometime today.

I had waited for quite a while when a man driving a white convertible pulled up to the curb. There was a pretty blonde woman sitting in the passenger seat. Before the man got out he leaned over and kissed her. When he turned toward the door, I almost fell off the bench. It was Maynard!

From the look of things, he and the woman waiting in the car had something going on because they acted VERY friendly. I was shocked and hurt for Harriet, who was waiting at home for a man who would probably never show up. He wasn't saving up money for his next visit home. He was cavorting around town with another woman!

"What a jerk!" I snorted as I spit disgustedly in the grass. The pittance he sent Harriet once in a while was no doubt to assuage the guilt he felt over having an affair.

Chapter 14

I readjusted the pack on my back and began walking down the street. I couldn't just sit there in the park forever. After several blocks I found myself in a section of the city that was rundown and dirty. It was dusk when I finally stopped and leaned against the side of a building, exhausted.

Tears trickled down my cheeks. What was I going to do now? I couldn't call Harriet. She would have questions about why I wasn't with Maynard. I just didn't have the heart to tell her the truth.

I took out a piece of bread, cheese and venison that Harriet had packed for me, and began nibbling at it, trying to think what I should do next. Fear began growing at the edges of my brain. Panic was its partner.

The old man was practically on top of me before I even knew he was there. He was filthy, and he seemed to be talking to people that I couldn't see. He had one eye that looked at the sky while the other eye tried to focus on me. He only had two visible teeth. My mind went numb, but only for a second. Then I fought like a wildcat.

He might have been old, but he was bigger than I, and stronger. With his knee in my back forcing my face into the pavement, he went through my knapsack throwing my things into the street while cramming my sandwich into his mouth.

He smelled so bad I gagged. I guess he thought I was going to vomit because he quickly stood up. I turned over and kicked him as hard as I could in the crotch. After that, running seemed my best option, so that's what I did.

Flying around a corner I collided with an old woman pushing a shopping cart piled high with rubbish. The old woman was wearing several layers of clothing, all dirty, and her straggly gray hair stuck out in all directions from underneath a brown stocking hat. She walked like her feet hurt.

She pulled herself together and started hollering at me at the top of her lungs. I was petrified that she had friends in the vicinity that would come running to her aid. Nobody came. She looked me up and down for several seconds as I stood like a statue with my back against the wall of the rundown building.

She started cackling like one of Harriet's hens. "Gert's my name, and that old coot was Richard. He's mostly harmless, but he is crazy. You must be new to the neighborhood. You look downright pitiful."

The boy disguise didn't fool Gert for one single second. When I hesitated and then said my name was Keith, the old woman burst out laughing, showing blackened gums and no teeth.

"Keith my ass," she said between snorts that ended in a fit of coughing. "You better stick with me, girlie. You won't last a minute on these streets by yourself! Keep the name though. It might fool somebody." Thus began the friendship of Gert, the bag lady, and "Keith" the lost boy.

Chapter 15

I was so tired and disheartened, I was unaware that we had turned down an alley. Gert was heading toward a dark corner in the back. There was rubbish piled high against the side of one of the buildings. I could make out broken chairs, old dilapidated book shelves, metal pipes, and other things I couldn't quite identify. I must admit it was an impressive structure.

A piece of black plastic was draped precariously over the top of the pile and tied to something in the corner. Gert made her way under the plastic, shoving me ahead of her. She pulled her cart in to block the opening.

"Welcome to my humble home," she said as she plopped down on a pile of rags. "Make yourself comfortable."

As my eyes adjusted to the dim light that filtered through the holes in the debris that made up the shelter, I noticed two things instantly. Stacks of old newspapers, and what looked like animal droppings. As I stared in horror, Gert told me the newspapers were for "insulation" and as for the other things, well, the maid had today off.

The next thing I noticed was the rancid smell. It made me gag.

"Oh, you'll get used to the smell," Gert assured me.

Over the next few weeks Gert patiently showed me the ropes. She told me which restaurants had the best garbage, the streets where old clothes could be found on the curb on Saturdays, and which corners to avoid altogether.

I was introduced to the local hookers. I knew what the term meant. I wasn't born yesterday, after all. Some were old looking with makeup caked into the lines on their faces. Others looked to be my age, but their eyes betrayed wisdom beyond their years. I guess they didn't see me as competition, so they could afford to be friendly.

I became Gert's right hand "man." I was small and lithe, well able to crawl into places Gert would never fit. She taught me how to steal food from the numerous open markets found along the docks. The stealing bothered me, but not for long. Survival became the name of the game.

Anything that wasn't nailed down was fair game for the other homeless people. Any clothes I found, I wore. My shoes never left my feet. The twenty dollars Harriet had given me I kept tucked inside my shoe under my foot.

The days ran together, one after the other, as Gert taught me everything she knew about life on the streets.

My fifteenth birthday passed without notice. It was just another day to get through.

Summer with its merciless heat turned into fall, and fall turned into winter. Gert said this was the hardest time of year for the homeless. Without adequate clothes and food, many succumbed to the frigid temperatures and malnutrition. Gert was right. It was bitter cold. When we weren't scavenging for food, we were huddled together in the shelter. My imagination became my best friend.

I imagined a tall handsome man with kind hazel eyes finding me amongst the trash. He would see my beauty beneath the dirt and grime, and fall madly in love with me. He would take me home to his castle where I would have fancy clothes, and eat food prepared especially for me.

Best of all, there would be a big, white tub where I could take long, luxurious bubble baths every day if I wanted. I would never be dirty or stinky again. My husband would never be unfaithful, having eyes only for me. We would have lots of children and all live together happily ever after.

It was so real to me I could almost feel the touch of his hand on my skin. Then Richard would belch or make some other obnoxious noise and my prince would disappear.

Richard had moved in with Gert and me for the winter, uninvited. He was alright once you got to know him, but that made an extra mouth to feed and less room in the shelter. On the up side, it was more body heat making it a bit warmer.

As the winter deepened, the stench of unwashed bodies crowded into a small space became overpowering. I was on the verge of being sick most of the time. Any excuse to exit the shelter was a welcome one, so it became my job to go out and find food. At least outside the air was crisp and clean. I would gulp in deep heaving breaths of fresh air, and feel better all around.

It was all Gert and Richard could do to keep the home fires burning. We had found an empty trash barrel on one of our foraging expeditions and dragged it home. We pulled the barrel as close to the shelter as we dared. By burning scraps of wood and newspaper, we kept a little warmer.

Gert had been coughing a lot and I was worried about her. Richard sounded like a horse with the heaves as he struggled to breathe, but that didn't stop him from taking the last few drags left in the cigarette butts he picked up off the street.

Harriet was often in my thoughts. She had been like a mother to me, even if for only a short time, and I missed her. She had probably asked about me by now, and Maynard could honestly say I had never showed up. I knew it would be painful for her to think some harm had come to me, and I wished there was something I could do for her; some way I could let her know I was okay.

Winter passed and Gert improved, but we lost Richard. He left one day insisting that he could find food and just never came back. One of the hookers told Gert that he had been found frozen to death leaning against a building only a block from our shelter. His strength had given out before he could make it "home." Gert and I took only a short time to grieve for our friend as life was cheap and we had our own survival to worry about.

Chapter 16

On more than one occasion, the pimp who "owned" the girls in the area around our block tried to ply me with sweet words and promises of a wonderful, easy life.

At first I was flattered, but Gert warned me what I could expect down the road if I let "Rooster" Adams persuade me to join his jolly band. He was a smooth talking, lying, SOB, according to Gert. All he wanted was fresh, young meat for his stable. I steered clear.

I had given up on the whole boy disguise thing. I just looked too much like a girl to be able to pull it off. Being filthy wasn't much of a deterrent either. It seemed men wanted what they wanted. Their leering and raunchy invitations bothered me more than I let on, but I learned to close my ears as I went about my business.

Drugs were always available if a girl wanted to "put out" to pay for them. Some of the girls did, and I saw the results. I watched one unfortunate girl younger than I overdose and die on the street. Eventually an ambulance came and got her. But it was too late.

Life was cheap. Nobody cared. I was a nameless, faceless, worthless, less than human being. If I disappeared, nobody would even notice; well maybe Gert. She would have to find her own food without me.

On the outside, I was a tough, smart-mouthed, street savvy teenager. But on the inside, my heart yearned for someone to love me. Sometimes it was almost a physical ache, the weight of it suffocating me. Deep inside, I believed there were good people in the world somewhere. Besides my parents, I had only known one. Harriet. Honesty, kindness, integrity; all traits she modeled.

"Loving and needing are not the same," she had told me. "Loving is giving. Needing is taking."

I realized Harriet had loved me. Gert needed me. I recognized the difference.

That hunger for affection and acceptance rose up in me at the oddest moments. Like when I saw old people holding hands, or when a fine lady stooped to give a tidbit of food to a stray dog. I believed love conquered all. Maybe this innocent quality is what made me easy prey for Donny Madison.

Chapter 17

Gert had sent me to check out the streets where used clothing was put out on the curb for pickup by Good Will. I knew the streets around "home" well enough, and had no trouble finding my way. I was about to turn down South Avenue when I saw police lights and a fire truck. *Wow, something serious must have happened*, I thought to myself as I peeked around a parked car.

I wanted to avoid the police at all cost, fearing they were still looking for me. I decided the clothes would have to wait for another day. I turned down a side street, and headed in the opposite direction.

It was getting dark, and I had wandered into an area that was unfamiliar to me. I walked another two blocks in the direction I thought would take me back to a street I recognized, but soon realized I was completely lost. A familiar feeling began in the pit of my stomach, and crawled up into my throat. FEAR.

There were apartment buildings and small homes on both sides of the street. People were sitting out on their stoops in the cool of the evening laughing and playing music. It looked like a nice residential area. Certainly not some place where I belonged! Maybe I could find someone who could give me directions.

There was a young man sitting on the steps of one of the buildings talking to an attractive woman. Her dress was a little too tight, and she leaned in a little too close when she laughed at something he said, reminding me of the hookers I knew.

The young man looked away for a second and spotted me walking down the street. He got up from the step, telling the woman he would "catch her later," and sauntered lazily up to me.

"You look a little lost kid," he said with an easy friendly manner.

He seemed nice, and he was very good looking with his blonde hair and dark eyes. He wore nice clothes; not flashy like Rooster's. No gold chains or cowboy boots. He had all his teeth, which gleamed white when he smiled.

He asked me if I had eaten lately, and I admitted that I hadn't.

"Well what do you know, I haven't either. Why don't you join me? There's a little bodega just around the corner."

We sat at a table in the back, and the young man told me to order anything I wanted, his treat. He said his name was Donny, Donny Madison.

I ordered a roast beef sandwich and a Root Beer. As I think back, it would be the last decision I would ever be allowed to make for a very long time. As I ate, Donny asked me about myself, and I was soon telling him way too much.

He acted interested in what I said, and it seemed nice to have a conversation that didn't revolve around which dumpster had the best Chinese food. Little did I know this was just an information gathering activity for Donny.

He told me very little about himself. All I knew was that he worked for Lewis Construction Company and had his own house and car. Today had been his day off, and he was in this neighborhood "visiting friends."

It was getting late. I said I needed to get going before it got too dark. When he asked where I lived, I was embarrassed to tell him I lived in a garbage pile on Henry St.

If I had stopped and thought for two minutes, I would have realized he could figure out on his own that I lived on the street just by the way I was dressed, and the way I knew I smelled!

This should have given me reason to question this whole situation. What could an older, well off guy like this, possibly want with somebody like me? I guess I was so desperate for something better, that I was blind to what was right in front of my eyes and should have been obvious.

I told him I lived on Jay Street, which was, in fact, a couple blocks from where I actually lived. He offered to give me a ride as it would be quite a walk. I hesitated for only a minute before I accepted.

When I thanked him for the food and the ride, I was surprised when he said, "Would you like to do this again sometime?"

Was this anything like a date, I wondered? *After all I would be 16 on my next birthday. That was old enough to date wasn't it?*

Since I had never actually been on a date I had no idea what was involved. I guess I would have to talk to Gert. Or maybe I should talk to Lucy, the hooker who worked our block. She probably had more experience in these matters.

I gave Donnie my best smile and told him I would like to see him again. I stayed in the shadows as I watched him pull away. Then I headed for "home."

Chapter 18

Over the next several weeks, when Donny didn't have to work, he appeared at the corner where he had dropped me off. I was flattered by his interest in me. He treated me like a lady, holding the car door open for me, and ordering for me from the menu when he took me out to eat. It didn't strike me as odd at the time that he never asked my opinion on anything, and we always did what he arranged. I thought he was just taking care of me.

He complimented me on my eyes and my hair. Frequently there were little gifts waiting for me on the seat of his car; a bracelet or a box of candy. I was starving for this kind of attention, and I was completely sucked in by his charm.

When I told Gert about Donny, and how I felt about him, she was skeptical. When I told Lucy, her eyebrows shot up and the concern on her face was obvious. I guess she decided it was time to have a heart-to- heart talk with me about men. A subject she was eminently qualified to address.

Lucy said she "knew" Donny. When the realization of what she meant by that sunk home with me, I was furious! She had slept with him for money! I knew this was what hookers did, but this was bringing that knowledge to bear on someone I knew... someone I loved!

How could anyone do…"that"…with someone they didn't love? I would never do it, I assured myself. *When I have sex it will mean something.* My own words would come back to haunt me one day.

She warned me that Donny could turn dangerously ugly without any warning or provocation. He could be very rough and he had hit her on more than one occasion.

"Men just aren't to be trusted," Lucy said. "They're all pigs who will use you, then kick you to the curb when they're finished. It's all a game to them. I don't think men are capable of loving anyone but themselves! Mark my words Kathy. Once he gets in your pants, he will treat you like dirt and you will be less than nothing. At least I get paid for it!"

"That's totally ridiculous," I replied angrily, my little know-it-all attitude rising to the occasion. "I think you're just jealous! He has always been very gentlemanly and courteous to me. I think you're telling me these horrid things because you are mad that he loves me and not you! You're only a hooker. What do you know about anything?"

What a cruel, heartless thing to say to someone who had been a friend to me and was only trying to protect me. Momentarily, my conscience pricked me. I had hurt her on purpose.

With tears running down her cheeks leaving black trails from her excessive eyeliner, Lucy walked away.

"I'm sorry, Lucy. I didn't mean that. I'm sorry," I called after her. But she did not turn back and I didn't see her for several days.

Being in love and being stupid, I justified Donny's interest in a prostitute by telling myself that if he had someone at home who loved him, he would never need a hooker. I was also very sure he would never hurt me.

Chapter 19

I would be 16 in two weeks. Donny said he had something special planned to celebrate. He had bought me a beautiful dress, shoes and a little jacket that matched; real girl clothes! I hadn't worn girl's clothes in a very long time.

When I showed my new things to Gert and Lucy, a knowing look passed between them that I didn't understand at the time. Gert just shook her head and made a disgusted burping noise. Lucy walked away without a word. Their responses hurt my feelings. Why weren't they happy for me? I was escaping this mess we called home.

Donny had told me he was in love with me, and when I asked him about Lucy he hung his head. In reality, it was probably to hide the smirk on his face! He took my hand, and told me how lonely he had been before he met me. His promise to never do it again sounded sincere. I believed him because I wanted to. It was an award winning performance on his part.

The night before my birthday all I could think about was the surprise Donny had promised me. He wouldn't tell me what his plans were, only that they were something "spectacular." I was in love, and my life was about to change.

Why hadn't I paid closer attention? Why hadn't I listened? Why had I been so blind...and stupid? I would ask myself these questions over and over again during the next three years.

I had convinced myself that Donny DID love me. Hadn't he told me so over and over again? He had asked me to marry him, hadn't he? He wouldn't do that unless he loved me, would he?

He had already purchased the license, and his friend Bernie was a Justice of the Peace. He would marry us without asking any questions. Everything was all arranged right down to the honeymoon. I felt so special that Donny would go to all this trouble just for me.

Donny had done his homework. He knew I didn't have any family, so there was no danger of anyone coming to look for me. There was also no one I could call for help in the event I needed it. I would be completely dependent on him for everything, which was just how he wanted it. I would make the perfect "wife."

I wanted a white dress and a church wedding, but I quickly gave up those notions. Donny seemed so anxious for us to be married. It made my heart melt to think he wanted me so much. Moving into his little house in a nice neighborhood was a dream come true for me, and I couldn't have been happier.

The day finally came and I said good-by to Gert and Lucy as Donny waited in the car. I was wearing my new outfit, and Gert did have to admit I looked lovely. I didn't take any of my old things. I wouldn't need them and I didn't want anything that would remind me of my old life.

I stuck the twenty dollars Harriet had given me in one of my new shoes. I had held onto it just in case. I smiled to myself. I would probably never need it now.

I was so incredibly naïve.

Chapter 20

It was about a half hour drive to the home of Bernie Olson, Justice of the Peace. He greeted Donny with a sly grin, and ushered us into his living room. His mousy little wife handed me a near-dead flower. The vows were exchanged without fanfare. Donny placed a cheap ring on my finger with the promise of a nicer one after we were settled.

We all signed the appropriate paperwork that Bernie had ready. Donny paid him, and headed for the door. The whole process had taken about 15 minutes.

I stopped and turned around. "Oh, I almost forgot to get that paper."

"Oh come on, baby, a piece of paper won't make us any more married will it?" Donny laughed as he tried to pull me toward the door.

I grabbed the marriage license off the table, quickly folded it, and stuck it in my pocket as Donny was having a final whispered conversation with Bernie. He hadn't noticed.

We drove through Boston for a short time until we arrived at a cheap looking motel. Donny had reserved the room all the way at the end of the building for our wedding night so we would have privacy. *How sweet*, I thought with a smile.

To say I was nervous was an understatement. Lucy had explained to me what would happen, but I was very unsure of myself. I hoped

Donny would understand and be patient. I wanted to please him, but wasn't exactly sure how to do that. I needn't have worried.

As soon as the door closed Donny threw his jacket over the chair and grabbed me. He pulled me tightly up against his body. He forced my head back and began kissing me roughly on the mouth.

This frightened me, and I pulled back staring up at him. He wasn't a big man, but he was certainly taller and bigger than I. He slapped me across the face knocking me backwards until the back of my knees hit against the side of the bed, and I fell. He was on me so fast I never had time to think.

Panic filled me as he ripped my dress open and dragged it over my head. What was happening? My mind was reeling. The words "dangerously ugly" flashed through my exploding brain, and I began to hit him with my fists.

This seemed to amuse him, but only for a few seconds. He laughed, quickly catching my wrists. He sat on top of me, easily holding me down as he adjusted his pants to accommodate what he was about to do. My mind froze. Bile rose up in my throat as he raped me.

When he was finished he laughed harshly. "A virgin," he shouted, "all the better."

I couldn't help it, I began to sob uncontrollably. Donny, being tired of the drama, hit me on the side of my head leaving me dazed and in pain.

He immediately rolled over on his side and began snoring. I quietly crawled from the bed and went into the bathroom. Closing the door, I looked at my face in the mirror. My lip was swelling and so was my eye. I was really sore "down there," and there was blood. Lucy had told me to expect that.

This was far beyond anything I had imagined. I was terrified. I was alone. I curled up in a ball trying to make myself as small as possible as I huddled between the toilet and the tub. Here in this sleazy motel, on a night that was supposed to be special and wonderful, a part of me died.

Donny woke up several hours later seeming to have gotten his second wind. When he yelled my name a wave of shock and nausea ran through me.

No, please. Not again!

He threw open the bathroom door. Seeing me crouched in the corner, he dragged me by my leg out into the middle of the bathroom floor. Fighting him proved pointless. He raped me again. I screamed inside my head, but nothing came out my mouth. The horror of the whole degrading, terrifying situation overwhelmed me.

The third time, I didn't fight. My mind went numb and I endured until it was over. In my head, I went to another place and another time. I was back on the farm, and Harriet was brushing my hair.

Chapter 21

Thankfully, Donny slept for the rest of what was left of the night.

"Pull your damn dress together, and let's get out of here," Donny snarled. "I have to be at work by 8:30."

This had been just another "good time weekend" to him. He hardly looked at me until we arrived at his house. He changed his clothes for work, and before he left he gave me orders to get the house cleaned up and have dinner on the table at 5:30 when he arrived home.

He slammed out of the house, locking the door behind him. When I was sure he was gone, I went through the whole house looking for a way to get out. I had lived on the streets before. I could do it again. Maybe I could even find my way back to Gert and Lucy.

The back door was also locked from the outside. All the windows were nailed shut. I couldn't find a hammer or screwdriver or anything I could use to pry them open.

Okay, I'll just break the glass, was my next thought. But the glass had some kind of covering over it. Or maybe it wasn't even glass. Maybe it was some kind of heavy plastic or something. Hitting it with a frying pan didn't make a dent. With a shock I realized I was a prisoner.

A second shock followed the first. *He must have been planning this all along!*

I knew I had better do what Donny had said or I would be in trouble. My strategy became to anticipate his every need thus avoiding the punishment that would follow if he had to ask or wait for anything. What I would learn over time was that his cruelty had nothing to do with my behavior. He just enjoyed hurting me.

He came home at exactly 5:30. He looked around the living room, pulled off his muddy boots and threw them in the corner. His hat and jacket followed. He ate the "slop" I had fixed for dinner, and dragged me to the bedroom.

This went on exactly the same every day for about a month. Then something changed. I didn't know why, but Donny began coming home later, sometimes staying away all night, which was fine with me. Was he tired of me? Was he out with another "Lucy?" *Poor girl.*

I learned to sleep in short naps, snapping awake at the slightest sound. At least he hadn't hit me again, and my bruises had faded.

He had gotten me a few clothes; not the right size, but at least they covered me up. His generosity, he told me, was because he didn't want to have to look at my skinny rack of bones any longer.

"You're only good for one thing, and I don't have to look at you to do that," he told me as he pushed my face into the mirror to reinforce the fact that I was a "sorry looking cow."

Things were relatively calm for a couple of weeks, and it made me more anxious than the yelling and the sex. Fear flickered through my consciousness all the time, ready to blossom into full blown terror at any given moment. I decided that's exactly what Donny wanted.

Chapter 22

One night he came home with a couple of friends, Art and Willie. They were policemen, and Donny had met them in a bar downtown. They would be regular "visitors," Donny informed me, and I had better make them feel welcome, or else. The threat was implied. I got the message.

Art was fat. His big gut hung over his belt, and he had to keep hitching up his pants. I was very uncomfortable with the way he leered at me as he wiped the sweat from his face. He was arrogant and loud, his language filthy, his gestures vulgar. Donny found him hilarious.

Willie was average and quiet. He couldn't quite look me in the eye, as if he were ashamed of something that was about to happen and was a reluctant participant.

Donny treated me like the slave I was, taking great pleasure in showing his pals how he could control me, and make me do anything he wanted. He rudely demanded I get some food for him and his new friends. They ate like the pigs they were.

Art and Willie left as soon as they had eaten, but not before having a whispered conversation with Donny at the door. I had a feeling they were talking about me because Art kept glancing my way, his eyes roaming up and down over my body. It made me shudder and feel sick inside.

I had been right to be apprehensive about Donny's friends. When Friday night came, they arrived early. I tried to blend in with the woodwork, head down, quietly going about my chores.

They sat around drinking beer, and their conversation soon turned to vulgar jokes and crude gestures. It wasn't long before Donny got up and dragged me into the bedroom.

He left me half naked on the bed. At least it was over for the night, that's all I cared. I couldn't have been more wrong. I heard the door open, and there was Art. My confused look made him laugh as he proceeded to do things to me. Horrible nauseating things, which I was sure he would never even attempt to do to his wife.

He was mean about it. He made it as painful as he could. He enjoyed doing it, and my screams didn't faze him in the least. Apparently, Donny didn't care either. He stuck his head in the door a couple of times, shouting encouragement to Art who continued until he could hardly catch his breath.

When he finally left the room, Willie appeared. At least he wasn't mean.

Chapter 23

Every shred of self-respect I had disappeared that night, and self- loathing took its place. I was so humiliated it was hard for me to hold my head up. I couldn't stand to look in the mirror, because what I saw revolted me. I was no better than Lucy. In fact, I was worse.

Donny told me later that his friends were cops, so trying to tell anybody what was going on would only get me in trouble. If I tried to leave they had the resources to find me and bring me back no matter where I ran. If I thought my life was tough now, it would be worse if he had to come looking for me.

"I know your scurvy bunch of friends on the street. I know where they live. I can arrange for unpleasant things to happen to them. It's all up to you, Kathy. Run if you want to."

With that said, he went to bed.

My friends! He would hurt my friends! How could anyone be so evil? It was a concept my mind could not wrap itself around.

I was still bleeding heavily the next morning. It felt like something was torn inside me. I didn't know what to do. Donny hadn't locked the door when he left. He knew I would never do anything to jeopardize my friends. It was almost like he wanted me to run just so he could have the fun of carrying out his threats.

I had discovered that when Donny flopped on the couch to watch TV, money would frequently fall out of his pockets ending up under the couch cushions. I had been collecting it and hiding it under a loose board in the closet.

The bus stopped just up the street at ten o'clock every morning. I slowly made my way there in time to catch a ride into the city. My hope was that I could find the hospital, get patched up, and make it home before Donny got out of work.

The nurse put me in a little cubicle surrounded by a curtain. When she asked my name and address I blurted it out without thinking. Too late, I realized I should have invented a story! I couldn't even look the young woman in the face. I was terribly embarrassed, and shame stained my cheeks.

Dr. Mark Goodwin was working the emergency room that afternoon. He was a tall, broad shouldered man with black hair and kind, smiling eyes. He had recently completed his schooling along with all the other requirements needed to be a full-fledged physician. He seemed full of enthusiasm with an unfailing desire to help others.

It was a very delicate situation. He tried his best to put me at ease, which was impossible. The outward signs of sexual assault were obvious, I guess. I certainly felt like my sins were written across my forehead for all to see. Before he began his examination he asked a nurse to be present.

She explained everything the doctor was going to do and she asked me questions I was not prepared to answer. Everything I said was written down, which worried me. I needed to be more careful!

I forced my mind to focus on only one thing, which was getting home before Donny. Refusing to say anything more, I turned my face away. I forced myself to concentrate on an ant making its way up the wall. I wasn't going to cry. I was done with crying. Nobody cared anyway.

After the exam, Dr. Goodwin told me that I was badly bruised inside. Fortunately, it was not life threatening. Little did he know, for me, it very well could mean my life! *What if Donny finds out?* That thought filled me with a new horror. My anxiety reached such heights that my teeth were literally chattering.

"Be careful for a few days, stay off your feet as much as possible, and refrain from intercourse until the pain is gone," were his instructions to me.

He went on to explain that there was always the possibility of pregnancy. I would need to see an obstetrician in about 3 months for a test. I wanted to laugh in his face.

He became very serious, and I could see the concern in his eyes when he encouraged me to press charges against whoever had done this to me. He wrote down the name of an organization that specialized in situations like mine.

I was given a bottle of pain medication from the hospital pharmacy that I could begin taking as soon as I got home. I hurried out the door, making it to the corner just as the bus pulled to the curb.

Donny found the bottle of pills I had gotten at the hospital. This prompted a search of my belongings. I should have thrown that piece of paper away! Why hadn't I? I tried to explain that Art had really hurt me, and I had gone to the emergency room.

"I promise Donny, I didn't tell them anything. Please don't hurt me. I will never tell! I came right back. I didn't run. I came right back. Please don't hurt me!" The words tumbled out chaotically as I did everything I could to plead my case.

The look on Donny's face told me what was going to happen next. When he threw me to the floor I tried to protect myself by curling into a ball, and covering my face with my hands. It was no use. He beat me unmercifully until I lay moaning on the floor.

Chapter 24

During Art and Willie's next visit, Donny showed them the paper about reporting abuse. Art was familiar with the organization listed in the information. When he was finished with me that night, he shoved the paper in my face.

"If you EVER report this, I will see that you have a very serious, painful accident. Understand?" he snarled, spit flying in my face.

For emphasis, he touched his lit cigarette to the skin on the inside of my arm. When I shrieked, he laughed.

"There's more where that came from if you talk."

I was indeed pregnant. I lost my first baby in the toilet. It wasn't much of anything to look at, but I grieved nonetheless as much for myself as for the lost child.

The days and weeks and months all blurred in together as I went from one day to the next. When my injuries were serious enough, Donny would sometimes take me to the emergency room himself. After all he didn't want to lose his "cash cow." Art and Willie never issued him a ticket for speeding or driving drunk, and in return they got to use me.

He always made a big show of telling the staff how clumsy I was. How I had fallen down the stairs or how I had run into a door. He didn't fool anybody. Dr. Goodwin was almost always the one who took care of me, and each time he tried to get me to press charges. I couldn't. I knew what would happen if I did. Donny had made sure I understood in no uncertain terms.

Sometimes the burns got infected, prompting me to sneak to the hospital after Donny left for the day. I would ride the bus paid for by my stash of couch-coins. The wounds were cleaned, and I was given antibiotics, which I had to keep hidden until I had taken all of them. I had learned my lesson well. The loose board in the closet was the safest place to hide things.

Dr. Goodwin told me he was extremely worried about me, but if I was unwilling to press charges, there wasn't much he could do. He would need my permission to speak to the authorities. I didn't dare allow that. The people in authority were part of my problem. His concern touched me. Maybe there was ONE decent man on the face of the earth after all.

Donny and his friends continued to abuse me, sometimes all three of them at once. I always fought, but they held me down. It was no use. I was told I deserved it because I was worthless and ugly. I was a stupid cow and only good for one thing. I should consider it an honor that two of Boston's finest even bothered with me.

"Nothing but a whore." That's all I was. Just like Lucy.

I wasn't allowed to give an opinion. I was knocked around more if I cried, and laughing was out of the question. There certainly wasn't anything to laugh about anyway.

I became dead inside. Every time Dr. Goodwin saw me, another piece of the person I was had disappeared. My eyes took on a sunken, haunted look. More often than not, I just stared at the wall as they treated me.

I was 18 when I lost my second baby and I was quickly pregnant for the third time.

The only bright spot in my life was Dr. Goodwin. He was so kind and gentle. He always talked to me like I was a human being. He tried his best to draw me out of the shell I had built around myself.

I would just look at him knowing the despair and hopelessness I felt must be written on my face. I would usually leave without making a sound. I had to catch the bus.

Chapter 25

Time passed, and each day began the same as every other morning over the past six months. I got quietly out of bed so as not to wake up Donny, scurried to the bathroom and threw up.

I had just turned nineteen. This was the first time I had managed to carry a pregnancy longer than two or three months. After my miscarriages, I didn't have any medical care, and I didn't have anyone to talk to, so I mourned the losses in silence and alone. But now a tiny life was hanging on.

On the one hand, I desperately wanted this child, but on the other hand, I was terrified about what kind of life it would have in a house ruled by my husband. I was painfully thin with the exception of my little round tummy.

My clothes hung on me effectively hiding my pregnancy, not that Donny ever really looked at me after his needs were satisfied. When he beat me, I curled up in a ball to protect the baby as best I could. I was not even sure who the father was as Willie and Art used me as often as Donny did.

It didn't matter. This baby was mine and I loved it without reservation. In my mind I called him Lucas. Little baby Lucas. When Donny was at work, I would talk to him about wonderful faraway places I had only seen on TV. I made up stories. I sang songs.

It was a boy, I was sure of it for some odd reason, and carrying on a conversation with him gave me comfort.

I was in a constant state of anxiety about what to do. I was positive that if Donny found out about the baby, he would be furious. He would probably beat me until I gave birth prematurely.

Maybe Dr. Goodwin would help me. He had tried every time I came through the emergency room, with one injury or another, to get me to leave Donny, and press charges. He just didn't understand how things were.

Donny had warned me more than once that if I ever told or tried to leave he would hunt me down like the dog I was, and kill me. To reinforce what he said, he had dragged me to the top floor of a building he was working on, and held me over the edge. He threatened to drop me to my death if he even <u>suspected</u> I was "up to no good."

I had no place to go anyway and no money except for my couch-coins. There was always the twenty dollars that Harriet had given me, but even with that, I wouldn't get very far. At least not far enough. I didn't have any friends, and I never went anywhere except to the hospital. Donny controlled everything; even getting the groceries. I was a prisoner. I lived in fear for my life all the time. Now I was afraid for my baby as well.

Chapter 26

One Friday afternoon Donny came home early with Art and Willie in tow. Each was carrying a case of beer, which did not bode well for me. Apparently the foreman had closed the job site early as they were ahead of schedule on the construction of a new skyscraper. Everyone was sent home, and told to enjoy a long weekend.

I began to tremble inside, but I didn't dare let my fear show. Averting my eyes, I kept busy in the kitchen. Donny put the beer in the fridge, slamming the door so hard it startled me. Panic prickled up the back of my neck.

"Get your lazy ass in gear," he yelled. "I'm hungry."

For emphasis, he hit me in the back of the head, almost knocking me down. I regained my balance by grabbing the edge of the sink. With shaking hands I began putting hamburger in a pan.

All three men had started drinking well before they arrived at the house. It continued through and after dinner. I could hear them in the living room laughing. They were watching a porn flick that Art had brought, apparently finding it hilarious. The combination of booze and porn made my situation extremely dangerous.

I was quiet as a mouse as I cleaned up the kitchen. I did my best to stay out of sight. When Donny drank a lot, thankfully, he usually just fell into a drunken stupor and went to sleep. Art, on the other hand, got meaner. Tonight Donny had Willie and Art to keep him awake and agitated.

From the kitchen I heard Art say, "Why don't you get your old lady in here, Donny. I feel like some lovin."

I froze. Donny came into the kitchen and yanked me by the arm into the living room. Before I saw it coming in time to duck, he backhanded me in the face so hard I fell backwards onto the floor.

Donny decided he wanted the first "ride" and was on top of me in a heartbeat, ripping my clothes off. Art enthusiastically cheered him on. Watching got him more excited. It didn't take Donny long before he rolled off panting from the exertion.

I looked up in time to see Art loosening his belt. Terror overwhelmed me, and my only thought was, *oh NO...my baby, my baby!*

Fueled by fear for my unborn child, and with adrenaline coursing through my body, I waited until Art was bending over me. His eyes were glazed. His slack lips were curled in a lewd, drooling grin.

"Ooohh baby, you're going to really love this," he slurred, just before I brought my foot up as fast and hard as I could into his crotch.

He howled in pain, grabbing himself as he doubled over. He lost his balance and fell backwards. He landed on the coffee table, which crashed to the floor under his considerable weight.

Willie had been half asleep on the couch. When he heard the commotion, he sat up rubbing his eyes. He stared in confusion at what he saw. I always fought them, but I had never done anything like this!

I turned over and started to crawl away as fast as I could. Donny wasn't as drunk as I had first thought. He jumped up, immediately grabbing me by my hair. He hauled me to my feet, and spun me around.

He kicked me so hard in the stomach that I went flying backwards through the picture window. I rolled down the bank in front of the house ending up in the street. I was dazed and I could feel something wet running down my face. I vaguely wondered when the rain had started.

Through a fog of pain and panic, I heard the three men yelling and laughing. They finally got into Donny's car, and went tearing out of the driveway leaving me in the broken glass and dirt. I thought I was dying and I was glad.

Chapter 27

I woke up in the Intensive Care Unit of Boston General Hospital, lying on my side with Dr. Goodwin bending over me. He was asking me what my name was, and did I know the name of the current president of the United States.

Hummm, that's an odd question, I thought as I tried to focus on his face…and couldn't.

Two days later I finally surfaced from a drug induced haze feeling like I had been run over by a train. Every muscle and joint in my body hurt. When I tried to move, dizziness incapacitated me. The pain that shot through my back felt like liquid fire. Laying flat was impossible.

My head had been shaved bald over the area where my scalp laceration had been closed. My eyes were swollen and discolored. Bruises in various shades of purple were everywhere, and speaking was painful as it pulled on the stitches in my upper lip.

One look in a mirror spoke volumes. It was a shock. As comprehension of the extent of my injuries washed over me, my first thought was for my baby. *Oh God! Please let baby Lucas be all right!*

In addition to my physical injuries, a deep pulsating fear throbbed every time my heart beat. *Will he come here and get me? Can anyone protect me? Will I ever be safe?* These thoughts cascaded through my mind like a waterfall.

When I was more awake and alert, Dr. Goodwin came and sat beside me, taking my hand in his. Tears prickled behind my eyelids. The kindness of that simple gesture rippled through me unexpectedly. He went over everything that had happened in detail so that I understood the seriousness of my situation. My condition was critical. My injuries were severe.

Apparently, a car had turned down the street. Seeing me in the road, the driver had gone to the corner phone booth and called for an ambulance. The police officers who arrived on the scene with the ambulance were covering this part of town as Willie and Art were off duty. They had seen Art's car parked in the driveway, and wondered what was going on. No one seemed to be around.

Upon entering the house through the broken window, they found empty beer cans everywhere. The living room was in shambles with the coffee table nothing but a pile of broken boards. It was obvious that some sort of struggle had taken place.

When the ambulance attendants called the emergency room to give their assessment, Dr. Goodwin answered. He was told it was a "scoop and run" situation. They were already en route to the hospital. He had recognized the address and was waiting for me when the ambulance pulled in.

On arrival in the emergency room, I was only semi-conscious and incoherent. I was bleeding profusely from a scalp laceration as well as a very deep gash that ran from top of my left shoulder across and down my back all the way to my right hip. There were also numerous other cuts and bruises.

My wounds had been embedded with dirt and glass, making it necessary to start a special intravenous line for delivering antibiotics. With a "dirty wound," they fully expected an infection. Two units of blood had been transfused to replace what I had lost, and I was getting intravenous fluids. X-rays had revealed a concussion, several broken ribs, and my pregnancy.

On examination, it was thought that the baby was at about six month's gestation. Anesthesia could be dangerous for the baby, but surgery could not be avoided.

It had taken a plastic surgeon several hours to debride the wound and flush out all the debris. Several hundred tiny stitches were needed to close the wounds on my back and scalp. A drain was left in place in the middle of my back.

The police were already involved due to the severity of my injuries, and the fact that I had been found in the street. The obvious evidence of a struggle inside the house led the police to believe that this was a crime scene, and I had been the victim of foul play.

At the time, they had been unable to find my husband. Even drunk, he was smart enough to realize that he and his friends had gone too far this time. He had apparently decided to go into hiding, probably needing the time to come up with some sort of alibi.

My injuries had been photographed for purposes of documentation, and the police had been canvassing the area for possible witnesses. So far, there were no solid suspects, but the investigation was ongoing.

Dr. Goodwin gently addressed the gravity of the situation with my husband, which the police, so far, did not know anything about. I would have to be the one to disclose this information.

"This time he almost succeeded in killing you. Something has to change, Kathy, and the authorities need to know. You likely will not survive another attack like this one," he said with concern etched on his face.

I knew what he said was the truth. I also knew he was genuinely worried about me. But what could I do? Dr. Goodwin didn't understand everything that had transpired. He didn't know it wasn't just my husband who had been abusing me. It would be my word against two policemen. I didn't think anyone would ever believe me.

Chapter 28

My condition finally stabilized, and Dr. Goodwin allowed the investigating officer to speak with me. At my request, he agreed to stay with me during this interview. My condition, although stable, was still precarious, and he didn't want me to be unduly upset. The first question didn't surprise me.

"Do you know the person who did this to you?" the late middle-aged detective asked, with his pen poised over his notebook.

I looked up at Dr. Goodwin. He nodded encouragement. "Go ahead, Kathy. Tell him."

Taking a deep breath, I tried to quiet the hammering of my heart so I could think straight. My mouth was so dry I could hardly get the words out.

"My husband, Donny Madison, did this to me. He works at Lewis Construction." I paused to gather my courage. "I have also been raped and abused by my husband's two friends."

When I whispered the names of the officers involved, both Detective Thorpe and Dr. Goodwin stared at me with mouths slightly open, disbelief evident on their faces. I looked down at my hands, which were clenched into fists in my lap.

"Are you sure about this young lady," the detective asked. "These are very serious charges. "

My head snapped up, and I looked the detective square in the face. Some of the feistiness I was born with came to the surface.

"Yes. I'm absolutely sure. They raped me! They hurt me! Not just this once, many times!"

I pulled up the sleeve of my hospital gown and turned my palm up so the detective could see the burn marks on the inside of my upper arm.

"Art Dawson did this to me! I have lots of other scars...." My voice trailed off and I looked away.

Dr. Goodwin verified that I did indeed have numerous old injuries that were, in his professional opinion, the result of repeated abuse.

"Do you want to press charges, Mrs. Madison?"

I swallowed and licked my dry lips. "Yes."

Detective Thorpe left to file three arrest warrants.

"My God, Kathy," Dr. Goodwin said after the detective left. "You should have told me!"

"But they said they would KILL ME if I told! They said they would hurt people I know. I believed them. I couldn't tell! I shouldn't have said anything now!" I wailed.

I was getting more agitated by the minute. Medication was injected into my intravenous line, and I slowly calmed down.

"I don't want you to worry about anything accept getting better, Kathy. Do you trust me enough to let me help you?"

"Yes, I guess so," I said with some hesitation.

He squeezed my hand. "Well, that's a start then, isn't it?"

Before leaving he gave orders to the nurses that even though he was going off duty, he would be in the doctor's lounge. If my husband should show up, he wanted to be notified immediately. Detective Thorpe was also to be called ASAP!

Chapter 29

Toward mid-morning the next day, sure enough, having left the hole he was hiding in, Donny found his way to ICU. Dr. Goodwin arrived in my room just in time to hear him say, "You lazy bitch, you'll do anything to stay in bed."

When Donny heard someone behind him, he whirled around coming face to chest with Dr. Mark Goodwin.

"When the hell can I get my wife out of here? She has work to do at home," he demanded.

I was awake, but pretended not to be. It would be safer that way. Dr. Goodwin calmly asked the nurse, who had followed him into my room, if she would step out for a few minutes. She left and closed the door.

Mark Goodwin was a good head and shoulders taller than Donny and at least 75 pounds heavier. He was also mad! He took Donny by the front of his shirt and slammed him against the wall. Through my nearly closed eyelids, I saw a look on Donny's face that I had never seen there before. Fear.

Dr. Goodwin put his face just inches from Donny's nose. Each word he said was spoken slowly and with emphasis.

"If she dies, I will see to it that you are charged with murder! I will do everything in my power to make sure you are convicted. You are nothing but a coward who preys on helpless women because you don't have the guts to take on a real man. Do I make myself perfectly clear?"

He let go of Donny and stepped back. Donny's face was chalk white, but he quickly regained his bravado. He always had to play the "big tough guy."

"I'll charge you with assault. You can't treat me this way. Just who do you think you f------ are anyway?"

"It will be my word against yours, you pinhead. Who do you think the police will believe?" Dr. Goodwin responded, his tone low and menacing.

At that moment, responding to the call made by the nurse to Detective Thorpe, the police appeared in the doorway. Donny was arrested, handcuffed, read his rights and taken away. Somehow I knew this wasn't the end.

Dr. Goodwin took a minute to get control of himself before he turned toward my bed. His face was flushed, but he was calm. He gently touched my shoulder, and I looked up at him.

As he did a quick assessment he asked if I was having any pain. He must have suspected I was, even though I said I was fine, because after he left, a nurse brought me a pill with some water. Soon I drifted off to sleep again.

Chapter 30

I woke up several hours later with a terrible pain ripping through my belly. My heart rate jumped. The cardiac monitor alarmed bringing the nurse on the run. I was having the baby. Right now!

Dr. Goodwin was paged STAT to my room. There wasn't enough time to transport me to the delivery room. I was ready to push! He arrived just as the nurse delivered the baby. Baby Lucas was extremely tiny and fragile. Dr. Goodwin wrapped him in a blanket, and put him on my chest.

My arms closed around my child. He only lived a few minutes, but it was long enough for a bond to be formed. When he died, my heart broke, and despair engulfed me. On Dr. Goodwin's orders, the staff left me alone for quite a while. I rocked my dead baby back and forth, letting my agony pour out in great heaving sobs.

The bleeding just wouldn't stop, so I was taken back to the operating room where a hysterectomy was necessary.

My will to live left me, along with the baby. I had been hanging on for his sake, and now there was nothing to care about anymore. I knew my little Lucas was dead. I didn't know where his body had been taken, and what did it matter anyway?

Dr. Goodwin tried his best to comfort me, but I was inconsolable. I continued to stare at the wall with tears coursing down my cheeks.

He told me I wouldn't be able to have any more children; the final blow. Donny had won.

My physical injuries slowly began to heal, but emotionally and psychologically, I was completely broken. I refused to eat more than a few bites, and I answered questions when asked, but other than that, I didn't say a word to anyone.

Chapter 31

I t had been about two weeks since I had been brought to the hospital. No matter how much I wanted to die, I just couldn't seem to do it. I guess my body wanted to live even if my mind didn't, so I slowly began to improve.

Everyone was so kind to me. Especially Dr. Goodwin. When I forced myself to eat a little bit, he would get a big silly grin on his face. He acted like I had accomplished some monumental feat by just swallowing custard!

He coaxed and prodded me. He brought me milkshakes and pizza. I finally gave in, and started eating. I had turned the corner toward living. I was moved to a private room, and since I was eating and drinking, the intravenous line was discontinued.

Some of the superficial stitches had been removed from my head and back, but since there was still discharge coming from the incision in my back, the drain had to stay for the time being. My condition had been downgraded, and I was no longer considered to be critical.

I was finally allowed to get out of bed with assistance from the staff. That was Dr. Goodwin's order. I was still as weak as a kitten, and he didn't want me to fall, possibly pulling out the stitches that remained. My temperature had hovered above normal for a few days, but an overwhelming infection had been averted.

"Dr. Mark," as I had decided to call him, was pleased with my progress.

I tried not to think about the future. I would have to leave the hospital sometime, but where would I go? How could I support myself?

Sleep was elusive. I awakened often during the night, thinking I heard a baby crying. Then the memories would sweep through my mind, and I would dissolve in tears again.

During one of my sleepless nights, I was lying on my side with my back to the door when suddenly a hand clamped over my mouth. A voice I knew all too well whispered in my ear.

"Time to go home, bitch, and get what's coming to you."

Donny hauled me roughly from the bed. He yanked out the drain that was still in my back. Blood immediately poured from the site. It began trickling over my hip, down my leg, and onto the floor.

He was arrested! Why isn't he in jail? My breathing came in great gasps as I stared into a face filled with rage. I felt lightheaded and ready to pass out. I was terrified! This time, I would die.

Change of shift. He couldn't have picked a more perfect time. No one was in the hallway, as the nurses were busy at the nurse's station giving a report on each patient to the oncoming shift. We went unnoticed as he pushed me ahead of him down the hall and around the corner.

I was barefoot and wearing nothing but a hospital gown. When my knees began to buckle, he swung me around and slapped me hard across my face, pulling apart the incision in my scalp that was just beginning to heal. The incision in my lip pulled apart, causing blood to run down my chin.

"You better walk, bitch, or I'll kill you right here," Donny snarled. "Then I'll come back and kill that big-ass doctor of yours. I'll pay him back good for the way he treated me."

He was out of control with blind fury. He was also very drunk. I didn't dare scream for help. Experience had taught me crying or screaming only made things worse. I knew he would hurt Dr. Mark, and anyone else who got in his way. I couldn't let that happen! By sheer force of will, I walked.

Donny had his car waiting at one of the hospital's emergency exits at the back of the building. He threw me in the backseat before slamming the door. He pulled away in a spray of gravel.

I was only semi-conscious when he pushed me into the house, and threw me to the floor on top of several days' accumulation of filth and garbage. I was bleeding profusely from my back where he had pulled out the drain. My face was covered with blood from my scalp and lip.

A haze of pain caused black spots to dance before my eyes, and I knew this was probably the end. The one thought that flickered through my mind was that I wouldn't get to see Dr. Mark again. I really liked him.

"You get this place cleaned up. Look at yourself. You're a dirty, ugly cow. Look at me when I'm f------ talking to you," he screamed in my face.

There was no way I could even lift my head. I felt like my arms and legs didn't even belong to me anymore. He gave me a vicious kick before slamming out the door.

I knew I would lie right here in this very spot, and bleed to death. The prospect wasn't all that unappealing. I just didn't care any more. Every last, tiny bit of the person I was had been destroyed. I sank into unconsciousness and floated between life and death.

Chapter 32

Once again I woke up in the Intensive Care Unit. I remember thinking, *why can't I just die and be done with it. I'm so tired of living.*

The intravenous line was back in plus another line with blood infusing. My mouth felt like it was packed with cotton, and my head was swimming. I heard a moaning sound, finally realizing it was coming from me. I spent two days in and out of consciousness before I rallied.

The nurse had let Dr. Goodwin know that I was back in the land of the living. The next time I opened my eyes, he was sitting beside me on the bed.

"Kathy! We were all so worried about you. How do you feel?" he said as he bent over me, his stethoscope on my chest.

Talking seemed like too great a task. I tried, but couldn't manage it, so I just shook my head the tiniest little bit, and closed my eyes. Just that little movement made me feel like my head would explode!

"Don't try to talk then, just listen. I'll explain what happened."

He pressed the button that raised my head just enough so that I could easily see him if I opened my eyes, but not high enough to make me feel dizzy. He held a glass of water so I could take a few sips, as he continued.

"It seems that one of the maintenance men had been late leaving work. When he turned the corner he saw a man shoving a woman along the hallway toward the rear emergency exit. He called out, but to no avail. He was too far away to catch the pair before they were out the door. He heard tires squealing as a car sped away. When he got to the door he saw the trail of blood on the floor, and immediately called security."

"Back on the unit, the next shift was making first rounds on each patient. When your nurse entered your room she found the bed empty, the drain on the floor, and a trail of blood out the door. She called security and paged me STAT."

Dr. Goodwin had taken one look at the room, and had a pretty good idea what had happened. *Why wasn't Madison in jail,* he had frantically wondered? *This looks exactly like something he would do!*

"I'm so sorry, Kathy. I should have anticipated something like this might happen. I should have taken extra precautions, but he was supposed to be in jail for God sake!

The look on his face told me that he blamed himself for what had happened. I desperately wished there was some way I could make him believe it wasn't his fault.

He had called the state police, and told them one of his patients had been taken from the hospital against her will. She was in serious danger, and in critical condition. He gave them my home address, and told them to have an ambulance meet them there.

When the state police and the ambulance arrived, they found me unconscious in a pool of blood. The paramedics worked on me at the scene, taking my vitals, putting ice on my face, and using pressure bandages to control the bleeding from my scalp, lip and back wounds.

An officer from the State Police asked me what my name was, and if I knew who had done this to me. I wasn't coherent enough to respond so they loaded me in the ambulance. With the lights flashing and the siren blaring, we headed for the hospital.

"When you arrived in the emergency room, and I saw what kind of shape you were in, I wanted to choke the bastard to death with my own bare hands. I have to admit I have never felt such rage before in my life," Dr. Goodwin said as he looked away briefly to regain his composure.

The plastic surgeon had been called once again, and he just shook his head as he looked at the area where the drain had been pulled out. He could put the wound back together, but there would be a scar; an extensive one. It would require careful attention.

He would take extra care when repairing my lip to prevent scarring as much as possible. My hair would cover the scar that would result from the scalp laceration. My back was his biggest concern. I was taken back to the operating room for the third time.

When the surgery was done, and I was finally back in my room, the state police were waiting. I was afraid of what they wanted with me. *What did I do now?* I wondered. *It must be something awful!*

Since Dr. Mark was standing close to my bed, I tentatively slid my hand into his. It was a great comfort to me when his fingers closed around mine.

Was I going to be arrested for something? I hadn't done anything wrong, but then, that hadn't mattered in the past!

Chapter 33

"**M**rs. Madison I am very sorry to have to inform you that your husband was killed this morning in a work related accident."

When Officer Gray delivered this news, I was stunned. It took several seconds for me to understand what he had just said. I stared at him for several seconds with a blank look on my face, my brain reeling.

Apparently, after Donny was arrested and booked, his one phone call was made to his boss, Maynard Lewis.

Maynard Lewis! Harriet's Maynard? How could that be? I was dazed, but that name got my attention! *Donny has been working for Harriet's husband all this time?*

At his arraignment, substantial bail was set, but Maynard, being the great guy that he was, posted the money. It wasn't long before Donny was released. It had been his word against mine as there wasn't any concrete evidence of his attack on me. No witnesses. Art and Willie certainly weren't going to incriminate themselves be telling the truth!

He had gone back to work, taking up his job right where he left off. He took the elevator to the 25th floor and walked out onto the I-beam. Picking up the riveter he had previously been using, he hit the start button. The piece of equipment roared into action and then jammed, throwing him off balance.

Witnesses would later testify that he tried to grab something, anything, to catch himself, but to no avail. He had fallen, his arms and legs flailing, down 25 stories. He died instantly.

"There will be an investigation," the officer assured me. "Again, I'm very sorry, Mrs. Madison." With that said the officer and his partner left.

What did this mean? I felt like I was in a time warp with everything moving in slow motion. Nothing made sense. Dr. Mark became my lifeline to sanity.

Art and Willie had been arrested at the police station. They had probably been shocked, to say the least. They never expected me to disclose their despicable activities. Art vehemently denied ever having anything but "casual social contact" with me. Willie wisely kept his mouth shut.

Neither of them could make bail, so they were still sitting in jail. Art was getting more verbal by the day proclaiming his innocence. It surprised me that their "brother officers" didn't anti-up and get them released.

Their Police Chief was seething with indignation. He had given a press conference assuring the good citizens of Boston that he would get to the bottom of these ridiculous allegations, and the truth would come out. He was sure his officers would be exonerated.

I had watched the press conference on TV with Dr. Mark. He was furious over the remarks made by Chief Finnerty. I was considerably upset to hear myself talked about like I was some kind of horrible villain!

Dr. Mark leaned over and kissed my forehead, something that was completely unexpected. My eyes filled with tears.

"I promise, Peanut. I'll make sure you're safe. I have a good friend who is a lawyer. I'm sure he'll help."

As I think back over the events of my life, I realize this was a pivotal moment for me. As I stared into the face of this good man, I decided to give humanity one more chance.

He had called me Peanut. I knew it was a term of endearment. He promised to keep me safe. I wasn't sure anyone could do that, but it touched my heart that he was even willing to try.

Over the next several weeks, I struggled to process everything that had happened.

Chapter 34

Attorney Oscar Schwartz was Dr. Mark's closest friend. They had gone to undergraduate school together, and had stayed in touch even after graduation. Mark had gone on to medical school. Oscar was drawn to a law career.

Both had ended up in Boston. Oscar worked as an associate in a prestigious law firm. Mark decided on a career as an emergency room physician at Boston General Hospital.

I guess Oscar hadn't expected me to look so young and pathetic! It took him a few minutes to feel comfortable interviewing me. His obvious distress brought a tentative little smile to my face, and that seemed to break the ice.

His area of expertise was criminal law. He had been waiting for just the right case to propel him into a full partnership at the firm. It would have to be something spectacular, like suing Lewis Construction for the wrongful death of my husband.

With my permission, Dr. Mark had given him a brief introduction into the circumstances surrounding my abuse and subsequent admission to the hospital.

Oscar was appalled. He had not lived a sheltered life; however, the extent of what had been done to me shocked him. He decided we should also bring a lawsuit against Art and Willie for their part in the abuse.

At the time, it was impossible for me to comprehend what impact all of this would eventually have on my future. All I was sure of was that Donny would never hurt me again, and for the time being, that was enough.

Oscar immediately began investigating Lewis Construction as well as Arthur Dawson and William Thompson. What he discovered proved most interesting.

Chapter 35

It was well known to everyone who worked for Lewis Construction that if you worked without regard for safety measures, you could work faster. Willing employees were paid substantial sums of money under the table if a project was completed ahead of schedule, and Maynard Lewis earned a nice fat bonus for his efforts.

The piece of equipment Donny had been using at the time of his death was of the poorest quality to begin with, and no attention had been given to the recommended maintenance.

Oscar discovered that there had been reports filed of other less serious accidents tied to the malfunction of this specific riveter. Mr. Lewis was well aware of the problem, but chose to ignore it. He fired people for complaining too loud or too long. "Just get the job done." That was Maynard's mantra.

Maynard had started out as the low man on the construction totem pole. He was clever and willing to do anything to get ahead. This quickly brought him to the attention of the company owner, Bruno Salinger, a sleazy, greedy character without a shred of decency. Maynard quickly advanced through the ranks and was soon a foreman with his own crew.

He took short cuts and used inferior materials, but he always brought his part of the construction project in under budget. The owner was very pleased indeed, and Maynard was compensated generously. "The Boss" began grooming Maynard for bigger and better things.

It wasn't long before he was second in command. Mr. Salinger, being close to retirement and in ill health, turned the company over to Maynard for an "undisclosed amount of money."

If you wanted work done in a hurry, and weren't too particular about the way it got done, Maynard Lewis was your man. His reputation grew as did his bank account.

The authorities had known about the shady business practices of this company for some time. They were just never able to get enough evidence to make charges stick, but up to this point, no one had died.

Co-workers of Donny's confirmed that he often bragged about all the extra money he made by walking the I-beams. It didn't matter how high up he was, he had what it took to get the job done.

So Donny was dead, and Harriet's husband, Maynard, was scum. Poor Harriet! I still missed her.

I wondered how I was ever going to pay all the hospital bills, but Oscar told me not to worry about it. Once we won the lawsuit, there would be plenty of money.

Chapter 36

D r. Mark spent as much time with me as he could, and I began to wonder if he lived at the hospital. He was a constant encouragement to me, especially when doubts and fear assailed me. He reassured me that Donny got exactly what he deserved! He also believed that Art and Willie would eventually get exactly what THEY deserved!

I was discharged from acute hospital care and moved to the rehab unit, where I began working diligently with the therapist to restore strength and flexibility to my back. The scar was already starting to contract, so the skin on my back felt very tight and sore. The exercises were painful, but necessary, and I tried my best.

Dr. Mark came to my room one evening, and sat down in the chair beside my bed. "If you're feeling up to it," he began, "I would like to talk to you about something I think is important."

Apprehension immediately filled my mind, and must have showed on my face. "Do you trust me, Peanut? I will never do anything that isn't in your best interest."

I nodded yes, so he continued. He wanted my permission to discuss my domestic violence situation in more detail with Oscar.

The next day, after therapy and a nap, Oscar arrived looking very dapper and business-like in a dark suit and red tie.

Mark began explaining the circumstances, going back three years, which had led to my hospitalization for such serious injuries.

Oscar's first question didn't surprise me. Why hadn't I tried to get away? When I explained the depth of the fear that had been instilled in me, and the threats that had been made, I could tell by his manner that hearing the details of my life greatly affected him.

He began asking specific questions; hard embarrassing questions. I did my best to answer truthfully. He wrote furiously on his legal pad as I spoke. When he seemed satisfied that he had enough information, he asked if I would give him permission to have full access to my medical records. I signed the release forms.

My file was brought to my room. I was surprised to see how thick it was! Dr. Mark had been meticulous in his documentation of my emergency room visits, as well as the necessary treatments. He had collected blood and semen samples and taken pictures of my injuries.

With every picture he saw, Oscar made a disgusted grunt until he had gone over the entire file. He shook his head and peered at me over the top of his round glasses. I saw compassion in his eyes.

The charges against Art and Willie would be rape, assault, depraved indifference, and dereliction of duty for starters. Oscar was sure he could come up with other charges once he gave the matter some thought.

He was going to take my case pro bono because of his friendship with Mark, not to mention the fact that the acts against me had been heinous. He felt justice should prevail.

He had not expected to invest himself personally. After all, this was just another case. But after listening to me haltingly describe the horror my life had been he was in my corner one hundred percent!

He began pacing back and forth across my room. "This is outrageous! People in law enforcement take an oath to protect and defend! These two officers are a disgrace to the whole department!

We'll just see how cocky they are once I'm through with them! Don't you worry. I'll handle everything!"

I believed him because I trusted Dr. Mark.

When I sighed and lay back against my pillow, Oscar awkwardly tucked my blanket under my chin.

He doesn't have much experience with women, I thought, as I drifted off to sleep. The whole process of re-telling had exhausted me, but I knew I had made a good friend in Oscar Schwartz.

Chapter 37

I learned a lot about Oscar over the ensuing weeks as we prepared my case for trial.

Oscar Schwartz was Jewish and came from "old money." He was financially set for life and really didn't need to work at all. However, he didn't think being rich was an excuse for being lazy. He was gifted in the areas of investments, the stock market and banking. He could have easily made a career in any financial arena.

There was just something about the excitement of the courtroom. He thrived on it. Oscar was a very ethical young man, and he loved the idea of "catching the bad guys and making them pay." He was like a little banty rooster when confronted with injustice, and he never stepped away from a challenge.

My case met all of his criteria. He decided that in order to put all his time toward winning the case, he would leave the law firm and open an office of his own.

A couple of secretaries and three paralegals were hired; all young and dedicated to pursuing justice. He rented some office space in the same building as his old employer.

He was as thorough in preparing his case as Dr. Mark had been in documenting the medical aspects of my numerous visits to the emergency room. No stone was left unturned when it came to finding evidence to present to the jury.

Oscar was an average looking young man, certainly not handsome. He was short, his hairline was receding a bit, and he had a rather prominent nose. After I got to know him better, I teased him about it. He took it good naturedly, stating that he was stuck with what his mama gave him.

I appreciated the fact that when discussion of the case got too heavy, he always did his best to lighten my mood. He would do one of his crazy, arm flapping dances, and sing an off-key tune he made up on the spot about something silly. It never failed to make me smile.

His voice was pleasant and well modulated, his suits impeccable, but not ostentatious. He presented himself as being humble and honest, and he <u>was</u> honest. Humble, maybe not so much.

Under that average exterior he was smart as a whip. He was also driven and fearless in the courtroom. He had the uncanny ability to "read" people, instinctively knowing when they were lying and when they were telling the truth. God help you if you were lying!

The papers had been filed and we had a court date. Oscar would handle all the preliminaries. He would let me know exactly what he needed me to do and when. In the meantime, I continued my therapy, and tried not to obsess over the prospect of going to trial!

In order to try and keep my mind occupied with other things, Dr. Mark suggested I use my time to study, with a goal of getting my high school diploma. He and Oscar went together and hired a tutor to help me. I threw myself into this task with a vengeance.

In the meantime, immediately after Donny's death, Maynard Lewis had circled the wagons. He assembled his highly paid legal team in the hopes that he could save his "sorry ass." At least that's what Oscar said.

Oscar "accidently" let it slip to a friend of his, who worked as a reporter for the biggest newspaper in Boston, that he would be representing the widow of Donny Madison in the lawsuit against Lewis Construction.

"Free publicity never hurts," he told me with an innocent grin.

He had an idea what might happen as a result. Employees of Lewis Construction would be coming out of the woodwork to jump on board with Madison's widow, hoping for some cash of their own.

As predicted, his office was soon inundated with calls from former, as well as current, employees of Lewis Construction. Each one wanted to know if they had a case against Maynard Lewis.

They claimed they had been "forced" to work without proper safety precautions in place. This made Oscar laugh out loud. He said his secretaries thought he had lost his mind.

He decided to file a class action suit against Lewis Construction on behalf of all these clients. If they were his clients, they would readily testify as to the unsafe practices at the job sites and the faulty equipment, thus solidifying my claim of the wrongful death of my husband.

By the time all was said and done, Maynard Lewis would be bankrupt. He was a slimy, deceitful, greedy man, and I knew he had met his match in Oscar Schwartz.

This will be a little justice for Harriet. She will probably never know it, but I would. Just the thought gave me a feeling of satisfaction.

Chapter 38

While he was preparing for trial, Oscar spent considerable time with me. I think he genuinely liked me, which amazed me. It was hard for me to believe I was a likable person.

I would be kept updated every step of the way through everything he did. During the Lewis lawsuit, he would not call me to the witness stand unless he absolutely had to, but he wanted me in the courtroom as much as possible.

He said I presented the perfect picture for the jury to keep in mind when they were deliberating. I was extremely nervous, but Oscar would tell me exactly what to do, and Dr. Mark would be with me.

As our court date drew nearer, I became more preoccupied with the "what if's," and Dr. Mark came whenever he had free time to provide some distraction. He brought a checker board and taught me to play. I was delighted with the game, challenging him at every opportunity.

I also loved books. Mark and Oscar brought me fiction, non-fiction, biographies, poetry; I couldn't get enough. One evening Mark brought me a magazine someone had left behind in one of the hospital waiting rooms. It was about boating and fishing. He thought I might like the beautiful pictures of faraway lands and endless oceans.

He was right. I was fascinated by the yachts and the ocean, never having seen anything like them before. I marveled at the glamorous women and tanned handsome men who caught huge fish while looking so happy. I told Dr. Mark I would like to go fishing someday on one of those boats.

I blossomed under the watchful eyes of my friends, Oscar and Mark. I became a favorite of the rehab staff because I was compliant with everything they asked me to do. They knew I tried my best, even when it hurt.

Good progress was being made, but the scar across my back remained raised, red and ugly, no matter what treatments the doctors tried. I was going to have to live with it the rest of my life.

Chapter 39

Jury selection was underway, and Oscar was a bundle of energy. The Lewis team of lawyers had never heard of Oscar Schwartz. He didn't have a reputation in town so they underestimated him. That was their first very costly mistake.

The day of opening statements arrived. Oscar wanted me in the front row of spectators, sitting alone. The very thought of this frightened me, but Oscar said Mark would be sitting just a few rows back. He would be keeping an eye on me.

He wanted me to dress simply with low heeled shoes, no makeup, and my mass of curly hair pulled back. Since I didn't have appropriate clothes for the trial, the nurses on the rehab unit got together, and with advice from Oscar, bought me some things to wear.

"Thank you so much," was all I could manage to stammer as unshed tears of gratitude brightened my eyes. I was completely overwhelmed by their generosity.

On the days that Oscar wanted me in the courtroom, he would drive me himself. He wanted to make sure I was seated where the jury could easily see me.

He was like a dog with a bone, and his tenacity in the courtroom took everyone totally by surprise. Not only was his knowledge of the law expansive, he seemed to have an uncanny ability to see the "loopholes" before the Lewis defense team had a chance to slither through them.

As I sat on the front row, dressed exactly as Oscar had suggested, I was impressed with how he conducted himself. I only knew him as Oscar, not really as Attorney Schwartz.

He was eloquent and articulate when presenting his opening statement. He told the jury that he would prove beyond a shadow of a doubt that the negligence of Lewis Construction was fully responsible for the death of Donny Madison, resulting in his young wife being left alone.

The jury saw exactly what Oscar wanted them to see; a demure young woman, now a widow.

Oscar had presented witness after witness who testified to having been required to work without regard to their personal safety. Several had used the exact riveter Donny had been using at the time of his death. The jury also heard testimony regarding the frequent malfunction of this specific piece of equipment.

The riveter was submitted as evidence.

Oscar carried out a little demonstration for the jury. He had the necessary materials set up in the courtroom. When he tried to operate the riveter it worked correctly for a few seconds, and then jammed, almost knocking him to the floor. The jury gasped in unison. I knew inside Oscar was ecstatic!

Also produced as evidence, were the work orders that had been submitted to have the riveter repaired or replaced.

Workers who had been present the day Donny had fallen to his death testified to what they had seen. Donny had been using the riveter presented as evidence.

It was now an established fact that the construction company was at fault. That was a done deal. No question. But there was one small thing that worried Oscar.

I had been only 16 when Donny had married me. Oscar said if he were a lawyer for Lewis Construction, he would try to prove that I wasn't, in fact, really married to Donny, and therefore not entitled to any compensation for his death.

He understood it was a very sensitive subject with me, but he needed to prepare me in case the defense used that tactic.

His instincts had been right again.

Now the lawyers representing Maynard Lewis were grasping at straws. If they could prove I was not married to Donny, no money would be awarded to me.

There would still be fines to pay, and small claims to deal with, but the biggest winner in all of this would be me, Kathy Madison. The lawyers knew Oscar would not settle for less than millions in damages, pain and suffering, loss of wages, etc, etc.

Oscar was not at all surprised when he was notified that I would be called as a witness; a hostile witness for the defense. Coaching me for the witness stand was pointless, as Oscar knew I would tell the truth even if it meant losing the case.

He explained to me what was going to happen the next day. I needed to answer only the questions that were asked and not offer any other comments. I understood.

"State your name for the record."

"Kathy Ann Madison," I replied.

I swore to tell the whole truth and nothing but the truth, so help me God. I must have looked small and vulnerable sitting there. At least, that's how I felt. I clutched my little purse trying to keep my fingers from visibly trembling. Was it important that I looked confident? I wasn't sure. I definitely didn't feel confident!

Attorney for the defense, Nathan Westlake, was tall and thin. His hair was slicked back with his head jutting forward, reminding me of a reptile. I wouldn't have been surprised if his tongue had flicked in and out as he started asking me easy questions in a deceptively friendly manner.

Where and when had we been married, did we have a honeymoon, how old was I when we married. I knew Oscar was on the edge of his seat listening carefully, trying to anticipate each question before it was asked.

Atty. Westlake was well aware of the other pending lawsuit against Art and Willie. He desperately wanted to somehow persuade the jury to see me in a different light. At this point, he must have thought the jury was sympathetic to my plight.

When Atty. Westlake asked if Donny and I had been happy together, Oscar jumped to his feet. "Objection," he shouted. "Relevance?"

The judge had both attorneys approach. The defense said it was imperative to their case to establish whether or not I had actually been married to Donny Madison.

Oscar said he agreed this needed to be established. But whether or not we were happy had no bearing on the charges brought against the defendant.

The judge agreed. The lawyers walked back to their respective tables. Oscar glanced at Mark. I had the feeling that both men were holding their breath. The whole case would depend on how convincing I could be to the jury.

Atty. Westlake quickly stepped up to the witness box, leaned toward my face, and shouted. "Tell the truth! You were never married to Donny Madison were you?"

His outburst startled me. I had not expected this kind of attack! I knew the color drained from my face as I stared from the attorney, to Oscar, to the judge. The judge kindly told me to answer the question.

"I was married to Donny Madison, and I can prove it," I said very quietly.

I opened my purse, and took out a folded piece of paper that neither Mark nor Oscar had ever seen. I carefully flattened it out, and handed it to Atty. Westfield.

It was a duly signed, dated and witnessed...certificate of marriage stating that Kathy Ann Martin was indeed wed to Donald J. Madison.

Atty. Westlake realized instantly that he had lost the case. He dropped his head as he handed the document to the judge. It was all Oscar could do to contain himself! He looked like he wanted to jump up on the table and do one of his crazy little dances!

He had never asked me if I had a marriage certificate.

Later he told me, shaking his head in amazement, "You learn something new every day, even when you think you already know it all."

Chapter 40

T he monies I would receive would be substantial. The construction company had made a LOT of money over the years, and when Maynard Lewis took over, the profits had skyrocketed albeit illegally.

His insurance company could come up with only so much to settle this case. He would have to pay the rest out of his own pocket, and Oscar wanted it all.

I couldn't quite comprehend that much money or how Oscar had arrived at the figure; something about expected wages over Donny's working years, pain, suffering…it was all Greek to me.

The best part, in my mind, was that dear "May" would be lucky if he could get a job as a janitor after this.

I asked Oscar if he would find my beloved Harriet Lewis. I wanted to do something for this woman who had been willing to take me in as her own child if circumstances had been different.

With a little investigating, Oscar found that Harriet had managed to survive on the farm, but not before selling off a good portion of the land, and all the cows. Currently, the farm could be bought by anyone who could pay the back taxes.

Out of the money I was awarded, I asked Oscar if I had enough to pay the taxes for Harriet. Oscar gave me an indulgent smile. He knew I had no concept of the amount of money I would be awarded.

"Of course you do, Peanut," he said. "I'll see to it."

I also wanted Oscar set up a fund or something that would provide Harriet with enough money to continue to keep the remainder of the farm intact for as long as she wanted to live there. Oscar said he could invest some additional money so that interest would grow, keeping revenue flowing into the fund.

Harriet would probably never know who her benefactor was, but I would know. It made me smile! One of those big, heart-stopping, eye-popping, dimple-dancing smiles that Oscar and Mark were the first to ever see.

Chapter 41

Every newspaper in the city carried the story of how this relatively unknown lawyer, Oscar Schwartz, had brought down the biggest construction company in the Boston area. He had gotten the biggest settlement for his client, Kathy Madison, that had ever been awarded in the whole state to date.

The other clients represented in the class action suit were also awarded smaller amounts depending on the injuries they had suffered. Oscar needed to hire at least two or three more lawyers to handle the clients that were now calling his office on a daily basis.

Harold Tweaks was brought on board as the head of Oscar's investigative unit. Harold was a college buddy who had specialized in forensics and criminal justice.

He had taken some serious ribbing, especially from Oscar, about his last name.

"Hey, it takes a big man to carry a name like this one," he had told Oscar with a grin.

Oscar would only hire people he knew and trusted. He wanted his law firm to be known for its integrity and fairness. He would only defend the innocent, and that's where Harold came in.

It was his job to substantiate the client's claim. If it was proven to be just, then all the assets of the Schwartz law firm would be brought to bear on the client's behalf.

At this point, his secretaries took messages from would-be clients, as Oscar's full attention was now focused on the second part of his plan. Art and Willie had knowingly and repeatedly perpetrated violence against me. Now it was their turn to pay.

As it turned out, the police department had already been conducting its own investigation. Their goal, of course, was to prove Art and Willie were innocent of all charges filed against them.

The Lewis Construction lawsuit, and the death of Donny Madison, was still fresh in everyone's mind. Was it just coincidence that Art's car had been seen at the Madison residence? They dug a little deeper into Art and Willie's association with Donny Madison and discovered they were all friends.

In the meantime, no grass was growing under the feet of Harold Tweaks. He had already spoken to neighbors who verified that Art's car was parked next door at least once a week, sometimes more often.

The old man who lived across the street was a bit of a busybody and liked to keep track of his neighbors' comings and goings. He was an odd little guy who enjoyed his chewing tobacco. As he talked to Harold he frequently spit in a coffee can he kept specifically for that purpose. His head bobbed up and down in excitement as he expounded on what transpired across the street.

He had seen a young girl limping down the street to the bus stop on several occasions, returning a few hours later. The dark blue sedan was parked in the driveway a lot, leading him to think it belonged to someone who lived there.

"I even seem 'em 'ere pooo-lice in uniform roll up in dey poooo-lice car, and go in and out of dat dare house all-a time. I often wonner why dey be needing the cops dare so often, but it ain't none of my bi'ness," he confided to Harold.

The officer who had been at the scene the night I went through the window was questioned extensively. He admitted he had seen Art's car parked beside the house that night.

Oscar had requested a search warrant for Art's house. When the warrant was executed, Art's wife had been terrified. She followed the officers from room to room, wringing her hands in distress. They finally had to ask one of the female officers to sit with her in the living room until the search was completed.

She was an average looking woman in her mid-thirties. Her hair was stringy and unkempt, and she had a haunted, trapped look about her.

Her eyes flitted nervously from one thing to another when Harold tried to talk to her about Art. She refused to say anything against her husband.

"My Art's a good man," she repeated over and over to Harold.

Pornographic videos and magazines were discovered hidden in a box at the back of Art's closet. Lewd pictures of very young girls were found under his mattress; not a very imaginative hiding place, especially for a cop!

On a hunch, Harold visited the bars the trio frequented. People like Art usually bragged about their exploits. Sure enough, the regular barflies knew Art, Willie and Donny well, and had shared many a drink with them.

And "yes," Art had often alluded to the fact that he had access to a "young dolly" that was a "fine piece of ass." With a smirk and a wink he regaled them with details of what he did to her. The more he drank, the more he talked. Not coincidentally, what he said matched exactly what I had told Oscar, Dr. Mark and Detective Thorpe.

Chapter 42

Oscar told me how important it was that I be completely honest with him. If we were going to win this case, I needed to tell him everything, even if I didn't think it was important. The tiniest little thing could make a difference, and we couldn't afford to be surprised in court. So I was completely honest with him, even when the telling of it shamed me.

He would just pat my hand. "It's okay, Peanut. You didn't do anything wrong. None of this was your fault!"

As more and more information came to light about the unsavory character of Art Dawson, the local police department did a complete turn-around in attitude. Oscar said it was called "saving face."

There was a statement issued by the Chief of Police a week after his press conference. He wanted everyone to know that the confidence of the people of Boston was important to him and the effective functioning of the department. The situation was being thoroughly investigated. Based on the facts, appropriate action would be taken - blah, blah, blah.

Oscar just huffed in disgust. He said the chief of police just wanted to be perceived as being willing to clean up his own mess once a problem had been discovered.

"Perception is everything, Peanut. He wants to keep his job!"

Both officers were in jail and suspended without pay, pending the results of the trial.

Art continued to proclaim his innocence loud and long to anyone who would listen, even from jail.

Willie kept his mouth shut. His apartment was also searched, and nothing of consequence was found.

"He just might be the weak link," Oscar mused. It was something to keep in mind when the trial started.

My medical records had been subpoenaed as evidence in court. Of course, Mark and Oscar had already gone over everything with me. Oscar made it clear that the pictures would be enlarged and everyone in the court room would see everything.

This was going to be very difficult for me, and Oscar wanted me to be prepared for the worst. The press would be cruel. Accusations would center on "she asked for it, she liked it." The whole thing would probably get ugly before all was said and done.

The case would rest on circumstantial evidence. There were no eye-witnesses to the actual events, so my testimony would be crucial. It would be essentially my word against Art and Willie's. Oscar would try to protect me as much as possible, but I knew it was going to be rough. Sometimes just discussing the case got me so upset Dr. Mark had to give me a sedative.

Both men were unsure if I could hold up under the cross examination, which was sure to be vicious. I was adamant. I could do it.

"If I don't stop them, who will be the next victim?" I tearfully asked Oscar.

Oscar said the case was ironclad, and short of everyone on the jury being a moron, he expected a guilty verdict on all charges.

Chapter 43

The jury selection was complete and the preliminaries were done. The courthouse was packed on the day the trial was to begin.

Oscar did a terrific job with his opening statement. He presented our case simply and clearly for the jury without fanfare or theatrics. He stated he would prove beyond a shadow of doubt that Arthur Dawson and William Thompson had repeatedly raped and assaulted his client, causing serious physical, emotional and psychological damage.

He further stated that the defense would try to persuade them to think that these fine, upstanding police officers were not capable of such cruelty. Their only crime was possibly picking the wrong friend in Donny Madison.

Their unblemished records would be presented along with any commendations they had received. Witnesses would expound on their excellent character; but the fact remained, they were indeed guilty of assault and rape.

When it was the defense attorney's turn to address the jury, he said exactly what Oscar warned them he would say. He reminded them that this would be my word against the word of two of Boston's police officers.

They could only convict if the prosecution proved without doubt that Art and Willie were guilty. He went on overlong while Oscar got more restless and madder by the minute!

Attorney Barton, for the defense, looked like a strutting little peacock. He was perfectly coiffed and manicured. His suit and shoes looked expensive. Being an eloquent speaker, he had a flair for the grandiose.

Some of the jurors seemed mesmerized as he pranced back and forth with one hand in the pocket of his trousers, the other moving with artistry as he spoke. Others yawned, unimpressed.

He put on a great performance as he spun his tale. I was a beautiful, married, young girl, awestruck by my husband's two important friends.

When my womanly charm and flirtatious advances were rejected, I cried rape and abuse. What better way to sooth my wounded pride?

Unfortunately, with my husband now deceased, he was not here to speak to the innocence of his friends.

"How convenient," he finished with a bow to the jury. As he returned to his seat he made sure the jury saw the look of sorrow he gave his clients. He shook his head sadly before he sat down.

Oscar was seething, his face set in stone.

I wanted to crawl under my seat. Nothing could have been farther from the truth. *Is this what justice is all about? Which lawyer can put on the best show?*

It was getting late in the afternoon. Thankfully, the judge called a halt to the proceedings. Court was adjourned until the following morning.

I was relieved. One day down. I had survived. But the worst was yet to come.

The following day, Dr. Mark Goodwin was the first witness to testify for the prosecution.

Oscar questioned him about his education, where he went to medical school, where he did his residency, his field of expertise, years of experience etc. I was told this was to substantiate his credibility to testify as my treating physician.

The enlarged photographs of my injuries from the abuse had the desired effect on the members of the jury.

I could hear gasps, especially from the women, as they saw picture after picture of a young girl, her face battered beyond recognition, cigarette burns in various stages of healing, bruises on her thighs, neck, arms...

Dr. Mark explained each picture and what treatment had been necessary. Without being condescending, he used terms the jury could understand. He answered each question Oscar presented with quiet confidence. His eye contact with the jury portrayed sincerity.

He spoke not only to my physical injuries, but also to the emotional state I exhibited each time I presented for treatment; classic behavior for someone who had been raped.

Atty. Barton objected.

Dr. Goodwin was not a psychiatrist, therefore not qualified to testify as to my emotional or psychological state.

Oscar came back with, "Dr. Goodwin has been an emergency physician at Boston General Hospital for many years. He has treated numerous victims of rape and violence. He is therefore, eminently qualified to make observations and speak to my client's emotional state."

"Objection overruled. The witness may continue," responded Judge Jerome Hackett.

I kept my head down and never looked up. It was like going through the whole thing all over again. Waves of nausea ebbed and flowed. It was all I could do to stay seated.

Mark's testimony took two full days.

During this time, Arthur Dawson let his eyes rove around the courtroom giving the appearance that he was bored with the whole proceeding. His lawyer whispered something to him on several occasions, and for a few minutes he would be attentive to what was being said.

Willie took advantage of the drinking water that was available on each table, soon paying the price, and squirming in his chair. The next day, he stared forlornly at a spot just over the judge's head and didn't touch the water!

Surprisingly, when it was Atty. Barton's turn to cross-examine Dr. Mark, he "had no questions for this witness."

Oscar's feeling was that the defense didn't want those pictures in front of the jury any longer than was necessary. They were too graphic; too "telling."

All of the witnesses that Harold had interviewed were sworn in one by one and testified to what they had seen.

Chapter 44

The old man from across the street was our last witness. His testimony put Art and Willie in uniform, driving their cruiser, at the house, on multiple occasions. It also put Art's own personal vehicle in the driveway frequently, and most importantly, on the day I was found in the street.

"State your full name."

The old man puffed out his chest, and sat up a little straighter in the witness chair. "Aloysius Leroy Whitley Sr.," he replied with pride.

"Do you swear to tell the truth, the whole truth, and nothing but the truth so help you God?"

"Course I does," he said with disgust written all over his face. "I is a God-fearin' man."

"Do you recognize the two gentlemen sitting at the defense table?"

"I seen 'um alla time, wearing dey po-lice uniforms, goin' in and outta dat dare house cross de street. Dey pull up in dey big ole po-lice car, lookin' all kinda like dem dare pee-cocks, struttin' up to de door."

He turned his head, and spit a long stream of tobacco juice on the floor to emphasize what he thought of them.

"MR. WHITLEY! NO SPITTING," the judge warned.

He glared at the judge, and then slowly looked back at Oscar. "Be wondrin' why de po-lice hafta be at dat house so much…"

"OBJECTION," shouted Atty. Barton. "Move to strike!"

"Sustained. The jury will disregard Mr. Whitley's speculations. Mr. Whitley, stick to what you saw, please."

Leroy whipped his head around toward the judge. "My 'pinion be wuth as much as yours I reckon," he snapped.

"MR. SWARTZ, control your witness!"

"I'm very sorry your honor. Leroy, what else, if anything, have you observed from your house across the street from the Madison home?"

"I seen dem two park a regalur car in de driveway. Dat big fat one alwis dribin'. Dey go inna house, come out afer while, de fat one hossen up he pants. Den sometimes I seen dat lil gal come stumblin' outa dat house, and she be hobblin' down de street to de bus stop. She come back later."

"Have you ever noticed anyone other than these two men coming and going from the Madison house?"

"Nope! Never! Alwis dem two."

"Now this is very important Mr. Whitley, so think carefully before you answer. Did you notice anything on the day in question when Mrs. Madison was found in the street?"

"Sho' nough did! Ain't gotta think 'bout dat. I know what I seen. Dat fat guy and him skinny fren come dat day early. Didn't see nothing de rest of de day. Den in de evenin' afta dark, I hears tires scretchin', and seen dat fat guy, de skinny guy an de guy who lib dere go fast down de street like de debil hisself was afta dem. Next ting I know, amblance, po-lice, de flashy lights all in de street. I seen dem put sompin in de amblance, and off dey go. Dat's what I seen," he finished as he sat back, resting his hands on his knees and looking very indignant.

Oscar, scratching his chin on the pretense of thinking out loud, said he wondered why, if there were police officers present during whatever altercation took place, a passer-by was the one who called for an ambulance.

"OBJECTION," screamed Atty. Barton, his eyes bulging, his face purple.

The jury was told to disregard Atty. Schwartz's comments, but that little kernel of suspicion was planted, just as Oscar had planned.

"That's all I have for this witness," Oscar said as he smiled at Leroy.

Atty. Barton quickly stepped forward. "It seems, Mr. Whitley, that all you do is watch your neighbors from your window. Why is that?"

"You mus be stupit er sompin'! I is an ole man. What I gonna do? Dancin'? Climbin' mountians? Got nuttin else to be doin', so I jus sit back an' watch."

Then Atty. Barton made the mistake of questioning the witness's eyesight, and his ability to identify the defendants, much less remember specific dates and times.

Mr. Whitley rose from the chair, stuck his scrawny neck out and yelled, "dey ain't nuttin wrong wit my eyes or my memry, you donkey's…"

The gallery erupted in laughter prompting the judge to bang his gavel several times to bring order to the room.

The witness was promptly excused, as Mr. Barton apparently decided to cut his losses.

Of course, Atty. Barton had tried to discredit all the witnesses on some pretext or another, but at the end of the day Oscar felt we had done well.

Chapter 45

Tomorrow I would take the stand. I was extremely nervous, and hardly slept a wink. Talking about my ordeal AGAIN, and in front of all those people! I couldn't bear to even think about it. I was utterly humiliated. I felt cheap and dirty. When no more tears were left, I stared at the ceiling the rest of the night.

I was sworn in, and took the oath to tell the truth.

Oscar had told me to look only at him. "Don't be tempted to look at Art and Willie. Art especially will do his best to intimidate you."

Very gently, Oscar began asking me questions. The first few were general questions about when Donny and I had gotten married, where we had lived; easy questions. My eyes remained glued to his face.

When the questions became more directed at the first time I had been raped by Art, I began to tremble. I knew Dr. Mark was agonizing over this, knowing how hard it was for me.

"Kathy, I want you to describe in detail for the jury what Arthur Dawson did to you."

Now that the moment had arrived, I didn't think I would be able to open my mouth, and say those words. I made the mistake of glancing at the jury.

There was a heavyset, gray haired woman sitting in the front row with her arms folded across her chest. She was looking at me like I was a filthy slut; something that put a nasty taste in her mouth. I recoiled as if I had been slapped.

A middle-aged man in the back row was looking at me exactly like Art did while he was taking off his pants! My cheeks burned with embarrassment. I quickly looked away.

What little I had eaten for breakfast now rose and lodged in my throat. I gagged, quickly putting my hand over my mouth to keep from vomiting.

Gaining a measure of control, I brought my eyes back to Oscar's face. I could see the pain there. I knew this was ripping him apart inside.

"Please, do I have to say?" I whispered.

"Speak up young lady, so the jury can hear," the judge prompted.

I turned, and looked up at him. "Please, I can't say those things out loud," I pleaded, knowing it was no use.

When he told me I had to tell the court what happened, my tongue stuck to the roof of my mouth. I couldn't speak.

Oscar went back to his table and poured a glass of water. "Could my client have just a minute?" he politely asked the judge as he handed me the glass.

"Oh, come on your honor. This is just a ploy to waste the court's time," Atty. Barton snorted loudly.

"Sit down, Mr. Barton. We can afford to be a little generous with our time, can't we?"

I had to grip the glass with both hands. I was shaking so hard the water splashed over the top, spilling onto my skirt. I finally managed to take a small sip. As I was handing the glass back to Oscar, it slipped from my grasp, and fell to the floor. The glass exploded sending water and shards of glass splattering all over floor, as well as Oscar's shoes.

Overpowering fear flooded my brain. Acting out of instinct born of terror, I was on my knees picking up the pieces of glass.

"Please, I'm sorry. I'm so sorry. Please don't hurt me," I whimpered.

For a few seconds, you could hear a pin drop in the courtroom with the exception of my gasping breaths and quiet sobbing. I frantically tried to gather the pieces of glass and wipe up the water with my bare hands.

Then there was blood. I had cut the palm of my hand on one of the larger pieces of glass. Oscar was instantly in motion, putting his handkerchief in my hand and calling for Mark. Oscar lifted me off the floor and sat me back in the witness chair.

Mark was there immediately, carefully peeling back the handkerchief to examine my injury.

"She will need medical attention," he said to the judge.

He didn't wait for permission, he just scooped me up and strode from the room.

"Your honor, I would like to request a recess so that my client can receive the medical attention she needs."

Of course, Atty. Barton objected, which didn't gain him any points with most of the jurors.

The request was granted with court to reconvene at two in the afternoon.

According to Oscar, Judge Hackett had been on the bench for many years. He had probably seen every reprobate known to mankind. He recognized genuine emotion when he saw it, as opposed to a contrived ploy to gain sympathy from the jury. My actions were reflexive as a result of repeated abuse.

My hand bled profusely, but the cut was not deep. While Mark was cleaning the wound and applying a pressure dressing, Oscar received a call from one of the court officials.

Willie had fired Atty. Barton, and was demanding to speak with Oscar!

Chapter 46

This was an unexpected turn of events and extremely unorthodox! Oscar hurried back to the courthouse to see what was going on, leaving me in Mark's capable hands.

He returned about two hours later with a crooked smile on his face.

It seemed Willie wanted to "come clean." He felt his actions were morally reprehensible. He should never have been an active participant in an activity that he knew was wrong.

Further, he should have put a stop to what was happening. He should have reported Art right from the get-go. He would not accept a plea bargain, telling Oscar he deserved whatever sentence the court handed down.

Oscar was stunned! I had told him from the start that Willie had not been the instigator of any of the abuse. He had never hit me or burned me. At the time, Oscar had found this hard to believe, but I had insisted that I didn't think Willie was mean. Art had bullied him into participating.

For whatever reason, Willie had grown a conscience, and Oscar couldn't have been happier. When he told me I would not be required to continue my testimony, the relief that washed over me at that moment was overwhelming. I hugged Oscar.

The jury was back, and we all stood as the judge took his seat.

Oscar stepped forward, informing the court he would not recall me to testify. Instead, another witness had come forward. He called Officer William Thompson to the stand.

Excitement electrified the spectators. A ripple of comments filled the room for several seconds before Judge Hackett regained control with several sharp raps of his gavel.

One look at Atty. Barton's face was enough to make my blood curdle. He was furious! Art looked like he might explode. His face was beet red. Sweat was pouring down his neck, and into his shirt collar.

Willie stated his name, and with his right hand on the Bible, swore to tell the whole truth.

Oscar began by reiterating for the jury and the judge what had transpired during the recess. He then asked Willie to repeat what he had said during their conversation prior to court reconvening.

All eyes were on Willie. He swallowed several times before he cleared his throat and began to speak.

"I am terribly ashamed that I have allowed these proceedings to go this far without speaking up. I not only witnessed my partner's repeated rape and abuse of Kathy Madison, I raped her myself."

Willie looked down at the floor. "I never hit her or burned her, but I did force sex on her. She always fought us. I helped hold her down because Art threatened to shoot me if I didn't."

He finally lifted his head and his eyes sought out mine. "All the testimony that has been presented by the prosecution is the absolute truth. Kathy, I'm so sorry." With that said, he hung his head.

The spectators went wild and the reporters covering the trial ran from the room to call in this latest development to their respective newspapers. They left too soon. The real action was about to begin!

Chapter 47

Seemingly, out of nowhere, three shots rang out.

With the first shot Willie's chest blossomed red. He fell sideways out of the witness chair. Oscar dropped into a crouch position frantically looking around for the shooter.

The second shot sent a bullet whizzing past my head. Mark pushed me to the floor covering my body with his.

A third shot went wild, hitting the woman who sat in the very last chair in the jury box. Her head exploded and her body flew backward from the impact, knocking the man behind her to the floor.

Pandemonium broke loose in the courtroom! People were screaming and running in all directions. Some were trampled trying to reach the exits. It was utter chaos.

It took three court officers to finally wrestle Art to the floor and disarm him.

All the while he kept screaming, "Willie, you bastard," and "you're dead, bitch. You liked it! You wanted it! YOU ARE DEAD! I have friends…" He was thrashing and spitting as he spewed his garbage all the way down the hall to the holding cell.

Ambulances were called, along with police reinforcements, to bring some semblance of calm to the scene. Several women were weeping as they huddled on the floor behind overturned chairs. The injured moaned in pain. The gentleman who had been sitting next to the woman who had been killed was sobbing like a child. The left side of his face and arm were covered with blood and brain matter.

Mark's first concern was for me. After Art was finally removed, he helped me to my feet. Then, realizing I was unable to stand on my own, he picked me up, and for the second time that day, carried me to the back of the room.

I clung to him with my face buried in his neck. I was in shock. He began talking calmly to me, reassuring me that everything was over, and he wouldn't let anything happen to me.

The events of the last ten minutes seemed to have happened in slow motion. I was disoriented and confused. I couldn't seem to get my thoughts focused.

Willie had taken the hit and fallen. Oscar said he saw a flash from the gun as a shot was fired in my direction, and he heard what Art was yelling. He turned around in time to see the woman fly over backwards from the impact of the third shot.

The next thing he remembered was hurling himself and his paralegal under the table where they had been sitting. Papers and evidence were scattered everywhere. The noise level rose instantly to a roar, and for the first time in his life, he admitted that his mind just wouldn't function.

He finally made his way back to where Mark was still holding me. "My God," he said, running his fingers through his hair. "How could this have happened?"

Chapter 48

One person died at the scene while several others received serious injuries. Willie was rushed by ambulance to the hospital where he went into surgery immediately. The shot, having been fired at an angle to the witness box, had only grazed his chest. He would live.

The police department reeled under the accusations of misconduct and possible complicity in conjunction with Art and Willie's activities.

The big question of the day was how did Art Dawson have access to a gun in the courtroom during a trial? It had to have been placed there by someone on the inside. The department scrambled to find explanations for what had happened. The whole city was in an uproar.

Court resumed two days later with the alternate juror sitting in for the woman who had been killed. Art was brought in wearing an orange jumpsuit and shackles.

It took exactly thirty minutes for the verdict of guilty to be handed down for the rape and assault charges. Sentencing would take place in two weeks.

There would be another trial for the murder of the juror and the attempted murder of Kathy Madison and William Thompson.

There would probably be other charges filed, perhaps even some against the police department, related to everything that had resulted from the shooting spree. Speculation was rampant about who had placed the gun in the courtroom.

With an abundance of eye witnesses to the shootings, including Judge Jerome Hackett himself, the district attorney had no doubt convictions would be handed down on all counts. He would be asking for life without parole.

Willie pled guilty. He was terminated permanently from the police department with loss of benefits and pension. He was sentenced without fanfare. Oscar thought he should rot in hell. He got 10 years.

The press was having a field day. My picture was plastered on every newspaper and rag in the whole city. The story even made the national news with pictures of Mark, Oscar and me filling the screen.

An intense investigation followed the shootings. The gun had been taped to the underside of the table exactly where Art would be sitting, probably just hours before the trial began. Someone on the inside had been an accomplice. Who?

If it hadn't been for my two dearest friends, Dr. Mark and Oscar, I would have descended into a pit of darkness and confusion from which I would never have recovered.

Over the days following the shooting, one of them was with me at all times. I was in seclusion and under sedation, still in the rehab unit of the hospital. All requests for interviews were declined.

The City of Boston, to avoid a lawsuit against the police department, offered a financial settlement to Oscar on my behalf. He accepted. He knew I would never survive another trial. I was much too fragile at this point.

Chapter 49

As I slowly recovered, Mark and Oscar spent much time in discussion over what would be the best course of action for me in order to keep me safe. I couldn't stay in rehab forever.

Obviously, Art had enough influence within the court system to have a gun planted. We had to consider the possibility that he had the resources to reach me even from behind bars. He had made threats. He wanted me dead.

Also to be considered was Maynard Lewis and his cohorts. By the time everything was said and done, they would be bankrupt and possibly looking for revenge.

The only viable solution was witness protection. Oscar made the necessary calls. The US Marshall's office usually didn't get involved with cases like mine. I wasn't a witness to a major crime per se. However, I definitely WAS in danger.

Oscar was very persuasive, and they finally agreed to put me in the program.

As soon as I was physically and emotionally well enough, the US Marshalls would move me into a safe house. From there I would be given a new identity.

I was devastated by the thought of being separated from Oscar and Dr. Mark! I knew I would never see them again. I also knew if I had asked them, they would have protected me 24/7 themselves for as long as it took, probably the rest of my life. They loved me. It was as simple as that.

But they were relatively young men and deserved lives of their own, not one tied by obligation to me. I couldn't be that selfish. I had changed over the past several years. Yes, I needed them, but I loved them more. With a heavy heart I finally agreed.

The plan was for everyone to meet in Oscar's office so that final good-byes could be said. I would then be removed to a safe house out of state, where I would stay until the necessary documents could be obtained and my indoctrination into my new persona was complete.

How would I support myself? The fact that I would have a LOT of money didn't really mean anything to me. I had never had money before. I was only 19 years old and hadn't even graduated from high school!

A female marshal, whose name was Amanda, was going to help me through the transition and answer any questions. I was at least thankful for that.

Chapter 50

The day came when I was taken to Oscar's office. I had insisted that Oscar continue to handle my finances. I trusted him. The marshals had reluctantly agreed under certain conditions, which they had worked out with Oscar.

He was never to have direct contact with me either in person, by mail or by telephone. I would be given a number after everything was arranged. It would give me access to my money through any bank in the US, any time I needed it.

My name would be slowly and quietly removed from all my assets. It would appear to anyone who checked that everything had been sold and/or liquidated.

The new account would be by number only. Oscar would monitor the activity, investing and managing, making the money grow. *At least he will know I'm alive.* The thought gave me a small measure of comfort.

Oscar said he couldn't do anything else for me, but he was determined to make me a very wealthy woman, completely self sufficient in every way.

We waited as long as we could for Mark. He must have gotten tied up with an emergency at the hospital. That was the only thing that could have kept him from seeing me one last time.

Oscar found himself squeezed in my tight embrace, the top of my head coming just under his chin. He wrapped his arms around me.

"I love you Oscar Schwartz," I said as I swallowed the sobs that were threatening to erupt. "Thank you for everything you have done for me. I will never forget you. Please tell Mark I love him too, and will think about him every day."

The pain in my face was heartbreaking to even the toughest marshal, and he turned away giving me a few private moments with Oscar.

Oscar held me for several minutes before he let me go. "You take care, Peanut," he said as tears ran unashamedly down his cheeks.

They put me into the back seat of a black, unmarked car with Amanda. As we sped away, I pressed my face and hands against the window.

I saw Mark's car pull up in front of the building. He got out, and with his white coat flapping in the breeze, he ran up the steps... too late. I turned my face to the corner and sobbed uncontrollably. Amanda tried to comfort me, but it was useless. There was no comfort that would ever be enough.

Chapter 51

My middle name was Ann, and I insisted on keeping it. I just couldn't bear the thought of losing myself completely! So I became Lauren Ann Reynolds two days after I turned twenty.

"Ann" as I decided I wanted to be called, spent the first week of her new life crying. I missed Mark and Oscar so much! Not a day went by that I didn't think about them.

A small town in Ohio became my new home. I had my own little house in a good neighborhood. Amanda would be with me for 6 months, and then I would be on my own. She would continue to check in periodically for a while until I was comfortable in my new life.

When I felt I was ready, all ties would be cut. I would either sink or swim on my own. After that first lonely week, I decided I would make Oscar and Mark proud of me. I would swim.

Along with my new name came a whole new family complete with parents and a sister. My parents, Charles and Martha Reynolds, were from Montreal, Canada.

My older sister's name was Patty. Patty had been born in Canada, but I had been born in the United States when my family had been vacationing, and my mother had gone into early labor. I was an American citizen.

Mom and Dad had died, and if anyone should check, there were gravestones in a little cemetery in my "hometown" bearing their names. After the death of our parents, Patty had married a French Canadian, and they had moved to France.

I had been a good student, graduating with honors from Taft High School. Sports had never been my thing, probably because my nose was always buried in a book. By all reports, I had been a happy, well-adjusted child. I had even had a dog named Napoleon.

None of this sat well with me. My whole life was now one big fat lie! I felt rather like a "fake" person floating in a sea of nothingness, unable to see the shoreline or touch the bottom beneath the loneliness.

Amanda did her best to calm my fears. She did everything possible to help me come to grips with this new person I had become. A little quiver of apprehension was never far from the surface, ready to blossom into full-blown panic at any provocation or perceived threat. *Will it always be this way?* I wondered.

She assured me that my tutor in Boston said that I had easily completed high school material, and, under normal circumstances, would have graduated. A transcript of my classes and grades had been provided to prove it, if I ever wanted to go on to college.

I had a social security card and a birth certificate. My new birth date was May 31, 1948, which made me 21 years old instead of 20, the legal age to do anything I wanted to do.

It seemed like the Marshall's Office had covered all the bases. Every single tie to my old life had been cut except for my bank account number.

Amanda went over and over and over my new identity. She made me repeat it until it came naturally from my lips. My hair had been cut short and styled differently than I had ever worn it. The color was changed to blonde without any hint of red. Glasses were the finishing touch, without any prescription of course, as my eyesight was fine.

When I looked in the mirror, a stranger looked back at me. Except for the vivid blue eyes and long lashes, I was a different person. The metamorphosis was complete. It was an odd feeling.

Checking and savings accounts had been opened at a local bank. Amanda came with me for moral support as I met with the bank manager in regards to my private account. It was the first time I had to answers questions using my "new" identity.

The interview went well, all things considered. I was proud of myself. I had managed to keep my nerves under control even though I was sure that at any moment I would be caught as an imposter!

The gas and electric were turned on, and the bills would come in my new name. Amanda taught me the rudiments of check writing, bill paying, grocery shopping; all those things I had never done before.

We shopped for furniture and clothes. We bought everything I would need to succeed in my new life. My taste for decorating ran toward the simpler things with my home soon taking on a cozy quality that appealed to me.

I passed the entrance exam enabling me to enter junior college. Education was important. That's what Oscar and Dr. Mark had told me. If I wanted to make my own way, I would need some kind of profession. I already knew I didn't want just any old job. I wanted to make a difference somehow.

Speaking of jobs, I got one in the local library after seeing a help wanted ad in the school newsletter. It didn't pay a lot, just enough to keep my cupboards stocked. Confidence in my ability to live on my own was something I sorely needed. This part time job was a step in the right direction.

Chapter 52

I had only been allowed to bring a few things with me. My most important possessions were the books Mark and Oscar had bought for me, and my boating/fishing magazine.

Amanda couldn't figure out why this particular magazine was so important to me, but oh well, everybody had their little quirks. She didn't understand that when I flipped through the pages, I remembered Mark sitting on the bed with me looking at the pictures and talking about how we would go fishing someday. It was my favorite memory.

I obtained a learner's permit, and Amanda taught me to drive. Much to my disappointment, I had to take the driver's test a second time before I passed. The first time around my nerves got the best of me! My first car, a little Rambler station wagon, certainly wasn't anything fancy, but it got me from point "A" to point "B."

Classes began, as did my job, and I tried to concentrate on my schoolwork. The librarian, Luella Dickinson, was a very nice older lady who took me under her wing. She was grateful for the help, patiently showing me what my responsibilities would be.

She became my only friend, and we often ate dinner together in the little café across the street from the library. I couldn't share my past with her, but I enjoyed her company. She didn't press me when my answers to some of her questions were vague.

We talked about current events, religion and politics; things that had never interested me before. She made sure I got "first dibs" on the new books that came into the library. The wisdom she had accumulated from years of working with the public was amazing, and she regaled me with humorous stories from her past experiences.

I liked her, but didn't allow myself to become overly attached. She, in turn, liked me and worried about me living alone. She frequently brought me homemade bread and cookies, insisting I needed a little "meat on my bones." This comment never failed to bring a sad little smile to my face, as I remembered Harriet saying something similar.

I worked evenings, which was a concern for me, as I had to go home after dark. Amanda had installed a couple of lights that turned on automatically at five in the evening, which helped considerably.

The locks on the doors and windows were probably excessive, but I didn't care. I needed to feel somewhat secure. Amanda gave me some lessons in self-defense, which didn't make me any less apprehensive. I was still hyper-vigilant, and jumped at every sound.

Amanda sternly warned me on several occasions that as long as I kept my face out of the newspaper, maintained a low profile, and minded my own business, I would be fine. I wasn't convinced. *Will I ever feel completely safe?* I wondered.

The fact that I was an attractive young woman brought several of the young men in my classes buzzing around. I didn't want anything to do with any of them. My life was complicated enough already, and what did I need a man for anyway? I was afraid of them in general.

The brash, slick, smooth-talking men reminded me too much of Donny. The boisterous, know-it-all types who eyed me up and down like a side of beef, sent fear screaming through my brain! That's how Art had been.

The quiet men appeared non-threatening, but they were just as dangerous! They were the ones who could never quite look me in the eyes, making me wonder what kind of plans they were hatching. It was best to avoid them all.

The bar had been set high, and my standards were non-negotiable. I didn't think there was a man on earth who could ever come close to Dr. Mark or Oscar. I had resigned myself to being alone and lonely for the rest of my life. However, I was determined to make the best of what I had.

My reputation soon became established as aloof and even snobby. The other girls avoided me, which was fine. I didn't want to get close to anyone ever again. It simply hurt too much.

Chapter 53

Amanda had gone on to her next assignment. She had promised she would check in at least once a month for a while to make sure everything was going okay. I had become familiar with my new life, and as long as I stuck to the rules, no one would be able to find me...would they?

I thought and thought about some way I could safely let Oscar know I was all right. I had practically taken an oath on my life that I would never disclose anything about my past to anyone, and I would not contact anyone from my past for any reason. But this was Oscar and Mark!

I had memorized the number that got me into my account through the bank. I knew Oscar was on the other end of that number. I knew he was the only one who would be working with the account. I went to the bank and withdrew $1,589.15.

It was an odd amount to withdraw, and I was sure it would catch Oscar's attention. If these numbers were correlated to the letters of the alphabet, 15-8-9-15 spelled OHIO. Oscar was smart. He would figure it out.

I felt a little better. I was attached, if only by a tiny thread, to the people I loved. I deposited 1,000 dollars of the money I had withdrawn into my regular savings account, just in case. I felt a little glimmer of a smile on my lips as I remembered Harriet.

Chapter 54

Years later, I would learn how Oscar and Mark managed life without me.

They got together every couple of weeks, and the conversation often turned to me. They wondered what my new name was and how I was faring on my own. They missed me terribly. I had become enmeshed in their hearts in a way neither of them could explain or had expected.

Oscar had left a message at Mark's office that said, "Meet me, usual place, noon." Mark's secretary gave him this rather cryptic message with a raised eyebrow.

At precisely 11:45 he flew out of his office and made his way to the donut shop near Oscar's building. Oscar was already waiting, hardly able to contain his excitement!

The napkin he turned toward Mark had the numbers 15-8-9-15 written on it. Mark thought his friend must have lost his mind, but attempting to look serious, he studied the numbers.

With a scowl, he tried to figure out what they could possibly mean. Oscar looked to the right and to the left making sure no one was nearby before he said one word, very quietly, O H I O.

*Okay, M*ark thought. *He really has lost it. Is there some conspiracy going on that I don't know about? Ohio. What's up with that?* Keeping a calm exterior, he waited for an explanation.

Then Oscar told Mark how this information had been relayed. Both men grinned. They felt better than they had since I was taken away. I was safe! The waitresses in the donut shop stared as two grown men laughed, cried and pounded each other on the back.

"I bet they aren't going to leave a tip either," one of the waitresses confided to the other. "I think they're both crazy!"

Chapter 55

I finished junior college in a little over a year by taking a full schedule of classes through the summer. I did the same to get my Bachelors Degree. My class schedule had been loaded with science and math, but since I didn't have a social life, there was plenty of time to study.

Taking a foreign language was a requirement for graduation, and I discovered I enjoyed the class very much. The instructor said I had "an ear for it." I became fluent in Spanish and French, French being my favorite. I also picked up a smattering of Italian, Russian and German.

I didn't bother to attend my graduation. What was the point? I received my diploma unceremoniously, in the mail.

A career in medicine was exactly what I wanted. I had given it serious thought and decided that since Mark had done so much for me, I wanted to give back in some way.

Reputable medical schools that offered a lot of the pre requisite classes locally was a perfect option for me. I knew I would have to do clinical work on site; however, I wanted to stay in my home in Ohio as long as possible.

I kept my job in the library, and used all of my spare time to complete one course after another. Every so often I withdrew money from my account, never following any pattern, and always for different amounts. It was the one thing that always made me smile.

A hospital in Virginia had accepted my application for continuing my education. I traveled there for an interview with my old fear rearing its ugly head. *Would I be good enough? Would someone recognize me? Was I a fool for even trying?*

My clinical schedule would be demanding and the hours would be long. It was all fine with me! Despite my fear, I was ready and anxious to start this new chapter in my life.

I looked into student housing, as well as apartments, near the hospital. I didn't plan to live in Virginia permanently, and didn't want to buy a house. I also asked about the possibility of some type of employment.

The house in Ohio sold quickly, my personal belongings were packed and a moving company would transport my furniture. I took several days to make the drive to Virginia. I had never had a vacation, and I wanted to see some of the country. It also seemed prudent to take time to relax before starting my new responsibilities.

Those few days away from work and study had been well worth it. I felt refreshed and excited. I had found a small, comfortable apartment that was within walking distance of the hospital. After arranging my things, it suited my needs perfectly. The landlord gave me permission to put extra locks on the doors and windows without asking too many questions.

The person in charge of personnel told me that when I wasn't busy with my clinical work, I could work as a regular employee, doing whatever needed to be done. It seemed like short staffing was always a problem, and I could work as much as I wanted. I was well satisfied with this arrangement. I would be getting paid for gaining experience.

I had transferred my financial business to a bank in Virginia. As soon as I was settled, I made a withdrawal of $13,152.25. 13-15-22-5 = MOVE.

That amount of money was enough to pay for the move, buy uniforms and other supplies, as well as to pay for a one-year lease on my apartment with discretionary spending money left over. I knew Dr. Mark and Oscar would be very proud of me.

Chapter 56

Being very conscientious about my spending habits, I was able to live on the salary I earned. I never needed to touch the money Oscar was managing for me. The withdrawals I made to send messages barely scratched the surface of the funds available to me.

My clinical work went very well. I found that I loved the interaction with my patients, and I thrived on the hectic schedule. Time flew by and soon I was a resident working long hours in the emergency room on very little sleep. I also did a residency in general surgery. I didn't have time to dwell on the past circumstances of my life. There was only time for work...and more work.

Resumes had been sent to several hospitals for permanent employment. I wanted to find a place to build a house of my own and put down some roots. I wanted to find some peace, if that was even possible.

I had decided I wanted to work for a privately owned hospital, having had enough of the tight fisted budgets of the not-for-profit organizations.

Working short staffed, with outdated, poorly maintained equipment, and an administration that seemed to be interested only in the "bottom line," was not how I wanted to practice medicine.

Dixon Memorial in Dixon, Vermont met all of my criteria. It was privately owned and funded. The equipment was state-of-the-art, and there was adequate staff to do the job without jeopardizing my license to practice.

My only worry was the close proximity of Vermont to Boston, MA. I was a grown woman and could defend myself; but I was still afraid. *Hide in plain sight,* I thought to myself. *Blend in.*

After a couple of interviews, I was offered a position in the emergency room. I accepted. My life was about to change again, this time, by my choosing.

Before I made the move to Vermont, just to be on the safe side, I decided I had to make myself into yet another person. Carelessness or becoming too lax and comfortable could very well cost me my life.

My hair had grown long again. I decided to straighten it and use temporary dye to color it dark brown. When I pulled it back in a tight bun at the back of my neck, it made me look more stern and older.

I knew my eye color was too distinctive, so I got contacts that hid the brilliant blue under dark brown. I kept the glasses. Lifts in my shoes made me appear taller, and wearing trousers hid my legs.

A white lab coat just a little too big was the finishing touch. I hoped it would make me look chubby. When yet another metamorphosis was complete, I thought I could have walked right past Oscar and he wouldn't recognize me.

A side benefit of my new look was that I was taken more seriously by my colleagues. After all, an attractive, petite, young-looking woman couldn't possibly be a good doctor.

Chapter 57

In my opinion, most men thought of themselves as irresistible Casanovas who only wanted hot looking babes for one reason. I was most certainly NOT interested in any man or his motives for being friendly. I had learned my lesson well.

I had made it a habit to covertly study the behavior of men in general. *Better to know my enemy,* I thought. What I learned did not impress me.

The conclusions I drew from my observations were that men weren't at all interested, and in fact, never noticed, dowdy women. I was happy to be included in the latter category. So, for the most part, I was left alone.

There was one more thing I felt I needed to do to protect myself. I needed a gun. I found just what I wanted in a little out-of-the-way sporting goods store.

It was small, but deadly, and easy to handle. It was inconspicuous in the holster that fit neatly in the small of my back under my shirt. I promised myself that I would never be left at the mercy of another slick, fast talking and abusive man ever again.

The background check done by the retailer went through without a hitch. Much to my relief, I was issued a permit to carry a handgun. *Must be the US Marshalls are as good as they claim to be!*

The owner of the store recommended a shooting range where I could take some lessons. As a student, I could use the facility any time I wanted to practice. The instructor would not only teach me how to properly take care of the gun, he would teach me to shoot with accuracy. I decided the lessons were a good idea.

I recalled some of the old lessons that Harriet taught me about hunting. These weapons were different from Harriet's old piece and I didn't think I would get the hang of it. It took some determination on my part, as well as many hours of practice on the shooting range, but I became a relatively good shot. I was confident I could defend myself if necessary.

When at work, I left the gun locked in the glove box of my car. Otherwise, I carried it with me where ever I went.

I rented an apartment about a fifteen-minute drive from the hospital. Renting forever wasn't an option for me. I was interested in designing and building my own house. I wanted a house that "fit" my personality, as well as met my safety requirements.

There was a piece of property for sale at the end of a dead end street in a nice section at the outskirts of Dixon. It suited my need for privacy perfectly and I made an offer. After some dickering, I was soon a property owner.

Now all I needed was a builder who would work with me, allowing me to have complete control over the design of the house. I knew exactly what I wanted, and I could afford to have it!

There was an ad in the newspaper for an architect who specialized in home security, so I gave him a call. After checking his references, I made an appointment to meet with him. He was well known for the quality of his work and his honesty.

Doug Hagan agreed to meet me at a local restaurant to discuss my requirements as well the cost involved. The sketches I had drawn gave him an idea of what I wanted. He offered to come up with a blueprint and a price quote for my approval, promising the house would be as secure as Fort Knox.

When the house was finished, I loved it. I made a withdrawal from my account; $8,151.35. 8-15-13-5 HOME.

Chapter 58

~~~
ᔔᗢᔔ
~~~

I t had been two years since I moved to Dixon. I loved my work at the hospital, rarely taking a day off. I quickly became a favorite with the staff. I could always be counted on to cover the shifts no one else wanted to work. Holidays were no problem for me. I never celebrated.

There was no one waiting for me at home, and except for going to the shooting range every other week or so, I didn't participate in any outside activities. My work became my life.

I often checked on the more seriously ill or injured patients even after they were admitted to a regular room, just to make sure they were progressing well. It gave continuity to my care that I thought was important. When one of my patients died, I attended the funeral whenever possible.

Since I could also provide general surgery, I was able to follow my patients from the emergency room to the operating room. None of the other physicians had an interest in this kind of "follow-through" care, as I called it, so I became popular with patients and their families.

It was not unusual at all for me to make home visits. I frequently checked on patients who were alone. Some had families who were unavailable, while other families were just unwilling to help. If long-term care was necessary, I made referrals to agencies that could address those needs. It broke my heart when no one cared; no one helped.

My life became predictable and safe, albeit very lonely. I considered getting a dog, but with the hours I worked it wasn't very practical. I remained cautious, keeping to myself most of the time. My books and my music were a source of enjoyment and comfort to me.

Dancing was something I found fascinating. I watched the competitions on TV whenever I could. The graceful movement and beautiful costumes appealed to me. *It looks so romantic,* I thought sadly. It was just one more thing I would never experience.

I toyed with the idea of taking some lessons. On the other hand, I realized it would require a partner; a male partner. I wasn't quite brave enough for that. I could deal with my male co-workers strictly on a professional level, but I was very afraid of anything personal.

Chapter 59

A call came into the emergency room one evening from one of the ambulances. They had been summoned to a residence on the far side of Dixon where a middle-aged man was suffering from chest pain, which radiated to his left arm and jaw. His color was ashen, and his vital signs were unstable. They were bringing him in.

He hadn't lived in the area long enough to have found a primary care physician, so I accepted temporary responsibility for him. When his name was relayed to me, my heart stood still for a few seconds, then jumped into my throat.

His name was Oscar Schwartz! What were the odds that Oscar had moved to Dixon! How was it possible that he was being brought to the hospital where I practiced! For a moment, I thought it was a cruel joke.

Mixed emotions cascaded over me one after another. I couldn't seem to catch my breath. *Don't be silly*, I chided myself. *It can't possibly be him. Can it?*

I ordered the preliminary workup that was required for possible heart attack patients, so that as soon as he arrived, the diagnosis could be made and treatment started as quickly as possible.

When the gurney rolled in I caught a glimpse of the patient. It <u>WAS</u> MY OSCAR! I struggled to control myself. I felt hot, then cold in quick succession. My mind reeled, my stomach heaved, and my hands were clammy.

Oscar needs me right now. I will deal with the emotions later! An element of self-doubt tried to creep into my mind. *Will I be able to save him? Am I smart enough? Good enough?*

There wasn't time to dwell on these conflicting thoughts, because a distraught middle-aged woman was hovering nearby. A nurse told me it was Mrs. Millie Schwartz.

While the patient was being transferred to a bed, and the tests were started, I introduced myself to Oscar's wife as the physician who would be taking care of her husband. I took a minute to guide her gently to the waiting room where we sat side by side, my arm lightly around her shoulders.

Apparently, Oscar had not been feeling up to par over the last week. This evening when the pain started she called the ambulance.

"Is it his heart?" Millie stammered with tears beginning to spill down her cheeks. "Is he going to die?"

"We will do everything we can to make sure that doesn't happen," I responded. "I promise I will keep you updated on his condition every step of the way."

A volunteer especially trained for exactly this kind of situation came over, and took my place beside the now sobbing Mildred Schwartz. I gave her a quick hug before I hurried in to Oscar.

As I entered Oscar's cubicle his chart was put into my hands with the lab and EKG results on top. He was having a heart attack, no doubt about that. I sent the nurse to get as complete a medical history on Oscar as his wife was able to provide. I specifically needed to know about any past heart problems, the medications he took, and the name of his physician in Boston.

What if his doctor in Boston is Mark?

Much to my relief, and great disappointment, I didn't know the doctor who responded to my telephone call. He gave me all the information I needed to safely begin treatment. He assured me he would forward all Oscar's records as soon as possible.

There was a look of confusion on Oscar's face when I introduced myself as Dr. Reynolds, but this was quickly replaced by pain. As I began my examination, I explained to Oscar that he was having a heart attack, and I would be giving him something for the pain as soon as I finished my clinical exam.

His hand grasped mine, just for a second.

"15-8-9-15," Oscar said through clenched teeth.

He knows who I am! My heart swelled, as tears backed up behind my eyelids.

"Yes, I understand," I responded, giving his hand a little squeeze.

Now I was worried. If Oscar recognized me, maybe my disguise wasn't as effective as I thought!

Will he keep my secret, I wondered in somewhat of a panic. Under sedation would he inadvertently give my true identity away? I had been so careful! Would I have to run <u>again</u>!

In the very next heartbeat I decided, NO! I was finished with running!

Chapter 60

Oscar told me later that he hadn't recognized me at all until I spoke. He immediately knew my voice. Even under his present circumstances he said he couldn't help but grin. *That's my girl; and a doctor no less.*

Thank God for by-pass surgery, because Oscar had three blocked arteries in his heart. He was in the right hospital for the job, as our thoracic surgeons were on the cutting edge of this technology, and our operating room was well equipped.

I checked in on him every day as his recovery progressed. He was going to physical therapy to gradually regain his strength. He was also serious about taking off the pounds he had gained since I last saw him.

In a couple of weeks, when he was finally ready to be discharged, I went to his room to have him sign the appropriate papers. When I got there, he was alone.

Oscar beckoned me to come close to the bed. As I sat down beside him, he took my hand in his.

"Your secret is safe with me, Peanut," he said with a wide grin. "I'm so proud of you."

I was overjoyed, and in another minute I would have been crying like a little girl! Fortunately, or unfortunately as the case may be, one of the nurses walked in to take his vital signs one more time before his wife arrived to take him home.

I desperately wanted to continue our conversation. I had so many questions, number one being; how is Dr. Mark?

Oscar must have read my mind, because he quietly said, "He's fine."

He handed me a business card, and very smoothly said, "Well Doc, thanks for everything. If you ever need a good lawyer, my office is in the Emerson building."

"I'll remember that," I answered, as I wished him well.

When I left the room, my heart was lighter than it had been in a very long time. I decided it might be a good idea to be established with an attorney in town…just in case.

PART 2

M. Bryce Peterson, The Beginning

Chapter 61

Thomas, Michael and Bradley Peterson were 10, 11 and 13 years old respectively when I was born on February 5, 1946. My brothers were robust, active babies that grew up to be rugged, handsome, athletic types who made our father proud. They excelled in sports, and never lacked for girlfriends. My mother spoiled the two younger boys, but Brad was more serious and self-sufficient even as a child.

My mom had grown tired of her hum-drum, stay-at-home mom life, so when Tommy started school she had gone to work. Against my father's wishes she became a waitress at the diner down the street from our middle class home.

She hated needing to ask my father for every dollar she spent, and she was resentful of the fact that she was expected to carry the load at home by herself.

Martin Peterson had not been her first choice for a husband, but her best friend had married the guy she loved. Martin had been her "husband by default." There was no meaningful communication between them, so their relationship grew more and more distant as each year passed. Mom became angry and bitter.

My father worked in middle management at a local business. He brought home his paycheck, and apparently felt that's where his responsibility ended. He left everything else to mom. She had to pay the bills, discipline us boys, monitor homework, keep up with the housework, as well as do all the cooking.

He seemed well satisfied with his life, often telling his buddies on poker night that even if his wife was somewhat cold, she always complied with his demands in bed. What more could a man possibly want? He couldn't understand mom's problem, and frankly, he didn't care. When she tried to discuss how she felt, he ignored her.

As you can imagine, neither parent was happy when mom found out she was pregnant with number four. This pregnancy was not easy like the other three had been. She was constantly sick and exhausted. The housework was never ending, my brothers were loud and often unruly, and my dad was disinterested and non-supportive.

With no desire to be bothered with another baby in the house, he blamed mom for disrupting his life with this unwanted pregnancy. HIS boys were his pride and joy. He was at every one of their games, and attended practices when he wasn't working. On the weekends, if they weren't in the backyard playing football or baseball, depending on the season, they were watching it on TV.

To make matters worse, I was sickly as an infant. I cried incessantly, or so I was told over and over again as I grew up. It became obvious to me as I got older that mom hadn't wanted to be tied down to another child just when she was starting to enjoy her own life a little bit.

Chapter 62

I always had food, clean clothes and a bed to sleep in, but I was also well aware that I was a disappointment to my parents. I tried hard, but never seemed to measure up. That's a heavy weight for a little boy to carry.

"Oh, for heaven sakes, Bryce. Your shirt is wrong side out! You're four years old, and you can't even dress yourself! I'll be late for work. GET IN THE CAR," Mom would scream. "You will wear the shirt like that all day and maybe you'll learn!"

If it wasn't my clothes, it was something else. I never left the house unscathed, and consequently spent the day with a knot in my stomach!

"BRYCE! Get down here RIGHT NOW and eat your breakfast. What are you doing up there? If I'm late again, I could get fired, and it will be your fault!"

Tears often threatened, but I refused to let them fall. That would only make things worse, and I would look like a baby! It only took once for me to learn a spanking would be forthcoming if I cried. I was dropped off at the sitters looking like nobody cared about my appearance or my well being, because nobody did.

Almost every morning in the car I had to hear the same thing over and over again.

"I am NOT about to give up having my own money, and some well earned freedom, just because I made one mistake and got pregnant with YOU. Do you understand me, mister?"

That panicked, tongue-tied feeling would rise up. "Y-y-y-yes, I under...I understand," I always replied quietly. "I'll t-t-try harder M-mom, I p-p-p-p-promise."

Chapter 63

First grade came as a relief! I could ride the bus! It stopped at the end of our street. Most mornings, if I hurried, I could avoid mom's lectures and threats. I became an expert at forcing my brain to wake up early so I could hurry through my morning routine, and be at the corner by seven.

There was a down side to entering first grade. Brad went off to college. He had been my protector against the roughhousing, and constant teasing, from my other two brothers. He had only been gone two weeks, and I was already paying the price.

It was great sport for them to tell Mom I had done something wrong so they could watch her punish me. Without Brad as a buffer, mom's resentment toward me ratcheted up a couple of notches.

I was a skinny kid who was always coming down with, or just getting over, some virus or other malady. If I was too sick to go to school, Mom would drag me to the doctor who prescribed pouring Cod Liver Oil down my throat. If she had to miss work, I was in big trouble! It only took one day of missed school to teach me to go no matter how bad I felt.

"Honestly, Bryce. Why can't you be more like your brothers? They were never this much trouble! Take a tissue and wipe your nose! That's disgusting! Now get upstairs young man. I don't want to hear another peep out of you."

With my head down, I would trudge up to my room on the second floor at the back of the house. It didn't do any good to argue with my mother. She was always right, and what I thought or how I felt didn't matter. I was better off if I just kept quiet.

I guess she didn't realize I could hear the comments she made to her friends, or maybe she wanted me to hear. It wasn't unusual for her to talk about me, in front of me, like I wasn't even there. I felt invisible.

"Bryce is nothing like his brothers," she would whine. "They were always healthy and energetic! Bryce is just so much work. He can't even speak properly! I sometimes wonder if he isn't brain-damaged or something."

These comments always elicited much sympathy and tongue-clucking from her friends. It was as if I got sick on purpose.

When I grow up and have kids I will NEVER treat them like Mom treats me, I would think as I lay on my bed staring at the crack that ran across my ceiling. *Who am I kidding? Nobody will ever want to marry me.*

Never big and tough enough for the sports my dad loved so much, he mostly ignored me. Mom had full reign. They fought frequently over me. Mom accused Dad of not taking any interest in my up-bringing. Dad yelled that I was HER son and HER problem.

"Why am I always the one to have to deal with Bryce? YOU ARE HIS FATHER," she would scream, as she burst into tears.

From then on he would ask the obligatory questions every day. Is your homework done? Did you do your chores? How was school today? As if by this "communication" he had done his "job" as a parent.

Chapter 64

When I was seven years old an incident occurred that would be burned into my memory for the rest of my life. Tommy was a senior in high school and Mike was still living at home, having procrastinated about applying to college. Brad would be graduating from college in a year, and was expected home for Thanksgiving in a couple of days.

Mike and Tommy were watching TV while I sat on the couch looking at a book. When Mom came stomping down the stairs, I stiffened. I must have done something wrong. She was mad.

"I found a pile of dirty clothes on the floor in your room, Bryce Peterson. Do I look like your maid?"

"I'm I'm s-sorry Mom, I f-f-f-forgot," I stuttered. "I'll...I'll go take care of them r-r-right now."

As I was putting my book down, she came around the couch and grabbed me by the arm, hauling me up until my toes barely touched the floor.

"I am SICK TO DEATH of you and your slovenly behavior," she screeched, her face red, her eyes bugging out. "I'm going to teach you a lesson once and for all!"

Chapter 65

She proceeded to pull down my jeans and my underwear. Tommy and Mike were immediately interested, and came over to watch.

The next thing I knew I was face down over the arm of the couch with my bare butt sticking up in the air.

"Tommy," my mother yelled. "Come over here, and give your brother a few good licks."

I was horrified, and not above begging. "P-P-P-P-PLEASE M-MOM! Don't. I'll be good. I'll n-n-n-never forget again! P-PLEASE M-M-M-MOMMY," I cried.

She didn't have to tell Tommy twice. He hopped up and began hitting me over and over again on my bare behind. I tried my best not to cry out, but after the first few whacks I was screaming from the pain and the humiliation. When his hand hurt too much to continue, and he was breathing hard from the exertion, he stepped back.

"Mike," I heard Mom say. "Now it's your turn. Teach your brother a lesson."

To Mike's credit, he tried to bring some calm to the situation. "Come on, Mom. Don't you think he's had enough?"

"I WILL DECIDE WHEN HE'S HAD ENOUGH," she shrieked. "You get up here and be a man."

Chapter 66

Mike had given me a couple of half hearted swats when the front door banged open. Everyone froze. Brad had come home early. He had heard my screams as he was walking up the sidewalk. As his eyes took in the scene in front of him, the vein in his forehead began to throb.

Brad had grown into a tall man, bigger and more muscular than either Mike or Tommy. He grabbed them by the front of their shirts like two rag dolls. He then proceeded to drag them up to within an inch of his nose.

"Just WHAT the HELL do you two think you're doing?" he bellowed, spit flying.

Tommy immediately began to whine. "Mom told us to do it, Mom told us to do it!"

Brad threw them to the floor and turned to Mom. Her face was white as a sheet, and she had backed up into the other corner of the couch as far from Brad as she could get.

He grabbed her by the wrist, and yanked her to her feet. "WHAT IS WRONG WITH YOU?" he yelled in her face, as he gave her a disgusted shake. "How could you allow this? Encourage this? INSTIGATE THIS?"

Apparently my father had been in the basement puttering with something, and when he heard Brad's voice he came upstairs to see what on earth was going on. My screams of pain had not elicited any response from him at all.

Brad heard him and whirled around, throwing mom up against his chest. His anger was barely controlled, and they both knew it.

"WHAT KIND OF A MAN ARE YOU TO ALLOW THIS TO GO ON UNDER YOUR ROOF? YOU SHOULD BE ASHAMED!"

"Now you listen here, Brad, this is my house and I will not..." and that's as far as he got.

Blood flew from his nose when Brad hit him square in the face. The blow drove Dad back against the far wall. Mom let out a yelp; then everyone stood stock still while Brad struggled to control his raging emotions.

Chapter 67

"Now I am going to tell you people how things WILL work in this house from this moment on."

Mom tried to interrupt.

"YOU SHUT UP! You don't deserve any consideration whatsoever in this matter. If ANYTHING like this ever happens again, I will personally call the police. I will have all of you arrested for assault on a child. Do I make myself perfectly clear?"

Everyone nodded yes, afraid to say a word.

"Further, Bryce will NEVER go without dinner. If I call here asking for him, I EXPECT TO SPEAK TO HIM or I will be on your doorstep madder than I am right now! He had better NOT receive any mistreatment as a consequence of what has happened here today! You make me sick. All of you."

He didn't wait for a response. He walked over to me, still bent over the arm of the couch. He gently picked me up, and carried me up the stairs. He didn't say a word as he laid me face down on the bed and left. When he came back he had several towels, which he had soaked in cool water. He placed them very carefully across my backside where raised painful welts were already visible. Sitting beside me on the bed, he waited for my sobs to subside.

"My God, Bryce. How long has this kind of thing been going on?"

He began to gently rub my back. When I winced, he pulled up my shirt to find several bruises in different shades of black, blue, purple and yellow.

"Who did this to you?"

Between hiccups and gulps I let it all pour out. I never stuttered when I talked to Brad.

"Mom did it. She uses one of Dad's old belts."

I told him about the many times I was sent to bed without anything to eat as punishment for some minor infraction at the dinner table. Most times I didn't even know the reason. I told him the way mom treated me if I got sick.

"And if I wet the bed she makes me stand out on the sidewalk in my wet pajamas holding up a sign that says, 'I wet my bed,' and sometimes it's really cold out there!" I wailed as the tears rolled unchecked down my thin cheeks.

"I am so sorry, Bryce. I should have been paying more attention. I should have done something sooner," he said as he tried unsuccessfully to hold back his own tears. "I didn't know it was this bad, but things will be different from now on. I promise!"

And things were different. From that day on, nobody laid a hand on me. I got supper every night, and there were no more threats or degrading comments. If I had an accident and wet the bed, I pulled off the sheets, put them in the hamper, and remade the bed. And that was the end of it. I became isolated in my own home. That was fine with me.

Chapter 68

A s I grew older I developed a passion for music, especially the piano. There was a piano in the auditorium at school. During study hall, if my homework was done, I would get permission from the music teacher to try and play. After several attempts, I discovered I could play by ear. It wasn't long before I was hammering out simple songs I heard on the radio.

The music teacher, Mrs. Atherton, happened to hear me one day. She sat down beside me on the bench, and began teaching me the rudiments of reading music. Suddenly a whole new world opened up to me.

She wanted to call my parents to arrange for piano lessons. This, of course, sent off flashing lights and warning bells in my head. I begged her not to call them. It must have been obvious to her that something was very wrong in the Peterson household. I was very grateful that she didn't ask any questions, and she never called my parents.

She did, however, continue to teach me when she had free time at school. She would sometimes look questioningly at me with sad blue eyes and pat my shoulder.

"I'm so sorry you can't take regular lessons," she would say. "I know how disappointed you must be. Maybe it will help you to know that you are my best pupil. I'm very proud of you."

All of the affirmation I hungered for, and never got, from my parents, I received from Mrs. Atherton. She was a continual source of encouragement to me. I was soon accompanying the chorus when they practiced. I tentatively began making friends.

Of course, Mom and Dad never came to one of the concerts, which didn't surprise me. As the years passed, I learned to persevere and even flourish.

Chapter 69

Tommy graduated and moved to parts unknown. Mike decided college wasn't for him, so he got a job in the company where Dad worked. He rented a room downtown preferring not to live at home. When either of them came home to visit, I stayed away. I had discovered the wonders to be found at the local public library, and spent much of my free time there.

Brad would call me right before he came home so I could be ready. He never came in. He would just pull up in front of the house, and honk the horn. I would sprint to the car with my duffle bag over my shoulder.

In a neighboring community we would rent a motel room, and for a few days my now stilted life with my parents was forgotten. We would catch a movie or go bowling. Over banana splits at the malt shop, he would regale me with tales of his college life. I was the only one he told that he was serious about Melanie. He knew I would keep his secret.

To my knowledge, he never spoke to our parents or our brothers again.

I could be myself with Brad. He would listen to me, and try to answer my questions.

My primary question was always, "Why do Mom and Dad hate me so much? I never did anything to deserve how they treat me."

It was one question he couldn't answer. "I don't know, Bryce. None of it is your fault. Try to remember that."

I told him about my friends, and some of the silly things we did. We found a church in town with a beautiful piano. Brad talked to the pastor, who was only too willing to give me permission to play. He was very surprised at my talent! He encouraged me to get a summer job, and start saving for college.

"I bet with your talent you could qualify for a music scholarship. Get a good education, Bryce. I know you can do it, you're a smart kid. Living at home with Mom and Dad sucks for sure, but you don't need good parents to make something of yourself. You don't have to be like them!"

I listened closely to the advice Brad gave me. *Could I really make something of myself,* I wondered? The thought gave me hope.

"Don't ever be afraid to stick up for the underdog, Bryce," he would say as he grabbed me playfully around my neck so he could ruffle my hair. "It's the right thing to do. A real man stands by his word, protects his family, accepts responsibility, and helps those who are less fortunate. Don't let what other people say bother you, little man. You're okay in my book."

I loved my brother, Brad. Throughout my life, I would recall all the times we spent together, and remember his words. I would not have survived without him. He was my hero.

Chapter 70

M r. Gregory, who owned the grocery store in town, hired me to bag groceries after school. He paid me 75 cents an hour plus a big sandwich, a glass of milk, and a piece of chocolate cake. It saved me from having dinner with my parents. There was always food on the table at home, but eating it was never a pleasant experience!

I worked a couple of hours at the store before heading to the library to do homework and study. I came home after the library closed. My parents never asked what I was doing out so late. Neither of them spoke to me at all unless absolutely necessary.

During the summer I worked as many hours as the child labor laws would allow, and saved my money.

Life went on, and I finished high school in the top 10 percent of my graduating class. I had been president of the chess club, I was well known in school for my musical abilities, and I had worked on the yearbook staff. I had friends, and my teachers liked me.

My accomplishments were small in my my parent's eyes, but all in all, I was satisfied with myself. I didn't intentionally hurt people, I showed respect to others, and I minded my own business. I had learned to depend only on myself, and I was proud of that.

Chapter 71

A fter high school, I was accepted at the college where Brad had landed a good job coaching football. I majored in business and minored in music. I knew this was an odd combination, but I wanted a career where I could support myself. I also wanted to continue with my music. It was an important part of my life, and my sanity.

Brad and Melanie had gotten married in the spring. The wedding was beautiful, and I was my brother's best man. They moved to a small, efficiency apartment just off campus. There wasn't much room, but Melanie said I was welcome to visit anytime. I could sleep on the couch.

The relationship Melanie and my brother had was something special. It wasn't long before I was an uncle to a beautiful little girl named Sarah.

I enjoyed my classes, and was a good student. A part time job working in a book store earned me enough money to rent a tiny, but adequate, apartment near campus.

Dorm life didn't appeal to me. I had lived a solitary life so far, and didn't see a need to change anything. Being a serious young man, I wasn't interested in the drinking and partying of my classmates, preferring instead to apply myself to my studies.

A local business in Dixon, Vermont hired me upon graduation from college. I rapidly advanced up the ladder through hard work and attention to detail, becoming known for my honesty and fair-mindedness. Brad and Melanie were very proud of me. When I was promoted to Assistant Vice President, they gave me a leather briefcase with my initials on it.

Chapter 72

Unfortunately, I began balding in my twenties, which didn't help my social life with the ladies. I was self-conscious about it, making me shy around girls. I was well liked in general, but almost never dated. A loving wife and children were things I wanted, but somehow that dream seemed out of my reach.

"Don't worry, Romeo. I just know there is a special girl out there somewhere just for you," Brad would assure me. "You will make a great husband and father someday. You certainly have had an example set for you of what NOT to do!"

Another coaching job in Connecticut came open for Brad. It was more money, and since he and Melanie were now expecting another baby, he felt compelled to take the position. He felt bad about the move and leaving me to fend for myself. I assured him I was a big boy now. I could take care of myself. Besides, he wouldn't be that far away. I could always visit.

As I look back, I wish he had been close by to give me advice on the turn my life was about to take. When I called, he was always willing to listen, but he was busy with his own family and career. I didn't want to keep pestering him with my problems. I should be able to handle things myself by now!

Chapter 73

I knew the young ladies in town considered me too plain looking and quiet to be much fun on a date, so the sudden attention of Monica Stratton, local socialite, greatly surprised me. She was the daughter of Edward G. Stratton, wealthy owner of Stratton Industry.

Mr. Stratton and I had crossed paths on a number of occasions related to business. Monica frequently accompanied her father to social gatherings, and acted as hostess for events held in their home.

Her mother had died when she was two years old, leaving Mr. Stratton a widower. I was always polite to Monica not realizing that she laughed at me with her friends behind my back.

Monica was considered to be a beauty by her peers. She was tall and buxom with dark hair and eyes. The old saying "beauty is only skin deep," certainly applied in her case. She grew up without the discipline and guidance that Beverly Stratton would have surely provided, leaving her morally and ethically bankrupt. Unfortunately, I discovered this after the damage was already done!

Edward, awash with grief over the death of his wife, gave in to his pretty little daughter's every whim. She was spoiled, and she expected to get what she wanted no matter what the cost to anyone else.

To my detriment, I was very naïve. I would learn much later that she was cruel and ruthless, no matter how innocent and beguiling she could be when it suited her purposes.

Watching me apparently became an obsession to this bored, self-indulgent young woman. I seemed to fascinate her. At the time, I was flattered, and completely unaware of the game she played to perfection.

Unbeknownst to me, Monica had made a bet with her two best friends that she could get me to marry her. I was just too "good," and I piqued her interest. She wanted to peel back that layer of goodness in order to see what was underneath. She confided to her friends that she certainly didn't plan to STAY married to me, it was the sport of a good challenge she loved!

Chapter 74

B eing a creature of habit, there were certain restaurants, art galleries and community events that I frequented. Monica made it her business to become acquainted with my schedule. She would show up at my elbow unexpectedly and turn on the charm. I was a sucker every time!

I was amazed that someone like Monica was interested in someone like me! I had seen her out about town with other men, and her preferences seemed to be for the flashy, hard-drinking, good looking men.

It embarrassed me on those occasions when she pressed her breast provocatively against my arm, which she did in public. I could feel the heat creeping up my face. I usually made some excuse to get away as quickly as possible.

It took me a long time to realize that this was great sport for Monica, and even upon that realization, I chose to ignore it. She was so convincing. She treated me like we were long-time, close friends. I desperately wanted it to be real. I <u>needed</u> it to be real!

When I received a printed invitation in the mail requesting my presence at the Stratton home for dinner, I was flabbergasted, delighted and terrified. It looked official and RSVP was requested. After anguishing over the very thought of spending an evening with the Stratton's, I finally called the number on the card, and said I would be happy to attend.

The night finally arrived. I was on time and appropriately dressed in my best dark suit and tie. I had assumed there would be other guests. I was wrong. I was the ONLY guest, and extremely uncomfortable being the focus of attention.

Monica made a grand entrance, fashionably late, looking slightly breathless and pink cheeked.

Her father told me with a conspiratorial wink that he had peeled off several large bills to pay for her dress, but he had to admit, his money had been well spent. She looked beautiful and I was captivated!

After dinner Monica "needed some air" and asked me if I would mind walking with her in the garden behind the house. When we were alone she boldly turned to me, and kissed me passionately on the mouth. I immediately stepped back. I began stuttering an apology, for what exactly, I wasn't sure.

I was even more stunned when she proclaimed her undying love for me. I didn't know what to do next. I couldn't breathe, let alone think! I needn't have worried. Monica knew exactly what she was doing. She soon had me persuaded that I couldn't live without her.

Chapter 75

⁂

One day Monica and I just "happened" to be shopping together, a pastime she could spend hours doing, when she pulled me into a very expensive, exclusive jewelry store.

The next thing I knew, I was practically signing my life away to buy the biggest diamond I had ever seen! Monica put on a real show for the other customers, throwing her arms around my neck, and calling me "darling." I didn't think about it at the time, but I don't remember actually asking Monica to marry me!

Monica used my inexperience with women to her advantage. She had expertly manipulated me into becoming engaged, while convincing me the whole thing had been my idea!

It wouldn't be until years later that I would learn that Monica and her friends had carefully orchestrated the whole thing. Monica must have realized if she gave me the opportunity to think things through, it would be a long time before she marched me down the aisle. By then, she would be bored with the game. She needed to move things along.

The engagement was announced in the newspaper along with a picture of the "happy couple." Monica looked beautiful, as always. I had a rather puzzled expression on my face. Everything seemed to be happening so fast with events spinning out of my control. Monica was like a whirlwind.

Of course there was a HUGE engagement party. Monica was the center of attention, just the way she liked it. The expensive champagne flowed like water, and the dancing went on all night.

I was still unable to grasp how this had happened, and after being introduced to so many people, everything was just a blur. The wait staff hired for the occasion, and on Monica's instruction, made sure my glass was never empty. Not being a drinker, I was soon off balance physically and mentally. My knees were wobbly and I felt lightheaded.

Through an alcohol induced haze I heard Monica say, "He's not much to look at, but he is SUCH a wonderful person inside when he's not drinking."

That should have been red flag numero uno, but I was in such a fog, I didn't see it; Monica had made sure of that. She clung to my arm, and to the casual observer, she appeared to be madly in love with me.

Chapter 76

M onica wanted a huge, grand wedding with all the trimmings. This was not anything that I wanted, especially after my painful experience at the engagement party. All I wanted was to simply marry this woman who, now that we were engaged, was all over me all the time!

I believed she really did love me! She would bring me to a feverish pitch with her kissing and fondling, then pull away promising that our wedding night would be spectacular. During those months before our marriage, I took many a cold shower!

I never discussed Monica with Brad. Of course I had told him I was dating her, and he had congratulated me when we got engaged. I guess I was embarrassed to go into the details of our relationship with my brother. I was a grown man, and should be able to get married without getting anyone's approval! Maybe, down deep, I knew he wouldn't approve.

The wedding plans were put together without consulting me about anything. When I offered an opinion, Monica gave me her best little pouty smile, and what I wanted was quickly dismissed. I gave in to her every time. After all, she loved me. She just wanted this day to be very special. I certainly had no experience in such matters, as she was a little too quick to point out.

Ed Stratton was a really nice man, and I liked him very much. In an odd way, he became a father figure to me. We spent considerable time getting to know each other. As time passed, he soon offered me an administrative position in his company.

I accepted. In a short time, the changes that I instituted brought harmony and teamwork to the employees who worked there. I tried to settle disputes fairly, and I was honest when negotiating contracts for the business.

At least at work, I was on firm ground where I knew what was required of me. I also had the experience I needed to perform my responsibilities well. Profits rose along with wages under my supervision

Ed Stratton told me over lunch one day, that he felt he could finally retire with his company in good hands, and his daughter's future secure. I had never felt more proud!

I enjoyed my work, and felt a sense of accomplishment with each new contract I acquired. I wasn't getting married for several months yet, so I threw myself wholeheartedly into Stratton Industry, soon making it one of the most profitable manufacturing companies in Vermont.

Machinery was upgraded, and work flow patterns were changed, making operations run more smoothly. As business increased, so did the need for more employees, one of whom was Bobby Rodriguez.

This young man appeared in the personnel office one day, pretty much without skills, but full of enthusiasm. He had made a lot of mistakes, and gotten himself mixed up with a gang in Florida.

He wanted to turn his life around so he had come north finally settling in Dixon. He was just the kind of kid, with the right attitude and motives, that I wanted working for me. I hired Bobby on the spot in the maintenance department.

As I did with all new employees after a month on the job, I took Bobby to lunch. I wanted to know how things were going with his work, and whether or not he needed help with anything. I never expected to hear his life's story, but I was more than willing to listen. He needed to talk, and I knew how that felt.

Chapter 77

Roberto Juan Rodriguez Sr. and his family emigrated from Puerto Rico when Bobby was thirteen years old. They settled in a small, mainly Hispanic neighborhood, outside Miami, Florida. Unfortunately, the living conditions were substandard, and jobs were few and far between.

Bobby's mother managed to find a job as a housekeeper in a neighboring town leaving Juan Rodriguez as the stay-at-home parent. His only responsibility was watching his three children. Juan preferred drinking cheap liquor. Bobby was left to his own devices. His two little sisters knew enough to stay close to home.

When Bobby turned fifteen he came to the attention of the Hispanic gang that was active in the neighborhood. With his "take no prisoners" attitude, and cocky self assurance, he easily became entrenched in gang life.

Being a little scrapper, he wasn't afraid of a fight, and he usually came out on top making him a favorite with the gang leader. His reputation in the gang, and with the local police, grew exponentially.

He had been picked up for petty crimes and loitering, but no one was ever able to pin anything on him that would put him away. Bobby became involved in bigger and more dangerous gang activity, managing to be elusive when arrests were made.

When the gang began talking about robbing a bank and shooting anyone who got in the way, Bobby began to take stock of his situation. He was no killer. He wanted more from life than a one-way ticket to prison.

To make a long story short, Bobby gathered his few belongings; his knife and all the money he had "earned" over the past year, and skulked out of town in the wee hours of the morning. He knew no one walked away from a gang. He had to get as far away as he possibly could before they realized he was gone.

He hitched rides until he hit the Florida/Georgia line, and then asked directions to the nearest bus station. He wanted to go as far north as his money would take him! He had just enough to get him to Vermont. The city of Dixon looked like as good a place as any to start his new life.

Chapter 78

He hit town around lunch time and he was starving. There was a soup kitchen not far from where the bus stopped, so he decided to check it out. To his surprise, the atmosphere was friendly, and the food was simple, but filling. Best of all, the price was right. What could be better than FREE!

A pretty dark skinned girl was serving up the food and Bobby, never one to waste an opportunity to talk to a pretty girl, started up a conversation.

Her name was Maria Sanchez. She was 18 and lived on her own in an apartment on the upper east side of town. She seemed reluctant to talk about her family, and Bobby knew firsthand about dysfunctional families. He didn't press her with questions. After all, he had some skeletons in his own closet.

She was taking night classes at community college, and after graduation, her plan was to get a secretarial position in one of the big companies in Dixon.

To support herself in the meantime, she was waiting tables in a local restaurant. She also felt strongly about giving back to the community, so she volunteered at the soup kitchen in her spare time.

Bobby stayed and helped Maria and the other volunteers clean up. As he walked her back to her apartment they got to know each other. She was "straight laced" in Bobby's mind, and conservative in her thinking. He found himself very much attracted to her.

From then on, Bobby ate lunch every day at the soup kitchen, and stayed to help clean up. He just couldn't seem to get enough of seeing Maria!

Bobby was diligent in looking for a job, and he was finding it difficult. He hadn't graduated high school, finding life in the gang much more exciting than getting an education. He also didn't have any job skills, unless hot wiring a car or robbing a gas station counted.

Maria said there was a class two nights a week at the library for people trying to get their high school diploma. Without at least a high school education, he would never get a decent job.

He got paid "under the table" for his dishwashing job, and saved most of his money. Living on the streets wasn't that hard if you were smart, and Bobby Rodriguez was smart.

Taking Maria's advice, Bobby began attending classes. He rapidly progressed in his school work, finding that by applying himself, he was a good student. Most surprising of all, he enjoyed it!

Chapter 79

The classes at the library would soon be over. Bobby had been scheduled to take the exam in a couple of weeks, giving him some time to review. He had studied hard, and was confident that he would pass. Maria laughed good-naturedly at him, telling him not to be so stuck on himself.

There was a big manufacturing company in town called Stratton Industry, and Bobby had seen an ad in the newspaper that they were hiring "unskilled laborers."

"I decided I definitely qualified," Bobby said with a grin.

Dressed in his best jeans and leather jacket, and with his charming smile in place, he entered the personnel department.

"I was totally surprised to get an interview that very same day with the big man himself," Bobby said as he gave me a sideways glance.

This characterization of me made me smile. I had never thought of myself quite that way before.

I had hired Bobby in the maintenance department with the understanding that he pass his GED exam. Walter Ackerman would be his boss, and I knew Walt would take Bobby under his wing.

Bobby told me with new enthusiasm, that now that he had a real job making honest money, his courtship of Maria would begin in earnest.

"She isn't like any other girl I have ever known," he said with a dreamy look on his face. She is not only beautiful, she actually has morals and principles! She's the kind of girl a guy like me might just consider marrying."

It seems when Bobby wasn't working, he spent every possible second he could with her. They went to the movies once in a while, but most of the time they walked in the park and talked. He admitted he couldn't imagine his life without her, and he hoped she felt the same way about him.

"Mr. P, I sure do appreciate you giving me a chance and all," Bobby said earnestly. "I won't let you down, sir. I promise."

Walt reported to me at the end of three months that Bobby had an irresistible charm about him, got along with everyone, showed up on time and worked hard. I was pleased, but then I never had any doubts.

Chapter 80

It was lunch time, and I was hungry. I decided to pass on the cafeteria food, although I frequently ate there, finding the food very good. It also gave me an opportunity to get to know the employees on a more casual level. Today I wanted to get away for a while. I had some papers in my briefcase, and wanted to look them over while I ate.

As I reached my car I happened to notice a disheveled looking kid going through one of the dumpsters that sat by the back door. When he saw me looking his way, he froze. This was probably a matter for security to handle, but something told me I needed to check things out myself.

He went back to his foraging as I approached.

"Are you looking for anything in particular," I asked, with what I hoped was a non-threatening, pleasant smile on my face.

He mumbled something unintelligible without looking up.

I tried again. "My name is Bryce Peterson. Is there something I can do for you, son?"

The boys head snapped up. I was taken aback by the hostile glare he gave me! Maybe this wasn't such a good idea after all!

"I ain't your son, and no you can't do nothing for me."

Undaunted, I asked, "Are you hungry? I'm starving and Billie Burgers has a great lunch menu. It's not far. Would you care to join me?"

The kid looked to be about thirteen or fourteen. It was hard to tell. He was tall but slouched as if he were trying to appear shorter. Several layers of clothes made him look bigger than he probably was. His long, dark, auburn hair was greasy, and tied back with a dirty piece of rag.

I must be out of my mind! I thought as I unlocked the car door. *I wonder what this kid's story is. He's obviously thinking over my offer.* I was surprised when he shuffled over to the car and got in. *He must really be hungry; poor kid.*

"I'll go this once, but I don't owe you nothing, understand?" he said with bravado.

"Understood," I said, raising my hands in an "I surrender" gesture.

Chapter 81

The short ride to the diner was a silent one. The lot was full, as expected. Fortunately, I found a parking spot on the street, avoiding a drive around the block. Billie's was a popular eatery for people who worked in the surrounding businesses. We were lucky to find an empty booth in the back.

"Order whatever you want," I said. "The food here is really good."

He continued to look defiantly at me over the top of the menu. "You don't exactly look like a burger joint kind of guy. What's your game?"

"No game. I just like the food. Oh, hi, Lil. I think I'll have a burger and fries. What do you want; er…I don't believe you told me your name."

"It's Luke, and I'll have the same only double."

The look on his face was an obvious challenge. He expected me to object to his order.

Lil raised her eyebrows at me, but quickly left to put in our order. Luke wolfed down his food like he hadn't eaten in days. Every now and then he glanced my way as if he thought I would take the food back or something. The meal passed in silence. I didn't pry. I figured when the boy was ready to talk, he would.

Chapter 82

From that time on, Luke was frequently loitering around the back door of Stratton's at lunchtime. I made a point of always checking. Dave, our daytime security guard, asked if I wanted the police called.

"I'd be glad to run him off for you, Mr. Peterson."

I looked at the kid kicking a stone around while he tried to look inconspicuous. I just didn't have the heart to send him away. Somehow, I identified with that lost, but hopeful look on his face.

Over time, Luke relaxed, apparently deciding I was harmless. Little by little he opened a window into his life. What I saw was heart breaking.

He lived in the projects down on the east side of town with his mother. The kids at school, when he could be bothered to go, called her a "dirty whore." Luke said he guessed they were right.

She entertained several gentleman callers every night except Mondays. That was her night off, so she said. What she did sickened Luke.

"Why would any man want to crawl in bed with that? And what kind of woman would let them do it, Mr. Peterson?" he asked with pain evident on his young face.

His mother was a skinny, sallow appearing woman who looked much older than her actual age of 35.

"She's probably got TB or something for all I know. She's always hacking and coughing," Luke said with his head down, avoiding eye contact with me. "She don't hardly eat nothing, and she smokes all the time. It's a wonder she ain't set the house afire!"

It was obvious she had never been much of a mother to Luke. According to him, she frequently allowed her boyfriends to use him as a punching bag if it would benefit her in some way. Once she even implied he could do "other things" for her friends. Apparently, some had kinky tastes, and liked young boys.

"I HATE her, Mr. Peterson. I HATE HER," he yelled trying very hard not to cry.

The kids had a name for him too. "Stupid moron." It looked to me like he intentionally reinforced this perception with behavior that rivaled the craziest whack job at Bingham, the local psychiatric hospital.

He was actually fifteen years old and six feet tall. He said he always wore his clothes too big, making him look fat and clumsy. He had perfected his shuffling gait until it was almost an art form!

"Good disguise, don't ya think?" he said. "Keeps people away from me most of the time."

I agreed. It was a great disguise. By the aroma wafting off the boy, he didn't bathe either. Another strategy, I assumed, to keep people at bay. Luke almost never looked me in the eye. I suspected he was hiding something, or maybe he really was mentally challenged. He was certainly socially inept, and his language could be quite colorful!

Chapter 83

It was obvious to me right from the start that Luke lived mostly on the streets. For one thing, why wasn't he in school? For the time being, I kept my questions to myself, but I became more determined than ever to help this young man if I could.

More than once, as I was paying the tab for lunch, I noticed Luke eyeing my wallet. I knew he would lift it if he got the chance. He wanted money. He probably really needed it. I decided there was something I could do about that, something honest that would hopefully put the boy's feet on the right path.

One day after eating hot dogs from a vendor on the street, I asked if he would be interested in doing some odd jobs around Stratton's to earn a little spending money. Luke nearly choked on his hot dog. The guilty look that came over his face told me loud and clear he usually just stole what he wanted.

I told him to think it over for a day or two. If he wanted the job, come by on Friday. The pay was $5.00 an hour.

The next day, promptly at noon, I opened the back door to find Luke standing there with his hands shoved deep in the pockets of his ragged jeans. I guess it hadn't taken him long to decide he wanted the job. It looked like he had tried to comb his mop of long hair, and his shirt was reasonably clean.

I shook his hand warmly.

"I'm glad you decided you wanted to come and work for me, Luke. We really can use your help."

Chapter 84

"The maintenance department is one of the most important areas in the whole company," I explained to Luke. "The people there are responsible for keeping the whole plant running smoothly. If one machine breaks down, the whole assembly line falls apart."

I introduced him to Walter, who would be his immediate supervisor. Walt smiled at Luke as he wiped his greasy hands on a rag he had pulled from his back pocket. He had been with the company a long time before I arrived, and he knew the inner workings of every machine in the plant. His knowledge, and his friendship, was invaluable. I depended on him.

One of the conveyers had been giving him some problems. He was trying to fix it without much success. If he couldn't get it to run properly, an outside mechanic would have to be called in.

"Can I take a look?" Luke tentatively asked.

"Sure, Luke," I said with more confidence than I felt. Have a go at it."

Luke looked the equipment over from every angle. Then he asked for a screwdriver, a wrench, and a short piece of wire. Walt gave me a questioning look. It was an expensive machine. If it were damaged further, the line would have to be shut down indefinitely.

The conveyer was soon lying in pieces on the floor while Walt and I looked on in amazement. Luke tinkered with a couple of things then quickly put everything back together. When he hit the start button the motor whirred good as new.

Walt clapped Luke on the back. "I've been trying to get that dang thing to work all morning. I could sure use your help on some other projects around here!"

Luke <u>almost</u> smiled as he was shown the employee locker room. He was given a locker with a combination lock. Also included for this job were three blue work shirts with Stratton's imprinted on the back. I told Luke I would have his name put on the front pocket just like all the other maintenance guys.

I told him he was to wear each shirt ONCE, then throw it in the laundry bin. The maintenance shop had its own laundry area where the shirts would be washed, pressed, and hung back in the locker room closet. The time clock was beside the door. Pay day was every Friday.

"I'll have Bobby show you to the personnel office. There are a couple of papers to fill out, tax forms mostly. You're under age, so we will need working papers signed by your mother. Do you think that will be a problem?"

Luke said his mother would sign. I didn't ask how that would be accomplished.

"That about covers everything doesn't it, Walt? Luke, do you have any questions?"

Luke's eyes shone as he shook his head. "Nope. No questions."

Just then Bobby poked his head in the office door. "You wanted me, Mr. P?"

"Oh, Bobby, this is Luke. He's going to be working with you in maintenance. I need you to take him over to personnel to do the 'new hire' paperwork."

"Yo bro, what's with all the hair?" was Bobby's first comment.

Luke stepped up to Bobby. "My hair is my business, man, so why don't you just go back to Mexico or wherever you came from."

I was ready to intervene, expecting a fight.

Bobby began to laugh. "He's okay, Mr. P. He's tough. We're going to get along great. Come on, yo, there's this cute girl who works in personnel. I'll introduce you."

Walt looked at me and shook his head. "Crisis averted I guess!"

From then on, Luke showed up at precisely three o'clock every day, trying to give the impression that he had been in school all day. Walt always had things for him to do. He showed Luke how to do the quality inspections, as well as the regular required maintenance for each machine. If Luke found a problem, he brought it to Walt's attention.

"Luke, you're one of the best mechanics I've ever seen. You don't need to check with me every time you find something wrong. I think you're quite capable of handling the needed repairs. If you can't fix it, then we really DO have a problem," Walt said with a grin.

Chapter 85

The local baseball team had made it to the finals, and Saturday was the championship game. I just happened to have two tickets, so I asked Luke if he wanted to go.

Luke said he LOVED baseball! I was pretty sure he had never been to a game before, and probably had never even played, but I understood pride. We agreed to meet Saturday afternoon.

Luke asked if I could pick him up outside Stratton's, apparently not wanting me to see where he lived. It took about fifteen minutes to drive to the stadium, with Luke staring at me the whole way.

"What's wrong?" I asked. "Did you have trouble getting permission to go today or something?"

"No, no problems," he replied as he nonchalantly turned toward the passenger side window. It's just that you look like a 'home boy' in jeans and a sweatshirt."

"I figured a suit and tie would make me look a little conspicuous," I chuckled.

The box seats were right behind home plate, not that this meant anything to Luke. *It's funny, I really like baseball. Too bad my father never knew,* I thought sadly as we took our seats. We ordered several hot dogs and root beer from the vendor who came around as soon as we sat down. We were ready for the first pitch!

We laughed at the bloopers some of the players made, and Luke seemed to be enjoying himself. I bought him a Dixon Dragon baseball hat, assuring him he would be able to see the field better without the sun in his eyes.

I talked about the game in such a way that Luke could pick up the rules, without feeling embarrassed because he didn't know anything about it.

Luke asked me to drop him off at the entrance to the park by the lake, which I thought was a little strange. Not wanting to pry, I didn't ask any questions. When he got out, I pulled around the corner behind some trees and watched.

He quickly glanced around to make sure no one was looking before he parted the dense, low-hanging branches of a large tree, and slipped out of sight. When he came out, the baseball hat was gone.

Well, what was that all about? I wondered as I drove home. *What kind of life does this kid have? All he needed was a chance. I guess that's all any kid needs; a chance and someone who cares.*

Chapter 86

It was 3:30 on Tuesday afternoon when I got a call from Walt. Luke hadn't shown up for work today, which was highly unusual. He had never missed work before. I had just hung up the phone from speaking with Walt when my outside line rang. It was Luke. He was out of breath, and talking so fast I could hardly understand what he was saying.

"Please come quick, Mr. Peterson! Something terrible has happened! I didn't know who else to call. Hurry! I don't know what to do!"

He gave me the address, and I was out the door. I met Luke at the corner of his street, which was closed to traffic with a police car blocking the road. Up ahead we could see an ambulance and more police cars with lights flashing.

I asked one of the officers if I could speak with the person in charge as this "young man" lived at the address behind the yellow crime scene tape. The officer made a call from his cruiser. I was relieved to see the Police Chief himself striding in our direction.

Chief Peter McHenry and I were well acquainted, having been on different committees together over the years. We shared a desire to better the community by reaching out to kids who were at risk, thus reducing delinquency, and the crime that went with it.

Pete had a grim look on his face as he shook my hand. Luke took a step closer to my elbow.

"Is this Luke Smith?" he asked me, finally looking at Luke. "Do you live at this address, son?"

Luke nodded yes to both questions.

Apparently, something had gone wrong when his mother had been trying to negotiate a good deal on some heroin. She ended up with two gunshots to the chest. She was dead when the police arrived.

Neighbors had heard the shots, and called for help. There were witnesses who saw a short, stocky, young, white male wearing jeans and a hooded sweatshirt, fleeing the scene. The Chief told Luke that it was only a matter of time before an arrest was made.

When the coroner's wagon arrived, the body was unceremoniously loaded inside. Luke would have to go to the morgue to make the positive identification of his mother's remains. He was doing his best to keep his "game face" in place, but I could tell he was scared to death.

At the morgue he looked for only a second at the woman who had given him birth.

He turned on his heel, and as he walked away he said, "Yep, that's her."

Chapter 87

On the recommendation of Chief McHenry, Child Welfare was more than willing to give me temporary custody of Luke. They would have a hard time placing him in foster care at his age, and with his sullen disposition.

I asked Luke if he wanted to come and live with me. There would be rules and school work. He didn't look too thrilled. On the positive side, there would also be lots of food, a clean place to sleep, decent clothes, and people who would care about him.

Luke hesitated for a couple of minutes, staring at me as if he were trying to decide if I meant what I said or not. His only other option was being put in state custody and living in a "home for wayward boys." He finally made a decision that would change the rest of his life. He came with me.

I asked if he had belongings he wanted to go get from his house. Instead, he asked me to drive to the park where I had let him off after the baseball game. He led the way as we walked to his hiding place. When I looked inside, it brought tears to my eyes. He had a couple of ratty, old blankets, a few cans of Spam, and a cardboard box where he kept his baseball hat. He slapped the hat on his head, and we went home.

He explained on the way that he hid the hat so his mother wouldn't take it away from him to give to one of her men friends.

Home for me was a boarding house at the outskirts of town owned by retired spinster school teacher, Gloria Hamilton, "Glo" to her Bridge-playing friends.

She was a short, stout woman in her late 60's with gray hair and sparkling hazel eyes. She immediately took a liking to Luke, and made arrangements for him to have a room.

As soon as Monica and I were married, she knew that I would be moving out. She said she would worry about finding another boarder when the time came.

I was well aware that Monica did NOT like the fact that I lived here in this "dump," but I had prevailed and stayed. I didn't think it would look right if I moved into one of the spare rooms in her father's house! I told her I was just trying to protect her reputation, to which she laughed and patted my arm.

Luke had almost fallen asleep at the supper table; understandable given the stress of everything that had happened. After he had eaten, he went immediately to bed, giving Glo and me an opportunity to discuss the best way to proceed with this new house guest.

I didn't go to work the next day. Instead, after a HUGE breakfast, and after the other boarders had left, I sat down with Luke and Glo for our first of many "family meetings."

Chapter 88

My philosophy was that everyone in a "family" should get to express their feelings and opinions without fear of any repercussions. Luke was surprised that this included him. The rules were laid down, including no more running around all over town doing God only knew what. He understood there was no compromise when it came to matters of personal hygiene, bad language and stealing.

Since Luke was so far behind in his school work, I asked Glo if she would be willing to do some tutoring. I would willingly pay the going rate. Being a teacher at heart, and missing the classroom if truth be told, she readily agreed.

Luke could go to Stratton's, and work with Walt after his homework and household chores were done. Luke looked at me, his blue eyes wide with wonder, and relief swept across his face.

"Welcome to the family, Luke," I said.

The funeral for his mother was the next day. Luke confided to Glo that he was dreading it. He didn't know why there even had to BE a funeral at all.

I paid for the casket and the burial plot. I had even found a minister who was willing to say a few words at the cemetery. Luke looked very uncomfortable standing by the grave staring at the box that held the body of his dead mother, while the minister read from his Bible. The words didn't mean anything to Luke, and they certainly didn't bring any comfort. Not a tear was shed.

Chapter 89

We started early. Shopping! Luke and I. Who would have thought? Yep, just two manly dudes out shopping!

First, he needed some decent clothes. Luke insisted that he pick out his own because after all, he had a certain persona he had to maintain. Within reason, I agreed. The sneakers were expensive, but the look on Luke's face when he tried them on was priceless!

"MAN, these shoes are cool," Luke assured me. "They are worth every penny you paid."

Luke had never owned a new pair of shoes.

"We can stop at the barber shop next, and I think that will about do it for today," I said as we were getting into the car.

Luke stopped in his tracks. "NO. I agreed to everything else, but I am NOT getting my hair cut."

I was surprised. It had been a long time since he had been so defiant about anything with me. I knew there must be a reason.

"Luke, what's wrong with getting a haircut. You might like it better short."

"My mother had one of her boyfriends' give me a haircut once. I looked like a FREAK," he yelled, his face distorted with pain and panic.

"Okay, how about this," I suggested calmly. "As long as you keep it neat and clean, you can wear it long."

Luke stared at me for a long minute. I knew the length of his hair wasn't important in the whole scheme of things. I didn't want to make it into a big deal that would create unnecessary friction between us. I preferred to pick my battles carefully over more important issues. This particular situation was obviously painful for Luke.

"It's a deal," he said as the panic receded. "Can we get something to eat now?"

Chapter 90

It was incredible what money and a top lawyer could accomplish in a short amount of time. Much to his amazement, Luke Smith, soon became Luke Peterson. As the papers were signed, a big smile spread across his face. I was surprised to see deep dimples in his cheeks. When I mentioned it, he gave me a withering look.

"They make me look like a sissy!" he told me disgustedly. "That's why I don't smile much. People might think I'm weak or something."

I tried to discuss Luke with Monica, telling her about his situation and the adoption. Monica just waved me off with a whatever, whatever attitude. She was busy planning the wedding and only half listened. The impression she gave was that she really didn't care anything at all about a homeless boy or what happened to him.

"What on earth are you talking about Bryce…adoption? We'll talk about it later."

But "later" never came, and this selfish preoccupation should have raised all kinds of red flags; however, I was in love and unfortunately, love is blind. I convinced myself that after we were married and things settled down, Monica would welcome Luke into our home.

I explained to Luke that Monica and I would be getting married in a few months and we would be gone away on our honeymoon for several weeks after that.

"Don't worry, Luke. I've made arrangements with Mrs. Hamilton. She'll make sure everything at home runs smoothly."

Luke didn't comment he just gave me a skeptical look.

He quickly settled into his new life of chores, school, homework and work at Stratton's. Glo kept me abreast of how the school work and chores were going. Walt told me that Luke had an uncanny aptitude for anything mechanical, and went about his work without needing much direction. I was pleased.

With the successful completion of each new work assignment, Luke began to take pride in his accomplishments. It wasn't long before word spread that Luke could "fix things," and other employees began to come to him for help. I could immediately see the change it was making in him. His self-confidence grew. He was also more at ease around people, although he still didn't "join in," preferring instead to stand back and watch.

I was quick to give praise. Everyone needs a pat-on-the-back for a job well done, and Luke was no exception. At first, he was embarrassed by the attention, acting as if he wanted to crawl into a hole out of sight. Over the ensuing weeks, he began to accept what I said with a smile, a bob of his head and a thank you. We were making progress!

Very few mistakes were made, especially related to his work. Luke knew more about the machines than I did! More often, problems arose with miscommunication. I treated Luke as I would any other employee. It was not just assumed that he was guilty of something. He was always given a chance to present his side of any problems that arose. This was something new to him, and he was leery at first. In the past, anything that went wrong had always been his fault.

Luke didn't know quite what to think about Bobby Rodriguez. Bobby poked fun at everyone including himself. Luke's hair was one of his favorite targets. Good-natured joking around had never been a part of Luke's life, but Bobby had a way of making him laugh even if he didn't want to! They were good for each other. As Luke became more confident, he was able to "give as good as he got." Bobby's heavily accented English became <u>Luke's</u> favorite target.

Bobby could do minor maintenance-related jobs, but he didn't have the knack for fixing things that Luke did. Bobby was a thinker; an organizer. He had started reorganizing Walt's office, making it more efficient. He also began prioritizing the work that needed to be done. He put out a schedule every morning so everything got taken care of in a timely manner. "Hot jobs," as he called urgent repair needs, were moved to the top of the list. The boys seemed to work well together even with all the fooling around. Walt was impressed.

Retirement was something Walt was looking forward to in just a few years. We talked it over and decided Bobby was ready for more responsibility. He became second man in charge after Walt, a position he was proud of and took very seriously.

Chapter 91

Today, Luke would turn sixteen. I knew he was really excited about it. Sixteen was a "rite of passage," one of the major birthdays he had informed me that morning at breakfast. He wanted to drive in the worst way. Cutting the grass with the riding lawnmower just wasn't enough anymore!

Of course Bobby teased him about being a baby.

Luke came back with, "You're lucky I give an old man like you the benefit of my considerable experience."

This bickering went on all the time. I knew it was good natured fun, and I was glad Luke had found a friend.

"Hey, Luke," Walt said that afternoon. I'm having a problem with one of the vending machines in the break room. Could you take a look at it?"

When the door of the break room opened, there were several of his friends yelling happy birthday, and holding out small gifts and cards.

A huge cake with his name on it, took up half of one of the tables. Carla, who worked in the kitchen/housekeeping department, had made it especially for him. There were candles and balloons…Luke was astounded. No one had ever celebrated his birthday before.

My present was a leather wallet and an application for his learner's permit. There was also a passbook for his own bank account with $100 already in it!

Bobby whooped and jumped in the air, promising to teach Luke to drive. I let both boys know that wouldn't be necessary, as I was going to do the teaching myself. Everyone laughed, including Luke and Bobby.

Later at home I explained about the bank account, and how money put there earned interest. Luke was very interested in all this and paid close attention. He was tight with his money. I knew he kept almost every penny he earned in a tin can under his bed.

Luke read every card he received several times, and marveled at the fact that he actually had friends. He couldn't wait to get to the bank the next day and put his money in his new account. He informed me that he was never going to be poor again!

Chapter 92

I wanted Luke to attend the wedding, but he adamantly refused.

"Are you kidding? I can't hang with all those snooty people," he argued. "Why can't things stay like they are? Just you, me and Glo?"

No explanation I gave could convince him that this would be a good thing for all of us. After the wedding and honeymoon, we would all move into the new house downtown. I knew he was extremely apprehensive about it. I did my best to put his fears at rest, which was hard as I had some serious fears of my own!

Monica became more testy and sharp-tongued as each day passed. I tried my best to be understanding. I continually told myself she was just under a lot of pressure. I hadn't been able to spend much time with her lately; she was always running here or there, talking with florists and caterers. She had numerous dress fittings, and the list of things to be done seemed endless.

Confused and frustrated, I felt like nothing more than an observer. I kept telling myself things would all work out. I NEEDED everything to work out. All I had ever wanted was to be happy with a family of my own.

More often than not, when I visited, I spent most of my time in the study talking with Ed. We became good friends over the ensuing weeks.

I finally gave up trying to be alone with my wife-to-be. She was just too busy, and frankly, appeared disinterested. This worried me, but I pushed these thoughts aside.

Chapter 93

The day of the wedding dawned bright and clear. I arrived at the church earlier then necessary, and began pacing back and forth in the little room that had been made available for my groomsmen and me.

My good friend, Pete McHenry, had agreed to be my best man. He did everything he could think of to keep my mind occupied. The wedding party was huge, but Pete was the only person I actually knew. All the others had been selected by Monica.

The time finally came. I couldn't believe it. In just a short time I would be married to the most beautiful woman I had ever seen. Pete and I lined up with the other men beside the minister.

The wedding march began, and the flower girl came down the aisle tossing rose petals from a little basket. The seemingly unending procession of bridesmaids followed. Then, finally, there was Monica on her father's arm. She was stunningly beautiful.

Her dress with its long train must have cost a fortune, enough to feed an entire third world country no doubt. Tiny pearls and diamonds sparkled on the long veil that covered Monica's face and flowed down her back to the floor. She was glowing as she nodded to friends and family.

Her father looked very proud and a little teary eyed as he handed his daughter over to me. I think it must have been a bittersweet time for him. He probably missed his wife, and wished she had lived to see this day.

The ceremony was long and arduous. There was much kneeling and standing and speaking of vows, but finally…

"May I present to you Mr. and Mrs. Bryce Peterson. You may kiss the bride."

Monica pulled away from my kiss just a little too quickly as she turned and lightly put her hand on my arm. Down the aisle we went to the cheers and clapping of the guests. I had never been happier!

The picture taking seemed to take forever. There were a LOT of pictures of Monica standing alone in many different poses. I felt awkward and out of place in our pictures together, completely overshadowed by my bride.

The reception was a repeat of the engagement party, only bigger and more elaborate. This time I was wise and didn't allow my glass to be refilled more than a couple of times. I wanted to enjoy our wedding night. After all, Monica had promised it would be spectacular!

Chapter 94

W e went directly from the reception to the airport, stopping only long enough to change clothes. We made it to the dock just in time to get on board the cruise ship. The honeymoon would be three weeks, and I had planned it carefully. I wanted us to be able to spend uninterrupted time together.

To my utter astonishment and dismay, Monica had somehow discovered my plans. She had invited at least fifty of her "closest friends" to come along! I could NOT believe it.

How could this have happened? I wondered as I stared in confusion at the group of people clustered around Monica. I thought we were finally going to be alone! That's exactly what I wanted...to be ALONE with my new wife!

We had spent our first night as husband and wife traveling, and upon boarding the ship, there were any number of things that Monica insisted she had to attend to. After all, she had to make sure her friends were comfortably situated in their cabins, didn't she? I thought that was a job for the ship's crew, but what did I know. I was extremely disappointed! Monica seemed to be oblivious to my sudden change in demeanor.

After dinner at the captain's table there was more dancing and drinking. Monica never stopped. It was after four in the morning when we finally made our way to the honeymoon suite. It was one of the larger cabins sporting a little balcony off the bedroom. The fruit, cheese and crackers I had ordered were on the table in the sitting room. It was all perfect! Or so I thought…

Monica made a huge fuss over getting ready for bed. She seemed to drag out her nightly beauty regimen forever. When she finally got in bed an hour later I put my arms around her and kissed her. I loved her, but I was nervous. I wanted to please her. I wanted to make her as happy as I was.

Her lack of response aroused my sympathy. After all, this was her first night with a man. But I was her husband now. She knew me; loved me. I couldn't understand why she seemed so uncomfortable. I would never do anything to hurt her, she must know that! I tried to be gentle. My efforts were by no means perfect, but the marriage was finally consummated.

Chapter 95

I leaned back on my pillow feeling a warm closeness to Monica that I had never felt before. I wanted to hold her close and go peacefully off to sleep. Instead, she sprang from the bed! Needless to say, I was confused and hurt. *What could possibly be wrong?*

The look she gave me was pure hate! She stood there with her fists clenched, and literally screamed in my face!

"That was, by far, the lousiest lay I have ever had in my life. If you think for one minute you're going to make a habit of it, you are sadly mistaken. Your slobbery kisses sicken me," she yelled with disgust written all over her face. "Whatever made you think you could satisfy a woman like me. Compared to the other men I know, you are the smallest, sorriest excuse for a lover I have ever seen!"

My mouth dropped open in shock. I was stunned and could only stare at her.

"I'm s-sorry," I finally stammered. "W-w-w-what if there's a c-child?"

"You idiot! Do you think I'm stupid," Monica shrieked an octave higher and a few decibels louder. "I used precautions. No little brat of yours is ever going to inherit MY money. NO, the Peterson name ends right here," she sneered sarcastically. "Now cover yourself up, I'm tired of looking at your pathetic little..."

Before she could hurl that final insult, I flung myself out of the bed and into the dressing room. I pulled on my clothes as quickly as my shaking fingers would allow. As I fled from the cabin I heard her laughing hysterically. After all, she had won her bet! The joke was on me!

Chapter 96

I wandered aimlessly over the various decks of the ship for hours. I saw lovers kissing in the moonlight and my heart shattered. *How could I have made such a huge mistake,* I wondered? Over and over again I searched my mind for the signs I should have seen, but didn't. What I came to realize in those long lonely hours was that I wanted to be loved so badly, I had been willing to overlook the obvious.

Images of her leaning in to me and whispering in my ear that our wedding night would be spectacular ran in circles through my brain. Well, at least she hadn't lied about that! It certainly HAD been spectacular. Bile rose in my throat as familiar humiliation washed over me. I had been SO STUPID!

There was piano music coming from a little bar on one of the lower decks where an elderly black gentleman was playing a soulful tune. I sat down at one of the small round tables and ordered a whisky sour. After one sip, I couldn't swallow past the lump in my throat, and I decided I really didn't like the taste of alcohol all that much. All the drinking had been Monica's idea.

I must have presented a pretty pathetic picture slumped over my drink with my head in my hands. It was the lowest moment of my life. I just wanted to be left alone to lick my wounds.

The sun finally came up on another day. As the old man made his way out of the bar, he gently patted my shoulder. I looked up into sympathetic brown eyes.

"Nothing stays the same forever, my friend," he said. "Things will get better."

I just didn't have the heart to go back to the cabin where I would surely face another of Monica's tirades. There was an empty deck chair in a secluded spot under the stairs leading to one of the upper decks. Feeling drained emotionally and physically, I threw myself down and fell into an uneasy sleep.

When I awoke the sun was bright in my eyes, and I knew it was well past noon. Going to the rail, I could see the lower decks. Sure enough, there was Monica, in all her glory, surrounded by a group of her friends. They were, no doubt, talking about my poor performance the night before. I had never felt so betrayed.

Taking this opportunity while Monica was preoccupied, I hurried back to our cabin, showered, shaved, put on clean clothes and made my way as far from Monica as I could get. I was hungry, and I needed to think.

What am I going to do? I asked myself. *What am I ever going to do?*

Chapter 97

From then on until the end of the cruise, I spent every evening in the piano bar with Gus Hendrickson, the piano player. It was never very busy, and I was sure Monica and her friends would never visit a dull little place like this so I felt relatively safe.

After the first two or three nights, Gus asked me if I played. When I said yes, he gave up his seat, and let me play as much as I needed to. It was a soothing balm to my wounded heart. It also brought calmness to my mind, which in turn helped me put things in perspective. I would just have to make the best of a bad situation, and when I got home I decided I would buy a piano. I hadn't realized how much I missed playing until now.

I managed to avoid Monica and her friends for the whole three weeks we were aboard ship. I knew I would have to face her eventually, as I had to disembark and take her home! The thought chilled me to the bone.

How am I ever going to live in the same house with this woman! And what about Luke? He will be living with us. She's NOT going to like it one bit, I realized with a jolt! Just thinking about all this made my stomach churn.

The day before we arrived back in port, I packed all my belongings while Monica was having her last hooray with her friends. I put my bags behind the lounge chair, which had become my "room."

I had on the clothes I would wear home. I wouldn't be able to shave, but what did it matter? Thinking about taking Monica home made me break out in a cold sweat. I sighed sadly and took a deep breath. I had given my promise. "Till death do us part." And I was a man of my word.

The next day was clear, sunny and beautiful. As soon as passengers were allowed off the ship, I took my bags to the car that was waiting for us. I went back to the suite, and squaring my shoulders, I knocked on the door. Not waiting for an answer, I entered.

Monica spun around when I asked if she was ready to go. Her eyes were bloodshot and her face puffy. Apparently she had celebrated long and hard the night before. She looked so pitiful, my resolve almost weakened.

She threw me a nasty look before pointing to her bags. I picked them up and started for the door.

"Aren't you going to escort me off the ship," Monica snapped sarcastically.

"No," I responded as I walked out the door.

I knew the plane ride would be excruciatingly painful. After all, I would have to sit beside Monica for six long hours. There were magazines for sale in the airport gift shop, so I bought a couple. I would at least have something to read, or pretend to read, thus avoiding unpleasant conversation.

Monica whined and complained every minute we were in the air. She demanded this and that all the way to Dixon. I flipped casually through my magazines and ignored her. I had resigned myself to how things would be, and had accepted the consequences of my mistake.

Chapter 98

Luke had missed me something awful. Of course he had Walt at work and Glo at home, but it just wasn't the same. He knew when I came home with my new wife we would all live in the big house we had purchased in an upscale section of the city. I knew he was dreading it; however, that didn't lessen his excitement at seeing me, which lifted my spirits a little.

Arrangements had been made for Glo to continue teaching Luke. I had decided to keep the rooms we rented at the boarding house for a while longer, giving Luke a "safe haven" if he needed one. Now I realized the wisdom of that decision!

I didn't see the point of making unnecessary changes right now. The move would be change enough. He could continue to spend as much time with Glo as he wanted. She loved him like a son, and he had become very attached to her.

As soon as the luggage was carried in I called Luke to tell him I was home. I tried my best to sound upbeat.

"Monica and her maid will be busy unpacking and getting things settled so how about you and me having dinner at Billie's? Pick you up at 5:50?"

"Sounds great," he replied enthusiastically. "How was your trip?"

I had anticipated this question, and had given much thought as to how I would respond.

"Tell you all about it over burgers and fries."

Luke may have his limitations, but he was a perceptive young man. He must have noticed some change in me.

"Hey, Dad, are you okay?" he asked as soon as he saw me, concern etched on his face.

Before I had left on my honeymoon, Luke had asked me what he was supposed to call Monica; and me for that matter. Up to this point he really hadn't called me anything except Mr. Peterson. I told him to just call Monica by her name, and he could call me anything he felt was comfortable for him.

He looked at me sheepishly. "I think I'd just like to call you Dad if that's okay."

"Luke, of course it's okay!" I had responded, as a big grin spread across my face. I couldn't have been happier!

As we ate, he spared no details telling me about all of Bobby's adventures and misadventures. Walter had been sick for a few days, but was better now. Carla kept him well stocked with homemade cookies at work, and Glo was really piling on the homework.

"Okay, Dad. Now it's your turn. I want to know everything," he said with his eyes glued to my face.

I never said a word about my relationship with Monica. What on earth was there to say? I couldn't tell Luke the whole thing had been a nightmare! After all, he was just a boy. I knew he would only be upset and probably very angry at Monica. It would definitely NOT be the best way to start our lives together as a family.

"The ship was like a floating city, Luke, it was incredible. The restaurants stay open all night and all day. There are all kinds of things to do including movie theaters, bowling alleys, aerobics classes, swimming pools…anything you could possibly want."

I did my best to paint a positive picture of the ship and life aboard. I don't think he fell for it. He didn't ask about Monica. I was grateful. Looking back, I think Luke was very capable of reading between the lines.

Apparently, Luke had discussed what his new living arrangements would be with Bobby. I knew he was worried about it. Bobby, usually full of advice on any subject, didn't know what to tell his friend. Luke would just have to wait and see!

Chapter 99

The "sleeping arrangements" that Monica had made for us were two bedrooms with a connecting door. Each bedroom had its own bath. It was fine with me.

On Friday afternoon I picked Luke up for the twenty minute drive to 1000 Park Lane. The house was HUGE with manicured lawns and beautiful flower beds. Monica's expensive red sports car sat in the driveway.

I introduced her to Luke, and noting the puzzled, angry look she gave me, I added, "Don't you remember? I told you several times about Luke and the adoption."

Puzzlement quickly changed to disgust and anger turned to fury. I couldn't understand her reaction. I had made it very clear that Luke would be coming to live with us after we were married. She stared back and forth between Luke and me for several seconds before she erupted.

"Get your filthy little retard bastard out of my house this minute! He is NOT living under my roof for one single second!"

I stood stock still, not able to believe Monica's outrageous behavior! I had expected that she wouldn't be overjoyed, but I never thought she would react in such a cruel and heartless manner toward a young boy.

The hurt look on Luke's face was something that would stay with me forever. He turned and ran. I was frozen to the spot where I stood gaping at Monica in disbelief.

As I turned to follow Luke, Monica snarled, "Don't you dare walk away from me!"

I paused only long enough for my mind to register her twisted, hateful look before I left the house without a word. I hurried down the street hoping to catch Luke before he got too far.

Luke was nowhere in sight! I knew he had lived on the streets, avoiding trouble by being able to melt into his surroundings. But I didn't know how he had managed to disappear so quickly!

I ran down the street frantically calling his name. I HAD TO FIND him! I had to apologize for this horrible mistake. There must be something I could do to make him understand that this in no way changed how I felt about him!

Having run out of places to look I returned to the house and got in the car. After driving around town for several hours, I was about to elicit the help of my friend, Pete, when I remembered a place in the park that Luke had often used as a hiding place when trouble was afoot.

Parking the car beside the entrance, I walked to an area where the tree boughs formed a canopy, and a tangle of prickly wild vines hid an enclosure. I pushed aside some of the vines, getting briers caught in my hands and clothes.

I shined a flashlight around inside the little "cave." Sure enough, huddled in the corner was Luke with his knees drawn up, and his head buried in his hands.

He looked up when the flashlight beam passed over him. Without saying a word, he moved over to make room for me to sit beside him. I had scratches across one cheek, my tie was loosened, and the top button of my shirt was open. There was mud on both knees of my trousers, and the elbow of my jacket was ripped.

Neither of us spoke for a long time.

Finally Luke broke the silence.

"Gee, Dad, you look like hell."

I didn't reprimand him for using the swear word. His language was the least of my problems right now!

"That's exactly how I feel, Luke. I am SO SORRY. I never expected her to act like that. I explained everything to her months ago. I guess she wasn't paying attention."

"I know it wasn't your fault, Dad, really I do," he replied sadly without looking up.

"You don't have to go back, Luke. You can stay with Glo. She'll be more than happy to have you. I'll come every day after work to see you. We will still go to Billie's every week, and we will have lunch together at work as often as you want. We are still on for baseball games and movies…please, Luke, can you ever forgive me? I promise I will make this up to you!"

Luke's eyes finally met mine. He just nodded, and I put my arm around his shoulders. We sat together like that until the sun was all the way up.

We crawled out of the shelter, and headed for the boarding house. I still had a few clothes there, so I cleaned up, and took Luke out to breakfast. When we got back to Glo's, I explained briefly what had happened. She didn't ask any embarrassing questions, she just gave Luke a quick hug.

"Of course you can stay with me, Luke. I'll watch after him, Bryce. Don't worry about a thing."

With a heavy heart, I went home to what I thought would be another ordeal I really didn't want to face. But I was committed to making this work for all concerned, no matter what it cost me personally.

Chapter 100

When I got home, the butler told me that Madame had not yet risen, but he had been instructed to show "Mr. Peterson" to the apartment at the opposite end of the house where my belongings had been moved.

When did I hire a butler? I wondered. *Well at least I won't have to deal with Monica right away. I'll go unpack my things and...*I couldn't think any farther ahead then that.

I knew the "other end of the house" had a little sitting room, a den, bathroom and a bedroom. It also had a private entrance with a parking spot by the door. I had assumed a housekeeper would reside in these quarters! I breathed a sigh of relief. At least I would be spared another bedroom fiasco and further humiliation.

I guess the housekeeper will have to make other arrangements, I thought grimly.

Wearily, I made my way to my new "home." I hung my clothes neatly in the closet, and arranged my personal things in the bathroom. Monica had thrown all my books and other possessions haphazardly in boxes. They sat in disarray in the middle of the sitting room.

Despondency settled over me like a cloak, as I sat alone on the small couch. I didn't bother to turn on any lights...

Chapter 101

Thanks to Glo, Luke passed his GED exam. I was very proud of him. For a graduation present I helped him pick out a used pickup truck. It was a bit rusted and battered, but it was exactly what he wanted. He was very excited about fixing it up. He couldn't wait to show Bobby.

He would have to maintain the vehicle, and buy his own gas. He would have to stick to a budget, but I knew he could do it. He had become very good at managing his money. He was growing up, and I was slowly allowing him more freedom.

Whatever Walt gave him to do at Stratton's, Luke did it without complaint. The other employees liked him, and he had a circle of friends, thanks in part to Bobby. They had both turned out to be good kids.

Bobby was always trying to get Luke dates with Maria's friends. He told Luke the truck would be a real "chick magnet." Luke wasn't so sure about that. He was extremely shy and uncomfortable around girls, plus I knew he was very suspicious of them. Part of that was my fault! I had exposed him to Monica's vile disposition.

"You just can't trust 'um, Dad," Luke explained to me over lunch one day. "Well except for Glo, Carla and Maria. They're okay. Girls are all about the drama and I don't need any. I've decided I'm never getting married!"

I had to smile to myself. It was as if he was the parent, and I was the child being lectured. *Maybe there's some truth to that,* I thought sadly. I hadn't made a very good choice as far as women were concerned. I certainly knew all about the drama!

"I know how unhappy you are, Dad, even though you never say anything. I wish there was something I could do about it," he said solemnly as he polished off his third burger. "If you ever need to talk about it, you know, man to man, I'll always listen."

Chapter 102

Baby Grand pianos were very expensive. I had looked around, and found just the one I wanted. I could afford it. I felt I deserved it...hell, I needed it to help preserve my sanity!

Monica and her friends went out to lunch and shopping every Wednesday afternoon, so arrangements were made for the piano to be delivered that day. It was beautiful. The sound was magnificent. The heaviness in my heart eased a little as I ran my fingers over the keys.

I had also found a painting of a young woman sitting at a piano, her hands gracefully poised over the keys. Her eyes were closed, as if she were being transported to another place and time. The artist's ability to capture the spirit of the unheard music appealed to me. I bought the painting and hung it on the wall over the piano in the den. Here with my music, maybe I could find some measure of peace.

Monica hated me. It was obvious. However, it seems I served a purpose for the time being. She knew her father was extraordinarily fond of me, and would probably be upset enough to cut off the flow of money he sent her way if she divorced me.

I wasn't as stupid as Monica thought I was. I knew she was seeing other men. She certainly didn't try to be discreet about it. In fact, she flaunted it!

Almost everyone in Dixon knew what was going on. Some felt sorry for me while others, I was well aware, laughed at me behind my back. No one ever heard me complain or make any comments at all about my wife or her behavior. All I had left was my self-respect. I refused to stoop to her level no matter what she did.

Chapter 103

We had been married three years when I got a call from one of the hospitals in Dixon. My father-in-law had been admitted. If this was a serious situation, I wondered why they had called me instead of Monica. When I asked that question, I was told calls to her personal phone had gone unanswered.

When I arrived at the hospital, I was told that Mr. Stratton was in the Intensive Care Unit. His condition was very serious. Ed only had one request of me, and that was to take care of Monica.

"It's my fault she is the way she is," he told me in a voice just barely audible. "I spoiled her. I let her run wild. But when her mother died…" He couldn't go on as he began coughing and choking.

Finally the spasm passed and he continued. "I should have done a better job with her upbringing," he gasped. "I'm sorry, Bryce. You're a good man and I trust you. Please promise me you will always take care of my little girl."

I promised him that I would always make sure she had what she needed. With this assurance, he relaxed and closed his eyes. When I called home, the butler answered. He was told to get Mrs. Peterson to the hospital as quickly as possible. Her father was dying.

To Monica's credit, she came immediately. She was at her father's bedside when he roused long enough to tell her he had always loved her, no matter what.

Monica wept bitter tears as she sat by the bed holding her father's hand. She had always known that he disapproved of the way she lived her life, but that had never stopped him from loving her.

Edward G. Stratton was an important man in Dixon and the surrounding towns. His funeral was packed with influential people from all over the state of Vermont.

Monica looked surprisingly attractive in her conservative black dress as she stood by her father's casket, and greeted the visitors. I stood beside her, feeling it was my duty to be there for support if nothing else.

I got her a chair when she appeared fatigued, and brought her a glass of water, which she accepted with a contrite look of gratitude.

Regardless of the problems between Monica and me, I had loved her father. It pained me that I had lost a good friend.

The grieving didn't last long. Monica was anxious for the will to be read. I knew she expected to inherit everything. When she was independently wealthy, my usefulness would come to an end. I had no idea what the future might hold. If she owned Stratton Industry…it could prove disastrous!

The lawyer had notified all those who were named in Ed's will when to be present for the reading. Monica was stunned to see several people, including me, in the lawyer's office.

"What is the meaning of this," she demanded. "I am my father's only child. Why are these other people here?"

Ed's lawyer had known the Stratton family for many years. He was well aware of Monica's rude, crude behavior as well as her recent activities since her marriage to me. His voice and demeanor were courteous but firm.

"If you will please take your seat, Mrs. Peterson, we can begin."

There were several small bequests to people who had worked for Ed faithfully over the years. He had also left a few thousand dollars to a charity he had supported.

When the lawyer began reading off the other assets: the investments, the bank account, the Stratton homestead where Monica had grown up, as well as Stratton Industry, a very smug little smile played across her lips. She was almost salivating at the thought of getting her hands on everything for which her father had worked all his life.

"Monica, you will get your mother's jewelry. According to the wishes of my client, Edward G. Stratton, the balance of his estate in its entirety will go to...M. Bryce Peterson. Anything you want, Monica, will be subject to his approval."

Chapter 104

M y mind reeled. I felt like someone had punched me in the stomach. I couldn't believe what I was hearing. It only took a second to register with Monica, and she was livid! She flew from her chair, knocking it into the old gentleman who happened to have the misfortune of sitting behind her.

"YOU BASTARD," she screamed in my face. "This will never stick. I'll see to that. You will not get my money! You had this planned right from the beginning; stealing my inheritance. I HATE YOU!"

Then she turned her attention to her father's lawyer. She let her wrath pour out on him informing him that the will was illegal.

"You buffoon," she screeched. "I am entitled to everything my father had. What kind of a lawyer are you anyway? Were you in cahoots with HIM all along?" she continued pointing a shaky finger in my direction.

The lawyer had expected this reaction from Monica. He was more than prepared for her outrage.

"Monica, sit down," he commanded in a voice that brooked no argument.

I was further surprised when Monica righted her chair and obeyed. Her face was almost purple with rage. Her chest heaved as she tried to control her breathing.

"Your father came to me over a year ago, and wanted to change his will. Anticipating your reaction, he asked me to make sure it was iron-clad and unbreakable. He requested there be three witnesses present. These well-known distinguished gentlemen can testify, if necessary, to his sound mind, and ability to make this decision. There is absolutely nothing you can do about it, Monica. I'm sorry."

I didn't think he looked sorry at all. In fact, I thought I detected a slight twitch of his lips that could be interpreted as a sly smile!

The lawyer told her he had a statement her father wanted him to read along with the will.

It began, "My beloved daughter, I know you are angry right now, but in time, you will thank me. Bryce is a fine man, and he has promised me he will care for you always. It is my hope that you will reconcile your differences with your husband, and live a long and happy life…" and that was as far as the lawyer got.

Monica jumped up, shrieked a curse against her father, and grabbed the letter. Before anyone could stop her, she ripped the letter to shreds, scattering the tiny pieces all over the floor. She then stomped from the room, slamming the door behind her.

Everyone was extremely embarrassed. They quickly concluded their business with the lawyer and left. I sat there bewildered. Atty. Richardson came over, and sat down beside me in the chair Monica had vacated.

"Well, that was quite a display wasn't it? I expected as much!" he said, with disgust evident in his tone. "I have some papers for you to sign, and when everything is said and done, you will be a very wealthy man, Mr. Peterson. If there is anything I can do to help you with this transition, please call my office. Oh, one more thing. The letter Monica destroyed was a copy. The original, which is in Ed's own handwriting, is filed with the will just in case she does try to cause problems. It's further proof that he thought highly of you, and wanted you to have everything!"

After the forms were signed I was given my copies. I thanked the attorney for his patience, and headed for my car. Thankfully, the lot was empty. Monica's red Mustang was nowhere in sight.

Chapter 105

I drove slowly home. The events I had just experienced left me feeling completely drained. Reconciliation with Monica would be nothing short of impossible now. I sighed as I pulled my car into its parking spot.

There was another surprise waiting for me when I opened the door to my apartment.

Monica was sitting on the floor leaning against the wall. She was disheveled and breathing hard. Tears had streaked her makeup, and she looked like a freak in a side show. A sledge hammer lay across her lap.

The room had been completely ransacked. The picture on the wall had taken a direct hit, breaking the frame. The picture itself had been ripped to shreds, and was scattered like confetti over the pile of rubble that was my piano.

The sledge hammer must have been heavy for her, but in her rage she had welded it with considerable power. She had pulled books off the shelves, and ripped out pages. My stereo had suffered the same fate as the piano. Even the clothes in my closet had not escaped her vicious attack.

I sadly surveyed my rooms, and what was left of my piano and other belongings. I didn't say one word. What was there to be said at this point? I calmly salvaged what I could, putting everything into a couple of boxes and a suitcase.

As I stepped over Monica's legs I paused at the door.

"Monica, you will be given an allowance each month, which will be placed in an account under your name at the bank. I expect you to stay within that limit. When it's gone, it's gone. You will not be extended any more money until the first of the next month. I will continue to pay the household expenses; however, I will no longer live under this roof. You can reach me for emergencies at my office through my secretary. Do you understand?"

She didn't look up. I left.

Chapter 106

Luke was growing up into a fine, responsible young man. He didn't need as much of my attention anymore. I had moved into a spacious 2 bedroom apartment in a high-rise in downtown Dixon within walking distance of Stratton's. He was given the option of moving in with me or keeping his room at the boarding house.

He decided Glo needed him, and he would stay with her. He had become her live-in maintenance man and protector. She had confided in me that she couldn't keep the place going without his help. I was proud of him for making such a conscientious and thoughtful decision.

For me, time dragged. I needed something to do that had meaning and purpose so I decided to go on the road occasionally to check in with my various subsidiaries, and find new contracts for Stratton's. I always let Luke know where I was headed so he could contact me if the need arose.

One day I decided to take a different route north and see some new scenery. It was late in the afternoon when I saw the sign for Cedarville, Vermont. I thought it might be a nice, quaint, little town where I could find a hot meal and a soft bed.

Much to my surprise, nestled among some trees, and sitting back off the road, I saw a rather non-descript building with a sign that said simply, "Vincenzo's. Dinner and Dancing." Since it sounded Italian, and I liked pasta, I pulled into the parking lot. Inside the door at the bar sat a white haired, portly gentleman who, upon seeing me, got up and greeted me with a big smile and a warm handshake.

"My name is Georgio Vincenzo," he said with flair, and a thick Italian accent. "I never see you here before, welcome to my humble establishment. Mama," he hollered. "Come meet our new guest."

For the first time in a long while, I felt at home.

Through the course of the evening, I got to know Rosa Vincenzo, who was only slightly less portly than her husband. She had the same ready smile and easy, welcoming manner.

Being the middle of the week, it wasn't very busy. I soon found myself seated in their cozy kitchen like I was family instead of in the dining room with the other guests. They must have sensed that I was carrying a heavy burden and needed a friend.

I had never tasted food so good, and complimented them on their hospitality as well as their cuisine. Through a one-way window between the private Vincenzo kitchen and the restaurant dining room/ballroom, I could hear music playing. There were several couples dancing on the large ballroom floor.

Georgio said the window was put in so they could keep an eye on what was going on in the dining room without actually needing to be there all the time.

"Mama and I, we are getting too old to carry the heavy trays of food, and wait on the customers. We have good people who work for us so we can relax and enjoy chatting with our guests. We have a good life here don't we, Mama?"

As we sat around the table after dinner, Georgio told me the history behind Vincenzo's. I could tell he was proud of what he and his wife had accomplished. They had worked hard and it had paid off.

Chapter 107

He and Mama had grown up in the same city in Italy. Her family had been wealthy, Georgio's lower middle class. Mama was a real beauty, and the boys flocked around her like moths to a flame.

Georgio worked in one of the more exclusive ballroom/restaurants in town as a waiter. He was a good looking kid with thick black hair and an easy grin, trying without much success to grow a mustache.

Rosa and her parents came there often to eat and to dance. Rosa was, by far, the most beautiful girl Georgio had ever seen. The very first night he laid eyes on her, he made the decision there and then that he would marry her someday.

Georgio smiled tenderly at his wife as he ran his finger down her cheek. Her eyes brightened with unshed tears, and she took her husband's hand.

It was obvious to me what kind of relationship they shared. It was that shared intimacy I craved. I envied them.

Georgio made sure that every time Rosa and her family came, he was their waiter. He was extremely solicitous of her parents while he made meaningful eye contact with Rosa as often as he dared. She was not unaware of his attraction to her, and she returned his gaze more often than not.

Rosa loved to dance, and she was never at a loss for a partner. Georgio watched and envied every single boy who took her hand. He desperately wanted to be the one that waltzed her across the floor. There was only one small problem. He didn't know how to dance.

Chapter 108

This was only a small bump in the road for a young, love-struck guy like Georgio. He took some dance lessons, borrowed a tuxedo, and the next time Rosa and her family came to the restaurant, he was ready. He had arranged for one of his off-duty coworkers to take his shift so that he would be free to make his move.

When the dancing began, he walked with confidence up to Rosa and asked her to dance. The rest was history. She never danced with anyone else all night. When she went home her dreams were filled with a brash young man with intense dark eyes who had held her in such a way that it made her tingle inside.

Rosa's parents wanted better for her then to be married to a waiter. They had already made some preliminary overtures to the wealthy parents of a nice young man in a neighboring town. They forbid her to have anything to do with Georgio Vincenzo.

Of course, young love always finds a way, and Rosa and Georgio found ways to spend time together. When they turned 18, they ran away and got married.

Rosa's parents were extremely upset. Refusing to acknowledge the marriage, they shut Rosa out of their lives. She loved her parents, and their actions hurt her deeply, but Georgio meant everything to her. Couldn't her parents see how happy they were? Wasn't marriage more than moving up the social ladder?

Georgia kept his job and Rosa went off to work for the first time in her young life in a general store as a cashier. They moved into a little flat near the restaurant, and at every opportunity...they danced.

They were an attractive, talented couple, which brought them to the attention of a band leader who frequently provided the music for the restaurant.

He told them about a dance competition to be held in a neighboring town. They scraped up enough money for the entry fee, and borrowed a car for the drive.

Much to their surprise, they won! And there was prize money! As their reputation grew, they entered more and more lucrative competitions. Much to their continued amazement they frequently finished in the top five. In just a few short years they were the European Champions!

They decided it was time to make their move to America. They had saved enough money for the passage, and soon settled in Vermont. Georgio was convinced they could succeed in this land of opportunity.

"To make a long story shorter, we bought this place for a song and fixed it up. We worked hard, didn't we Mama? But it's been worth it. We are happy and content with life."

Mama had learned to cook, and was soon preparing a buffet style dinner. Their restaurant became known for its authentic Italian food in a homey, comfortable atmosphere.

They found a young musician with a small band who was willing to provide music for a reasonable price. It turned out to be a good partnership, and Vincenzo's Restaurant added a ballroom.

Georgio and Rosa began dancing competitively again, and the reputation of Vincenzo's grew.

"We have retired from dancing, except in private," Georgia said as he winked at his wife. "The restaurant still provides a good living for us to this very day," he finished as he hugged his still beautiful Rosa.

Along the way they had a baby girl; their only child. According to Rosa, her father spoiled her rotten. But the truth was they both doted on her. Her Papa called her his Little Rose, and she was currently away at college.

I looked at this happy couple, and wished with all my heart my life had turned out differently. I was still young, only thirty-five, but I felt twice that. Sometimes my heart was so heavy I didn't think I could survive another lonely day.

Under Mama Rosa's gentle prodding, I had told them everything. It was a welcome unburdening. They just listened while giving me much needed support and sympathy. Their home became an Oasis in my otherwise desert of a life where Luke was the only bright spot. They treated me like a son, even giving me my own room. I found the peace I needed, and I loved them dearly.

Chapter 109

One day, out of the blue, I got a call at work from Monica. "I hear there's a little Italian restaurant in Cedarville that you frequent. I've decided I'm going to go check it out," she sneered. "Some of my acquaintances have told me the food is very good, but I'll be the judge of that myself. You can either take me or I will go with my friends. Either way, I'm going."

Wondering how she had heard about my comings and goings, I didn't respond immediately.

"WELL? Are you deaf as well as stupid? Make the damn reservations you moron. I want to go on a weekend," she yelled, hanging up before I had a chance to say a word.

With Monica's declaration of her intentions, I decided if I was present maybe I could prevent her from doing too much damage. Reluctantly, I made the reservations. I knew once she got something in her head, she meant business. She would go whether I did or not. Her friends had willingly participated in her escapades in the past, and would not hesitate to do so again.

I had never dreaded anything so much in my life. Luke advised me to stay home. Let Georgio handle Monica. But I simply couldn't do that to my friend. Instead, I warned him to be prepared for anything.

Chapter 110

The complaints never ended during the hour drive to Cedarville. The mood for the evening was set when we pulled in the parking lot, and Monica called the place a "dump."

Georgio and Rosa were dressed in evening clothes as the weekends attracted a more "upscale" crowd. They both looked wonderful to me. My stomach churned over what I knew was about to happen.

Being his usual cordial, pleasant self, Georgio took Monica's hand as I introduced them. He started to tell her it was a pleasure to meet her when she snatched her hand back and almost spit in his face.

"Can't you speak intelligible English? I doubt if anyone can understand your gibberish. Just how long have you been in this country anyway?" Monica snapped sarcastically. "And where did you get those God-awful outfits? At the Good Will?"

She looked them up and down like they were garbage, disgust written plainly on her face. I wanted to slap her!

Monica swept past them and demanded to be taken to her table, which, of course, wasn't close enough to the dance floor and had to be changed. She found fault with absolutely everything from the tablecloth, to the waitress assigned to our table, to the "spots" on the water glasses. I wanted to crawl into a hole someplace!

Of course the food was slop. She told the wait staff to take it back, and bring her something that was fit to eat. The meal was painfully long. I just pushed the food around on my plate, praying the night would end soon.

People were staring and whispering behind their hands, which didn't seem to bother Monica at all. In fact, I knew from prior experience that she enjoyed watching me squirm.

Chapter 111

While the band warmed up, Monica said she had to use the "powder room" before the dancing started. "I just hope the place isn't filthy. You never know with foreigners. They can be so dirty," she informed me as she flounced away toward the lady's room.

Oh please, God! Please don't let her want to dance, I begged an Almighty that I wasn't sure was listening or even cared what was happening to these good people. I certainly had no reason to believe he cared about what was happening to me.

When the music began, Monica decided that we were going to dance. She grabbed my arm, and began pulling me to my feet. Rather than cause a scene, I got up and followed her onto the dance floor.

Before we were married she had insisted that I take dance lessons so that we could dance at our wedding reception. I had thoroughly enjoyed it, and had become quite proficient. We had danced together once...and that was enough. I knew this was going to be unpleasant at the very least.

When I tried to hold her in my arms, she shook herself disgustedly as she pulled my arms where she wanted them to be. She proceeded to literally drag me around the floor making us look as ridiculous as she possibly could. Of course, it was all my fault.

Why should this behavior surprise me, I thought fleetingly as perspiration began to bead on my upper lip.

In the middle of the song, she stopped.

"You clumsy ox," she screamed into my face. "You call yourself a dancer. You have two left feet, your hands are too sweaty, and I cannot dance with such a buffoon any longer," she concluded as she left me standing alone in the middle of the floor.

The other couples on the floor backed away from us. They opened a path for Monica as she stalked off the floor, head high, like she was some Grand Dame leaving her subjects in her wake. I wanted to die.

The band leader tried his best to keep the music going, but everyone's eyes were on Monica and me. The music haltingly stopped as everyone stared.

She commanded that her wrap be brought to her immediately. She then ordered me to take her home. I was only too willing to comply. I stopped long enough to apologize profusely to Georgio and Rosa. I knew they were extremely upset, not so much for themselves, but for me! I only hoped this incident didn't cost them future business. Not one word was spoken on the way home. I realized Monica had accomplished her goal. Once again, she had made me look like a fool.

Chapter 112

The hour's ride back to Dixon had given me time to collect my thoughts, deepening my resolve. I would not tolerate this behavior ever again. I was done being the nice guy. Consideration of her feelings was no longer possible for me. *Does she even have feelings,* I wondered?

Her hand was on the door knob as I grabbed her arm, and brought her around to face me. I guess she could tell by the look on my face that I had had enough. Her satisfied smile quickly faded.

"If you EVER go near the Vincenzo's again or cause them any problems whatsoever, your allowance will be cut in half. I will take away that car you love so much, and you can use public transportation for all I care. The household staff will be dismissed. You will have to do your own cleaning, or live in squalor. Eat or don't eat, it's your choice. Any questions?" I finished without raising my voice.

By the look on my face, Monica must have realized I wasn't kidding. She threw herself out of the car leaving the door hanging open. She stomped up the sidewalk and disappeared into her house.

Back in my apartment, I sank onto the couch. With my head in my hands, I wept. How could I ever face my friends again? Was it her intent to destroy everything that held meaning for me? Apparently so.

Several days later I received a call from Mama Vincenzo that eased my mind and my heart.

"Bryce, my boy, I just wanted to know that you were okay. Papa and I are worried about you. Please, you come back soon. You will always be welcome."

Chapter 113

B obby and I had just finished going over the rotation schedule for the next month when my secretary buzzed me.

"Sorry to bother you, boss, but there is a woman on the line asking to speak with you. She says it's urgent, and that she works for your wife. Do you want me to put the call through?"

It was Mrs. Buckley, Monica's housekeeper, the tenth one she had hired. All the others had quit after just a few months. *This woman must really need a job,* I thought as I took the call!

"I'm so sorry to bother you, Mr. Peterson," she said, with a nervous quiver in her voice. "Please don't think I'm a busybody who listens to other people's conversations, but I happen to overhear Randall, you know, Randall Kaplan the butler? He and your wife were talking about doing something awful to your son! Madame wants your boy beat up! She wants drugs found on his body! I'm afraid Randall has friends who could very easily arrange that!"

It was obvious she was upset. I tried to calm the poor woman by assuring her that she had done the right thing by calling me. I would certainly handle the situation. I also told her Monica would never know who had given me this information.

My stomach heaved as I put a shaky hand to my face. I must have looked like death warmed over because Bobby was at my elbow in a flash.

"Mr. P! What's wrong? Did somebody die or something?"

After explaining the situation to Bobby, my first call was to my friend Pete at the police department. It seems the name Randall Kaplan was well known to the Dixon police. He had been arrested several times for assault and battery; each time, all charges were mysteriously dropped. The suspicion was that he had friends who were willing to do a little leg-breaking on his behalf.

They also knew he was involved in dealing drugs, but could never seem to catch him in the act. Pete would put the street cops on alert. In the meantime, I called Walt and asked him to send Luke to my office.

Why does it not surprise me that Monica would be associated with someone like this! How has poor Mrs. Buckley survived in that house? Thank God she is a moral, ethical woman, I thought as I paced back and forth in my office waiting for Luke to arrive.

I would move heaven and earth to protect Luke, but I knew Monica wouldn't stop until she got what she wanted. I was sure everything would be arranged so that her name would never be connected to whatever happened. I wondered where she had gotten the money to pay Randall. This kind of man didn't do something for nothing!

When I explained things to Luke, he shook his head in disgust.

"Don't worry Dad. I'll be on the lookout. I can take care of myself."

"I won't let him out of my sight for a second," Bobby promised. Luke just rolled his eyes heavenward.

"What? You think you're going to be my guardian angel or something, Bobby? I really appreciate the thought man, but no thanks," Luke said as he punched Bobby's arm.

This little interchange did give me an idea however. After the boys left the office, I called Pete back, and asked if he knew of people who could be hired to discretely watch over my son 24/7. I knew it would be expensive, but I could afford it and I wanted Luke safe. If something happened to him because of Monica, I hated to think what I might do! I had never been a violent man, but if something terrible happened I would never forgive myself or Monica!

I worried constantly even though I knew Pete's people were in place. Luke didn't seem to suspect he was being followed everywhere he went. When he was in for the night, two guys were sitting in a car parked down the street from the boarding house. I didn't see the point of telling Glo. She couldn't do anything about it, and she would only worry.

Chapter 114

B obby spent as much time with Luke as his job responsibilities would allow. I tried to persuade Luke to come stay with me, but he didn't want to leave Glo alone and defenseless. It was a very tense next couple of weeks. Then I got a call from a nurse at Dixon Memorial Hospital, which changed everything.

When I arrived in the emergency room, the nurse told me that apparently Monica had been feeling ill all day. Now vomiting accompanied severe pain in her belly. Her yellowish complexion led the doctor to suspect some kind of liver problem.

I could hear familiar cursing and screaming coming from inside the treatment area. I knew immediately it was Monica. I felt sorry for the nurses, and anyone else having to deal with her, even if she was really sick!

The thought suddenly struck me that this might just be a ploy to distract me from protecting Luke! She was not beneath doing something exactly like this! But my fears in that regard were assuaged when, an hour later, a nurse once again came out to speak with me.

"The doctor is with your wife now. Blood work and scans are currently being done to diagnose what is wrong with her. As soon as we know anything, the doctor will be out to talk with you," she assured me. "Is there anyone I can call? Or can I get you some coffee or something? You may have a long wait."

"I would prefer to wait until I have more information before calling my family," I responded, "but I will take the coffee. Thank you so much."

I waited for well over 2 hours before a short, dark-haired woman wearing glasses entered the waiting room with a patient chart in her hands. I stood immediately hoping she was going to let me know when the doctor would be ready to speak with me.

Much to my surprise she introduced herself as Monica's doctor, Dr. Ann Reynolds.

PART 3

Ann and Bryce

Chapter 115

Ann sat down next to Bryce on the couch, and put a gentle hand on his arm.

"I'm afraid I have bad news for you, Mr. Peterson," she said quietly. "Your wife has cancer, which has already spread to several of her vital organs. There are no treatment options available for her. All we can do is try to keep her comfortable. I'm so sorry."

All Bryce could do was stare at Ann, bewilderment evident on his face, as he struggled to comprehend what she was telling him. He didn't know how he should feel. Right now he was just numb.

Having been in the position of giving bad news to family members before, Ann understood his confusion.

"We will be moving her to a room on the oncology floor in just a few minutes where she will be more comfortable. I will be happy to take you there. Is there anyone I can call for you?"

"No...no, I'll call my son, Luke, after she's in her room," Bryce managed to say.

"There's a waiting area with a small kitchen at the end of the hall. The coffee pot is always on. The fridge and cupboards are stocked. There are also small rooms with cots and linens if you need to rest, but don't want to go all the way home. Feel free to use anything you want," she continued. "You may come and go as you please. A nurse will always be available to answer any questions."

She gave Bryce her card, assuring him he could also call her at any time.

"You can also reach me through the hospital switchboard," she said as she stood. "If you will come with me, Monica should be in her room by now."

The relationship between Mr. and Mrs. Peterson was not clear to Ann. One thing was obvious, they lived apart. The staff had called him at a different number than the home phone number listed on Monica's chart. He had come immediately so he must feel some responsibility for her. It was a bit puzzling; however Ann had seen stranger situations with families over the years.

He was tall, thin and bald. His eyes were sad; his face was drawn as if he carried the weight of the world on his shoulder. Ann's heart went out to him.

I hope he's not sick himself, she thought as she led the way to Monica's room on the second floor at the end of the hall.

Reluctantly, she left him sitting in the chair by the bed. He hadn't asked any questions or made a comment. It was an unusual reaction to this serious situation, and Ann was concerned about him.

Chapter 116

H e may not have been communicating with Ann, but his mind was working at top speed. He made a mental list of everything he would need to do in the morning.

The house would need to be checked and secured. The staff would stay on for the time being. Monica's bank account would have to be checked and any outstanding bills would need to be paid. And that's as far ahead as Bryce could think at the moment.

He left around midnight. Ann assured him that she would call if there was any change in Monica's condition.

He was exhausted and depressed as he headed back to his apartment. *One more thing. I'm just so tired. Will my life ever be normal? I don't even know what normal is! Will I ever find happiness?*

The nurse had called Ann twice during what was left of the night. The patient would require almost constant monitoring. When she roused she became very agitated. She had already pulled her intravenous line out.

Her vocabulary was profane, and she fought the nurses to the point that she had to be restrained in order for care to be given. Based on her current behavior, Ann began to think the cancer had already spread to her brain. Surprisingly, the X-ray of her head was unremarkable.

I will need to speak with Mr. Peterson about getting someone to stay with her 24/7. Maybe she will settle down if her family is with her, Ann thought as she wrote in Monica's chart. *I hope Mr. Peterson is getting some sleep. He looked like he was about to collapse.*

Bryce arrived early the following morning. After a brief discussion, it became clear to Ann that no family would be available to sit with Monica.

"Are there people available who can be hired to stay with her when I can't be here?" Bryce asked as he looked out the window, not quite able to meet Ann's eyes.

"Of course. I would be happy to arrange that for you, Mr. Peterson," Ann said. "There is one more combination of medications I can try, and hopefully she will get some relief."

The new medicine worked, thank God! Monica finally fell into a restless sleep. It was a relief to Bryce that she wasn't constantly screaming! After a few hours of that, his nerves were frayed, and his head was splitting.

Chapter 117

The house at 1000 Park Lane was quiet when Bryce arrived. He hadn't been in the place since Monica had destroyed his suite. Little had changed except that there weren't as many pictures and decorative items displayed as he remembered.

Randall was nowhere to be found. His rooms were empty, and his clothes gone. Mrs. Buckley was waiting at the door having seen Bryce pull in the driveway. She informed Bryce that when she arrived for work that morning, the lights were on, the door was unlocked, and nobody else was there. She had no idea what was going on.

When the situation was explained to her, she said the appropriate words to express her condolences, but it was obvious to Bryce that the woman had been browbeaten by Monica. He was surprised she had stayed.

He asked her if she would consider staying on until he knew more about what would be necessary in the future. She readily agreed, as Mr. Peterson had been kind to her.

Arrangements were made at Stratton's so that Bryce could be at the hospital as much as possible. He was hesitant to put a stranger at Monica's mercy should she wake up. However, the new medication kept her fairly quiet, and Bryce finally decided it was safe to hire people to sit with her.

He would spend a few hours at work every day doing only essential tasks. All the other things would be delegated to Bobby, who had become his right hand man. Between his secretary and Bobby, he felt satisfied that everything would run smoothly in his absence.

He made sure he spent time with Luke every day.

Luke was glad Monica was sick! She deserved to be darn sick in his opinion, one he didn't express out loud. This whole sorry business was already taking a toll on his father, and that bothered him a lot. He had no intention of visiting her in the hospital. If truth be told, he hoped she would die!

Chapter 118

When Ann went off duty, she would stop to check on Monica on her way out, frequently finding Mr. Peterson sitting quietly by her bed. When Monica roused she spewed every manner of vile filth against him.

She criticized everything from his bald head to his hairy chest to his pitiful performance in bed to his pathetic, inadequate manhood. Monica used very colorful, unladylike expletives, which made Ann's ears burn!

Bryce just sat there and took it, never responding in kind. He was courteous to the staff, and very respectful of her, paying close attention to what she said. He always apologized when he thought he was taking up too much of her time, thanking her repeatedly for her attention to Monica's needs. Ann had known only two other men like him…

It had been two weeks since Monica had been brought to the hospital. The staff was surprised she was still hanging on, the whole ordeal taking its toll on Bryce. Ann was becoming more and more worried about him!

Being a physician who was concerned about the family as well as the patient, Ann knew Mr. Peterson was trying to deal with this situation completely alone. She hadn't seen any family members at all. Ann knew he had a son, but hesitated to ask about him, not wanting to pry.

Bryce was thinner, his color was gray, and his eyes had a haunted look that really bothered Ann. She decided she could at least see that he ate one good meal a day.

Chapter 119

Ann enjoyed preparing tasty, nutritious food. That's just what Bryce needed right now to maintain his own health. Using hospital plates, she fixed meals at home. The coffee pot in the lounge was always filled with her special blend. She suspected Bryce to be the type of man who would object if he thought she was going to any extra trouble for him.

The meals were delicious, and Bryce decided hospital food wasn't as bad as he thought it would be. Since this was an oncology unit where families spent a great deal of time, he thought the meals must be a benefit for the families of the terminally ill.

As the days passed, Monica hung on to life like a dog with a bone. More often than not, when Ann's regular shift was done she would head to the second floor. In the evenings, Bryce was always there.

Monica's disease was now rapidly progressing. She slept more and more, which was a blessing to everybody. Ann began spending time getting to know Bryce. The more she got to know him, the more she liked and admired him. She found him to be a kind, intelligent man who certainly didn't deserve any of the treatment she had witnessed.

She began to look forward to spending time with him, often touching his shoulder as she said good night before heading home. She wanted so much to bring a smile to his face. Lately, much to her delight, her efforts were rewarded. Her feelings toward this man surprised her. They were completely unprofessional.

What on earth is wrong with me, she thought as she lay in her bed at night, wondering about this quiet, decent man.

Chapter 120

Monica had been in the hospital 6 weeks when Ann was paged in the middle of the night. When she arrived in Monica's room she knew the end was near, and asked the staff to contact Bryce.

When he arrived, Ann explained what was happening, and what he could expect over the next few hours. Bryce took up his usual spot by the bed. Ann stayed close by.

All the staff knew this was not unusual behavior for Dr. Reynolds. She frequently spent this much time on a case if the family was small, and appeared inadequate to the task of watching a loved one slowly slip away. No one realized just how much she really cared!

Without fanfare the end finally came at 03:47 hours in the morning. Ann was sure Monica would have been disappointed that her passing hadn't caused high drama and much anguish. Then she chided herself for such an unkind thought! She notified the funeral home herself, and gave emotional support to Bryce before sending him home.

The funeral announcement appeared in the newspaper the next day. Ann arranged her work schedule so that she could attend. Bryce stood alone at the casket looking calmly resolute. Not many people showed up. Monica's friends came briefly to the calling hours, but none could be bothered to sit through a boring funeral.

The house on Park Lane was sold. The housekeeper was given a generous severance having more than earned it. Bryce assured her he would give her an excellent recommendation if she needed it in securing other employment.

With Randall Kaplan in the wind, Bryce wondered if Luke was still in danger. He cautioned Luke to remain vigilant, as he himself would. Pete advised Bryce that since the gravy train trail had dried up for Mr. Kaplan, he was probably gone for good in search of other lucrative situations to exploit. Pete thought it was safe to cancel the 24/7 surveillance.

Bryce began trying to pick up the strands of his broken life. He was so lonely and so tired. It was all he could do to get through each day.

Ann, in the meantime, had resigned herself to the fact that she would never see this man again, which was probably for the best. She hadn't realized how much she enjoyed his company every day. It was funny; she just couldn't seem to get him out of her head.

Chapter 121

Without the constant stress that went along with Monica's antics, Bryce found he didn't have much to do in his spare time. It surprised him when he caught himself thinking about Dr. Ann Reynolds!

Her patience and kindness to Monica had impressed him. She had never seemed to get angry or frustrated although Monica certainly gave her good reason to feel that way! Monica had spit on her, verbally abused her, and in general, treated her horribly. Ann calmly took it all in stride. She did everything in her power to make this dreadful woman comfortable.

He had greatly appreciated her attention to his needs as well. Maybe he should drop by the cafeteria at the hospital someday. The food was outstanding, it was close to work, and just maybe he would bump into her! After all, he never properly thanked her for all she had done for him.

It took several weeks for Bryce to get up the nerve to visit the cafeteria. He was extremely anxious about entering the hospital at all. The memories of Monica's stay were still too fresh. Despite his nervousness, he went through the cafeteria line keeping an eye out for Dr. Reynolds.

He brought his tray to a table in the corner. With the first bite, he realized this was definitely NOT the food he was given while Monica had been a patient. It was edible, but barely. He left a bit confused. It had been a waste of time all the way around, as he never even caught a glimpse of Dr. Reynolds.

As Ann entered the cafeteria that day, she immediately saw Mr. Peterson going out the door. Short of yelling his name and looking like an idiot, she couldn't get to him in time to say hello.

She was mystified at the disappointment she felt.

I wonder if something's wrong. Was he looking for me? Oh, for heaven sake, that's foolishness. I wonder if I should call him. Would that be too forward? Even unprofessional? Of course it would be, what am I thinking!? All these thoughts tumbled through her mind as her heart fluttered in her throat like a moth trapped behind a glass.

Chapter 122

I t had been three peaceful months without Monica. Bryce was feeling relatively "normal," whatever that meant. He went to work, came home and ate a simple tasteless meal. He listened to some music or read before going to bed early, only to lie awake staring at the ceiling.

The time he spent with Luke was priceless. He looked forward to it every week; burgers at Billie's, just like when Luke was a kid. But Luke was busy with his own life and activities, just as it should be. However, it often left Bryce feeling lonesome and at loose ends.

When he was getting ready for bed one night, he felt a little ache in his side. He poked around in the general vicinity of the pain finally deciding he must have pulled a muscle or something. It would probably be gone in the morning.

It wasn't better in the morning, if anything it was worse. He had never been one to baby himself, so he just went through his morning routine as usual, arriving at work right on time. By mid-afternoon it was really hurting, and he grew concerned. By evening he was in intense pain. He decided it might not be a bad idea to have it checked out.

He called for his car, and drove the short distance to the hospital. Unable to stand up straight at this point, he was barely able to make it to the door under his own power. The attendant saw him coming, and immediately put him in a wheelchair.

He was soon in a bed with a nurse bending over him. Things happened quickly once inside the treatment area, as protocol was followed for investigating "belly pain." It didn't take long to determine he had a "hot" appendix. He was terrified!

Chapter 123

A fter a relatively quiet evening in the emergency room, Ann's shift ended at midnight. As was her usual routine, she ran down the list of new patients currently being treated to make sure there was adequate staff to care for them.

Her heart nearly stopped when she saw the name Bryce Peterson. Without giving away the emotions that were boiling just under the surface, Ann asked the nurse if a physician had been assigned to him yet. She was told that his workup was in progress with some of the results already on the chart. He had appendicitis. The on-coming physician would see him shortly. Not good enough in Ann's mind. She took his chart signing on as his doctor.

She went immediately to his bedside. His eyes were closed, and a grimace of pain tightened the lines of his face. She gently touched his hand. When he realized who it was, he gave her a small smile of relief. He knew he was in good hands.

"Try not to worry, Mr. Peterson. I'm going to get that appendix out of there and you'll be fine," Ann said as she studied his chart.

She did a cursory physical examination, her hands gentle on his skin. Bryce knew he would be okay, he trusted Dr. Reynolds. He was given preoperative medication before being wheeled to the operating room. As he descended into unconsciousness, he thought it was a shame he had to get sick just to see her again…

Scrubbed and gowned, Ann soon had a scalpel in her hand. The appendix had not ruptured; she had gotten it in time.

Chapter 124

The procedure went well. Bryce woke up in the recovery room just as Ann was checking the dressing over his incision.

"Well, hello, sleepy-head," she said as she pulled the covers over him. She put her hand on his forehead. "You're going to be just fine. How do you feel?"

"Like I've been run over by a truck," he whispered thickly, feeling like his mouth was full of cotton.

"Would you like a few ice chips?" she asked.

He managed to nod yes. Ann very carefully lifted his head, and spooned in a little crushed ice. When she decided he had had enough, she gently lowered his head back on the pillow.

When she touched his face, his eyes opened.

"Is that better?" she asked quietly as she adjusted the blankets.

Again, all Bryce could do was nod yes. He thought she looked like an angel. The thought flickered through his mind that maybe he had actually died and gone to heaven. As he fell into a deep, restful sleep, he pictured her face in his mind. It comforted him.

Chapter 125

His vital signs remained stable over the next few hours. Although he continued to be somewhat groggy, he roused easily, so Ann had him moved to his own room.

She stayed around until he was awake enough to take more ice chips that she carefully spooned into his mouth. His lips were very dry, so she gently applied lip balm.

Bryce had never received tenderness at a woman's hand. It was a whole new, somewhat embarrassing, experience for him. Ann was surprised by his shyness. It was oddly endearing to her.

With the help of the mild analgesic she had given him, Ann was confident he would sleep through the rest of the night. Barring any complications, he should be able to go home the next day. She rested in the doctor's lounge after giving orders that she wanted to be paged if Mr. Peterson had any problems. She dozed off with a smile.

By mid-morning she took a few minutes to check on Bryce, fully expecting to find him awake and alert. Instead, he was still groggy and very upset!

The minute he saw her he began pleading his case.

"Ann, they aren't going to let me go home! I can't stay here. I have to go. Please Ann, please tell them to let me go!"

His use of her first name pleased Ann more then she cared to admit. Her heart did a silly little flip. *Oh my goodness. What is the matter with me,* she thought as she hurried to his bedside.

He was so distraught that Ann promised to investigate what was going on. His chart revealed that the internist, who had taken over his care after surgery, would not release him until he was more alert. Since he lived alone, his ability to care for himself was a priority. Dr. Braxton was not sure he was capable of doing that yet. He was also running a low-grade fever that would need to be monitored for a while longer.

Dr. Braxton responded promptly to her page. After the usual formalities, they had a discussion about their mutual patient.

"I cared for the late Mrs. Peterson a few months ago, so I am somewhat familiar with the family. I would be happy to see that he gets safely home. In his present state of mind, I really don't think he will get adequate rest if he stays here. I can keep an eye on his temperature over the next few days, and with some rest, I think he'll be fine.

It sounded reasonable to Dr. Braxton. He said he would write the necessary discharge orders based on Ann's willingness to take responsibility for the patient. Bryce relaxed as soon as she told him that she would be taking him home. She didn't think he even heard the rest of what she said, he was fast asleep again.

This was not the first time Ann had taken a patient home. She frequently made house calls, so her offer was perfectly understandable to Dr. Braxton. He was happy to get this man discharged, as he had a full case load already.

Getting a week's vacation wasn't a problem, as Ann hardly ever took any time off. By leaving work a little early, she had time to stop at the grocery store. She was pretty sure Bryce's cupboards were probably bare. Then she ran home to change her clothes.

Ann pulled her little blue jeep up to the discharge door just as an aid helped Bryce out of the wheelchair. As he wedged himself into the passenger seat, a grimace of pain crossed his face. Ann immediately put her hand on his arm.

"Are you okay? I'll give you something for the pain as soon as I get you home."

Chapter 126

I t was only a 10 minute ride to the Covington apartment complex where Bryce lived. When Ann stopped in front of the building, the doorman hurried out to help Bryce from the car. Another young man carried the groceries.

Roscoe, the old doorman, introduced himself to Ann, and offered to park her car.

Well, well, well. What do we have here? Mr. Peterson has never had a woman in his apartment. I wonder who she is. Not bad looking either, he thought as he took her keys and headed for the jeep.

Bryce leaned heavily on Ann's shoulder to walk. With her arm around his waist, they made it ever so slowly to the elevator. He was pale and shaky when they got to his door.

The recliner in the living room seemed to be as far as Bryce could go for the time being. As he relaxed back against the soft leather of the chair, Ann made him comfortable under a warm blanket she found draped over the back of the couch. The Tylenol she gave him would help with his discomfort. He sighed deeply as he closed his eyes. Bringing him home had definitely been the right decision. Maybe now he could rest.

She put the groceries away as she looked around for what she needed to fix something for him to eat. Everything in the kitchen was neatly arranged making her search for a large stew pot successful.

As she put together her own recipe for chicken soup, she took a cursory look around the apartment. It was sparse and cheerless. There was an expensive looking, brown, leather couch that matched the recliner where Bryce was contentedly dozing, and a coffee table.

Several books were neatly arranged on shelves above a small entertainment center housing a tiny TV and a sound system. No knick-knacks, no artwork on the walls…nothing to make this place feel homey. *How depressing,* she thought as she stirred the soup.

There was a picture on the coffee table of a smiling young man she assumed must be his son, Luke. *Nice looking kid. I wonder why he hasn't been around. He never came to the hospital. I wonder if he even knows his father has been sick.*

On a whim, Ann had bought some flowers from a street vender near the hospital. She put them on the table in a glass of water. Looking around at the sadness that lived here, she was glad she had thought to buy them.

Chapter 127

After about an hour nap, Bryce woke up feeling somewhat better. As the soup simmered on the stove, Ann took his temperature. It was normal; a good sign. She asked all the usual "doctor questions," and when she was satisfied that he was doing alright, she asked if he was ready to eat a little something.

Standing under his own power was still very difficult for Bryce. He was embarrassed to need her assistance to walk just a short distance. She seemed to understand. She slipped her arm around his waist, guiding him into a chair at the table.

"This soup is delicious. Ah...it tastes a lot like the food you gave me in the hospital when Monica was sick," Bryce said after the first couple of spoonfuls.

Ann saw understanding, and something else she couldn't identify, bloom in his eyes. She quickly looked away as she busied herself pouring coffee.

They ate in silence, neither of them knowing exactly what to say. It could have been awkward, but somehow, it wasn't. It was comfortable.

After he finished eating, Bryce was exhausted. Ann asked if he wanted to go back to the chair or to bed. This time he opted for bed. He managed to get up slowly on his own. Ann was all business as she carefully helped get his clothes off and his pajamas on.

Chapter 128

Ann tucked him in bed and, as if he were a child, she put her lips to his forehead. He didn't feel warm; that was a good sign. She immediately felt silly, but he appeared to have fallen asleep.

Bryce was NOT asleep! That tender gesture brought tears prickling behind his eyelids. It was a reaction he never expected.

It didn't seem to matter how tired he was; now he couldn't fall asleep. He heard one of his favorite smooth jazz albums playing softly in the background. Water was running, and dishes rattled as they were washed and put away. He liked the peaceful feeling these sounds generated. Finally, he fell contentedly to sleep.

Bryce woke up once during the night to find Ann dosing in an easy chair she had pulled up close to his bed. He tried his best to get up without disturbing her. He didn't have any way of knowing the reason she was such a light sleeper. She was immediately awake.

He needed the bathroom. He was thankful that he managed this activity by himself even though Ann was not far away, ready to assist if necessary. The last thing she wanted was for him to fall, possibly pulling his incision apart.

"Dr. Reynolds, I can't thank you enough for all this. I appreciate it so much," he whispered when he was safely back in bed.

"It's no problem at all," she assured him. "And you really don't have to call me Dr. Reynolds. Ann is fine."

There was something different about this man. He didn't make any demands, and he didn't seem to have any expectations of her. This puzzled her. In fact, he seemed surprised by any kindness!

Ann would occasionally look up in time to catch him watching her. He would quickly look away with an almost timid smile on his face. She got the impression he wasn't quite sure what to make of her. The feeling was certainly mutual!

Neither of them had previous experience in the ways of love. All either of them had known was pain and betrayal. They didn't realize they were in the process of falling in love.

Much to Ann's surprise, she found she thoroughly enjoyed taking care of him, fixing his meals, and puttering around his apartment. It almost felt natural in an odd way. The feelings it aroused frightened her, and made her happy all at the same time.

What is wrong with you girl, she chided herself. *He's just grateful, that's all.*

Bryce wasn't recovering as quickly as he should. Ann knew he was medically progressing nicely. There were no signs of infection. His temperature had remained normal since he had been home. However, he should be up and around without so much difficulty by the second day after minor surgery. About all he could do was eat and sleep.

Ann had no idea how long he had been married to Monica. She guessed probably years, since Luke appeared to be an adult. If he had been subjected to what she had witnessed in the hospital for all that time, he was probably physically and emotionally depleted.

No wonder he's so completely wiped out. What a shame. He's such a nice man. He deserves better, she thought as she perused the books on his shelves.

She saw many titles she recognized and some she didn't. She picked out a book of poetry, and brought it to his bedside to read while he slept.

"We are one
In your eyes
I see my own reflection

One heart, one soul, one mind
It comes from somewhere
Deep down within
Where I end, you begin
It's a magic so few ever find"
By R. McKown

That's so beautiful. I wish someone would love me like that, Ann thought wistfully. She found a scrap of paper on the bedside table, and stuck it in the book to mark the page.

Bryce slept straight through the night; Ann didn't. She sat curled up in the chair beside his bed, spending most of the night staring at him like a ninny. She watched the rise and fall of his chest as she listened to the soft snore coming from his lips…and wondered…

Chapter 129

Ann was up early preparing breakfast. As her hands scrambled eggs, her mind mulled over the events of the past couple of days. She was so absorbed in her own thoughts, she wasn't aware that Bryce had gotten up. He was leaning against the archway into the kitchen watching her.

When she turned around to put a dish of fruit on the table, she saw a man standing there. She jumped back as her instincts kicked in. In the process, she dropped the dish. It shattered on the floor sending glass and fruit skittering every which way.

"I'm sorry, I'm so sorry," she stammered over and over again as she stood with her back pressed against the sink, her hands gripping the counter.

"Ann, it's okay! I didn't mean to startle you."

Her hands trembled as she cleaned up the mess. Her stomach churned in an old familiar way as she looked wildly around for an escape route. Finding none, she just stared at Bryce, her heart pounding. Her rational, grown-up mind told her she didn't have anything to be afraid of, but her heart still raced and she could hardly breathe.

My God. What could have happened to her in the past to elicit this level of panic, Bryce wondered as his mind raced to come up with something to say or do to put her at ease.

"The coffee smells wonderful," he finally said. "Why don't you join me for a cup?"

He walked to the table, and pulled out a chair for her.

As her fear gradually dissipated, she regained her composure. *I thought those old reactions were behind me,* she thought to herself as a deep blush colored her cheeks.

"I'm so sorry," she whispered, so appreciative of his thoughtfulness.

Bryce touched her hand. "It was only a dish," he said quietly.

She brought her eyes slowly up to meet his. In that moment, she realized with a jolt, that she loved him.

Bryce was having his own revelation as well. He wanted nothing more than to pull her close, and tell her everything was alright. She didn't have to be afraid. He would make sure no one ever hurt her again. *I think I love her,* he thought as he poured the coffee. *How stupid can I possibly be! I feel like a schoolboy with a crush!*

Luke had called every night since Bryce came home. He usually visited in the afternoon when Ann went home to take a shower and change clothes. He obviously didn't want to run into her. She briefly wondered why, but knowing Monica, she put two and two together. Understanding followed quickly!

It seemed that during Luke's visit, his father talked a LOT about Dr. Reynolds. Luke was skeptical. He didn't trust ANY woman where his father was concerned!

Chapter 130

It had been a week that Ann had stayed with Bryce under the pretext that he wasn't quite ready to be on his own yet. Her vacation time was over, and she had to get back to work in the morning. The thought of not seeing him every day was very disturbing to her. She really didn't want to leave!

Bryce, on the other hand, could have done a lot more for himself a lot sooner, but he was thriving on the good food and the attention. He had never been pampered in his life, so this was a new experience for him. He had to admit; he really liked it…a lot.

Ann had given him her business card with her home phone number on the back. He was the only person to have her home number, except for the hospital. She told him to call if he had any questions or problems. Even as she said the words she knew they sounded too business-like, and she wanted to kick herself!

She had wanted to say please call me sometime. I would love to hear how you're doing. But that sounded too personal or something.

As she stood in front of the elevator waiting for the door to open, she looked back. Bryce was just standing there, holding her card in his hand with a funny, endearing look on his face. With a lump in her throat, she rode down to the first floor.

Without her, Bryce felt like all the fresh air had been sucked out of his apartment. It was so quiet, so... empty. He slumped in his recliner wondering if he would ever see her again short of having some health crisis.

Chapter 131

Ann went to work every day as usual. She did her job, but somehow life wasn't crystal clear anymore. It was blurred around the edges, and she knew exactly why. She had fallen in love with Bryce Peterson; a hopeless situation...or so she thought.

It was not intentional; she hadn't meant to fall in love. It had just sort of happened. In the middle of the night when she couldn't sleep, she wondered if he was alright; if he missed her as much as she missed him. Then she berated herself for having such foolish thoughts. Still...she waited in vain for her phone to ring.

Weeks turned into months, and Bryce never called. She felt like a love-sick teenager thinking he would. She needed to just forget about him. This, she discovered, was easier said than done.

Bryce had picked up the phone every single day with every intention of calling Ann. Several times, he had even gone so far as to dial the number. But he just couldn't do it. He didn't want to humiliate himself.

Whenever Luke and Bryce spent time together, sooner or later the conversation turned to Dr. Reynolds. Luke didn't have much experience with women, but he recognized the love-sick look on his father's face every time he said her name.

Luke decided something needed to change. After all, if nothing changes...nothing changes.

Chapter 132

L uke was not about to allow his father to fall into the clutches of another woman like Monica, so he decided to do some investigating.

Unbeknownst to his father, he was taking classes in Criminal Justice at the local junior college. This gave him access to all kinds of information that otherwise would not have been available to him.

He found out Ann had dual citizenship; Canadian and US. Her parents were deceased, and she had a sister living in France. He knew where she went to high school, college and medical school. He even knew she had a dog when she was a kid. The background check he ran was clean as a whistle. She had never even gotten a parking ticket.

Estimating her age, he went to the library to the section where old newspapers were archived. He pulled out papers that carried national news, and began flipping through the pages. He never found the name Ann Reynolds.

One article, having nothing to do with Dr. Reynolds at all, caught his eye as the story was front page news for several weeks. A very young girl had lost her husband in a construction company accident. A huge lawsuit had been filed against Lewis Construction Company by some attorney named Oscar Schwartz.

As he read on, he discovered she had also been violently abused by her husband and two of her husband's friends, who were police officers!

That was a slap in the face for Luke. He respected law enforcement. That police officers would be involved in something like this was incomprehensible.

He read every article he could find covering the trials. There were also pictures that made his stomach feel a little queasy to see the effects of the brutality she had suffered. The trial had ended with a shooting in the courtroom.

There were numerous pictures of the young girl with her attorney, and her doctor, Mark Goodwin. Luke could only shake his head in disbelief.

One of the last pictures he found was of a beautiful girl with curly hair and huge eyes staring directly into the camera. The look on her face was one Luke knew he would never forget even though he had never known her.

She had been the innocent, young victim of horrible violence. The haunting sadness and fear caught in this picture put a lump in Luke's throat. In the future, if he ever doubted his career choice, he would remember this girl's face.

The articles ended abruptly without any follow up stories; nothing. It was as if this girl had evaporated into thin air.

Chapter 133

H e had discovered a great deal about Ann's background, which was important of course. However, the information he had gathered was pretty lean when it came to anything personal or more current. Luke decided to casually ask around. He would visit the hospital, and keep his eyes and ears open.

What he discovered was that everyone seemed to like her. As he sat in the cafeteria drinking horrible coffee and eating an equally horrible donut, he overheard snippets of conversations from patients and families. They loved her! If the care she had given his father was standard for her, he could understand why.

He decided some undercover sleuthing activity was in order, and on the pretext of needing a doctor himself, he asked the woman at the front desk where he could find a good physician. He didn't have one and was having some health issues.

"I've heard there's a Dr. Reynolds who is good. Could I get in to see her?" he asked with an innocent smile on his face.

"Oh my goodness, honey," a middle-aged woman responded. "She is one of our most popular doctors. She is highly regarded by all the staff. She works in the ER, and doesn't have her own practice, I'm sorry to say. She's great though. I happen to be personally acquainted with her," she continued with pride. "I wish she did have a private practice. I would go to her in a heartbeat."

She handed Luke a paper. "Here is a list of internal medicine doctors. You will just have to call their offices to see if any of them are taking new patients. Good luck."

Luke politely took the paper. He thanked this pleasant, chatty woman who had told him all he needed to know. *But what about friends? Was she already involved with somebody?* He would just have to put "part B" of his plan into action, and see what happened.

His father had told him she was attractive, had short, dark hair, brown eyes and her voice was… "melodic." *Oh brother*, Luke had thought at the time. *He's got it bad alright.* But this description wasn't much to go on. It could fit any number of women. Since Luke had never actually met her, he would have to go with only what his father said, and he was probably exaggerating. Love was blind, so they say.

Luke elicited Bobby's help in his little endeavor. Bobby made a suggestion that was a bold one.

"Hey man, just call the hospital, and ask her out. Take your father along. Just don't tell him she is going to be there. Then sit back, and watch the action."

Chapter 134

L uke and his father were eating lunch in Stratton's cafeteria one day when Luke decided to take the bull by the horns, so to speak.

"So Dad, have you talked to Dr. Reynolds lately?"

Bryce looked up a little too quickly. "No, why would I?"

"Because it's obvious you're in love with her," Luke stated, never missing a bite. "You should ask her out."

For several seconds Bryce didn't say anything, his sandwich half way to his mouth.

The expression on his face was a vulnerable one as he blurted out, "I have to admit, I'm crazy about her. But what would she want with someone like me?"

Bryce dropped his eyes from Luke's as he tried to continue eating. He had spent considerable time thinking about her, trying to assess his true feelings. He decided too much time had elapsed. He had missed the window of opportunity when he could have called. She, no doubt, had forgotten about him. She probably had lots of admirers. After all, she was an attractive woman.

Bobby was right. Action had to be taken, and Luke knew exactly what he was going to do.

Chapter 135

It was three o'clock in the afternoon. Ann was exhausted after a double shift in the emergency room. It had taken a couple of hours to finish her paperwork. She was definitely looking forward to a hot shower, and something to eat before falling into bed.

She had just pulled on her coat when her secretary, Julie, poked her head in the door.

"Oh good, you're still here. There's a young man on the phone who is insisting on speaking with 'Dr. Reynolds'. He says it's urgent. His name is Luke Peterson. Do you want to take the call? I know you're tired, and want to get home."

In a voice Ann hoped sounded calm she said, "That's okay. I'll take it."

Her heart had immediately rocketed into her throat. This call could only mean one thing. Either Bryce was hurt, sick or worse. She loved him so much she couldn't wrap her mind around the fact that something could have happened to him.

Julie left, closing the door quietly. Ann dropped her medical bag to the floor beside the coat rack as she ran to grab the phone. As Julie put the call through, she sank into the chair behind her desk with her legs feeling like rubber.

She took a couple of deep breaths as she tried to control her emotions well enough to speak coherently.

"Hello. This is Dr. Reynolds."

A very rich timbered, deep, all-business-no-fooling-around voice said, "This is Luke Peterson, Bryce Peterson's son."

Without any pause to allow for a response he said, "I want to know exactly what your feelings are toward my father."

This was certainly not what Ann had expected to hear. Taken off guard, she just blurted out how she really did feel. "I absolutely adore your father."

A huge sigh of relief could be heard on the other end of the line.

"Well, that's good because my dad is crazy about you. He just doesn't have the nerve to ask you out. So I'm asking you to come with me to Billy Burger for dinner. Dad will be there. He thinks I'm bringing my new girlfriend."

Ann hesitated for only a millisecond before she replied, "What time should I be ready?"

Chapter 136

L uke arrived promptly at five o'clock in a rusty, dilapidated old truck. When Ann opened the door, he stared at her for a full minute.

I know this face, he realized with a shock! The picture in the newspaper had been grainy and old, but the face, the eyes; they were the same! *What the heck is going on!* He recovered quickly, and continued with his plan.

"Dad said you were attractive; he was wrong. You're drop dead gorgeous."

Ann's face turned practically purple with embarrassment, and several awkward moments ensued. She didn't know what to say. She just stood there with her mouth slightly open, staring up at this very tall, out-spoken young man.

His rational for this behavior was just to see her reaction to such an outrageous compliment from a relative stranger. Would she "come on" to him? That's what he had expected. That's what Monica would have done.

Under the guise of being a little mentally slow, he had discovered he could get away with saying some pretty outlandish things. He was pleased with how she responded.

" Er...ah...thank you, Luke. Shouldn't we get going?"

She managed to get her jacket buttoned correctly, which was a major task considering her hands were shaking.

"Dad said your hair was dark and your eyes brown," he casually commented.

She had been in such a tizzy by the time she got home, she had taken a shower, washing the color from her hair. She had also forgotten to put the brown contacts back in! She realized with a jolt, that she looked like... herself!

"Contacts and hair dye," was her off the cuff response, which happened to be the truth.

During the ride into a rather unsavory part of town, Luke told her that since she had done emergency surgery on his dad, he had talked about her a lot.

"Dad said you really cared about what happened to him. I know that you took care of...Monica," the name came out like it tasted bad on his tongue. "So you must know how she treated him. He didn't deserve any of it you know."

It was a bit embarrassing for Ann to hear all these things Bryce had said about her. Inside she was thrilled.

"The hang-dog look on Dad's face when he talks about you was enough to convince me that he is indeed in love with you," Luke finished almost apologetically.

Luke knew he was taking a huge risk here, so he went on to explain that after years of marriage to a woman like Monica, who routinely rode around town on her broom, his dad deserved a good woman who truly loved him.

Ann had to smile at his description. It was certainly accurate.

Luke had surprised himself. He had never spoken like this to anyone, let alone a woman. But to secure his father's happiness, he had to come out of his shell and fast. It looked like his efforts had been worth it. She smiled.

Bryce would already be at Billie's, having taken a cab from work. Luke and his dad had been coming to this particular diner since Luke was fifteen years old. It was one of their favorite spots. It was also not the best place to park a nice car on the street.

The food was great, and the portions were generous. Thursday's special was meatloaf, Luke's personal favorite. But the place was run down, and a couple of the lights were out on the blinking sign over the door. Ann's reaction to this less than classy place would tell Luke a lot about her.

Monica wouldn't have been caught dead eating here and rubbing elbows with the common riff-raff. Luke was glad she was dead. He hoped it had been painful.

It seemed to Luke that his father tried his best to be invisible, having been totally humiliated in public by Monica's outrageous behavior. From what he had observed so far, he decided Dr. Reynolds was cut from a completely different cloth.

Luke did all the talking on their ride across town. Ann just listened while her heart ached for Bryce. She determined there and then to make things as easy as she possibly could for him.

Chapter 137

W hen they finally arrived at their destination, Luke asked Ann to walk behind him into the restaurant so that his father couldn't see her until they reached the table.

"I don't want Dad to bolt," Luke chuckled as he opened Ann's door. "This is gonna be great!"

Ann felt weak in the knees, but managed to walk obediently behind Luke. They got to the end booth where Bryce was just hanging up his coat with his back toward them.

Luke stepped aside just as his father turned around. A myriad of emotions flashed across his face. Ann and Bryce stood there staring at each other, time standing still, for what seemed like an eternity.

Luke finally broke the silence with a hearty, good natured laugh.

"Well, Dad, I guess you already know my date."

Luke skillfully maneuvered Ann into the bench seat next to his father, and sat down opposite them.

He folded his hands on the table, and looked at them like they were disobedient children, sitting sheepishly side by side.

"Dad, are you really crazy about Ann?"

Bryce responded in a choked whisper that Ann could hardly hear.

"Yes."

Luke turned to Ann. "And do you really adore my father?"

She couldn't believe this was happening. Her cheeks burned and she could hardly swallow. She finally managed to say, "Yes, I adore your father."

"Well alright then, I've done the hard part, now you two have to do the rest," Luke said with a big smile, feeling extremely satisfied with his efforts.

Bryce was stunned. His eyes went from Ann's curly strawberry blonde hair to her blue eyes and back to her hair. It was obvious he didn't know quite what to think about this current situation. He didn't have a clue as to what to do or say next. Ann was in a quandary herself and not much help.

Luke immediately recognized the look on his father's face. He understood the cause for the confusion. "Contacts and hair dye," he casually said as he nonchalantly perused the menu.

Fortunately, they were spared the need for conversation by Lillian or "Lil to her friends. Lil was a big, unattractive woman who waited tables while her husband cooked. They owned this restaurant, and worked hard to keep their customers happy. They just didn't make quite enough money to spiff the place up. She, of course, recommended the meat loaf.

Conversation was stilted at first. Ann couldn't help glancing at Bryce every once in a while, offering a shy smile. She was so happy to see him. What she really wanted to do was throw her arms around his neck. She decided that wouldn't be very lady-like. Bryce probably really would bolt!

She's more beautiful than I remember! I should say something... do something, but what? She adores me? How can that be? Bryce could only manage to stare.

He looked into her eyes with frank amazement. She gently touched his arm. This seemed to have been just the right response as it brought a huge smile to his face. He certainly wasn't like any other man Ann knew.

They were like two kids on their first date accompanied by a chaperone. In essence, that's exactly what they were; innocent to love.

Chapter 138

The food came giving everyone something to do. It was delicious, and Ann made a point of complimenting Lillian.

Luke magnanimously picked up the tab with an exaggerated flourish, which was humorous to watch, and made Bryce and Ann smile.

Then Ann did something she never dreamed she could, or would, do. She asked Bryce and Luke if they would like to come to her house for brownies and coffee. She just couldn't bear to let the night end so soon.

Luke was enthusiastic about accepting for himself and his father. After all, he did love brownies.

It was a tight fit for the three of them in Luke's truck. With Ann in the middle, she and Bryce were pressed together from shoulder to knee. They both felt paralyzed as they struggled to control the emotions that were running rampant, hindering any rational thought.

Bryce was finding it difficult to breathe. The meatloaf he had eaten for dinner was lodged in his throat, making it hard to swallow. He wanted to escape, but no power on earth could have pried him from the truck. He handled this dilemma by staring straight ahead out the window. Beads of perspiration were beginning to pop out on his upper lip.

Ann knew she had to do something to put him at ease no matter how unnatural it might feel to her in the beginning. She realized that, right here, right now, was her last chance. She had to make it count. Under any other circumstances, she would never have dared be so bold.

She moved just enough to put her shoulder behind his. She tucked her arm under his elbow, sliding her hand down the inside of his arm until her fingers interlocked with his; then she held her breath.

As his fingers closed around hers, the tension left his body. In the gathering darkness, Ann could only make out his profile. She could tell he was smiling.

Out of the corner of his eye, Luke saw what had just happened.

Very smooth move, Doc! I guess I can entrust Dad into your keeping. My work here is done!

Conflicting emotions were bombarding Bryce like gnats on a hot summer night.

Her hand is so small. Her skin is so soft. What does all this mean exactly? She smells SO good, and she is so beautiful. I wish this ride would never end…I wish we would hurry up and get there!

His stomach did a flip, dislodging the meatloaf. Thankfully, he could now swallow, as he tried to slow his breathing and heart rate. He wanted to savor this moment for as long as possible. Not daring to think about the future…he concentrated on "right now."

They arrived at Ann's house without incident; nobody jumped screaming from the truck, or passed out from lack of oxygen to the brain.

The truck was high for someone as petite as Ann. Short of taking a flying leap to the ground, she needed help. Bryce looked up at her, his eyes never leaving her face. Putting his hands at her waist he easily sat her feet on the ground. She was as light as a feather.

Suddenly realizing what he had just taken the liberty of doing, he quickly let her go and stepped back.

Oh, no, Mr. Peterson. You aren't getting off that easy, Ann thought as she took his hand. A persistent tug encouraged him to come with her down the sidewalk to her front door.

Once inside, Bryce helped her with her coat receiving a slow smile in return. Things got a little easier as Ann busied herself making the coffee and getting out the brownies.

Luke suddenly remembered urgent business he had to attend to.

"This can't wait until tomorrow," he said as he gave his father a wicked grin and a wink. "You can take a cab home can't you, Dad?"

"Oh, wait, Luke," Ann said.

Both men stopped instantly. They stood as if they were rooted to the floor. Bryce immediately thought she didn't want to be alone with him, while Luke was sure his plan was foiled.

Ann handed Luke a plate of brownies wrapped in cellophane.

"You can bring the plate back any time. I hope you like chocolate."

The relief on both their faces could have been comical in any other situation. At this moment, it was just sad to think that one cruel, thoughtless woman had damaged them both.

"And thank you so much for the date, Luke," she said quietly.

Luke just nodded and smiled. He couldn't think of a witty comeback at the moment! So off he went, leaving Bryce and Ann wondering how this had all happened!

Chapter 139

D etermined to make the best of the opportunity that had been handed to her, Ann's heart settled into a somewhat normal rhythm.

As the coffee perked, she offered to show Bryce her home. She explained that the house had been built to her specifications.

"The windows are bullet proof, one way glass. I can see out but no one could see in," she explained.

There were security cameras along each side of the house with monitors in the den so that she could always see what was happening outside. The exterior doors, including the sliding glass door to the deck at the back of the house, were double bolted as were the windows.

Bryce listened intently, never interrupting. He had a million questions he wanted to ask, but didn't quite dare. He was still processing his good fortune at the evening's turn of events.

The rooms were decorated with country patterns and colors. An overstuffed, comfortable couch and chairs were arranged around a stone fireplace. There were large bookcases on each side of the TV. An oval shaped coffee table sat in front of the couch.

There was music playing in the background through an incredible sound system, having come on automatically when the door opened. The lights were programmed to turn on promptly at dusk, whether Ann was there or not.

Along the baseboard throughout the house, there were tiny lights so it was never completely dark. Ann was terribly afraid of the dark. Bad things had happened in the dark...

The floors were heated as Ann was partial to kicking off her shoes at the door and going barefoot. The heat and air conditioning were regulated to keep the house at a comfortable 72 degrees year around.

Bryce was impressed by her collection of books; old leather bound volumes of poems, short stories, novels and biographies. As he recognized some of the titles and authors, he began to relax. Several of his own books had been destroyed during Monica's wrecking spree. He hadn't had the heart to replace them, leaving his library sparse to say the least.

Ann watched his face as he went through her albums. They had similar tastes in music as well. When he looked at her and smiled, Ann had never been so happy.

Bryce was in a bit of a predicament. *Is this beautiful, petite, soft spoken, slightly self-conscious woman the same one who took out my appendix, and cared for me so efficiently? Would she be offended if I ask her all the questions I have buzzing around in my head? What should I do?*

Several awkward moments followed with both of them looking at the floor when Bryce finally asked, "Why all the security?"

Her answer quickly cut through some of his self-consciousness.

Her eyes became the size of quarters as she looked up into his face. Her insides began to quiver.

"Because I'm so afraid," she whispered.

He hesitated for only a second before taking her hands in his.

"Can you tell me why?" he said in quiet seriousness.

"Maybe I can," she whispered as the coffee pot sounded its alarm.

Chapter 140

Over coffee and brownies Bryce steered the conversation to less stress-filled subjects giving Ann time to re-group. His thoughtfulness touched her deeply.

He began telling her about his work at Stratton's. He told her about some of the people who worked for him, and how much they had come to mean to him. He seemed more at ease as she listened attentively.

She began picking up the empty cups and plates. She was surprised when Bryce offered to dry if she would tell him where everything went. They did the dishes together in companionable silence.

When the kitchen was tidy, Ann suggested there might be something on TV worth watching.

"Let's sit where it's comfortable," she said as she led the way to the living room.

Her couch was situated perpendicular to the fireplace and across from the TV. Bryce offered to start a fire.

"Oh, Bryce, that would be great. I love the fireplace, but I work so many hours I don't get to enjoy it as often as I would like."

It was warm and cozy as they sat side by side on the couch. The TV was on, but neither of them was really interested in watching it. Luke was a safe topic of conversation, and Ann told Bryce about the great lengths he had gone to in order to arrange their "date."

Bryce laughed and shook his head. "He must be taking lessons from Bobby at work. It sounds like something they cooked up together. I'm so sorry if it upset you."

Cautiously, she put her hand on his arm. He looked at her hand, then up at her face, and slowly covered her hand with his.

"I was only upset because my first thought was that something had happened to you. I couldn't bear that, Bryce; if something happened to you."

She slid her hand into his. Tentatively, she leaned her head against his shoulder. Words weren't necessary for quite some time as they sat together, hand in hand. Shivers of pleasure crawled slowly up her spine.

He's so handsome! I love his eyes. When he smiles, it turns my insides to jelly. I wonder if that's normal. I've never been in love before. His hands are so gentle. I wish he would kiss me!

This must be a dream. I can't be sitting here with her like this. I wonder how she would react if I kissed her hand? Do I dare do that? I admit it. I love her! I WANT to kiss her!

Chapter 141

From the little bit that Luke had revealed to Ann, along with what she had personally witnessed when Monica was in the hospital, she knew this man's heart had been intentionally destroyed. Somehow she wanted him to know she understood.

She decided the best way to do that was by sharing her own pain. Besides, if they were to have any kind of relationship, it had to be based on honesty. He needed to know about her; who she really was.

There was no small risk involved. Once he knew about her past, he may decide he would be better off without her. Could she handle that? Never seeing him again by his choice?

She knew it would devastate her beyond belief; however, she felt strongly that he deserved to know the truth. After the telling, what would be…would be.

"Bryce, can I talk to you about something important?" She hesitated for only a second before continuing in a voice just above a whisper. "I want to tell you why I'm so afraid. It's something you should know before you decide if you want to see me again."

There was sudden apprehension in his eyes, as he immediately put his guard up. Past experience had taught him to expect sharp criticism for some unknown wrong he had probably unwittingly committed.

His rational mind quickly took over. *This is NOT Monica.*

"You can talk to me about anything, Ann. I promise I won't be angry."

With his attention focused on her obvious distress, he didn't think twice as he brought her hand to his lips and kissed her fingers.

"You don't need to be afraid."

He was completely unprepared for what followed. It made his own painful past seem like a picnic by comparison!

Chapter 142

She looked away. She swallowed several times before she had the courage to bring her eyes back to his. She held his gaze for several seconds before she turned her face away again, and stared out the window.

Everything came spilling out. The accident that took her parents, the series of foster homes that followed, her narrow escape from Roger, the locket he had ripped from her neck...

It was a bit easier to tell him about the time spent on the farm with Harriet. It had been the one pleasant memory from her traumatic past; in fact, the only bright spot. She told him how much she still thought about Harriet. This kind hearted woman had become a surrogate mother to her for a short time.

The child welfare people had been relentless in their search for her. She finally fled to Boston where she survived by living as a homeless person amid piles of garbage. She told him about her tenuous friendship with Gert and Lucy. They had tried to help her; she just hadn't listened leading to her final, almost fatal, mistake.

Her marriage to Donny Madison was something that she had pushed to the far recesses of her mind, hoping someday to push the memories into oblivion. She hadn't talked about any of this for almost twenty years.

Now the moment had come. This was the worst of it. She put her shaking hand over her eyes for a few seconds before she could continue. Her voice trembled as she told Bryce about her marriage at age sixteen to Donny, the repeated rapes, the abuse, the cops who used her, the terror that was her constant companion…she didn't leave anything out.

She couldn't keep her chin from quivering when she spoke about the babies she had lost, especially Baby Lucas. The utter desolation she still felt was evidenced by the look of pain that tightened her face.

"Dr. Mark let me hold him for a little while before he was taken away. I don't know what happened to his body; if it was buried somewhere or just tossed in a dumpster."

A solitary tear rolled down her cheek. The thought of her precious baby rotting in a dumpster with garbage was almost more than she could bear.

Bryce was stunned by what he was hearing. *My God! How did she survive,* he thought as he struggled to keep his expression from showing the horror he felt.

She clung to his hand to keep from drowning in the devastating power these memories still held over her. She didn't dare look at him, fearing she would see loathing and judgment.

She told him about how she missed her only friends, Dr. Mark Goodwin and attorney Oscar Schwartz. They had literally saved her life.

When Donny was killed in a construction accident, she explained how "Dr. Mark" had persuaded his good friend, and aspiring criminal attorney, Oscar Schwartz to represent her. Upon hearing her story, he promptly filed a lawsuit against the construction company for the wrongful death of her husband.

"Oscar believed in me. He defended me with every available resource he had. After winning my case, he invested the money I was awarded so that I could support myself and live independently," she continued. "He later brought rape charges against the two police officers who had abused me."

She then described what had happened in court; the shooting, the threats, the panic, the whole horrifying, degrading, humiliating thing.

"When a verdict of guilty was handed down, my life was in danger. One of the police officers screamed threats at me as he was being dragged from the court room. He said he had friends who could get to me and finish the job."

"Oscar also considered the owner of the construction company a threat. After the award settlement, he was bankrupt and blamed me."

Ann took a chance and looked at Bryce. "The only avenue open to me was entrance into the witness protection program. Kathy Martin was gone as if she had never lived, and I took her place. Fear drove me to change my appearance and buy a gun."

For the first time in a very long while, she wanted to cry.

"I really don't have dark hair and eyes. I had to reinvent myself in the hopes of blending in. The security precautions in my house make me feel only minimally less afraid," her voice trailed off...

She continued to look at Bryce with wide, frightened eyes.

"I'm so sorry I have deceived you, Bryce. It was never my intention to hurt you in any way. If you decide you don't want to see me again, I certainly understand. I won't do anything to try to hold you," she finished as she looked away and stared into the fire.

Chapter 143

B ryce sat unmoving. He was unable to think of anything to say that would be remotely appropriate under the circumstances. He was horrified by the events of Ann's life.

How did she ever survive with her sweet spirit still intact? She was a defenseless young girl for heaven sake! I can't bear to think of anyone hurting her! How could she possibly think I wouldn't want her because of all that happened to her? In truth, I want her all the more! I want to take care of her, protect her...

Finally, Ann pulled her eyes back to meet his. Raw emotion was written plainly on her face.

"I have just one request," she finally said, still unable to keep the tremor from her voice. "If you choose not to see me anymore, please never reveal my true identity to anyone, as it would compromise my safety."

Before Bryce thought about what he was doing long enough to allow his own insecurities to prevail, he pulled Ann onto his lap and held her close. He stroked her hair and whispered in her ear that he loved her.

Her sobs erupted against his shoulder as tears she had not allowed to fall for many years, spilled down her face and soaked his shirt. She cried until she fell asleep against his chest, the telling of it exhausting her.

He continued to hold her until he too dosed. During that time of shared grief, healing began in both of them.

Ann woke up just as the sun was peeking through the window. She was nestled in Bryce's lap, her arms around his neck, her face pressed against his. She knew he was awake as he touched her cheek, and pushed a stray curl behind her ear.

They were so incredibly comfortable sitting as they were. Neither really wanted to move. However, some sort of explanation would be necessary if they were both late for work, something that rarely ever happened with either of them. Reluctantly, Ann disengaged herself from arms only too willing to hold her forever.

As Bryce ate the breakfast Ann prepared for him, he told her he had never eaten anything so delicious in his life!

"It's only eggs and toast, silly" Ann said as she held his face in her hands and kissed his cheek tenderly.

From then on Bryce and Ann spent as much time together as possible. They both began the long process of learning to trust. As they grew closer, the old wounds became less painful. A new found happiness began to take root that was far beyond anything they could ever have imagined.

Of course problems arose from time to time, rooted in past events. They had agreed right from the start to keep the lines of communication open. They would not sacrifice the love they had found by being stubborn and taking offense where none was intended.

As Bryce shared the events of his life with Ann, she began to understand why he had a hard time initiating any kind of intimacy. She became determined to do everything she could to let him know that she welcomed his touch.

In turn, he understood why Ann occasionally flinched when he raised his hand unexpectedly. His response was to constantly reassure her that he would never hurt her.

They talked. They understood. They accepted. They loved.

When Bryce took Ann to meet his brother, Brad, he knew he didn't have to worry about her causing an embarrassing scene by belittling him or making inappropriate comments. His brother loved her immediately.

"You picked a winner this time, Bryce," Brad told him as they were getting ready to leave. "I have a feeling you two are going to be very happy."

It was obvious to anyone who saw them together that the love they shared was something very special indeed.

Chapter 144

B ryce knew exactly where he wanted to propose to Ann; down by the lake. There was a secluded bench under an oak tree down near the water's edge. He knew it was one of her favorite spots to sit and watch the ducks.

He had bought the ring weeks ago. It was three diamonds, one larger with a smaller one on each side, in an antique setting. It wasn't anything like the huge, gaudy thing that Monica had demanded.

Before he popped the question, there was one more thing he had to tell her about himself. It brought him shame to think about it, much less have to admit it. However, she had been starkly truthful with him about her past, and he wanted nothing less than to be as honest with her.

The day they had planned the trip to the lake dawned cloudy and damp. Ann could tell Bryce was disappointed so she hugged him tight.

"We'll be together, Bryce. That's what counts," she assured him.

He was smiling by the time they put the picnic basket in the back seat and headed south.

By the time they arrived, it was pouring. Ann didn't care. She was with the man she loved, and nothing could dampen her spirits. They sat in the car, ate their sandwiches and listened to music on the radio. For dessert, Ann asked Bryce to show her what the kids thought was so great about "parking." He did. She was breathless and the windows fogged up...

Finally, Bryce turned to her, and told her there was something he wanted to ask her. He pulled the ring out of his pocket, intently watching her face. When she saw what he was holding, she gasped.

"Oh, Bryce, it's beautiful!"

He couldn't quite look at her when he told her that before she decided to accept the ring, there was something he had to tell her. He looked out the window and back at the ring in his hand.

He didn't seem to know how to say what was on his mind. It was obvious to Ann that something was really bothering him. She put her hand gently on the side of his face. He slowly lifted his eyes to meet hers.

"Whatever it is, Bryce, it will be alright. We'll be okay."

He took a deep breath. "I can't...what I mean is...I won't be able to...no matter how much I want to..." His voice trailed off as he gave up trying to explain and looked away.

Ann hadn't forgotten the hateful comments Monica had made about his "manhood." With this background information, she suspected she knew what he was trying to tell her.

"Bryce, look at me," she said softly.

The agony he felt was in his eyes, and it made her heart ache. When she touched her lips to his, he gave her a sad little smile.

"Speaking as a physician who has examined you, I can assure you that you are a fully functioning healthy man," she said in her best doctor voice. It is also my opinion as a physician <u>and</u> a woman that you are very much above average in <u>every</u> way, and I happen to love you just the way you are."

His head came up a little. She could see a flicker of hope beginning to surface as his eyes met hers.

"I have only known rape and violence so I don't know how I will respond to making love, but I <u>am</u> sure of one thing; when the time is right, we will both be just fine."

Tears came to his eyes. The lump in his throat made it hard for him to speak, but he finally managed to get the words out.

"Ann, will you marry me? Please?"

"Bryce, of course I will," was her immediate response.

Bryce slipped the ring on her finger.

"If you don't like the setting or the stones, we can take it back and you can pick out what you want."

She clasped her hands to her chest.

"Oh no," she said. "You picked it out especially for me and that makes it very special to me! I love it, Bryce. It's perfect!"

A big smile spread across his face. With rivulets of rain running down the windshield, and the smell of bologna still hovering from lunch, he had never felt happier in his life.

Ann stared at the ring and finally said, "Do you have some idea when you would like us to be married?"

"You can have whatever you want, whenever you want, where ever you want," he answered with sincerity, his hand still holding hers.

"No, Bryce. This is OUR wedding. It should be what we both want."

"Well then, I don't want to wait too long," he said with a sheepish grin.

Ann smiled. As she put her arms around his neck, she whispered in his ear.

"Neither do I!"

Chapter 145

They discussed a few possible dates and venues as they sat cuddled close together in the car with the rain pounding on the roof. None seemed satisfactory.

Suddenly, inspiration struck. Bryce had planned to take Ann to Cedarville to meet Rosa and Georgio Vincenzo. They were leaving the following morning, and staying a few days so Ann could get to know them.

"Bryce, why don't we just get married in the morning on the way out of town? We were planning on staying with Georgio and Rosa for a few days anyway, it could be our honeymoon!"

He loved the idea!

When they got home from the lake, they called Luke to tell him the news. He let out a whoop that could have easily been heard in the next county.

"Can you meet us at the JP's on the edge of town on Kingston Rd. at 10 tomorrow morning?" Bryce asked excitedly. "I want you to be my best man."

"Okay, Dad, but do I have to wear a suit?"

He was still laughing when he hung up.

Ann didn't sleep a wink all night, and she was pretty sure Bryce was having the same problem. Each in their respective homes, they packed and paced and thought about what was to come. Ann wasn't at all nervous, she trusted Bryce implicitly. She just couldn't wait to never have to say good-bye again!

Ann was ready when his car pulled in the driveway. It was very cold for November and the sky was overcast. Yesterday had been cold and rainy. Today was crisp and clear with snow flurries sputtering in the air.

Just in case, Ann had packed some warm clothes including fur lined comfortable boots and heavy socks. She had learned long ago to prepare for unexpected circumstances!

Bryce put Ann's bags in the trunk next to his. This all seemed so surreal. He couldn't seem to stop smiling, and it made him feel a little bit silly. He wondered briefly if any of the neighbors were watching.

He helped Ann into the car, and buckled her snugly into the seat belt. He was whistling a jaunty little tune as they drove through town.

Bryce was wearing dark trousers and a sport jacket with the top button of his shirt open. Ann thought he looked very handsome. There was a sparkle in his eyes and a spring in his step, but best of all, he looked self-assured and confident. Ann knew it had been a very long time since he had felt that way about himself. It made her happy just to watch him.

Ann was wearing her favorite tweed skirt with just a hint of blue in the pattern. A flattering, form-fitting, blue sweater that matched her eyes completed her ensemble. Her pumps had 3 inch heels, which brought the top of her head even with Bryce's shoulder.

"The shoes enhance the attractive curve of your legs," he informed her with a wink and a smile. "I am quite sure there has never been a more beautiful bride!"

They reached the home of the Justice of the Peace just as Luke was getting out of his truck.

For just a second, visions of another JP, on another day, in a different town flitted through Ann's mind trying to gain a toe hold.

"Are you okay," Bryce asked.

Having become attuned to the way her mind worked, he had sensed what she was thinking. He wanted to be absolutely sure she wanted this as much as he did.

"I couldn't be better," she replied happily as she linked her arm with his. "Let's go get married!"

Chapter 146

When Bryce rang the bell, they were invited in by a round, friendly, elderly woman. Right behind her was her equally round, jovial husband. They immediately reminded Ann of Mr. and Mrs. Santa Clause.

Bryce had called ahead so Judson Perry knew why they were standing on his doorstep. He ushered the three of them into his living room with a flourish. Mable Perry handed Ann a small bouquet of silk flowers that she kept handy for just such occasions.

As they took their places in front of Mr. Perry, Bryce gave Ann a quick hug, stepped back, and took both her hands in his. His eyes searched her face for any sign of fear or doubt. There was no hidden agenda or self-serving motive lurking there and he relaxed. He had told Mr. Perry on the phone that they wanted to say their own vows.

Bryce cleared his throat, and with tears now streaming unabashedly down his face, he began to speak.

"I never expected to find a woman like you, Ann. One who so perfectly completes me. Your love has made me a whole person and when we are apart, I feel as if a piece of my own body is missing. I can't imagine my life without you. I promise to love and protect you in sickness and in health, in good times and bad, forever."

Luke handed his father the wedding ring. Bryce kissed her hand, and slipped the plain gold band on her finger next to the engagement ring.

Emotion swept through Ann like a tidal wave. As she looked into his eyes and saw the tenderness there, she was barely able to speak. She could not describe in words the enormity of her love for this man.

"Bryce, my love, I have been waiting for you my whole life. You are my prince charming; my white knight. You have rescued me from a life of loneliness and despair. You are truly the other half of me, and I will love you forever. You are as important to my existence as the air I breathe. I promise to love, protect and obey you through whatever comes our way now and forever."

She pulled a gold band from her pocket. It had been purchased several months ago when marrying Bryce was still only a dream. She carefully slipped it over his knuckle.

The JP pronounced them husband and wife. Bryce didn't waste any time kissing his bride. It seemed as though this was the culminating moment in both their lives. All the pieces of the puzzle had fallen into place, and their future together was crystal clear.

And so it was that Lauren Ann Reynolds and M. Bryce Peterson became husband and wife.

Not to be outdone, Luke picked Ann up and twirled her around.

"Does this mean I get to call you 'Mom' from now on, and come over for free food all the time?" he asked with a hearty laugh.

Luke had watched his father slowly change into a living, breathing, happy man, and if for no other reason than that, he loved Ann. But it wasn't only that. She had treated him like a son from the beginning. She had accepted him just as he presented himself without trying to change him. There had been an empty spot in his heart that only a mother's love could fill. Ann filled that spot perfectly.

Ann's mind went back in time to when she had held her dying premature baby in her arms. She had named him baby Lucas. Wasn't it ironic that God had given her another Luke? And he was just about the age her son would have been right now.

She was awash with emotion, and Luke didn't know if maybe he had inadvertently crossed some unknown boundary.

"Luke", she said, as tears sparkled on her eyelashes. "I would be honored to be your mother."

Chapter 147

⌒⌒⌒

The hour ride north on Kingston Road passed quickly as Ann and Bryce chatted or sang along with some of the tunes that played on the radio.

This wife of mine is perfect in every way, but she sure can't carry a tune in a bucket, Bryce happily thought to himself. Every now and then he would glance at her simply to make sure she really was sitting there beside him, and this wasn't just a dream. He didn't know it was possible to love another human being so much.

They talked about what a fine young man Luke had become. At 20 years old, he was a good looking kid standing six foot, five inches tall. The cleft chin and dimples in his cheeks gave him a boyish charm that continued to be a target for kidding from Bobby. His eyes were the same vivid blue as Ann's and his hair had a touch of auburn. In fact, he could easily pass as her natural born son; a thought that made her smile.

"Luke is a wonderful, thoughtful, moral young man, Bryce. All because of the example you set for him. You should be very proud."

Bryce, well versed in the ploys of deceptive women, knew she was sincere, and he humbly accepted the compliment with a shy smile. God knows he had never received one from Monica!

The conversation turned to where they were going to live. Bryce had his apartment, and Ann had her house. She told him she would live in a grass hut or a pup tent as long as they were together.

"I think I can come up with something a little better than a grass hut," Bryce laughed.

"<u>You</u> are 'home' to me, Bryce," Ann whispered. "Where we live really doesn't matter."

Knowing that Ann was serious about wanting his opinion, he had anticipated her question and had given the matter some thought. He knew there was some property not far from Rosa and Georgio that had been on the market for at least a year. What he really wanted was for them to build a home of their own...together.

As they drove slowly past the acreage, they saw the realtor's sign. Ann wrote down the name and number. A dirt road appeared to wind its way into the property, so they decided to check it out.

They were pleasantly surprised with what they found. There were some open grassy areas along with stands of several varieties of trees and patches of underbrush. The land seemed to stretch all the way back to the foot of the Greenwood Mountain range.

From the look of it, there might even be a lake. Ann could see the possibilities immediately. It was secluded and quiet, while at the same time, not far from town. Dixon was about an hour south. The town of Cedarville was just fifteen to twenty minutes north. It was perfect.

They followed the road until they found a place wide enough to turn the car around. It seemed like a good spot to get out and stretch their legs for a few minutes. It was breathtakingly beautiful. Ann loved it. She knew by the look on her husband's face that he loved it too.

My husband's face. WOW. This is for real! I can hardly believe it! All I want to do is drink in the look, the smell, the feel of him. And his voice! I could listen to his voice forever, even if he were just reading from the telephone book. I can't get enough of being with him... I can't get close enough, she thought as she looked up at him.

It was cold and Bryce wrapped his arms around her. She leaned back against his body. It felt natural. It felt right. It felt safe.

"We could put the house right over there on that knoll," she said as she pointed to a clearing some distance from where they were standing.

"Oh, Bryce, this is going to be wonderful! I'm SO excited!" she exclaimed as her eyes danced with delight.

"As soon as we get to Georgio's, I'll call Herm, and have him contact the realtor. He can make an offer for the property on our behalf," Bryce said. "I have no doubt he will get the best possible price for us."

Herman VanHouten, Esq. had known Bryce for many years. When Bryce had needed a friend during the "Monica years," Herm had steadfastly stood by him, never telling him what to do, never criticizing. He could be counted on to keep a confidence, and Bryce trusted him.

They made their way back to the main road, and turned toward their final destination. Ann was excited about meeting Rosa and Georgio, as Bryce had spoken of them frequently. She knew they were his very dear friends, supporting him during the worst time in his life. She was very grateful.

"I hope they like me," Ann said quietly. "Bryce, do you think they will like me?"

"What's there not to like!" Bryce chuckled as he patted her knee.

Chapter 148

B ryce had told Ann about Rosa and Georgio's daughter. She had been an attractive, intelligent, only child and the light of their lives. She had come home from college for vacation not feeling well, but she had been sure her Mama's cooking and some rest was all she needed. When she didn't respond to conservative treatment, she was taken to the hospital in Cedarville where she had been diagnosed with bacterial meningitis.

Most young people were able to fight off the disease with the help of antibiotics, but Anna Rose just couldn't seem to do it. When she died, her parents fell into a state of shock and sorrow from which they would never completely recover.

Bryce had gone to the funeral and had stayed a few days with them afterward. He had to leave to be back at work, but he had telephoned often. He visited whenever he could get away, and thought they were holding their own.

Vincenzo's was a large establishment, being a very popular dance spot. People came from all over Vermont to dance to the best bands, and eat the best Italian food in the entire state.

As they drove around to the back door, Bryce noticed how run-down the place looked. He immediately felt sorry that he hadn't checked in with them sooner. With everything that had been happening in his own life, time had just gotten away from him.

He knocked at the door. Several minutes passed before they heard someone coming.

Chapter 149

Bryce was shocked when the door opened. It was past noon. The Georgio Vincenzo Bryce knew would have been up for hours busy with restaurant business. Instead he stood there in his robe and slippers, unshaven, with his hair sticking up at odd angles. He had always been such a dapper little man, always very conscientious about his appearance! Now he just looked old and tired.

When he saw Bryce, his eyes lit up and he yelled, "Mama, come look who's here!"

Georgio threw open the door. "Come in, come in," he said with much hand waving and theatrics. "And who is this lovely creature?"

Bryce recovered quickly from his initial surprise over how much Georgio had changed, and proudly introduced his wife.

"Your wife!" Georgio exclaimed. "Mama, come quick. Bryce has brought his new wife home to meet us."

With that Ann was engulfed in the arms of the old man as he kissed both cheeks. He then held her at arm's length to get a better look.

"What a beauty you have found, my boy, and one look at your face tells me you are very happy."

Rosa Vincenzo came hurrying forward wiping her hands on her apron. She too looked older, and there were lines on her face that

Bryce didn't remember seeing there before. His heart was heavy as he looked at these two people who meant so much to him.

"Mama, what do you think? This is Bryce's new wife."

Rosa greeted Ann with caution. She had good reason to be suspicious, as she had been on the receiving end of Monica's foul tongue and cruel behavior. Ann understood completely and promised herself that she would win the older woman's trust before they had to return to the city.

"It's such a pleasure to finally meet you both," Ann said as she hugged Rosa gently. "Bryce has told me so much about you."

When Bryce asked if it would be all right if they stayed a few days, Georgio could hardly contain his excitement.

"You are welcome to stay as long as you want! Come, come. You know, Bryce, my home is your home," he said as he motioned them forward.

"And if it's okay, I need to use your phone. There's an important call I have to make."

"You know where the phone is," Mama responded.

There were a few awkward moments of silence while Bryce made the call to his lawyer. Ann took this opportunity to hang up her coat and smooth her hair, giving Rosa a shy smile.

Bryce soon returned, easing the tension.

"Herm will handle everything," he whispered as he squeezed Ann's hand. "I didn't tell him about you, I want that to be a surprise!"

As Bryce went to the car for their bags, Ann was ushered into the kitchen. The Vincenzo's had been just about to sit down to a late lunch, and there were delicious smells emanating from the oven.

Mama, in her brisk manner, got two more plates down from the cupboard.

"Can I help with anything?" Ann asked quietly.

Mama stopped in mid-stride, and looked up in surprise.

"The silverware, cups and saucers are over there," she said as she pointed in the general direction under the counter.

Ann was busy helping Mama in the kitchen, and Bryce was busy bringing in their bags, so Georgio took this opportunity to get cleaned up. He quickly changed into trousers and a sweater. He combed his hair, waxed his mustache, and now looked quite presentable. His heart had lifted the minute he had laid eyes on Bryce.

He had looked out the window as he passed by on his way back to the kitchen. Snowflakes were falling. *Hummm, it's early for snow,* he mused.

The bags were taken to a room that Bryce used whenever he visited, and finally he and Georgio were sitting down at the table.

Ann poured the coffee for everyone while Mama watched in amazement. The food was dished up, and when everything was ready, Georgio bowed his head.

He thanked God for bringing Bryce home with a wonderful little wife…

"Oh, and bless this food," he added almost as an afterthought.

As they ate, Bryce filled them in on everything that had been going on in his life. Georgio interjected questions and laughed when Bryce told him of the most recent antics of Luke and Bobby.

Mama kept quiet. She intently watched the interaction between Bryce and Ann. She noticed how often Ann looked at Bryce, and it was obvious unless you were completely blind, that she adored him.

When their eyes met, Bryce would catch his breath for a second, as if the sight of her smiling face was the most beautiful thing he had ever seen.

Out of the clear blue Mama asked, "So how long have you two been married?"

She almost laughed out loud when Bryce looked at his watch and said, "About four hours."

Chapter 150

Mama and Ann did the dishes while Bryce and Georgio argued good naturedly about everything and anything. They had a close, comfortable relationship and it showed.

Georgio noted how many times Bryce glanced toward the sink where his petite, attractive wife was helping Mama.

Ahhhhh, the boy's in love. I'm so glad. He deserves to be happy, Georgio thought as he stroked his ample mustache.

After Mama and Ann finished with the dishes they joined the men. For Mama, it was so good to see Georgio finally alive again. For Ann, Bryce looked happy and relaxed. The two women shared a look that said more than words could have expressed.

As they talked, no one noticed that the snow had been coming down steadily all afternoon. They were surprised when they turned on the TV to learn that a "Nor'easter" was fast approaching, and travel advisories were already in effect.

Georgio sprang to his feet, pulling Bryce along with him.

"Come on, Bryce! There is much to do to get ready for a storm like this. We need to bring in wood, the generator will need to be filled with fuel, and the water pipes will need to be drained throughout the building so they don't freeze!"

Georgio and Rosa had been through storms like this before, and had everything they needed. The "jenny" would keep their rooms at about 60 degrees. Old fashioned oil burning lamps would provide enough light to maneuver around the small apartment. Mama would not have a problem cooking on the large wood burning stove in the corner of the kitchen; she had been doing it for years. All the other rooms would be cold and dark. Ann hoped Mama had plenty of heavy blankets.

Suddenly everyone got strangely quiet as all eyes turned to Ann. It seemed they were waiting for some reaction, probably based on Monica's past performance. Even Bryce was a bit tense.

Ann wrapped her arms around him as she looked up into his face with a smile that always made her dimples dance.

"Honey, we're going to have a snow adventure. Isn't this exciting?"

Her use of that term of endearment in front of his friends put a lump in his throat as Bryce hugged her close, and pressed his face into her hair for just a second.

I think she must be an angel, Georgio thought as he gave Mama a look that told her he was well pleased with the choice Bryce had made this time around.

"Let's go you two, go change your clothes. Everybody has to help."

Chapter 151

I t was quite late when everything was buttoned down to Georgio's satisfaction. He was in the mood for drinking coffee and chatting.

Rose was a wise woman. She realized, as newlyweds, Ann and Bryce probably wanted to spend some time alone. She gave Georgio a "tisk, tisk" with a raised eyebrow that told him this was not the time for chatting. With a wistful look in his eyes, he pinched Mama's cheek and acquiesced. He remembered what it was like to be young and in love.

There was a big comfortable couch in a cozy little area in front of a huge fireplace along one side of the dining room/ballroom. It lent a certain old world charm to the room and Ann liked it very much. On the pretext of keeping wood on the fire, they settled on the couch.

Bryce pulled Ann down onto his lap. It was her favorite place to sit. She found by sitting on his lap, his face and hers were at the same height, making some activities much easier. He drew her close and she shut her eyes, letting her head drop to his shoulder. She was perfectly comfortable nestled against him, and the way he was holding her, she knew he felt the same.

Without the pressure he had been under for the past several years Bryce was completely relaxed and content. It was still amazing to him that Ann loved him and wanted to be with him.

He ran his fingertips ever so lightly down her cheek. *I would be happy beyond words to hold her like this the rest of my life*, he thought as he marveled at how easily she adjusted to the curves of his body.

He was taken off guard when she whispered, "You can kiss me if you want to."

He chuckled. Ann opened her eyes and smiled. Before he thought about it overlong, he decided to take her up on the offer.

He kissed her with such tenderness she practically melted into a puddle. He had never kissed her quite like this before! She couldn't think about anything other than the feel of his mouth on hers, and the warmth of his breath on her cheek.

"Ooohhhhh, Bryce," she sighed against his lips. "You sure know how to kiss a girl!"

He drew back, and the vulnerable look in his eyes told Ann just how much that comment meant to him. Then she remembered Monica's cruel insults about his kissing ability. Her arm crept around his neck as she drew his mouth down to meet hers again.

She kissed him with all the pent up frustration, loneliness and passion that she had never expressed to any other man. She achieved the desired effect, and Bryce responded in the way only a man can.

Just as they were about to repeat the process, a booming voice came from the kitchen doorway. "Are you two letting the fire go out? Who's ready for a game of checkers?"

They grinned at each other. The fire had definitely not gone out. Bryce reluctantly stood Ann on her feet and got up; somewhat unsteadily...

Chapter 152

B ryce stacked a couple of chunks of wood on the fire before they walked hand in hand to the kitchen where Georgio had the checker board all set up for a game.

He challenged Bryce to a match. Ann could play the winner. There was a mischievous twinkle in his eye as he rubbed his hands together, as if warming them for battle, and made his first move.

Bryce slid over on the bench seat opposite Georgio and Ann cuddled up close to him. Her thigh rested against his, her arm went around his waist. Every now and then she gently rubbed his back. She couldn't help herself. She had wanted to do this for such a long time! She loved being close to him; touching him.

The checker game was the farthest thing from his mind as Bryce felt like his shirt was on fire. When she touched him, he couldn't seem to breathe. He didn't know if he could stand it if she didn't stop, but prayed that she never would.

Georgio was oblivious as he began explaining the finer points of his playing strategy to Ann. She really did try to concentrate on what he was saying, but her thoughts kept wandering to other things.

Bryce lost the game, much to Georgio's delight, and now it was Ann's turn to play. Bryce rested his elbow on the table, and leaned forward according him a vantage point from which to watch the face he loved most in the whole world.

Ann still couldn't believe he thought she was beautiful. She had been told so many times in the past that she was an ugly, worthless cow, that she had come to believe it herself. Those words tend to painfully stick, making the words Bryce spoke to her all the more precious.

She was VERY conscious of him watching her, and when he began curling a strand of her hair gently around his finger, it felt like pins and needles were disrupting her brain function. *Georgio must think I'm a complete dolt,* she thought to herself as she lost one checker after another.

Rosa looked on with great interest, as she sipped from a cup of hot tea. She loved Bryce like the son she never had. She had long grieved for him over the way Monica treated him, praying that somehow God would intervene. It looked like her prayers had finally been answered.

She watched Ann closely. *She anticipates his every need, and is eager to please him. She is also very affectionate to him without being crass or vulgar. Her speech is refined, her voice, soft. Certainly no foul or inappropriate language…that's a relief! She is quite lovely in every way. A true lady,* Mama thought as she took another sip of tea. *I like her,* she decided.

It wasn't long before the lights flickered and went out. Everyone held their breath until the generator kicked in with a whine. The kitchen was cozy and warm, thanks to the wood burning stove. Fortunately, Mama had lit the oil lamp just minutes before the power went off. Georgio brought out his pipe, soon filling the kitchen with the wonderful aroma of cherry tobacco.

This is what "family" feels like, Ann thought as she looked around the table. Bryce was thinking exactly the same thing!

One lamp provided just enough light to make the ambiance perfect, as Rosa brought out the homemade apple pie with big wedges of sharp cheese. The last of a pot of coffee was still hot.

Georgio had a small, battery-powered radio he kept on hand for just these occasions. He fiddled with the knobs until he finally got a station, albeit mostly static. What little they could make out informed them that the storm was steadily picking up force. At least a foot of snow, or more in higher elevations, now covered the area from Dixon north through Cedarville all the way to the state line.

The snowfall was expected to continue until the following afternoon when the temperature would drop to well below freezing. Windy conditions after midnight would result in blowing and drifting snow causing visibility to be almost zero. The state police, in conjunction with the weather advisory people, had already declared a state of emergency. No one was going anywhere any time soon.

Gee, Bryce thought. *Isn't that a shame? We're snowed in.*

Chapter 153

T he bricks Rosa had put under the stove were toasty warm when Bryce and Ann slid them to the foot of the incredibly soft bed in their room. They were both feeling a bit self-conscious about how to proceed as this was new territory for them. The weather conditions made the decision for them.

They stripped off their clothes, diving under the covers quickly enough to avoid dwelling on the fact that they were naked. They both had significant body image issues as a result of past mistreatment, so they had discussed their wedding night during the drive north.

They had agreed that the intimacy part of their relationship might take some time, and that was perfectly okay. Nothing could change how they felt about each other.

The room was very cold and body heat was essential for comfort. After all, the bricks could only do so much. They needn't have worried. They loved each other deeply; the bond of trust was unwavering. Sweet, innocent love happened spontaneously under the blankets, and as Ann had promised, they were both just fine.

For the first time in her life, Ann willingly gave herself completely to a man. She wanted more than anything else to please Bryce having waited, what seemed like a lifetime, to hold him like this. She had tried to imagine this moment, but her fantasy fell far short of the real thing.

Bryce in turn gave of himself with her satisfaction his highest priority. It was still hard for him to believe she was really his wife; that she really loved him. He marveled at her desire for him. She held nothing back. She made him feel…he couldn't even describe it. He only knew that he would give up his own life to protect her.

They were both completely satiated as, in the lazy afterglow of love, they fell asleep wrapped in each other's arms.

Ann woke up once during the night realizing that Bryce was already awake. He had slept only a few hours. Now he couldn't resist caressing her hair, and kissing the top of her head. With a deep sigh, she snuggled as close to him as she could get, and slept soundly for the first time since she was seven years old.

Bryce lay awake for a while thinking about what an amazing turn his life had taken. He was exceedingly thankful for the woman God had saved specifically for him. The soft, smooth texture of her skin, the light fragrance of her hair; he knew there wasn't another woman on earth like her. They had both been through so much it only made them appreciate each other more.

There were advantages and disadvantages to having the room Bryce and Ann occupied. Since it was an "inside" room, and next to the kitchen, it was a tiny bit warmer. It was also as dark as a tomb.

Ann was terribly afraid of the dark. Bad things happened in the dark, so she clung to Bryce. He understood, and gently cradled her against his chest as he kissed away her fear. He knew she didn't realize what her dependence on him did for his self-esteem. She had given him back his masculinity.

"I'm here sweetheart," he murmured in her ear. "You don't ever have to be afraid again."

Chapter 154

When they awoke again, without light from outside, they had no idea whether it was noon or midnight. All they could hear was the whistling and moaning of the wind, which had picked up sometime during the night.

They were snug and warm under the covers, and one thing led to another. The wind, the snow, the cold, nothing mattered as they explored each other's body.

"In case I'm ever in a dark room with 100 naked men, I need to be able to recognize you by feel," Ann teased.

With her hands lightly caressing his body, Bryce felt like he may very well lose his mind, but he willingly gave her full access until he couldn't stand it any longer!

He finally laughed, "Well, in that case, if I'm ever in a dark room…" and he began to gently explore her body.

Ann began to giggle as he slowly moved his hand down her back.

All of a sudden she stiffened. "Bryce stop," she said in a panicked little voice.

Bryce quickly pulled back, assuming he had done something wrong.

"NO, NO," she cried out. "Bryce, please don't let me go, just don't touch my back. My scar! It's so ugly!"

Understanding immediately flooded his mind. The problem had nothing to do with him personally. In that moment of pristine clarity, Bryce made a conscious decision not to sacrifice their relationship on the altar of his past experience. He needed to put his insecurities aside so that he could focus on Ann's obvious distress.

"It's okay, I won't let you go," he said softly as he once again enfolded her in his arms, rocking her slowly back and forth. "Would you like to talk about it?" he said gently against her hair.

"Only if you kiss me first," she responded.

He kissed her tenderly. She sighed, content with the knowledge that he loved her and would listen.

She had told him about the scars on her body. He had only seen the one on the back of her neck just at her hairline, and the one on the inside of her upper arm. They were both from cigarette burns.

"I'm sorry," she began a bit hesitantly. "My back is so...ugly. It makes me feel ashamed. I tried to do the exercises I was taught at the rehab center, but I never had anyone to massage ointment into the scar to keep it soft. I would have had to explain what happened. I just couldn't do that. So, it has adhered to the tissue underneath. It hurts sometimes when I move a certain way..." Her voice trailed off as she buried her face in the curve of his neck.

"Will you let me touch it?" Bryce asked, waiting for her to give permission.

She finally nodded yes. He began at her left shoulder, and moved his hand down over the scar. When he got to the middle of her back, there was a rough, firm, ridge of scar tissue that extended to her right hip.

My God, Bryce thought as he gently held her close to his heart. *How could any man do something so cruel to an innocent young girl? The scars on her heart and mind must be as bad, or worse, than the ones on her back. Somehow I have to make her understand that I love every little thing about her, regardless of the scars. I love each breath she takes that causes her chest to rise and fall. I love every sigh that parts her lips and the softness of her skin. I love the texture of her hair, and the way her dimples wink in and out when she smiles. The thought of anyone hurting her in such a terrible way makes me feel physically ill!*

All these emotions coursed through his mind and heart as he could only imagine what this scar must look like. It was no wonder she was so self-conscious about it. He wanted desperately to do something to help her.

"Do you think if I rubbed it with cream of some kind every night, it would help?"

"After all this time, I don't know," she answered. Her voice so soft he could hardly hear her.

"Sweetie, it wouldn't hurt to try, would it? As soon as we get home, let's give it a go, okay?"

His willingness to accept her as she was, damaged goods, was almost incomprehensible to Ann. *"How could he possibly love me so much?"* she wondered.

"Oh Bryce, thank you so much!" she breathed against his lips. She kissed him and once again, nature took its course.

Chapter 155

T he wind waxed and waned over the next hour or so and during one of the lulls, they heard pans rattling and Georgio loudly expressing his opinion about something or other.

Mama called him an "old coot," and then they heard laughter before the wind picked up again. They decided it must be morning.

Georgio had given Bryce a good sized flashlight so he and Ann could at least find their way around the dark room. He turned it on to find Ann's face only inches from his own, her hair in tangles, and her eyes squinting against the sudden light.

The sight of her in all her "naturalness" was incredibly delightful to Bryce and he couldn't resist kissing her...several times. She told him they would need to practice all this a lot so the technique would be perfect. He agreed.

With goose-bumps running rampant, they cleaned up as best they could with cold water from a pitcher Mama had provided. They were only too happy to hurry back into their warm clothes.

Just as they opened the door to the kitchen, they collided with Georgio, who was just headed out.

He did his best to sound gruff. "I thought you two were going to stay in bed all day. I'm starving, but would this old woman feed me? Oh, no. I had to wait for you!"

He couldn't quite pull off the gruff part because of the sparkle in his eyes. Without thinking, Ann hugged him tightly for a second. He got a puzzled look on his face, which quickly changed to a wide grin.

Mama just clucked her tongue, and shook her head. "Old fool," she muttered.

Intimacy changes people. Ann and Bryce were no exception. It was apparent in the way they looked at each other that something special had happened.

Bryce could hardly look away from her long enough to find his chair at the table. When their eyes met, a slow blush crept up Ann's cheeks as a smile came to her lips. It was as if they shared the secrets of the universe.

Seeing the hairbrush in Ann's hand, Mama hesitated only a second before she pulled a stool in front of the stove. She motioned Ann to sit down. Taking the brush, she began to slowly work the tangles out of Ann's hair. This simple act had an enormous impact on everyone present.

Georgio got a faraway look on his face, recalling a memory he had tried to bury over the past several months. When he looked back at his wife, he saw tears running down her cheeks. Their beloved daughter had sat on that very stool in that very spot while her hair was combed and braided. It seemed like only yesterday to Georgio.

As Mama worked on the knots, her mind also went back to the daughter she missed so much. Her hands and her heart remembered this task that had once brought her such joy.

Ann was lost in the memories of her own mother brushing her hair, putting in the bows and barrettes, especially the pink ones that were her favorites.

They had been married for less than 48 hours, and being a witness to the bond that was developing between Ann and Rosa right before his eyes gave Bryce a new appreciation for his wife. She wasn't hard and bitter. She was warm hearted and giving.

Bryce knew that most people, having experienced what she had, would have become critical and self-absorbed. Ann had retained an innocent quality that her brutal past had not stripped away. It was one of the reasons he loved her so much.

When Ann finally looked up, Bryce saw the emotions rippling across her face. As their eyes held across those few feet that separated them, the feelings that suddenly ignited in Bryce were unexpected. He had been convinced he could never respond to a woman like a real man.

I could really get used to this, he thought as he tried to maintain his composure, and act natural while fireworks went off in his body.

Chapter 156

G iving Ann a gentle push, Mama told her to go sit with Papa. The casserole was ready, and she knew everyone was hungry. Ann took her place between Bryce and "Papa" while Mama set a hot breakfast casserole in the middle of the table.

It was obvious Mama could cook on a wood stove because the casserole smelled wonderful. Ann was surprised when under a biscuit type crust she found sausage, potatoes, scrambled eggs, onions and some things she couldn't identify, all mixed in a creamy sauce. It was no wonder Georgio had such a robust figure.

Everyone was silent, wrapped in their own thoughts, as they ate the first few bites. Then Georgio looked around the table.

"Mama, please forgive me for drowning in my own sorrow while I left you to grieve alone. Can you ever forgive me?"

Georgio went on to tell Bryce and Ann about the weeks following the death of Anna Rose. He gradually sank into such complete despair that the restaurant remained closed, as he had no desire to even get out of bed, much less run a business.

Rosa had done her best to console him, but her own grief was overwhelming. With his indifference toward her, she finally gave up.

"If you and Ann had not come when you did, I am afraid to think of what might have eventually happened," Georgio said as he patted Mama's hand. "I love you old woman. You know that don't you?"

Mama could only nod her head, too overcome with emotion to speak.

Bryce put his arm around Ann, and then rubbed the back of her neck. The most brilliant smile he had ever seen was his reward.

When the table was cleared and the dishes washed in melted snow water Georgio clapped his hands loudly, causing Ann to jump and reach for Bryce. After smoothing his generous mustache he slapped his hands on the table and stood up.

"Well, we have things to do, we'd better get moving!"

Pails of snow needed to be brought in to melt by the stove. The water would be used for washing and drinking after it had been boiled. More wood needed to be uncovered from the pile outside, and brought in for the stove in the kitchen as well as the fireplace in the ballroom.

They scurried for their coats and hats. Bryce apparently kept a heavy winter jacket here because he soon looked like a marshmallow man wearing a red stocking hat. Ann could hardly suppress a giggle as she covered her mouth with her hand. Bryce gave her a sideways, injured glance, pretending to be offended.

While Mama busied herself around the kitchen, the three of them went outside in the blowing snow. Ann had missed so much of her childhood that she couldn't resist making a snowball, and lobbing it in Georgio's direction.

This brought a funny little look to his face, and the battle was on. Bryce finally won when he tackled Ann, and tossed her in a nearby pile of drifted snow.

He pulled her to her feet as she sputtered and laughed. "I'm going to get you when you least expect it," she threatened.

"Promises, promises," he answered with a wink.

Ann filled the pails with snow as Georgio and Bryce handled the wood. After several trips back and forth to the house, Georgio was finally happy with the results, and called a halt to the work. It was time for hot cocoa and Mama's sugar cookies.

A blast of cold air followed them in as they knocked the snow from their boots. Bryce opted to keep the hat after he rolled up the sides over his ears. This struck Georgio and Ann as very funny, and they teased him good-naturedly.

"I don't have a mop of hair to keep my head warm," he responded with a laugh as he made a grab for Ann.

She let out a shriek and hid behind Mama, who tried her best to act disgusted by all this juvenile behavior.

I sure feels good to be happy, Mama thought.

Chapter 157

T he hot cocoa was much appreciated, and the cookies were beyond belief. As they munched away, Bryce asked Georgio what he knew about the property up the road.

He didn't know much more than Bryce did. It included about 200 acres, having been for sale for over a year. Georgio was surprised some big company from the city hadn't scooped it up for a song, and turned it into condos or something.

As Bryce laid out his plan to buy the land and build a house, Georgio clapped his hands with delight.

"Mama, our kids are going to live right up the road. How about that?"

Ann could never take the place of his Rosalina (little Rose). She was lost to him forever. But as Georgio felt life blossom in his heart, he knew this was the next very best thing!

The fire in the other room needed tending; at least that's what Bryce said. He didn't think he could possibly do it without Ann's help. They put on their jackets, and headed to the ballroom hand in hand.

The large room was so beautiful with its highly polished, hardwood floors, Ann couldn't resist twirling around with abandon, arms extended, like she was ten instead of thirty-eight. When she was breathless from this activity, she dropped a curtsey in front of Bryce, and proceeded to throw herself into his arms.

"Bryce, I dearly wish I could dance," she gasped. "It always looks so graceful and romantic on TV, but I don't know how."

An anxious, somewhat unsure, look came over his face. This usually happened when some unpleasant memory of an event from the past was licking at his heels.

"You...have never...danced?" he asked with some hesitation.

"I never went to a prom, I've never been to a ballroom, well, except for right now, and I just know I have a dancing spirit," she finished with a sigh.

Even though it was freezing, perspiration had beaded on his upper lip, and his posture became as taught as a bow string. Then Ann remembered him telling her about the last time he had danced in this ballroom...with Monica. She immediately understood his anxiety.

Her heart ached for him. She gently pulled his face down to her level, and kissed him soundly. I don't have to dance, my love. Let's go put some wood on the fire. We can sit for a while."

As she turned to walk away, Bryce caught her arm, and pulled her to his chest. One hand went just below her left shoulder blade while the other hand gently took hers, holding her in a perfect "closed" dance position.

"Just follow me," he said quietly.

He began to walk slowly forward, and then guided her easily in a small circle. Following him seemed like the most natural thing Ann had ever done. Soon they were gliding around the ballroom floor to music only they could hear.

Everything else faded away. Ann was only conscious of his arms holding her tight, the rhythm of their bodies moving as one, and his eyes gazing into hers with a look that touched her very soul.

Unbeknownst to them, Georgio and Rosa were watching from the kitchen doorway, hatching some plans of their own.

Chapter 158

Time passed all too quickly for Ann and Bryce. After only five short days, the storm had blown itself out. Bryce wanted to give the crews another day to get the roads safely passable before they headed home.

As soon as phone service had been restored, they called Luke to let him know they would be headed home the next day. Bryce was surprised when Luke told him that as soon as the state of emergency had been declared, he had contacted the hospital to let them know Ann wouldn't be able to come in, probably for several days.

He and Bobby sent the employees at Stratton's home as soon as the snow had begun to fall in earnest. Everything had been buttoned up nice and tight before the full fury of the storm hit. This didn't surprise Ann. She knew he was a very capable young man, even though he tried hard not to show it.

"The roads are all open now, Dad. The parking lots at work are ploughed, the sidewalks are shoveled…everybody's back to work accept you."

Bryce could hear the smile in his son's voice.

"Okay, okay. I'll be there tomorrow. I've been busy."

When Luke hung up, he was laughing.

Bryce just shook his head as he ran his finger across Ann's forehead and down her nose.

"I always thought Luke was, well, somewhat limited. I guess I was wrong! But you're not surprised even a little bit are you?"

Ann just smiled up at him.

At breakfast the morning they were to leave, Georgio handed Bryce a thick manila envelope. Bryce looked perplexed when Georgio insisted he open it. Inside was the deed to Vincenzo's Restaurant and Ballroom!

Bryce was stunned. His protests fell on deaf ears.

"Consider it a wedding present," Georgio announced with his usual flair. "Mama and I don't have any other family, only the two of you. We want you to have everything. Just let Mama and me stay here as long as we are able. Please, just accept it. Make an old man happy."

Bryce had a "what-do-we-do" look on his face that tugged at Ann's heart. He was such a good man. She knew he wouldn't do anything unless it was in the best interest of Rosa and Georgio.

Bryce, at this point, was so dumbfounded by the generosity of this gift, he didn't know what to say! Ann finally came to his rescue.

"Of course we want you to stay. We wouldn't have it any other way! But you have to promise to help us get the restaurant open again," she said as she hugged her "Papa."

Bryce quickly recognized the wisdom in this request. His mind immediately began mulling over some ideas. As they lingered over coffee, in no hurry to leave, Bryce threw out some suggestions for the restaurant.

"We'll be talking to a contractor in Dixon about building our house. Maybe he would be willing to take a look at the restaurant in regards to upgrades and repairs. Georgio, you could oversee the work on the restaurant, while Ann and I are busy getting the house underway.

Georgio looked at Mama with excitement in his eyes, something Mama hadn't seen in a long time.

"Mama, did you hear that?"

Chapter 159

Over the past several days Ann and Bryce had spent considerable time dreaming out loud about their plans for the future. Bryce decided to keep his apartment in the city so that they would have a place to stay when they needed to be in town.

They would live in Ann's house until it was sold, putting it on the market after the first of the year. She knew Oscar would get top dollar for it. He would be only too happy to handle all the details. That money would be rolled over to help cover the cost of the new house.

When Bryce had leased his apartment several years ago, it was already furnished so all he would have to move were his personal belongings. He was planning to do a lot more of his work from home, and Ann assured him her house had enough room to accommodate an office for him. They would start looking around now for new furniture to be moved into the house in Cedarville as soon as it was done. Ann's current pieces would then be used to furnish the apartment.

She was going to resign from the hospital in Dixon, giving them a month's notice. She would have her hands full with everything they were planning to do. Just packing up the house would be a monumental task. She was excited and the future looked bright. She hardly dared hope it would last...

Ann could apply for privileges at Cedarville Memorial Hospital after they were settled. Ideally, she had toyed with the idea of opening her own clinic; the Goodwin-Schwartz Free Clinic and Bryce thought it was an excellent idea. He even volunteered to be her secretary.

There were a myriad of other things that had to be done. First on the agenda, they would both need to talk to their respective lawyers.

They made it back to the city without incident even though it was still very slippery. It was only an hour's drive from Cedarville to Dixon, but with the road conditions, it took much longer.

It was around five o'clock when they reached the outskirts of town, and they were both tired and hungry. *Andre's* was on the way so stopping for an early dinner sounded like a great idea.

They weren't wearing the required evening clothes to be able to sit in the main dining room, so they sat at a secluded table in the bar. When Bryce introduced Ann as his wife, Andre's eyebrows shot up in surprise. Monica had frequented his establishment often. His recollections were vivid.

Stepping forward, Andre gallantly kissed Ann's hand in true European fashion. He was astonished when she spoke to him in fluent French. It was the first time Bryce had known his old friend to be speechless.

This 60-year-old self-proclaimed bachelor was immediately smitten. He took their order himself, and personally supervised the preparation of their food. When it was done to his satisfaction he served it with style.

Bryce was highly amused as he watched Andre flutter around Ann, making sure she was comfortable, refilling her water glass, adjusting her napkin in her lap...she gave Bryce a "help me" look.

"Thank you so much, Andre. This looks delicious. We will let you know if we want dessert."

Andre reluctantly took this as his cue to go greet his other guests, but he did look back at Ann several times. *Oh my goodness*, Bryce thought. *This will be fodder for future teasing.*

It was as if Ann could read his mind because she gave him her sternest glare, and for a few seconds, she actually managed to pull it off.

"He's just being nice," she insisted.

Bryce just shook his head as he tried to keep from laughing.

Chapter 160

The next day they headed to the Emerson building, which was the financial center in Dixon. It was also where the most prominent lawyers in town had their offices.

As they rode the elevator to the sixth floor, Ann admitted to Bryce that she was a little nervous about meeting "Herm."

"Oh honey, you'll be fine. Herm will huff and puff a little because I didn't tell him sooner, but he'll like you, don't worry."

When they stepped into the finely appointed lobby of the VanHouten law offices the secretary looked up, immediately recognizing Bryce. When she saw Ann her expression changed from open and friendly to guarded. She never took her eyes off Ann as she pushed the intercom, and notified Mr. VanHouten that Mr. Peterson had arrived.

Hummm, Ann thought. *She must have known Monica.*

They walked down the hall to an office on the right and knocked.

"Come in, come in Bryce. How..." Mr. VanHouten stopped in mid-sentence with his mouth open when he noticed Ann standing beside Bryce, her hand in the crook of his arm.

"Herm, I would like you to meet my wife, Ann. Ann, honey, this is my good friend Herman VanHouten."

Without so much as acknowledging her outstretched hand, Herman choked and sputtered.

"How could you have gotten married without talking to me first? A background check should have been done. What about a prenup? She could take everything you have!"

Bryce felt his friend had crossed the line with his ungentlemanly reaction and comments. Nonetheless, he understood the sentiment behind this behavior.

"Herm, I would gladly give her everything I have if she wanted it." Bryce said as he pulled Ann close to his side, and touched her cheek.

This exact scenario will probably be played out again in Oscar's office, Ann thought, as she again put out her hand to Herman.

"It's a pleasure to meet you, Mr. VanHouten," she said, as she firmly shook the hand that was reluctantly extended. "You certainly have my permission to check out anything you think is necessary. Please feel free to speak with my attorney. His offices are in this building. Maybe you know him. Oscar Schwartz?"

"THE Oscar Schwartz?" Herman managed to squeak out. "The Lewis Construction lawsuit Oscar Schwartz? He's your lawyer?"

Now Herman stared openly at Ann. It wasn't hard to see the wheels turning.

"I KNOW YOU!" he said as he expelled the breath he had been holding. "You're Kathy Martin! I followed the trials. I saw your pictures... I think I need to sit down," he finally managed to say before he collapsed into the chair behind his desk.

Now it was Ann's turn to be stunned. Every bit of color drained from her face as she sagged against Bryce. He caught her just before her knees gave out, and helped her to a chair. He stood behind her with his hands resting on her shoulders.

"I think we all need to take a minute," he said looking at Herman. "Herman, I'm going to have to ask for your word, not only as my attorney, but also as my friend, that you will never divulge anything I am about to tell you to anyone, for any reason."

Herman could only nod. Ann could only tremble. Bryce was steady as a rock.

Chapter 161

"Yes, Ann <u>WAS</u> Kathy Martin. After the trials, she was placed in witness protection for her safety as a direct result of the threats that were made against her life. She became Lauren Ann Reynolds. She is a physician at Dixon Memorial Hospital, and that is where we met. She was Monica's doctor. When I needed surgery early this spring, Ann took out my appendix. To make a long story short, we fell in love and here we are."

For several painful minutes, no one spoke.

"Maybe you're the one who should have required a prenup, Ann," a disgruntled Herman finally said, knowing she must be a very wealthy woman. "Does Oscar know about this?"

Herman decided to put his misgivings on the back burner for the moment, but Ann had no doubt he would definitely do some checking.

Bryce eased the tension by smoothly turning the conversation to a safer subject.

"What about the property in Cedarville, Herm? Were you able to buy it? "

"Oh, ah, yes, I got a hell of a deal for you too. The realtor couldn't wait to be rid of it. The owner put a couple of stipulations on the sale making other potential buyers unwilling to put out that kind of money."

Herman flipped open a file he had pulled out of his desk drawer.

"First, the parcel of land can't be divided into smaller lots and sold separately. It also can't be used for an apartment complex or strip mall or anything like that. I assured the seller that you were buying the land to build a house, and you were planning to live there. He was satisfied. Congratulations! You're the only one with money enough to buy it!"

Bryce wanted the property to be in both their names, which caused Herman to pause for a moment. He finally agreed to draw up the appropriate papers, handle the bank details, and let them know when the closing would take place.

"Herman, thank you so much," Bryce said with sincerity. "We were really counting on getting that property. Now we can go ahead and talk to the builder!"

As they were leaving, Herman took Ann's hand in both of his.

"Bryce looks happier than I have ever seen him, and I have to assume it's all because of you, my dear. You can count on my discretion, and I hope we will be good friends."

"I'm sure we will be," Ann responded warmly. "And thank you for looking out for my husband's best interests all these years."

As an afterthought, she turned back to Herman. "We are meeting with Oscar at two this afternoon. You are welcome to join us. You could ask any questions you have, and we will need you both in order to work out our joint finances. Would that put your mind at ease?"

"That would be wonderful, Doctor...er...Kath...Mrs. Peterson..." Herman stuttered.

"Please. Call me Ann."

Oscar was in for a big surprise.

Chapter 162

Their appointment with Oscar was later in the afternoon, and as they drove home they discussed the fact that Ann had been so easily recognized. Granted, Herman was about Oscar's age and followed high profile cases making him more likely to connect the dots, but still...

They decided Luke needed to be brought into the loop. He was an adult now, and if anything were to happen, Bryce wanted to make sure Luke was not taken by surprise.

Luke came to the house immediately when his father called saying they needed to discuss an urgent matter with him. His worried look made Ann wish they had told him sooner, and not just because her secret had been discovered.

There were some cookies in the cookie jar. It didn't matter to Luke that they were a week old. He brought a plate full to the table and sat down.

"Okay, what's up, Dad?" he said around a mouthful.

Bryce sat down opposite Luke, and Ann tried to keep occupied getting Luke a glass of milk. It still upset her to have to recount her life. She certainly wasn't proud of it.

Pouring a glass of milk took only seconds no matter how hard she tried to drag it out. Soon she was just standing there wringing her empty hands, and looking back and forth between these two men that she loved so much. She suddenly realized that if Luke turned his back on her, she would be crushed.

Knowing how distressing this would be for her, Bryce pulled her down onto his lap, and she buried her face in his neck, not wanting to meet Luke's eyes.

Bryce didn't go into every gruesome details, he just gave Luke the facts such as they were, ending with their meeting with Atty. VanHouten.

"As part of the witness protection program agreement, Ann wasn't supposed to tell anyone her true identity. However, before we were married, she told me everything. She wanted to give me an 'out' if I didn't want to become involved. Now, we're entrusting you with this information, Luke. We're a family and you should know," he finished. "Do you have any questions, son?"

Ann held her breath and looked up.

"Well dad, I have a confession of my own to make," Luke began, looking sheepish. "Before you two got married, I did some investigating, you know, to make sure you weren't getting involved with some kind of floozy or fortune hunter or something."

"No worries on that account," he said as he gave Ann a grin. "I estimated your age, Mom, and went back to the old newspapers in the library. I didn't find one word about a Dr. Ann Reynolds," he continued as he munched on the stale cookies as if they were fresh baked.

"However, I happened to come across several articles about a young girl named Kathy Martin. I read about both trials, and looked at the pictures. The events were so tragic, her face stayed with me. The first time I saw you, I knew who you were, and what had happened to you. It was a shock to be sure, but I didn't tell anybody what I discovered, not even Bobby."

He took another mouthful of cookies and a gulp of milk. "I'm glad you told Dad when you did though."

Looking Ann square in the eyes he said, "I respect you all the more because of it. I'm glad you're telling me now, and don't worry, Mom. I've got your back."

They both laughed at the look of utter disbelief on Bryce's face as he absorbed this new information.

"Well, I'll be…" he mumbled, shaking his head.

Chapter 163

L uke decided he would like to meet Mr. Schwartz, so he called off work, and went to change his clothes. He would meet his parents in the parking lot of the Emerson building.

An appointment with "Dr. Reynolds" was on Oscar's schedule for the afternoon. He knew it must be important, as she almost never came to his office. She called him from time to time, always to his private number from a phone booth in different locations around town.

He had to admit, she had learned how to cover her tracks. A lifetime living in fear had honed this skill. He shook his head sadly. *It's too bad. She deserves so much more.*

When Oscar opened his office door to receive "Dr. Reynolds," he was surprised to see Bryce Peterson standing beside her with his hand under her elbow. He was even more surprised to see a very tall, handsome young man, and another attorney he vaguely recognized, completing her entourage.

He knew Bryce immediately having seen him interviewed several times on TV in connection with Stratton Industry. He was also well aware of Monica Peterson's shenanigans around town before she died.

Oscar's first thought was in regard to Ann's safety. Because of the work Bryce did in the community, he was frequently in the public eye, exactly where Ann should not be. This concerned Oscar, causing him to wonder what her relationship was to these men.

He hugged her warmly as he commented on how good she looked. When she introduced Bryce as her husband, Oscar was astounded!

Processing this information, as well as dealing with it emotionally, took Oscar a few seconds.

"Peanut," he said with an exasperated groan, "what in the world were you thinking. You should have talked this over with me first."

Bryce and Ann just looked at each other and sighed. They had already been through this lecture with Herman. It's not like they were teenagers.

When Ann introduced Luke as their son, Oscar was even more perplexed.

"It's alright Oscar. Bryce knows everything. He won't let anything happen to me. I'm safe. Really I am. You don't have to worry about me anymore," she said as she touched her friend's hand.

"I've worried about you for half my life. I'm afraid I can't stop now," Oscar answered with a sad little smile.

She wanted so much to put his mind, and heart, at ease. "You may already be acquainted with Atty. Herman VanHouten. His offices are also in this building. He is the Peterson attorney, and I thought it would be a good idea for you two to meet."

"Yes, yes, good to formally meet you, Mr. VanHouten," Oscar said as the two men shook hands. "I'm sure we will have many opportunities to work together from here on out. It seems these two have pulled a fast one on both of us!"

It came as no surprise to Bryce that Oscar loved Ann. Not romantically of course, but like a big, overly-protective brother. He was also well aware of the extent the man had gone to for her safety.

"I'm eternally grateful for everything you have done for Ann," Bryce said. "She has spoken of you often with great affection, so I feel like I know you already. I think we can all work together to continue to protect her, don't you?"

A look of overwhelming relief passed over Oscar's face. He knew Bryce by reputation only, and respected him a great deal. He would be happy to get to know him on a more personal level. It was obvious the man absolutely adored his little Peanut. You would have to be blind not to see that. It was also obvious that the feeling was mutual.

"You've got the best little gal in the world, you know," he commented to Bryce.

Bryce slipped his arm around Ann's waist. "I know," he said as he smiled at her, giving her a little squeeze.

Then Oscar turned his attention to Luke. "And just where do you fit into this picture, young man? I know you aren't Ann's biological son, although the resemblance is uncanny!"

Luke smiled good-naturedly as he shook Oscar's hand. "I just got lucky when my Dad found Ann."

Thank you, Luke, Ann thought. *What a thoughtful answer.*

Over the next hour, Bryce told Oscar of their plans to move to Cedarville. He explained what security measures were going to be incorporated in the building of their home. In addition, Ann would be under his watchful eyes, and Luke was also very protective of her.

The boy's certainly big enough to do the job, Oscar speculated to himself as he evaluated the situation.

Oscar was satisfied that Ann's safety would be in the best of hands. Maybe now he could finally relax and enjoy life. His poor wife had taken a back seat to a woman she didn't know, for reasons she probably wouldn't understand, that Oscar couldn't share with her anyway. He had justified it all under the guise of "lawyer-client privilege." He was going to make it up to her, he promised himself.

Ann couldn't help herself, she had to ask. "Do you talk to Dr. Mark much?"

The few times she had been in this office Oscar had avoided discussing anything but current business.

"The walls have ears," he had always said as a way of dismissing the subject.

But Ann had to know if Mark was doing all right. Was he still in Boston? Had he ever gotten married? Was he happy? There would always be a special place in her heart for Dr. Mark. He had saved her life and given her freedom. She knew Bryce understood that her feelings for Mark in no way compromised her feelings for him. They were two separate things.

Ann could tell by the hesitation in his voice that Oscar didn't want to talk about this. Apparently, they had eventually grown apart, having different career paths. It had gotten too painful for them to talk about the past so they just didn't.

Oscar let Mark know every time there was a message in bank withdrawals so he would know Ann was okay, but that was it. After he had moved to Dixon, and accidently found her, he thought it best to keep that information to himself.

Ann got the impression Oscar wasn't telling her the whole truth, which made her worry even more.

Chapter 164

L uke went with Ann and Bryce for Thanksgiving with Rosa and Georgio only because Ann asked him to go. She knew he was leery about meeting them, after all, they were a part of the "Monica past," as he called it.

Georgio and Rosa welcomed him with open arms making him feel right at home. It wasn't long before he was rummaging through Rosa's cupboards looking for the goodies he knew she baked just for him.

Then Christmas was right around the corner. Ann hadn't celebrated since she was a little girl when her parents were still alive. The holidays always made her sad, and she preferred to bury herself at the hospital, covering for her colleagues who were married with families. This year would be different. She was so excited!

Luke was equally enthusiastic. When they were all together at Thanksgiving, he had asked Georgio if they could have a huge tree with lots of decorations for Christmas.

Georgio had just rolled his eyes. "I suppose we can if that's what you really want," he said gruffly, as though it would be a terrible imposition.

Bryce knew underneath Georgio and Rosa were thrilled that Christmas was going to be observed with all the trimmings, including a sumptuous meal.

It wasn't long before the "family" holiday gathering grew to include Bobby and Maria, and of course, Gloria Hamilton. Luke said she didn't have any family of her own, and she would be lonely on Christmas. He had also invited Carla and her husband John. They had been reluctant to accept his invitation. They were black. John was in a wheelchair. How could they possibly fit in?

Luke was not someone who gave up easily, and he kept pestering Carla until she finally agreed to come on one condition. She could help do the cooking.

"The more the merrier!" was Georgio's reaction to this news.

Ann knew Luke and his dad had always exchanged gifts, but the celebrating had been subdued. This would be Luke's first real Christmas. Excitement crackled in the air as shopping for the perfect gifts became an obsession.

It brought joy to Ann's heart as she watched Luke and Bryce with their heads together...plotting. When they noticed her watching they stopped talking immediately, and gave her big innocent smiles. *Hummmm*, she wondered. *Just what are they up to?*

The whole gang arrived in Cedarville a few days before Christmas, giving Luke and Bobby time enough to find the best tree in the whole state of Vermont, according to them anyway. It really was magnificent!

They had cut down the biggest one they could find, and it now stood in the middle of the ballroom. Everyone helped with the decorating while Mama and Carla kept the hot cocoa and cookies coming. It became John's job to untangle all the Christmas lights. He was thrilled to have something he could do from his chair.

To everyone's astonishment, Bobby and Maria slipped away for a few hours on Christmas Eve...and got married! Heaven only knows where they found a preacher who was available and willing during the holiday, but they managed somehow. *When all else fails, love will always find a way*, Ann thought to herself. This was something she had learned over time, and believed with all her heart.

Bobby apologized profusely for not telling anyone. He just couldn't wait a second longer to make his beautiful Maria his wife. Maria smiled shyly as she looked up at Bobby. Bryce and Ann had suspected for some time that this outcome was inevitable. Now it was one more reason to celebrate the season!

As they were busy congratulating Bobby and Maria, Ann thought she heard...sleigh bells! She tugged Bryce toward the window. Bryce threw Luke a glance, and a raised eyebrow, which was a signal that their carefully contrived plan was about to come together.

What Ann saw when she peeked out the window was a huge sleigh pulled by four beautiful horses. They were impatient to be off as evidenced by their stomping and pawing of the snow.

"Everybody, get your coats! We're going for a ride! It's Christmas Eve," Luke hollered. "This is your surprise, Mom. What do you think?"

Ann was speechless as she hugged first Luke and then Bryce. Her heart was full, and she was so incredibly thankful for all the people in her life who loved her.

The ground was still covered by a thick powdery layer of snow left over from the storm in early November, so arranging for the sleigh and horses hadn't been too difficult, albeit expensive.

Everyone bundled up, even Mama and Georgio, and piled into the sleigh. Carla and John offered to stay behind since they didn't want to cause any inconvenience getting John into the sleigh. Luke would have none of it. They were all going or nobody was going. He just picked John up out of his wheelchair, and sat him on the seat in the sleigh beside Mama.

"There you go, John. No sweat man!"

When everyone was settled under the heavy blankets that had been provided for their comfort, the driver whistled to the team and off they went. He knew all the untraveled back roads, so they didn't have to worry about possible traffic. The horses were familiar with the route, and pranced along at a good clip.

Soon Georgio began singing in Italian one of his favorite Christmas songs. Mama joined in, and it was truly beautiful. The stars were sparkling on a black velvet sky, and the moon was huge and hanging low, providing enough light to make the ride a wonderful experience. Other Christmas carols followed and everyone joined in the singing.

Ann sat cuddled up against Bryce, snug and warm. As she looked at each precious face she asked God to protect them. She loved them all so much. The fear that clutched her heart for a second was not the fear for her safety she had lived with all her life. It was the fear that what she had found would somehow be snatched away from her. She decided she would live each moment to the fullest. The future was... not today.

Christmas dinner was unbelievable. Ann had never seen so much food in one place at one time except at the supermarket. Mama had lots of help from all the women, so everything came together at precisely one o'clock on Christmas day.

The men had set up a long table in the ballroom so everyone could sit down together. When everything was ready, Georgio stood up and cleared his throat.

"Me and Mama, we have much to be thankful for this year. Yes, we lost our little girl and there will always be a bit of sadness in our hearts, but we have gained all of you! We did not think we would ever feel alive again...we are very grateful. Thank you Lord," he finished as he blew his nose on a big, white hankie and wiped his eyes.

There was not a dry eye in the place and several minutes of quiet reflection followed.

"The food's getting cold," Georgio announced and everyone dug in.

They had decided not to open gifts until evening. That would give some of them time for a nap, and for the younger folks, including Georgio, a rousing checker tournament.

It was hard to find a quiet corner where Bryce and Ann could be alone as there were good natured accusations of cheating, and much laughing coming from the checker games. They managed however, and Bryce pulled a sprig of Mistletoe from his pocket and held it over Ann's head.

"Merry Christmas, my love," he whispered as he took her in his arms, and gave her one of "those kisses."

Happy tears trickled down her cheeks as she looked into his face. "Oh, Bryce," she sighed as she ardently returned his kiss. "Merry Christmas to you too, sweetheart, and I'll have something special for you later, when we're alone," she hinted with a sparkle in her eyes.

Chapter 165

Oscar and Herman had gotten to know each other well and after much discussion, they had recommended that Ann and Bryce form a corporation. This would cover Stratton Industry, Vencenzo's Restaurant and Ballroom, and any other future business ventures, knowing Ann's desire to open a free health care clinic. Their individual investments would be separate and managed by their respective attorneys.

Georgio, Rosa, Bryce, Luke and Ann were in complete agreement and Peterson Enterprise was birthed. They collaborated, based on what each of them wanted to see as the future for their joint efforts, and came up with a plan.

In early March Bryce felt they were ready to get everyone together to present, what they felt was the best direction for their business. They knew the specific individuals they wanted as part of their management team.

The meeting was set for two o'clock on a chilly Saturday afternoon. Mama Rosa, insisting nobody could think properly on an empty stomach, had invited everyone for lunch at noon. It turned out to be a wonderful idea.

The actual meeting convened closer to three, as there was much horsing around between Bobby and Luke. Everyone was laughing as Mama tried to bring some semblance of order to the group, making them laugh all the more. The camaraderie was exactly as it should be, and Bryce was pleased.

He had previously introduced everyone to Doug, who was a bit overwhelmed by this boisterous gathering. He was easily accepted into the "fold" and soon settled in, enjoying the good food as well as the good company.

Now Bryce went around the table explaining why each person's gifts and talents were required if this business venture was to get off the ground. It was understood right from the start that this was a team effort, and no one person was more or less important than any other.

Doug was the first to present his findings as to the need for renovations and repairs. He had already had extensive discussions with Bryce and Georgio so he was aware of what they wanted.

He had drawn up some sketches, tacking them up on a board that Georgio provided. The end of the building, which had previously been small motel rooms, would be turned into office space and a small gym/workout room.

There would be four small bedrooms including the one Bryce and Ann used when they visited. On the other side of the ballroom, an addition would incorporate two apartments. Bobby and Maria would move into one of them.

A new modern kitchen with updated appliances would take the place of Mama's wood stove. There would be preparation tables, extensive cupboards, storage space, at least two industrial sized refrigerators, and a walk in freezer.

Mama was aghast. She couldn't even imagine such a kitchen. Georgio assured her she would have her own little kitchen in their refurbished apartment so she was content.

Georgio and Rosa's apartment would be expanded and modernized. Mama could decorate any way she wanted, and she would have her own private little kitchen. Mama tried to negotiate to keep her wood stove, but she was overruled. It was dangerous and hauling wood would eventually be too much for them to handle.

Instead of being long and narrow, their new area would be square. It would be across the hall from the rooms Bryce and Ann shared. The hallway between the two areas would lead to a back parking lot for family and employees only.

An industrial sized generator would keep the power on in the event of another major storm. That had been one of Georgio's requirements.

The fireplace would stay at one end of the ballroom. It added an ambiance that Doug had never encountered in this kind of establishment. Georgio and Rosa had gathered the stones, one by one, before building began. It had taken a long time but the result was worth all the effort. It was beautiful and handcrafted with love.

The ballroom area was already good sized however the "stage" section would be moved back, providing more room for dancing. Behind the stage would be several small dressing rooms, storage space, and a lounge complete with snack bar so that members of the band had a place to relax between sets.

The lighting, electricity and plumbing would be updated throughout the building for safety as well as aesthetics and efficiency. The front of the building would be changed to incorporate a huge awning extending out from the main entrance over a circular driveway so that guests could easily disembark in inclement weather. The entry doors would be wide and electronically controlled for easy access.

A newly designed sign would go over the front of the building. A smaller version of the sign would go on all the company vehicles. *Vincenzo's Restaurant and Ballroom*; plain and simple, but elegant.

Bryce had purchased land across the road from the restaurant where a large parking lot and a garage would be constructed. The garage would be big enough for two limos and at least five cars. There would also be a mechanic's bay and space for mowers, plows, etc.

Finally, Doug went over the security measures that would be put in place to protect, not only the buildings, but the guests and those who would be living on the premises.

Everything was similar to what Ann had in her house in Dixon only this would be on a much larger scale. The monitors for the security cameras would be located in the security office. They could also be accessed on computers in other strategic areas of the building.

One-way, bullet proof glass would be in all the windows, specific lights would come on automatically at pre-determined times, and the locks on the doors were activated by thumb prints; not keys. Only a "family" member could unlock any door. The private living quarters in the building could only be accessed by the people who lived there or by security in the event of an emergency.

Chapter 166

It had become immediately apparent at Christmas when everyone had gotten together, that if John agreed to become part of the team, he would need to be more mobile. Ann made a mental note to research electric wheelchairs and discuss it with Bryce. She was fairly certain John wouldn't accept what he thought was charity. He might, however, accept it if Bryce assured him it was a "business expense."

Finances, business regulations, tax requirements, payroll, in other words "keeping the books," would be under John's purview. This was something for which he was eminently qualified. He was currently doing private accounting work, which wasn't very satisfying or lucrative. He had been enthusiastic when Bryce had asked him to attend the first meeting of Peterson Enterprise.

Carla would be in charge of anything having to do with housekeeping and food service. The wait staff and cleaning people would answer to her. Of course, Mama Rosa was encouraged to participate as much as she wanted. Bless Carla's heart. She had a way of making Mama feel the kitchen could not be run successfully without her input.

Reservations, phone calls, minutes of meetings etc. would fall to Maria. Being a very creative individual, she was also free to help in any other area where she saw a need.

Bobby would be the organizer of, pretty much, everything that happened under this roof. He seemed to have an uncanny way of always knowing what to do and when to do it. He could be counted on to keep things running efficiently under any circumstances.

Furthermore, he had the ability to sell swamp land in Florida to Eskimos if the motivation was right. When the restaurant was ready to open, he would be responsible for the advertising and promoting.

As head of security, Luke would work with Doug on the installation of all the security systems. In this position, he would need to have a working knowledge of these systems as well as how to maintain the many programs. He was extremely excited about this opportunity. His parents didn't know yet how qualified he really was to handle these responsibilities. They would have a big surprise in a couple of months!

Georgio, Rosa, Bryce and Ann would be the "board of directors," so to speak. Georgio and Rosa were not educated people, but education doesn't always equal good sense. They had experience in running this kind of business that would prove invaluable. Their age was not a factor.

Bryce and Ann, Rosa and Georgio would not collect a salary per se. Rosa and Georgio would continue living in their rooms where all their needs were met. Additionally, they both collected social security. They were quite comfortable.

Bryce and Ann would have their own home just up the road, and Bryce owned Stratton Industry. If Ann decided to work at the hospital in Cedarville, she would collect a salary there.

Everyone else who worked for Peterson Enterprise would earn a healthy salary, and if this wild plan succeeded, salaries would go up accordingly. This meant Bobby and Maria would each have an individual income as would Carla and John.

Bobby couldn't pass on the opportunity to agitate Luke.

"Good reason to get married bro. More dinero. You better start looking."

Luke laughed and shook his head. Getting married was the last thing on his mind. He was young and happy, had all the money he needed, and drove a "badass" truck. What did he need with a woman? Besides, he didn't think he would ever find a woman like his mom. She was darn near perfect in his eyes.

Everyone would have health insurance benefits, a stipulation Ann insisted upon. They also decided to add enough room for Ann to have a small office and patient treatment room on the premises. Any health problems she couldn't handle in this setting would be covered by the insurance plan at the hospital in Cedarville.

Chapter 167

When the whole plan was laid out, Bryce asked if there were any questions. Everyone sat dumbfounded. Bryce adjourned the meeting asking everyone to go home, think about everything he had presented, and let him know if they wanted to be part of this great adventure!

The next day, everyone to the man, or woman as the case may be, called Bryce. They all wanted in.

Bobby and Carla would continue at Stratton's for the time being. Their recommendations would be considered when hiring replacements.

Since Ann and Bryce had gotten married, Bobby had been in charge at Stratton's and he wasn't sure if he wanted to keep those responsibilities. He would have to wait and see. He suspected that, at least in the beginning, Peterson Enterprise would take most of his time and energy.

General oversight for Stratton's would, of course, continue to fall to Bryce, and since he wanted to work from home, Bobby was looking into computer technology that would allow him to do just that.

John would need to start immediately getting all the appropriate paperwork in order to open the business. There was a lot involved, and John was eager to be able to finally apply his knowledge to something worthwhile.

Luke would need to start immediately as well. A lot of the inside renovations at Vincenzo's could be done in cold weather so he worked with Doug. He would check in with Walter at Stratton's once a week and help him as needed.

If the rest of the winter was mild, outside work could be started at the restaurant as well as on the house that Bryce and Ann had designed. They were so excited! They spent considerable time looking for just the right furnishings and accessories for their new home.

If the house in Dixon sold right away, they would live in the apartment until their house in Cedarville was finished. Things were moving forward at a rapid pace, and so far, the weather was holding.

Chapter 168

It was almost the end of May. Everyone had been diligently going about their tasks working toward a grand opening for the restaurant at the end of June.

Doug hadn't taken on any other construction jobs through the winter and spring as these two projects were keeping him busy enough. It was slower going in the restaurant because he was working with an existing structure. The house, on the other hand, was going to be finished ahead of schedule.

Ann was so excited when Doug offered to do a walk-through. The inside was close to completion. The things that needed to be finished on the outside, landscaping and such, would require warmer weather, and could wait until after the opening of the restaurant.

The half mile long curving driveway was currently gravel. It would be paved later. All the security was in working order, as was the computer Bryce would use for work. The furniture they had picked out would be delivered as soon as all the interior painting was finished. Everything looked good so far. They were pleased.

The house in Dixon had sold, as promised, for an incredible amount, which went a long way toward paying for the new house. Everything had been packed up weeks ago, and moved to the apartment. Bryce and Ann had been staying with Georgio and Rosa for the short time before they could occupy their new home.

Chapter 169

◦◦◦

For about a month, Luke had been away a lot, and was being very secretive about it. Bryce and Ann were curious, but allowed him time and space, knowing he would talk to them when he was ready.

He finally asked them if they would be free the following Monday night. He wanted them to meet him at the Hudson County Courthouse Building in Freeport at 7 o'clock. He had also invited the rest of his "family."

Bobby, Maria, Carla, John, Glo, Pete McHenry, Rosa, Georgio, Bryce and Ann had all put on their best clothes, and were sitting in the front section of the large meeting room in the court house. None of them knew what was going on, and nobody had seen Luke all day.

The chief of the Hudson County Sheriff's Department, in full dress uniform, stepped to the podium. Clearing his throat, he welcomed everyone to the 37th graduating class of the Hudson County Police Academy.

The only one who seemed to know what was going on was Pete McHenry. He was sitting there with a very smug grin on his weathered face.

The police chief continued by saying he was proud to introduce the cadet with the highest grade point in the class as well as the highest scores for police work in the field, Luke Peterson.

Luke stepped out from behind the curtain, his hair cut short and wearing a dress uniform that fit him perfectly. With a confident stride he walked forward to accept his diploma. He then walked to the first seat in the row behind the chief, made a smart turn to the front, and stood at attention.

Everyone's jaw dropped...well, except for Pete's.

Ever since Luke was young, Pete had taken a special interest in him. He had a soft spot when it came to kids who had three strikes against them from birth. He had always suspected there was more to Luke than showed on the surface.

He had been pleased to help Bryce obtain custody and later adopt Luke. When, as a young man, he had come to Pete asking for help getting into the police academy Pete was thrilled. He did everything he could to pave the way. Tonight, his efforts were rewarded. He was very pleased indeed.

The rest of the graduates were called by name as they came forward to receive their diplomas. Speeches followed. Awards were handed out. Luke got the academic award, the field work award as well as one for marksmanship. Each one he accepted graciously.

Bobby couldn't wait to tease his friend. Luke would have to be prepared to beat the girls off with a stick now!

Bryce was so proud he could hardly speak.

Gloria Hamilton and Ann had always known Luke had the potential to be anything he wanted to be.

Rosa and Georgio were beaming and talking in Italian while Carla and John marveled at being included in this highly emotional, excitable, affectionate...white family.

After the ceremony, Luke was immediately surrounded by his unorthodox "family" with everyone talking at once.

Bryce and Ann hugged him tightly. "We are so proud of you son, but then, we always have been," Bryce said as he wiped his eyes with the back of his hand.

Bobby slapped him on the back.

"You sly dog, you. Why didn't you tell me you was d' fuzz?"

Rosa pinched his cheeks jabbering something about his hair and uniform.

Georgio shook his hand, and clapped him on the shoulder.

"What do you think, Mama? Our grandson is the police!"

Maria kissed him on the cheek. Luke was like her big brother, and she thought the world of him.

Glo couldn't stop smiling. *I helped him become what he is*, she thought proudly to herself as she too kissed him on the cheek. *What a good boy!*

Carla and John didn't know quite what to do so they just congratulated him.

They all went back to the restaurant and celebrated long into the night, wanting to hear every detail of Luke's experiences.

Chapter 170

The house was ready. Ann had just received a call from Doug letting her know that all the interior work was done, and the furniture was in place. Bryce could tell by the look on her face that she was extremely excited about more than just the move.

Ann had given him strict orders to stay away from the house the next morning, which greatly amused him since she had never given him an order before. Early the next day Ann left by herself, something else she rarely did, always preferring to be with him. *Hummmm,* Bryce wondered. *What is this all about?*

A large moving van was just pulling into the driveway as Ann got there. It took them almost an hour to set up what she had purchased. Upon her return to Bryce she was humming an off-key little song, her eyes dancing with delight.

The afternoon held several surprises for both of them. Each gave to the other out of the love they shared, purchasing gifts with great thoughtfulness.

Bryce helped Ann out of the car in their garage, always a gentleman even when they were in private. Ann had commented to him once how much she appreciated it. He had informed her that she always acted like a lady, and should always be treated like one; a point he had reinforced at the time with one of "those kisses."

After he opened the door between the garage and the house he gently picked her up in his arms. She was a bit surprised, but enjoyed it none the less.

"I have to carry you over the threshold," he said. "It's tradition."

Ann took the opportunity to kiss his cheek and the side of his mouth before giving him one of the kisses that sent shivers up and down his spine.

"Are we going to do this every time we come home?" she teased as she placed another kiss in front of his ear.

"Absolutely!" he declared with a soft smile.

It was then Ann noticed the smell of fresh paint mingled with… fresh cut flowers. Bryce sat her on her feet and took her hand, leading her through the entry way and into the great room.

On the island in the kitchen was a huge arrangement of red roses, her favorite flower. She cupped one of the about-to-open buds in her hands as she took a deep breath of the intoxicating fragrance.

"How beautiful!" she exclaimed as she turned her eyes to Bryce. "However did you manage this?"

"Oh, I have my ways," he replied with a secretive smile. "Besides, I had a little elf that helped me."

They looked around the great room with satisfaction. Ann felt Bryce jerk and gasp. *Aaahhh, he spotted my surprise.* Her heart leapt with excitement.

In the alcove in front of a floor to ceiling window, next to the fireplace, stood a baby grand piano. Bryce slowly walked around it, admiring it from every angle. He drew his hand across the highly polished, cream colored finish with amazement in his eyes.

"Oh, my word," he breathed. "Where did you ever find this?"

He was so enthralled with the piano he hadn't yet noticed the picture on the wall. When he finally did, tears began streaming down his face.

In a gold frame was a picture of a young woman, her hands gracefully hovering above the keys of what looked like this very piano. The young woman bore a striking resemblance to his wife.

"Sit down, sit down," she urged. "Play something for me."

Bryce sat down and she slid in close to him on the bench. His fingers ran lightly up and down the keys. *Wow. Someone who knew what they were doing tuned this instrument,* he thought as he began to play one of Ann's favorite classical pieces.

As Ann listened, she let her head drop to his shoulder. He was happy so she was completely content. When he finished playing, the long slow kiss he gave her turned her bones to jelly.

Bryce had thought this was something that was lost to him forever. He never would have purchased another piano on his own. The memories were far too painful. Ann had restored this joy to him, and he thanked God once again for her.

"Come on, Love, let's look at the rest of the house," Bryce said enthusiastically as he pulled her to her feet.

On the mantle over the fireplace were peach colored roses. On the large round dining room table, they were yellow.

Ann ran her hand along the smooth marble countertops as her eyes traveled over the appliances, everything blending together symmetrically.

The den where Bryce would work from home was in order with the computer up and running, thanks to Bobby. The security cameras were operational, and the monitors were on the wall over the large oak desk.

A brand new washer and dryer were at the ready in the laundry room. The open shelves fully stocked.

The guest bedroom, with its own bathroom, was attractively appointed. So far, everything was absolutely perfect!

As they entered the master bedroom suite, Bryce could hardly contain his excitement.

There were vases of white roses along the built-in dressers. The queen sized bed was made. The comforter was one Ann had admired, but hadn't gotten because she thought it was too expensive.

She bounced up and down on the bed, giving Bryce a wicked grin. Their clothes hung neatly in the closets. They would need to make a trip to the apartment, and bring back a few more things they wanted in the new house.

The bathroom had double sinks and a huge shower. There were enclosed shelves with plenty of places for extra towels, bed linen and cleaning products.

At the very back of the suite was a small room where Ann had put her makeup table. She hadn't been back there in a while as this room wasn't necessary to finishing the rest of the house.

It was now painted pink and white, colors which Bryce said suited her femininity. In front of one window was a large, white, claw foot bathtub with candles and pink roses on the window sill. She could take a bubble bath any time she wanted.

"Bryce! Honey, the tub is plenty big enough for two. How wonderful!" Ann exclaimed. Bryce actually blushed.

In front of the other window was an antique writing desk with its own small chair. Bryce had found it when he and Luke had been poking around the flea markets in the area looking for tools to fill out Luke's tool box. The chair cushion was new, and the desk had been refinished and painted white.

On the desk was a small black velvet box tied with a pink bow.

"Go ahead. Open it. I bought it just for you," Bryce said quietly.

Ann tugged off the bow and opened the box. What she saw took her breath away. It was a heart shaped locket with small diamonds encrusting the edges.

"With love" was engraved on the front. When she turned it over the words "always and forever, Bryce," were engraved on the back.

Her eyes filled with tears as with trembling fingers, she opened the tiny clasp. When the locket opened, on one side was a picture of Bryce. On the other side a picture of Luke.

"Push right here," Bryce instructed as he showed her a tiny area concealed in the delicate floral pattern on the locket.

When she did, both sides where the pictures were, flipped open to reveal miniatures of her mother and father hidden underneath!

Her eyes flew to Bryce's face. "How did you...where...Oh, Bryce," she cried flinging her arms around his neck.

No one saw the happy couple for several days.

Chapter 171

The bathtub, the writing desk, the comforter; those things had been the easy part. Oscar had a fit when Bryce asked him to find pictures of Ann's parents. He was the only person Bryce knew with the resources it would take to pull it off without linking anything back to her. Money was no object, Bryce wanted the pictures.

Oscar finally relented. It had taken some extensive research of old records in her hometown, some maneuvering and scheming, but the look on her face made it worth the effort as well as the money.

The hand crafted locket had been especially designed with the hidden compartment by a friend of Andre's. It had taken an act of God to get Luke to pose for the picture.

As for Ann's surprises, she had heard Monica bragging about how she had destroyed the piano and picture that had belonged to Bryce. *What a hateful, hurtful thing to do*, she thought. After she and Bryce began seeing each other, she didn't know how, but she promised herself she would replace these items if she could figure out a way.

So the new Steinway baby grand piano had been in the making long before they were married. This instrument was one of a kind and made specifically for Bryce by a fourth generation piano maker whose ancestors had immigrated to the United States from Stockholm, Sweden.

The gentleman's wife had become seriously ill when they were visiting in Vermont. Ann had taken care of her. He was so grateful he told her if there was ever anything he could do for her, just ask. She had asked for the piano, and paid top dollar for it. He had stopped work on all his other projects to make this piano for Bryce.

Ann provided a paint sample and told him what she wanted. The sharp and flat keys were dark brown ivory instead of the traditional black. The cream colored finish was an exact match to the paint used on the walls of their home.

The artist who had painted the original picture that Bryce had loved so much still lived in the area. Ann had commissioned him to paint another. When she explained the situation, it had been his idea to use her likeness. Now she was glad she had let him talk her into it. Bryce absolutely loved it!

Luke had been co-conspirator to both of them. Privy to all the plans, he had been sworn to secrecy by his father and his mother. At times, he said it had been hard to juggle everything without giving something away!

Chapter 172

⚬⚬⚬

Vincenzo's was finally ready to open. It had been decided, for the trial run, to open only Friday and Saturday nights the first week. Thereafter, they would be open Wednesday through Saturday.

Wednesday and Thursday would be less formal with the cost per person less expensive. The food would be home-style with a variety of dishes like fried chicken and mashed potatoes, which was Carla's forte. They would try different styles of music, and all suggestions would be considered. They would be flexible and go with what worked.

Friday and Saturday nights would require formal evening wear with guests paying top dollar for a romantic evening of dinner and dancing until 1AM. In the past, Vincenzo's had been widely known for its excellent authentic Italian cuisine. Mama's original buffet style was tried and true; they would stick with it.

Reservations had been pouring in! So far, no one had quibbled about the prices, which were comparable to any upscale restaurant in Dixon. Bobby had really out-done himself with advertising. Something he didn't let anyone forget.

Andre had recommended a band he had started using as a back-up to his own musicians. The leader was new to the business, therefore affordable and available.

At Bobby's insistence, he and Bryce had spoken with Jimmy O'Brien personally before hiring him. They had been impressed and Andre had assured them the band had a "great sound."

Jimmy was young and inexperienced. Even with Andre's recommendation, Bobby had misgivings. The music was a huge part of the overall "Vincenzo Dining Experience," as he called it, and none of them had actually heard the band play.

"Well, none of us has experience in this area except for Mama and Georgio," Bryce commented. "I say we at least give him a chance."

Everyone finally agreed. Jimmy O'Brien and his band, "*The High Notes*," were hired.

A trip to *Claire's in* Dixon was in order. Bobby suggested they all needed "new duds" for the grand opening. They had spared no expense to make this a "classy joint," as he so eloquently phrased it, and they should look their best.

Claire's was a privately owned shop in Dixon that catered to the dance crowd with formal wear, shoes, accessories; anything a person needed to make a good impression when out on the town.

Ann had gotten to know Claire Lafontaine several years ago when she was looking for properly fitting shoes and dresses. She was so petite it was hard to buy off the rack and still look like an adult. Claire and Ann had become friends.

She was delighted to be asked to outfit the whole group for this very special night. The men would need black tuxedos, each a different style. The women wanted similar style gowns of different colors. Mama wanted black, to hide her not-so-girlish figure. Maria wanted red, which Bobby thought made her look "hot." Yellow looked beautiful with Carla's dark complexion, and Ann's dress was sapphire blue. Bryce said it exactly matched her eyes.

On opening night the family gathered for a light early supper. The doors would open at 6PM sharp. As Georgio thanked God for the food, he also asked for favor over their endeavor that evening.

They were all too nervous to eat very much, except for Luke. He couldn't think of anything that would result in him being too nervous to eat Mama's cooking; a comment which eased the tension, and brought a smile to Mama's face.

The plan was for Georgio and Rosa, Bobby and Maria and of course, Bryce and Ann to mingle with the guests. They would stop at each table to chat for a minute making sure everything was satisfactory before moving on.

How they presented themselves on this first night was extremely important. It would either make or break the business. They wanted Vincenzo's to be known as a quality place to dine and dance. It was important for romance to emanate from everything that was done in keeping with their mantra *The Vincenzo Dining Experience.* Bobby had said it once and everyone liked it. It stuck and was included in all their publicity.

Carla needed to be in and out of the kitchen supervising food preparation. She would make sure the buffet table was always clean and the serving dishes full. As time went on, and the kitchen help became more familiar with their responsibilities, Carla could spend more time in the dining room with the guests.

John would verify reservations from a special podium that Doug had constructed specifically to meet his special needs. He would make sure all the guests were escorted to their tables by one of the wait staff.

The wait staff had been hand-picked by Carla. She knew each one personally. Their uniforms were individually tailored so that they fit properly and looked professional.

Carla had taken suggestions from each person as to what they would like their "look" to be. They came up with fitted, black, tuxedo trousers with white shirts and suspenders for the guys. The girls chose knee length, short sleeved dresses, each in a different pattern of black and white, under crisp white aprons.

They looked wonderful and were well-paid. They could voice their opinions and make suggestions that were seriously considered. If a problem arose, it was addressed immediately and handled fairly. All this made for happy, hard-working, loyal employees.

Since the meal was buffet style, they moved among the tables refilling water glasses, bringing beverages, clearing empty plates; in general, seeing to the comfort and satisfaction of each individual at their assigned tables.

A separate group of kitchen helpers kept the food coming, making sure the hot food was hot and the cold food was cold. They were dressed exactly like the wait staff and were just as important.

Luke would greet the guests at the door, and keep his eyes open for any problems that might arise. He believed a major part of adequate security was good communication, and since he was the only security person, he had to be able to depend on Bobby, Bryce and Georgio if he faced something he couldn't handle by himself.

Each man was outfitted with a hidden earpiece. Their wrist watches contained tiny microphones. The watch Luke wore was more sophisticated. He could speak with everyone at once or with just one specific person. In the event of any disturbance, it was each man's responsibility to take care of his wife <u>first,</u> and then assist Luke as necessary.

Several off duty police officers had been hired to man the parking lot. They were well trained and eager to make some extra money. Luke could also count on them for help in the event of trouble. Ann knew her safety was always a priority for Bryce and Luke even though it was never discussed openly. The more well-known Vincenzo's became, the greater the danger that someone would recognize her. It wasn't that they were looking for trouble, they just wanted to be prepared for any eventuality.

Chapter 173

Jimmy O'Brien and his small group of musicians arrived early in the afternoon, giving them plenty of time to set up their instruments. They played a couple of songs to get a feel for the room, impressing everyone with their talent.

Bobby breathed a sigh of relief. So far, everything was going according to plan.

While waiting backstage until it was time to play, Jimmy was restless. He began walking around checking out the area designated for the band.

Nice setup, he thought as he opened a storage closet door. To his surprise, on the back shelf were several trophies of different sizes all bearing the names of Rosa and Georgio Vincenzo!

It seems they had been European Ballroom and Latin dance champions in the late forties, early fifties! *Wow, the portly old guy with the mustache and his wife were dance pros! Who would have thought? This might prove to be useful information down the road,* Jimmy thought to himself as he started mulling over some ideas for the future...

At six o'clock the guests began to arrive. Luke, looking extremely handsome in his tux, greeted everyone at the door. John took over from there, checking reservations. The wait staff guys and girls were lined up beside John. They seated each guest and returned to the end of the line.

The buffet tables looked fabulous. Carla and Mama Rosa had certainly outdone themselves tonight. The guests were told they could help themselves to whatever they wanted, as much as they wanted, at their leisure. One guy and one girl were available behind the tables to assist as necessary. They would notify the kitchen when some dish was running low. If there was a spill, it was cleaned up immediately and a fresh, white tablecloth was laid down.

When the first grand rush slowed to a trickle, the wait staff was free to attend to their individual section. They each kept on eye on John so that when new guests arrived at different times, they could be seated without waiting. The dining room seated 200 people. 150 reservations were taken. The other 50 places were kept open so it was possible to get in without making a reservation if one wanted to take the chance.

Of course Georgio was in his glory. He greeted many old friends and former customers, making everyone feel at home. Mama looked beautiful with her white hair piled on her head, her hand in the crook of her husband's elbow.

Bobby and Maria! What a striking couple! Maria was shy at first, but Bobby made up for her quietness with a ready smile and light conversation. His arm was frequently around her waist.

Bryce knew several couples from his community work, and from business at Stratton's, so conversation ebbed and flowed pleasantly for everyone.

Ann was the only one who was a bit uncomfortable at times. Several people she knew on a professional level from the hospital were there; some recognized her, some didn't. She looked different and she was on the arm of a very important personality in Dixon. As the evening progressed, with Bryce holding her hand, she began to relax and enjoy herself.

Bryce kept glancing at her with frank appreciation in his eyes. He told her later she had been the star of the evening, but then, she knew he was prejudiced.

Chapter 174

All too soon, it was nine o'clock; time for the dancing to begin. The thought of dancing in public still gave Bryce the cold sweats. The time was now. The band had taken its place. His beautiful wife was looking at him with admiration in her eyes. This wasn't their living room where they often danced to their favorite music. This was for real; there was no going back.

Jimmy was a very charismatic young man, and as the wait staff moved the tables back, he made everyone feel welcome on the dance floor as the first song began.

Andre was right. His band was excellent. They could play the old traditional songs as well as the newer more contemporary music. Everyone appeared to be having a great time.

Without hesitation, Ann stepped into Bryce's arms and looked expectantly up at him. Before Bryce had time to worry too much about it, they were gliding across the floor as one. She followed him without effort. Their chemistry was magic, and Jimmy O'Brien noticed immediately.

It was easy to see exactly how they felt about each other just by watching them together. It was as if they were alone on the dance floor. In fact, if Bryce had outright kissed her, no one would have been surprised.

Okay, Jimmy thought. *This is good. This is very, very good. I wonder if they have ever danced competitively.*

The night had been a huge success. There had been a few glitches in the kitchen, certainly not the fault of anyone on the kitchen staff. The process would just need to be tweaked a little bit.

There was one wardrobe malfunction with Maria's dress. Fortunately Glo was good with a needle and thread. She had wanted to come and help in any way she could. It's a good thing she was there.

Everyone had worked hard and it showed. Georgio received many, many compliments from old customers who were happy he was open for business again.

Conversations had been overheard about how wonderful the band had been. The wait staff got compliments about the food and the service; the tipping had been generous. Overall, they couldn't have been more pleased!

They made corrections and adjustments where needed, and life in their new career path fell into a smooth routine for all of them.

Jimmy stayed on as the official band for the ballroom. His reputation grew as more and more people visited the restaurant. Vincenzo's was fast becoming one of the best ballrooms in the area.

As expected, some changes were made along the way. Wednesday became Country Western night with everyone dressing accordingly. Thursday night was good ole rock n'roll. Friday and Saturday nights remained Ballroom and Latin dancing with formal evening wear required. Every night was booked solid for weeks in advance.

Chapter 175

Time was divided between Stratton's and Vincenzo's for Bobby. He seemed to thrive on this hectic work schedule. Maria was equally busy with her many responsibilities as John's secretary. Ann confided to Bryce that she worried that they weren't finding the "alone time" every couple needs.

Bryce chuckled. He knew her so well. Of course she was concerned. He assured her that they were young and seemed to have boundless energy. He was also relatively sure, by the way they looked at each other, that they had plenty of "quality time" together.

Bryce worked from home traveling to Dixon about once a week. Ann always went along. They stayed in the apartment overnight, and ate at Andre's. He was always exceedingly happy to see them.

Bryce usually couldn't resist an opportunity to tease Ann.

"I see how it is," he would say with a contrived injured look on his face. "Andre used to be my friend. Now he's only interested in chatting with you."

She knew he was only kidding. She would lean over and whisper in his ear. "Don't you worry, my love. I'll give you all the attention you will ever need just as soon as we get home."

Chapter 176

The Cedarville Police Department had offered Luke a part time position upon his graduation from the Academy. He told his parents he was sure he could handle this part time work as well as security at Vincenzo's.

He vacillated back and forth over what to do about his job at Stratton's, finally coming to the conclusion that all the travel time involved was a waste. Stratton's could find another maintenance person. He wanted to do what he loved so he accepted the position with the police department.

His only concern was for Gloria Hamilton. She had been so good to him through his younger years. He was the only boarder at her little boarding house now. She was getting on in years, and Luke wanted to make sure she was comfortable and cared for in her old age.

Bryce suggested they offer her one of the extra rooms at Vincenzo's. When Luke spoke with her about it, she readily accepted. She put the boarding house up for sale, and was soon a regular at the family meetings.

She proved her worth to the girls with regard to maintaining their wardrobes. She was not bashful about commenting when she thought the cut of a dress was a little too low or the skirt a little too tight. She wanted all "her girls" to look like ladies, not "trash."

Thanks to Ann's commitment to "just in case," learned years ago from her dear friend Harriet, an apartment had been built over their large three car garage at their home. It was perfect for Luke; half way between the restaurant and the police department. He was so busy they rarely saw him except when the restaurant was open and at family meetings.

Carla and John were one hundred percent loyal to Bryce and Ann. They had moved into the apartment next to Bobby and Maria, devoting their time completely to the efficient operation of Vincenzo's.

A suitable replacement had been hired to fill Carla's position at Stratton's leaving her more time to spend with Mama Rosa. Between the two of them, new savory concoctions were appearing on the buffet table, much to everyone's delight. The kitchen worked like clock-work under her capable management.

John was kept very busy with his new responsibilities handling all the paperwork, including payroll, necessary for Vincenzo's to operate in the black. Bryce was extremely pleased with his dedication and work ethic frequently telling him how invaluable he was to their overall success. John's confidence grew by leaps and bounds.

The new high-tech wheelchair went a long way toward making him feel like a "man" again. It gave him the ability to "stand" independently, something he hadn't been able to do since before the accident. The first time he "danced" with his wife was an incredible moment.

There was also another reason for the Peterson family to celebrate. Under the encouragement and medical guidance from Dr. Reynolds-Peterson, John and Carla were expecting their first child.

The Benson's were overjoyed. They had never dreamed it would be possible for them to be parents. A boy would be named John Bryce, nicknamed JB. A girl would be Melissa Ann. Bryce and Ann were honored when they were asked to be the God parents.

Chapter 177

Nine months passed quickly for John and Carla. The pregnancy was an easy one, and as Carla got bigger, John got prouder. He fussed over his wife to the extreme. Sometimes she confided to Ann that he was driving her crazy.

As the time got closer, John became more and more anxious about the delivery. Bobby said he was going to wear the wheels right off his chair if he didn't calm down.

When the first labor pain struck, Ann thought John was going to faint. Carla just shook her head. She got him a glass of water, and a cool cloth for his forehead. Bobby and Luke found this hysterically funny, and would probably never let John forget it.

Luke offered to drive them to the hospital in his squad car when the contractions were 5 minutes apart. Bobby wanted the lights and siren, but Luke drew the line. No sirens...well, okay, he would hit the siren once, and the lights would be flashing. The rest of the family would follow them to the hospital and wait.

After 12 hours of labor for Carla, eight pound John Bryce Benson came into the world screaming at the top of his lungs. John didn't know whether to laugh or cry...he ended up doing both. The new Mom and Dad were exhausted, John more so than Carla. They were so incredibly happy. As John held his son in his arms, Ann would always remember the look on his face when he thanked her for making it possible.

JB was a happy, well-loved little boy, never at a loss for someone to hold and cuddle him. Before he was 6 months old he had a career planned as a lawyer, a police officer and a professional baseball player, with outfits for each. Ann personally thought he looked the cutest as a baseball player.

Chapter 178

The only thing to mar the first year after the opening of Vincenzo's was the passing of Gloria Hamilton.

She was in her 80's when she moved into Vincenzo's. Ann kept a close eye on her health issues. She was able to get around and feel useful for quite a while. Everyone loved her, but Luke was her pride and joy. He was like a son to her.

Luke made sure he spent time with her every day or so. When she became ill, and took to her bed, he was beside himself with worry.

Ann had known for some time that she had a heart condition. Her medications had been adjusted to give her maximum comfort, but the problem was serious and she was elderly.

It was a Sunday morning when her breathing became labored. Ann gathered the family together to explain what was happening.

Glo wanted to speak with Luke alone. He sat beside her on the bed; her hand in his. To this day, no one knows what she said to him, but it seemed to give him comfort after the first shock of losing her.

When he emerged from her room they all knew she was gone. This tall, strong, police officer sobbed like a child on his father's shoulder. He arranged for the funeral himself.

He asked his father if he could bury her on the 200 acre Peterson Estate, as it had come to be called. John looked into what would be necessary to have a cemetery on private property. He knew there would be special requirements, as well as reams of paperwork to be completed. Bryce was willing to do whatever was necessary including pay any fees that might be required. The county finally gave permission.

On a grassy hillside that overlooked the lake, Gloria Hamilton was laid to rest with her "family" gathered around. Colorful flowers and trees were planted along a stone path leading to the small cemetery. A bench was placed close to her grave so that anyone who wanted to could sit and reflect in this quiet, beautiful spot.

She was sorely missed by everyone, especially by Luke. She would always have a special place in each heart. None of them would ever forget her kindness and generosity. For the first weeks after her death, Luke spent a lot of time sitting on that bench...

Chapter 179

There was a special delivery, legal-looking envelope waiting for Luke at the post office about a month after Glo's death. The reading of her will would take place in Attorney Burlington's office in Dixon one week hence. Luke made arrangements to be there.

When he arrived at the lawyer's office, he was the only one present. The lawyer wasted no time explaining that Gloria Hamilton had left all her earthly goods and assets to Luke Peterson.

Luke was flabbergasted. He didn't know Glo had anything to leave anybody. Apparently, she had lived a frugal life, and saved her money. When the boarding house was sold she added that money to her account.

Luke was the beneficiary of almost $100,000.00!

The family sat around the table that night, stunned. Luke just couldn't believe she had left him everything. It was too much. He had been just a street kid with nothing. He just shook his head as tears slid down his face.

"Yo, Bro! You better watch out now. Some chick will be wanting to marry you for your money, not just for your handsome mug and snappy uniform!"

Bobby could always be counted on to offer a sensitive and caring comment, and Luke smiled in spite of himself.

Soon everyone was laughing, and telling their favorite memories of their good friend Gloria Hamilton. Luke just listened, occasionally wiping a tear from his eyes. He was so grateful for his family, even Bobby; The Latin Jug Head, as Luke frequently called him.

Chapter 180

I t didn't take long for everyone to realize just how much they had come to depend on Glo for a multitude of little things. She had been an excellent seamstress, keeping all their costumes in good repair. She made sure everything was sent to the dry cleaners on schedule, buttons were sewn on tightly, and hems were never ragged.

Carla had incorporated several of her recipes into the Wednesday and Thursday night buffets. Her scalloped potatoes had become a favorite. She frequently helped out in the kitchen if one of the regular staff was ill or had vacation time.

She had been the kind of person who went about her tasks quietly and efficiently, never demanding or impatient. Everyone missed her tremendously. She had become a part of the family. Not a week went by that someone didn't put fresh flowers on her grave.

With the first wardrobe catastrophe, it was decided someone would need to be hired to take on the responsibilities that Glo had handled so effortlessly. Maria suggested it would be nice if this person could also help with hair and makeup.

There was a young woman who worked in the beauty shop in Cedarville where Ann got her hair trimmed who might be a good candidate for the job. Ann made a mental note to speak with her the next time she visited the salon. Her name was Asia Kim.

Chapter 181

L uke was late to the Wednesday family meeting. That almost never happened. Ann had been a little worried about him since Glo's death. He had gone from an easy-going, fun-loving young man to one who was quiet and introspective. She wished there was some way she could help him.

When she asked what was bothering him, he always replied, "Nothing really."

They decided to give him ten more minutes, and then start without him. John needed some papers he had left in his briefcase at the apartment, and he decided he had enough time to go retrieve them. Ann made another pot of coffee while Mama put out another pan of coffee cake.

Bobby had just helped himself to a nice big piece when a commotion could be heard at the back door. It sounded like a dog barking. Then there was some scuffling and yelling. It sounded like Luke! Everyone jumped up, and rushed to see what was going on.

Sure enough, it was Luke. He was wrestling a good sized dog that was not happy about being on a leash. The dog was probably the ugliest, scrawniest pup anyone had ever seen, and his coat was matted with mud.

"Oh for heaven's sakes," Mama muttered as she hurried forward grabbing the leash from Luke's hand.

"You stop it right this very minute," she said sternly to the dog with a quick jerk on the leash.

Much to everyone's surprise, the dog promptly sat down, and looked expectantly up at Mama.

The dog then followed her obediently inside. He stood quietly as if awaiting further instructions.

"You have to treat them just like children," Mama said confidently. "With a firm hand."

Everyone was extremely impressed with this little demonstration. Mama looked very satisfied with herself as she sat down at the large round table, and poured herself a second cup of coffee. The rest of the family took their seats, careful to avoid the dog. They were all anxious to hear the story behind Luke's new friend.

Chapter 182

I t seems the police department had received an anonymous complaint from an irate gentleman about animals being abused at a farm outside town. Luke and his partner were sent to check it out. The farm looked run down and deserted. No one answered the door when Luke knocked.

Barking could be heard coming from one of the out buildings, and the officers headed in that direction. What they found sickened both young men. In the doorway of a rickety shack was the carcass of an adult female dog. By the smell, she had been dead for several days. She had obviously been shot in the head.

Toward the back of the building, inside a filthy cage, were three younger looking dogs. Two had not survived. The third puppy was barely alive, but tenacious enough to have hung on against all odds. Luke figured the adult dog was probably the mother of the three puppies.

It didn't take much effort to pry the door of the cage off its rusty hinges. The poor pup stood on shaky legs and whined. He looked so pathetic Luke decided then and there to bring him home.

On the way back to the station, Luke stopped and bought a bag of dog food, a bowl, a collar and a leash. He had to keep pushing the hungry pup away as he poured food into the bowl. "Butch" never lifted his head until the bowl was empty, then he drank all the water Luke gave him.

The preliminary paperwork was quickly completed, and the next shift would follow up with trying to find the owner of the property. It was probably a lost cause, as whoever had been living there was long gone. No one else wanted the dog. If Luke didn't take him, he would go to the animal shelter, and no doubt be euthanized.

"I just couldn't leave him there," Luke said quietly as he patted the dog's head. "His name is Butch."

"It's up to you Georgio," Bryce said.

"You will have to be responsible for him," Georgio responded, trying to sound stern. "No messes in the house. No barking. He can't be on the furniture. No running amuck all over the place...and I guess that about covers it," he stated firmly.

Relief spread across Luke's face. "I wouldn't have it any other way. Thanks!"

Mama got up and went to the kitchen. Soon pots were rattling and water was running. When she returned several minutes later, she was carrying a bowl of something that looked and smelled like gruel. When she sat the bowl on the floor, Butch came over and sniffed briefly before wolfing it down to the last drop.

"I found a lost puppy once when I was a little girl," she said with a wistful faraway look in her eyes. "My papa wouldn't let me keep him. He said dogs were too dirty and carried diseases. The gardener took him away, and I never knew what happened to him."

It seemed Butch had found an ally and a new home. Ann was glad. Luke was obviously already attached to the mangy pup, and it would be good for him to have something to focus on instead of dwelling on his recent loss.

A trip to the vet's the next day proved frustrating and expensive. Even in his weakened condition he was lively enough to give old Doc Browne a run for his money. It was all Luke could do to hold him still for the examination.

Doc thought he was probably between 6 months and a year old, it was hard to tell in his emaciated state. He looked as if he had some Mastiff, and maybe German Shepherd, in his pedigree. He was going to be huge when full grown, and he was one ugly dog.

Luke forked over the money for shots and worm pills. He stopped at the county building on the way home where Butch was summarily licensed and tagged. A bath was next on the agenda.

When Luke stated his intentions, everyone gathered in the back yard to watch what they were sure would be a very interesting undertaking. Luke and Bobby rolled out the hose. Butch cocked his head to the side as Bobby took the leash, and offered to hold the dog while Luke did the washing.

With the first squirt of water, Butch bolted and knocked Bobby flat on his back. Luke dropped the hose and the bottle of shampoo as he made a dive for the dog's collar. With no one holding the hose, it kicked and bucked spraying water in all directions.

The ladies decided it would be much safer, and dryer, to watch from the kitchen window while the men tried to corral the wet dog. It was a pretty funny sight. Mama just shook her head, her eyes sparkling with amusement.

Butch found all this to be great fun! It was a new game, and he didn't want it to end! An hour later, clean, dry and comfortable, Butch lay snoozing on the floor, worn out by all the running and jumping. Bobby and Luke were exhausted and soaked to the skin.

"Ah, the joys of pet ownership," Mama said in Luke's ear as she handed him a towel.

A huge grin slowly spread across Luke's face, and Ann's heart filled with joy. Butch was a blessing in disguise. Ann decided she would start saving her scraps for the big dog.

Chapter 183

ᙡᓚᖇ

Training began immediately. Being smart, and eager to please his new human family, Butch was soon learning the rudiments of good canine behavior. However, being the stubborn little cuss he was, he had many a go-round over one of Georgio's favorite slippers. Since that was the only thing he seemed to want, Georgio finally gave up, and let him keep it as long as he left everything else alone.

"Must be something about the smell," Mama teased while Georgio grumbled.

K-9 Search & Rescue was something that Luke had pursued in his studies at the Academy, and Butch appeared to have a knack for sniffing things out no matter where they were hidden. With further formal training, Luke thought Butch would make an excellent working dog for the police department; however out of the ordinary he might look.

Cedarville didn't have a K-9 unit so Luke took Butch back to the Hudson County Sheriff's Department requesting he be allowed to join one of the classes with his dog. Since Butch was a stray he didn't exactly "fit in" with the purebred German Shepherd squad. Luke took a lot of good natured ribbing from the other cops.

Approaching 70 pounds, and still a puppy, Butch was bigger than most of the other dogs. He was also fearless, and well able to hold his own in all the agility training. When it came to tracking, he could follow a scent practically anywhere, soon earning the respect of the other officers.

The goal of all this training was to establish a K-9 unit in the Cedarville Police Department. Luke had known from the get-go that Butch had potential. All he needed was the training, and the opportunity to prove himself.

One of the instructors was a HUGE, black, ex-marine with a scar that ran from the corner of his left eye to the corner of his mouth. He was as tall as Luke, and outweighed him by easily 50 pounds of solid muscle.

I wonder how much this guy can bench press, Luke thought upon being introduced to the man. *I think I would rather be his friend than his enemy!*

He was as fierce looking as the dogs he trained, and about as friendly. It was said by some of the other officers that he had seen heavy action in the Middle East, had been awarded several medals for bravery, and "didn't talk much." As far as Luke could tell, he didn't talk at all, only grunted and glared. He was "a hell of a cop" though. That counted for something.

What must have happened to this man to make him so...afraid? Luke wondered. Considering how the man carried himself, afraid might not be the best choice of words to describe him, but for some odd reason, that's how he struck Luke. Always defensive. Always guarded.

Apparently, Bruce Watson had worked with dogs in the military, and was considered an expert in the field. Luke wanted to learn all he could so this gave him the opening he needed to befriend this unfriendly guy. From his own past experience, Luke knew that what showed on the outside wasn't necessarily an accurate picture of the person on the inside.

The big advantage Luke possessed was Butch. Bruce admired the dog tremendously. He also admired Luke for the attention he gave to his dog's general care as well as his training. When Luke went to Bruce for suggestions on better ways to handle specific situations, a friendship of sorts began to develop based on mutual respect.

All too soon, the course was over. Armed with his new badge as a K-9 officer, and a certificate proclaiming Butch as a "Police Dog," Luke went back to Cedarville to give his pitch to the Chief of Police, Franklin Stevens.

The Chief agreed to give Butch a try on the condition that the department would not provide any food, vet care or supplies. Luke would be held liable for any damage the dog might cause. Luke agreed.

Chapter 184

⁓⁓

Butch became a well-known personality in Hudson County, not only for his size, but for his intuitive way of integrating himself into a situation, often defusing it before actual police force was necessary. The Chief begrudgingly admitted he was a good addition to the department. Luke had hit his stride. He was going to be okay.

The golden years were satisfying and happy for Georgio and Rosa. They still missed their little Rose at times, but it was no longer an all-consuming, life-altering grief. They were surrounded by people who loved them, they had purpose, and they had meaningful work to continue to do as long as they desired. They were content.

Little JB was the center of the universe for John and Carla. They were looking forward to more children, and maybe a house of their own. John was confident about his ability to provide for his family, and Carla was very proud of him. The burden of responsibility for everything had been lifted from her shoulders. She loved her husband and her son dearly. Their world was complete.

No matter what happened, Bobby and Maria would always land on their feet. They were driven to succeed, and they thrived on hard work. They were loyal to a fault to their adopted "family," and devoted to making sure Peterson Enterprise prospered. They loved each other deeply and maybe, some day, when they were ready, there would be a little boy or girl to complete their lives together. Until then, "Yo! It's ALL good," as Bobby was fond of proclaiming.

And what more can be said about Ann and Bryce. As they faced the ups and downs of their life together, one thought was always foremost in their minds. *When all else fails*, love will always win.

The Sweet Ever After Series presents Book 2,

∽∾

All That Matters.

Follow Bryce and Ann Peterson as they are drawn into ballroom dance competition where constant publicity draws attention from one of Ann's old enemies.

Additional security is necessary and Bruce Watson joins Peterson Enterprise where meeting Asia Kim is unavoidable.

Anika and Victor, a young Russian couple, become part of the Vincenzo Ballroom dance team after a violent start to their lives in America.

A reunion between Ann and Dr. Mark brings some shocking revelations.

The little Peterson Cemetery on the hill welcomes other residents, and Luke falls in love.